A DISTRAUGHT TEENAGER CHARGED
WITH MURDER.

A WOMAN LAWYER WHO BELIEVES
HE'S INNOCENT.

AND ONE PIECE OF EVIDENCE THAT
CAN DAMN HIM...

IF SHE DOESN'T HIDE IT FIRST.

· HIGH PRAISE
FOR PERRI O'SHAUGHNESSY'S
OBSTRUCTION OF JUSTICE

"CAPTIVATING . . . A BEAUTIFULLY PLOTTED NOVEL . . . grave robbery, an unsolved hit-and-run accident and a bizarre death on Mount Tallac are jumbled together to create a story that has so many unexpected twists and turns that not even the most jaded mystery fan will be bored by *Obstruction of Justice.*"

—*Monterey County Herald*

"THE ACTION IS FAST AND FURIOUS."

—*Publishers Weekly*

"[A] mystery within a mystery novel . . . This book, with two fast action story lines that work well together, provides readers with a roller-coaster ride into the hearts and minds of all the characters. *Obstruction of Justice* is a tale not to be missed."

—*The Midwest Book Review*

"A COMPELLING STORY with some great courtroom drama and a likable heroine."

—*Library Journal*

"*OBSTRUCTION OF JUSTICE* GRABS AND HOLDS THE READER FROM THE VERY FIRST PAGE."

—*Elwood Call-Leader* (Ind.)

Please turn the page for more extraordinary acclaim. . . .

Dell Books by Perri O'Shaughnessy:

MOTION TO SUPPRESS
INVASION OF PRIVACY
OBSTRUCTION OF JUSTICE

OBSTRUCTION OF JUSTICE

PERRI O'SHAUGHNESSY

ISLAND BOOKS
Published by
Dell Publishing
Bantam Doubleday Dell Publishing Group, Inc.
1540 Broadway
New York, New York 10036

This novel is a work of fiction. Names, characters, places, and incidents either are the product of the author's imagination or are used fictitiously. Any resemblance to actual persons, living or dead, events, or locales is entirely coincidental.

ISBN: 0-440-22472-1

Reprinted by arrangement with Delacorte Press

Printed in the United States of America

Published simultaneously in Canada

July 1998

10 9 8 7 6 5 4 3 2 1

OPM

The authors gratefully acknowledge the following people and organizations: Nancy Yost, our agent at Lowenstein Associates Inc., for her outstanding support, professionalism, and editing assistance; Marjorie Braman, our editor at Delacorte Press, for her steady support, hard work, and excellent editing; Patrick O'Shaughnessy, attorney at Rucka O'Boyle Lombardo & McKenna, for reading the manuscript and making many helpful suggestions; Jeffrey L. Sellon, P.E., forensics electrical engineer, for kindly contributing his help as a lightning expert; the makers of the Public Broadcasting Service television series *Nova,* for the show titled "Lightning"; Jeffrey P. Schaffer, author of *The Tahoe Sierra* (Wilderness Press, 1979), for information regarding trails on Mount Tallac; and, always, our families. Any factual errors, naturally, are the fault of the authors.

PART ONE

Love and murder, they're still a few hours apart.
Love and murder, I feel it
coming with the dusk. . . .

—Henry Miller, "The Tailor Shop"

1

THE MAN AND WOMAN LEFT EARLY ON THAT SUL-
try mid-August day, and had already been walking
through the pine forest of the lower elevations for several hours.

The jagged purple mountain they were climbing had
stood fast against Ice Age glaciers, though walls of ice
had scoured its sides into grooved cliffs and left rubble
at its feet. It had brooded over the southwestern portion of Lake Tahoe for three million years, one of the
Sierra peaks that divide California and Nevada.

In the year and a half since Nina Reilly had opened
her law practice in the rough-and-ready town of South
Lake Tahoe, she had watched Mount Tallac from her
west-facing office window whenever her mind was
troubled, its eternal presence soothing and anchoring
her. She thought of it as her mountain, and she wanted
to climb it. Although snow blocked the trail until the
middle of July, the routes up the mountain didn't demand any technical knowledge, just a strong pair of
legs, and a backpack for those determined to camp out.

For a long time, though, Nina hesitated to make the ascent. She wanted someone who had been there before to take her up the first time.

So she waited, leaving the mountain to chance. Then in July of her second year in the California Sierra, while serving as defense counsel in her second grueling murder trial, her respect for Collier Hallowell, the deputy DA prosecuting the case, grew into a more personal interest. And she learned that he had climbed Tallac. So she called him and asked him if he'd like to go up with her, and he told her to bring her sleeping bag because the Perseid meteor shower would make its annual glittering return that weekend. They could watch it from the top of the mountain.

"Nina," Collier called over his shoulder. "Stop thinking so hard. You're making me tired." Nina, who had been talking steadily about the impact the computer was having on privacy laws, plodded up the steep trail behind him, swiping from time to time at the gnats dancing in front of her sunglasses. She absorbed the mild reproof, thinking that the hike was revealing plenty about her—that lately she could talk only about law, for instance, and that today she couldn't keep her mouth shut.

"Sorry," she said. "I guess a few years of sitting under fluorescent lights have made me slightly cockeyed. I'd like to turn my brain off, but I've forgotten how. It just keeps rollin', rollin', rollin'—"

"Try looking around you. What do you see?"

Well, she saw Collier's strong, hairy calves pumping away in front of her, his gold wristwatch, his pack swaying gently with the movement of his body, his red baseball cap—but this wasn't what Collier was getting at. He wanted her to appreciate the landscape they were walking up and out of, and that was difficult because she was keeping up solely by gluing her eyes onto his legs and moving her own legs accordingly. She wasn't like the strong, fresh-faced hikers who had just passed them, striding resolutely downward like workers in an old Soviet poster.

She glanced down at her arms, pale even this late in summer. Her back ached and her lungs labored. She would fit better into a poster for *The Phantom of the Opera,* wan and hollow eyed, haunting the dingy courtroom halls day and night—and she had moved to Tahoe to escape the rat race!

"Well?"

"Okay. I see trees, rocks, shadows, dirt, brush. A fat little animal just skittered off the trail in front of us. What the heck was that? And we have gnats. Many, many gnats. I hate gnats."

"That was a marmot," Collier said. "A rodent that lives in the rocks. Cute little bugger, don't you think?" He trudged on in an easy rhythm. It wasn't fair. He was hardly puffing. She was sucking up all the air for ten feet around her.

He waved his hand around and went on: "Red firs. White firs. Jeffrey pines, huckleberry oaks, thorny snowbrush, manzanita. Smell that? Tobacco brush, very aromatic." Then, pointing off into the sky, he said, "The moon."

Sure enough, the moon floated out there in the blue, just as if the sun hadn't put it to bed long ago. "There. Right next to it. The dot of light. Venus."

"You're kidding!" She craned her head upward, shading her eyes with her hands. "I don't see it."

"Try to catch it with your peripheral vision."

"I'm looking. I'm looking." Now, staring into it, Nina saw a sky made up of bright, swimming pixels. Up here, at about eight thousand feet, the star-filled vacuum showed through the deep blue transparence, creating a weird, vertiginous feeling.

"I don't see it. I don't like looking through the sky like that," she muttered, turning her eyes with relief back to the familiar muted greens and browns around her.

They came to a broad level area crossed by a dried-up creek. Ahead, through the trees, Nina saw a streak of shining water that must be Floating Island Lake. Patched with snow, the towering dark rock wall beyond it led toward the summit.

Boulders circled the water's edge, which was nicked with sandy inlets here and there. Nobody seemed to be around, though the Tallac trail had a reputation for getting overcrowded in August. "Bad mosquitoes last time I was up here," Collier said, wriggling out of his pack and setting it against a speckled stone. Then he helped Nina wrestle hers off. She watched him smooth out a sandy place for them.

He had said little so far. She wondered if he was thinking about his wife, Anna Meade, today. She knew he had come with her up this same trail four years before. They had camped near the summit and watched the meteors, and a year later she was dead, killed in a hit-and-run accident. Another lawyer, who knew him well, had told her the lights had gone out for him then and never come back on. That was Collier now—remote, though always kind.

She spread out her towel and Collier unpacked the sandwiches and water. Sinking down on the sand with a sigh of relief, she held her arms around her knees and gazed out at the shallow water.

He handed her a turkey sandwich, and in the process leaned over and seemingly accidentally brushed his lips against hers. It was so unexpected that she dropped the sandwich.

"Look what you made me do." While she said this, she was running a finger along her lower lip, amazed and stirred up a little. She dusted off the sandwich, took a bite.

"You looked so delectable," Collier said.

He finished his sandwich, took a long drink of water, and lay down on his side, facing her. The sun beat warmly down. "Let's pretend we're on Olympus, and it's five thousand years ago," he said. "The gods are watching as we picnic in the sacred grove."

"Aw, Collier, you've got a mystical streak. I'll have to think of a way to use it against you in court," Nina said with a laugh.

"So you don't feel it? The stillness, like something's watching?"

"It must be a marmot looking for crumbs. There are no gods. We're on our own."

"Never," Collier said. "There has to be a heaven, and a hell for the bad guys. And there has to be a goddess of justice who fixes all the mistakes we make down here."

"Justice with a capital *J*," Nina said. "Toward the end of the Scott trial, the night we had dinner together, you made that toast. And you said—"

" 'May it prevail over all the bullshit.' That's always my toast."

Nina ate her sandwich, reflecting that she was having a good time. Collier, who had unlaced his waffle stompers and taken off his socks, was engrossed in flexing his toes. His feet were long and narrow, elegant almost, the soles reddened from the miles walked in his boots since seven A.M.

"You know," she said a little diffidently, "if we, uh, became friends, it could really complicate things down below."

"How so?"

"You know. You being a DA."

"Why? I'm not allowed to hang out with defense attorneys? I socialize with several of them."

"But the other ones are all guys. It's different. People will talk about us."

"If you think that, why did you call me up and ask me to climb Tallac with you?"

"I don't know," she said. Then she surprised herself by blurting out, "But I guess I've seen you knock down other people's defenses in court so effectively, I decided to give you a crack at knocking down mine."

He put an arm around her, the first time he had done that, and she felt a current run between them, as if they were natural allies who belonged together. She felt excited but also skittish, wary. "I didn't mean that the way it sounded!" she went on.

"Defenses, defenses," Collier said. He pulled her down gently onto her back and held her hands against the sand with his. His eyes were gray, outlined in black. His lips were coming toward her now and she couldn't look anymore, and then they were on her mouth.

He kissed her lightly, but when she turned her head a little he followed her mouth, not letting her slip away, not giving her space to think, releasing some of the intensity he usually hid under his casual manner. She allowed herself to taste him, feel his slightly scratchy cheek, to enjoy his way of touching her. But still a part of her hung back. She was sensing something experimental in the kiss. His lips felt cool.

He released her.

She scrambled up. Her sunglasses had fallen off, and so had his hat. He reached for it, sitting up.

"You all right?" he asked. "What is it?"

"Collier, how many women have you . . . been with since . . . since your wife died?"

He stood up too. He was a tall man, solidly built, his dark hair under the cap already graying around the ears, a serious man. Nina suddenly realized that she was somewhat afraid of him, which was probably why she had thrown herself into this situation with him. She always drove full speed ahead toward the things she feared, and she didn't always come out unscathed.

"Why do you want to know that?" he said.

"I'm just trying to figure you out."

He smiled. "I'll never let you do that. As for your question . . ."

She got busy pulling on her pack again, her eyes looking away but her ears scanning for the answer like a bat's.

"I haven't been with anyone. Haven't kissed anyone, held anyone, loved anyone. For three years. Does that scare you?"

"Yep," Nina said. "I'll be honest. It scares me a lot. So now let me ask you a question."

"I'm listening."

"Does it scare you?"

His eyes told her nothing. "*Scare* isn't exactly the word," he said. "Let's get going."

★ ★ ★

They moved southwest above the lake, beginning the climb to the saddle of granite they could see far above them, while Nina racked her brain to think what the right word might be. The trail crossed Cathedral Creek, dry in the August heat. Collier continued his running forest ranger lecture. "Currant. See there? Western serviceberry. Do you smell all the sagebrush around here?" He plucked a branch of the nondescript bush and rubbed it into her hand. "Sniff it."

The fresh aromatic smell shamed the gray powder moldering in a spice bottle at home. She tucked the sage sprig into her pack, thinking guiltily that Andrea, her sister-in-law, had been doing almost all the cooking lately. "I'll rub it on chicken and bake it," she said. "And invite you."

After another steep climb they came to the juniper-covered top of the saddle, just west of a rocky knoll. Lake Tahoe displayed itself for them, the casinos on its southeast shore jutting like concrete fingers from the forest that stretched around the immense bowl of water. As they studied the wide-angle vista the lake turned to pewter, the mountain ranges rimming it turned dark, and a sharp, warm breeze gusted through the trees around them. A solid cloud passed by and they watched its oval shadow flit swiftly across the lake, darkening the places it passed over like the negative of a spotlight.

Voices from the trail told Nina that they weren't alone any longer. A group of hikers came straggling up to their lookout one by one, led by a strong-looking bald man with a set, hard expression on his face, wearing a heavy aluminum-frame pack and olive-colored golf hat. Behind him came a boy and girl in their late teens, both astonishingly tall and attractive, look-alikes with their fair hair and sunglasses and long legs in hiking shorts. The girl wore a black T-shirt that said WHATEVER. The girl and the man, who appeared to be her father, were arguing, the girl's voice protesting, the man's caustic and commanding. The boy, who must have been her brother, lagged behind as if reluctant to get involved.

A few moments later they were joined by a woman in shorts with a tennis visor over her curly black hair, stumbling and breathless, and another man, grim-faced and weathered, wearing a blue and green bandanna around his neck.

Nina and Collier stood aside to let the group pass and take in the best view, but though they walked over to the standpoint, the hikers weren't interested in the scenery. The tension between the girl and the man occupied them completely. Only the woman in the visor bothered to nod; to the others, Nina and Collier might as well have been rocks.

"We better hustle," Collier said as they moved back onto the trail. "Those clouds make me nervous." As he spoke, another cloud shadow drifted over them like a warning, heading west toward Desolation Valley Wilderness. The wind flowed across the lake from the Nevada desert, picking up speed as it traveled over the water.

"Don't tell me it's going to rain," Nina said.

"Maybe rain. Maybe thunder. Maybe worse."

"Should we go on?"

"Now, that doesn't sound like you."

"I'm only worried that you'll say we have to go back," Nina said. "We've been in a thunderstorm together. Do you remember?" They had met at the law library the year before, during an intense thunder-and-lightning display. Collier had said, "Makes me feel small."

Now he said, "I remember that storm. I respect the natural forces that rule in this place. This time, if the sky falls, we get wet."

"We have a tent."

"Nowhere to pitch it on this trail. C'mon."

They pulled on their packs again and resumed climbing, Nina casting one last glance backward at the unhappy people still standing on the rocky ridge.

The trail led past another small lake on a flat, just before a steep two-hundred-foot slope that led to smooth rock where fresh, cold water ran down. They followed it upstream, glad to be on a level stretch, looking up every once in a while toward the cumulus clouds massing like mushrooms in the east. The trail now rose steadily up the sloping floor of a cirque toward its headwall, which held snow in every crack. Several trails, formed through continual use over the talus, passed dirty patches of leftover snow.

Not far behind them they could see the small figures of the other hikers. "Not . . . a . . . happy . . . group," Nina said between breaths.

"It's a hard climb," Collier said. "The guy in front with the big backpack—the father, is my guess—sounds like the domestic-tyrant type to me. Maybe he's the only one who wanted to come, but it's hard to say no to a man like that."

"What about the second man?" Nina said. "He didn't look like one of the family."

"Hard to say," Collier said. "How are you doing?"

"Sweating more," Nina said. "Is it my imagination, or is it getting a lot more humid?" They both paused and looked up again. The drifting clouds were now clumping rapidly into ominous thunderheads.

"Shit," Collier said. "The summit's dangerous in a summer storm. Almost guaranteed to pick up a lightning strike, since Tallac is the tallest mountain around. I don't know what to do. We're only about four hundred vertical feet from the top."

"Oh, let's keep going," Nina said. "If we don't go on now, we'll miss the whole experience, the night on the mountain, the shooting stars, all because it might have rained. If anything happens, we can always dive into a ditch. We're supposed to be having an adventure."

"I don't think we should assume there'll be a ditch handy just because we need one."

They had stopped again on the narrow crest trail. A thunderhead had settled weightily above, poised to dump directly on their heads. Turning to look behind them, they could see the group they had run into before making the same ascent, coming up toward them.

A last ray of sun shot through the clouds, landing on the shining heads of the two young people, who had drawn together. They made a glorious sight, bursting with vigor and spirit like golden eagles perched on a narrow cliffside path, ready to spread their wings and fly lightly off the mountain to soar over the forests of green below. Their radiance was framed by the darkly threatening mountain backdrop. The dramatic contrast brought them into brilliant focus, as if even the sun paid homage.

Still at the front of the group, his shirt sticking to his body in the warm moist air, the bald man flicked angrily at the insects swarming around his face. He was sweating copiously. He said in a challenging voice to

Collier, "Giving up?" His mouth moved into a cold smile.

"Considering it," Collier said.

The man tilted his head back, examining the sky. He rubbed his cheek with his hand. "It's looking real bad," he concluded, and his voice held a gloom that suggested he meant more than the clouds above. "Goddamn ugly." He drew the words out, nodding to the group standing behind him, who tensed at the profanity, silent and alert to his every move, as if they were waiting for something else from him, something worse.

He said in a slow, deliberate drawl to Collier, "You wouldn't want to get your hairdo all wet." He had the belligerent look of someone who enjoys insulting strangers. The rest of the group seemed to hang back, as if to say, he's not with us.

Collier straightened up, stared back. The air between the two of them bristled.

Nina said quickly, "Are you going on?"

"Of course we are. We're almost there. A little rain never hurt anybody." He gave Collier another long, aggressive stare, but the woman in the visor sat down suddenly on the trail and let out a sigh of exhaustion, and his hostile attention turned to her. "Quit malingering, Sarah. I'll get you in shape yet."

"It's my feet, Ray. I'm sorry."

" 'It's my feet, Ray,' " the man said in falsetto, mimicking her. "Here we go again. Whining and complaining. Rubbing my nose in it. Making sure I don't get to forget it even for one lousy minute. Dr. Lee says you have to walk. So walk, damn it."

The girl hugged herself with her bare arms. "Dr. Lee never said Mom could climb a mountain. He didn't mean that."

"She'll do what I tell her to."

"You're such an asshole,'" the girl said in a low voice.

"What'd you say? Huh? What'd I just hear you say?"

"I said, 'you're such an asshole,'" the girl said, her chin jutted forward, her eyes filled with angry tears.

Before the rest of them could react, he gave her a stinging slap that sent her reeling toward her mother, who put her arms around her. "Big-mouth Molly," he said, looking around in an almost shamefaced way. "You see how she baits me?"

"I ought to break your face for that, Ray," the man in the bandanna said, his fist raised.

"Shut up, Leo. Or I might start wondering why Sarah insisted you come along."

"I said I'd come with you," Sarah said, stumbling to her feet. "Please, Ray. Don't start anything." The girl helped her, hand on her cheek, holding her head high.

The boy took the light pack Sarah was carrying and swung it over his shoulder. He wore it and the heavy pack on his back lightly. Nina couldn't see his eyes under the green sunglasses. "Come on, Mom. Let's go down," he said.

"You're not going anywhere with her, Jason," Ray said. He stepped forward and grabbed Sarah's arm. "You're all so worried about this sorry woman, you can finish the climb with us. Because we're going up."

"Really, I'm okay," the woman said apologetically to the others. Beads of sweat stood out on her lip. "Let's just do what Ray says."

"That's better," Ray said. He turned back to Collier. "Go ahead, run back down like a scared rabbit."

Collier said, "As a matter of fact, we're heading up. It's looking a little better. C'mon, Nina."

"With pleasure," Nina said. They walked off, leaving the group standing there rigid and unspeaking, as if anger had turned them to marble.

They climbed on, north and up, doing the Swiss Army step, one step for each breath. They were almost at ten thousand feet now. They avoided looking at the sky, as though ignoring the clouds would make them go away.

A swell of delayed anger washed over Nina. "Jerk," she muttered as she fumbled her way through the loose rock. Between the ugly little family scene they had just witnessed and the threatening weather, she was starting to feel oppressed.

She followed Collier a little to the east to a weather-beaten clump of conifers. He poked his stick into a pile of old snow cached against a tree.

"We could wait out a storm here," he said.

"Under a tree?" Nina said. "I should have known better than to climb a mountain with another lawyer. I thought everyone knew trees are dangerous if there's any lightning."

"The main thing is to get below the summit as fast as you can if the weather breaks. At least here we'd have some protection from the wind." They both looked upward. The sky had turned murky, lightless, almost sooty, and the breeze felt stronger, but there were still no distant rumblings or flashes. They could see the pointed summit just two hundred feet up and away.

"What do you think?" Collier said. "We're practically there."

"Go for it," Nina said, and he nodded.

"I suppose we'll meet our friends up there. They'll be following one of the parallel routes upward. At this point the trail hardly exists, anyway; it's just a scramble."

"I can hardly wait," Nina said. "I felt like breaking his face too."

"I didn't think we ought to—you know, get involved. The other man won't let it happen again. Need a hand?"

"Certainly not." They began the scramble, northeast to the brink of a dangerously steep avalanche chute, then diagonally northwest. In places they could not avoid the snow, and once Collier slipped on an icy patch that had somehow persevered into August, catching himself just before tumbling headfirst down the slope.

The hike so lightheartedly begun had degenerated into an ordeal. Nina wanted to finish and retreat quickly to the cluster of conifers two hundred feet down. The unpleasant mood of the other hikers had affected her. She didn't want to spend the night up there anymore, especially not with those folks. And the weather . . .

She climbed the last few steps up the dark, friable metamorphic rock, weary but excited. Collier, already at the top, dropped his pack on the ground, his hair blowing in the stiff wind. Someone had assembled a cairn of rough-edged stones in the center of the solid sheet of granite.

"You wanted to spend the night *here*?" Nina called. The wind blew hard and steady, almost forcing her back, and it was warm, peculiarly warm.

Collier didn't answer. He seemed transfixed by the scene, andesite-capped Mount Rose in the northeast, almost eleven thousand feet in altitude, the granitic western slopes of the Carson Range in Nevada in front of them across the lake, and on the South Shore, the casinos now considerably diminished, Legos abandoned by some giant kid. Below them many small, shadowy lakes spotted the long, lateral moraines.

"The glacier advancing down to the ice sheet over Tahoe was at least a quarter-mile thick, and it wasn't that long ago," Collier said over the noise of the wind, and just then Nina felt a plump raindrop land on her lip.

She held out her hands, palms up, saying, "Hey, Collier—"

"The scene must have been even more incredible fifteen thousand years ago—"

"Collier!"

"What?"

"Rain!" More raindrops landed on her hands. She held them out mutely, and Collier's eyes widened.

"Okay," he said. "We made it. Now let's get out of here." His words were punctuated by a rolling, harsh noise that blasted up the mountain toward them. At the same time they saw, directly in front of them but several hundred feet out in the air, a sight as magnificent and terrible as the mountain they were now trying to escape, a bolt of lightning thrown down from the layers of clouds, met from below by its jagged twin.

As the bolts crashed together, crackling and hissing around them, the hairs on the back of Nina's neck stood up. Clapping her hands to her ears, she tried to flatten herself, but Collier was grabbing her by the shoulders and turning her toward where the trail must be, extinguished in the torrent of rain that had suddenly begun falling. "Hold on to my pack!" he yelled.

Half-blind in the downpour, they groped their way frantically down toward the avalanche slope. The booming, rolling, noise never let up, as if they were trapped inside a big drum, more percussion than sound. Now and then a clap rent the sky and almost knocked them off their feet. More lightning flashed around the mountains, but now it had coalesced into a glaring sheet of light across the underbelly of the storm.

Collier held out his arm and stopped Nina, pointing toward a small boulder with an overhang. They hustled over and crouched under the rock, tearing off their packs and putting them in front for protection and then peering fearfully out at the frenzy. The din was incredible. The temperature plummeted, and hailstones began to batter the ground, gusting into their inadequate shelter and bouncing off the rocks outside like a blizzard of ricocheting BB pellets.

Nina unzipped her pack with clumsy fingers, managing to pull out a dry flannel shirt to shield their faces as they crouched behind the packs. Even shouting was impossible. For an endless ten minutes they curled up and buried their heads like animals, enduring the worst of the storm.

At last there came a sinister lull, and they pulled down the shirt, now heavy and stiff with melting hail. The light shooting through the clouds dimmed. Below the slick rocky ledge Nina saw remote trees flattened as if a meteor had passed by. She rubbed her numb hands, thinking, It's over, we made it. . . .

She turned her head to tell Collier, and he looked so funny, his hair was standing straight up, and then there was the smell of ozone and that awful tension in the air again, of something building, building up to intolerable stress, cracking . . .

She heard a bang just before a terrific gash of lightning struck about seventy-five feet above, right at the summit rocks. They saw only the upper segment, blinding and terrible. They both yelled and clutched at each other.

And as they gaped out into the appalling light, their eyes shocked and dazzled, deafened by the thunder reverberating all around, they saw a body catapulting past, blown off the mountain, falling toward the rocks below.

2

THE SPECTRE OF A MAN WHIZZING BY IN BLURRY
silhouette was followed by another torrent of cold rain
turning to sleet that washed away the horrific image.

Had it been a hallucination? Nina blinked, saw a
bright tree with zigzag branches inside her eyelids, and
turned to Collier, who pointed outside, then at himself, and pulled open his own pack, finding a thin
poncho folded tightly into a tiny nylon bag. He tugged
it out, spread it enough to find the neck opening, and
hung it around his neck.

Ice water spilled into their hidey-hole. Nina grabbed
Collier's arm and shook her head, shouting, "No!
No!" but the noise of the wind and rain picked up her
words and hurled them away.

"I'm going after him!" he yelled back. Somewhere
her mind registered that she could hear him again.

"Me too!" she hollered, a foot from his ear.

"Too dangerous!"

"Then stay!"

He ignored her, crawling out on hands and knees,

head down, leaving her with the packs. The wind had quieted for the moment, as if it, too, had been taken aback at the last lightning strike. The sleet became colder, lighter. Coasting in on a cold gust, heavy white flakes of snow began drifting down.

Cursing the mountain, Nina tied the flannel shirt over her head, bent to get out, and tried to follow Collier, but she found herself in white fog. She couldn't see ten feet away. She didn't know which way Collier had gone. He couldn't see through this mist any better than she could. What if he fell? What if she couldn't find him?

She made it about twenty-five feet before she knocked her knee into a sharp rock and had to sit down suddenly. Wet snow soaked through her clothes to her shoulders and legs. She touched her freezing fingers to the cut, but couldn't tell how bad it was.

The swift succession of changes in the weather and atmospheric pressure, the afterimages burned into her retinas, and the temporary deafness from the thunder combined with the pain in her knee. She was going to pass out or get sick. But she had to find Collier!

So she crawled back under the crag again to take stock. Huddled safely out of the weather once more, she opened her pack again, searching for dry clothes to heap on her shivering body.

Her hand closed over her cellular phone, the new one she took everywhere and had stuck in the front pocket as they were locking up the car.

No way. No way!

"What the hell," she muttered, pushing the power button.

Orange light glowed on the phone's face. It beeped. She listened. She heard a dial tone.

She punched in 911. Nothing happened.

Closing the phone, she pushed in the antenna, hot tears of frustration on her cheeks. Try again, Nina, she told herself. Don't give up.

She tried the whole procedure again, this time more slowly. No reply. Nothing but the sound of dead air.

Peering out into the fog, she listened for some new sound that would tell her where Collier was, some sound that would remind her that she was not all alone on the top of a mountain in a monster storm. She might just lie there and die. She might freeze to death in August in California, which would surely be one for the record books.

She checked her limbs for numbness, but her fingers and toes burned with the cold. She didn't want Collier to find her scrunched up under this rock, a beatific smile on her face from the warmth that she had heard crept up on people who were freezing to death.

A more distant clap of thunder interrupted her foggy meditations. The center of the storm was moving on, leaving the whiteout.

She sat back again, aware for the first time of blood spreading all over her pant leg. She opened the phone again to its spineless beep. She punched in the numbers, giving the little machine plenty of time to comprehend each one individually: 9 . . . 1 . . . 1.

Each beep of the buttons sounded weaker. She stared at the numbers. She read the labels. "Idiot!" she shouted. She had forgotten it again! "Send!" The magic *send*!

She punched it.

A calm female voice answered.

★ ★ ★

By the time the medevac helicopter arrived from Reno, setting off a flurry of fresh new snow, the clouds had broken up and blue sky showed above just as before. Two men in uniform jumped out and ran up to Nina, who sat on a rock next to her pack combing her long, wet hair, a bedraggled Lorelei.

"You okay?" They spotted her injury immediately. One of them ripped her jeans above the cut, examining her leg with expert speed, introducing himself as Sven. He cleaned the cut, pronounced it relatively minor, sterilized it, and covered it with a clean bandage as gently as a mother. While he worked on her, her voice returned.

"Boy, am I glad to see you guys. There are two men halfway down the slope. One of them is the man I think must have been struck by lightning. The other one is my friend, who went down there to help. I think I know which way they went. Let me show you." She heard herself jabbering, and didn't care.

"How's that leg feel?" asked Sven, substitute mom.

"Fine. The blood had me scared, but I can walk."

She led them to the edge of the slope, testing her leg gingerly and finding it really not too bad. They could see the two figures several hundred feet below. Collier waved. The other figure lay motionless.

"We can't get any closer, Dave," one of the technicians said. "Let's get the stretcher. What kind of shape are you in, miss?"

"Fine! Perfect!" The memory of her panic under the crag embarrassed her only a little. People did die on these mountains all the time. Look at that poor man lying down there, his life gone in an instant. They should have turned back. A perverse spirit had taken hold of them, and now—

"You need dry clothes. There are some in the chopper, and you can share them with the others as soon as we take a look at the injured guy."

"Sven, Dave, when we get back down, I'm going to do something for you. I'm going to . . . make you a cake!"

The men grinned. "Lemon frosting," Dave said.

As they talked, they had been unloading their equipment and lacing on hiking boots. While they prepared themselves, a second chopper landed not far from the first one. A man introduced himself as Mike and took charge, directing the technicians. Nina, watching them, said, "Let me help."

"The slope is steep and slick. It's nasty," said Mike.

"You might need another pair of hands."

He made an instant decision, bringing over a sling-like red contraption and a length of cable, and said, "Okay, we're going to rope up. Put this on."

"What is it?"

"A Whillans harness. Put your legs through here, pull it up around your waist, and put this 'biner through the front tab. Here, I'll do it." In a moment she was wearing the harness and he was tying her to the rope with a complicated knot at her waist. The EMTs got into their harnesses and Mike said, "Let's go."

They began making their way down the slippery rockfall, Nina third in line and Mike in the back. "There are other people caught up here," Nina said between breaths. "The storm was terrible. They could be hurt too."

"One at a time," Mike said. "Don't worry. We won't forget anyone."

"The lightning . . . it was horrible. He flew. I saw it, but I still don't believe it," Nina said.

"Take it easy. It's all over now."

The story seemed even more incredible now because, returning to its earlier state of apparent benevolence, the sky had cleared and the sun shone down, pure and golden in the afternoon. Yet the Tahoe Sierra gleamed white, as if it were December instead of August. Her watch said four o'clock.

After about ten minutes of slipping and sliding down the rocks, they could hear Collier. "I tried for a long time. Half an hour at least," he called plaintively. He sat next to the unmoving body, completely spent, his forehead matted with wet hair.

They slid down the last few feet to a level layer formed by a rock outcrop that had piled up loose rocks, making for unsteady footing. Nina stepped carefully over a rift, and reaching Collier, put her arms around his soaked shoulders. His face was drawn into the lineaments of deep sorrow. He buried his big head in her shoulder and said, "I breathed in and out a million times. I did it perfectly, perfectly. But she never moved."

"It's all right. Shhh. You did everything you could."

"She's dead," Collier said. "Isn't she?"

"She?" Nina said. She looked over at the face she had been avoiding, the singed eyebrows that she had seen from the corner of her eyes, the skull with a few flaps of flesh left that had once been . . .

Molly and Jason's father. Ray, they had called him. He was obviously dead, his clothing hanging in black tatters, his bulky pack still stuck like a succubus to his back, a bit of burned wire hanging from the frame.

"Anna," Collier said. He wiped his mouth, started to cry.

Yelling came from up above. The man called Leo slid toward them, taking great, sliding steps that moved him down the slope twenty feet at a time. Collier pulled away from Nina, putting his knees up, one arm hiding his eyes. Nina looked over at the dead man. The technicians seemed to have dumped more equipment than their packs could carry all around the man, some of it on his body, including two black paddles, which they held against his chest. . . .

"Clear!" Mike shouted, and they all moved back.

The dead man seemed to leap into the air. Then he fell back, while Mike listened to his chest through a stethoscope. "Again," he said. Dave held the paddles tightly to Ray's chest, and the dead man heaved up again and again. . . .

"Oh, God. Ray," Leo was saying. "His wife and kids are up there on the mountain somewhere. Is he . . . ?"

"Stay back," Mike said. The technicians continued to work doggedly over the man.

Finally Nina said, "Where's the rest of your party?"

"I don't know. We got separated when the storm struck."

"C'mon, Ray, c'mon," Nina heard Sven say. She couldn't watch anymore. She could hear them grunt, hear the noise of air artificially expelled.

"Is your friend hurt?" Leo asked.

"I don't know," Nina said, turning back to Collier. "It's not Anna, Collier. It's a man. Anna's been dead for a long time." Collier didn't respond; he wasn't moving at all, and a stab of apprehension went through her. "Look," she said, getting Sven's attention. "I want to take him back up."

"He's in bad shape, isn't he?" said Sven. "Need a hand? If you want to wait, we could come back and take him up in the stretcher."

She helped Collier to his feet. He followed her lead. "No, we'll make it up from here. I'm not sure about making it all the way down the mountain, though."

"We can take two plus one on a stretcher in each chopper," said Dave, still working on the body. "If nobody else is injured, you get first dibs. The three of us can wrestle the stretcher up. Go ahead."

Leo, who had been watching the proceedings from a few feet away, said suddenly, "Ray is dead, isn't he? I'll be damned."

"Yeah, I guess we've lost him," Mike said, rising wearily. "Let's get him on the stretcher, Dave. We'll all go up together. Safer going uphill."

"Collier, come on now." Nina took him by the arm, leading him across the split in the rocks, wondering how he had made it down there in the storm. He stopped on the other side, massaging his temples and eyes with both hands, as if to rub away his confusion.

Trying to determine the easiest route, squinting their eyes against the treacherous sun, they looked up.

Standing near the summit above them, still and silent, the dead man's family was watching.

3

TWO DAYS LATER, NINA WAS STILL LOOKING AT Tallac, but once again from the safe distance of her office window. Almost all the snow had melted. She remembered that groove, that ledge of light-colored rock, but the avalanche slope near the summit was hidden behind a jade-colored ridge.

She turned away. She would never feel the same about that mountain.

Sandy Whitefeather, her secretary, knocked and came in with a new stack of files to supplement the pile accumulating on Nina's desk.

"The coroner's office called," she said without preamble. "There's a meeting at two this afternoon. They want you to come, along with the other people who were on that hike. They said to tell you it's not an inquest, just an informal inquiry."

Sandy set the files down and stood in front of the desk, arms crossed, resplendent in a brilliantly colored Hawaiian shirt over white pants and tennis shoes. A large, formidable woman of indeterminate age, she knew everybody in Tahoe, and nothing fazed her. Her smooth, dignified face and dark hair, which she usually wore pulled back in a severe style, made her look like pictures Nina had seen of Liliuokalani, the Hawaiian queen, but Sandy was actually a member of the Washoe tribe native to Tahoe and the high desert near Carson City. She ran Nina's schedule. She ran the office. And she wanted to run Nina's life, but that Nina stoutly resisted.

"I guess I should show up, then," Nina said. "I wonder if Collier will be there. He hasn't called back, has he?"

"No. But your dental malpractice did. Ed Mills. He wants to know if you got a response to our settlement offer yet."

"Did we?" Nina said.

"And that right there says it all. You haven't paid a lick of attention to your cases so far this week. Maybe you should go home if all you're going to do is mope."

"I'm not moping, I'm brooding," Nina said. "There's a big difference. Moping is an unfocused sort of thing. But brooding, that's productive. I don't quite understand what went on up there, and I can't stand not understanding."

"You don't have time to brood," Sandy said. "You're a lawyer, not a poet, and that's how you get your money to pay your secretary, so please, call Ed back. And Mrs. Bindhari's husband refused to bring the kids back Friday night. She's getting frantic. She wants to see you right away. And you have a Settlement Conference Statement due out today on the Texaco case. Also, you asked me to order a lemon cake from the bakery, but didn't you tell me you were planning to bake one yourself?"

"I know what I told you. I know what I promised. The truth is, I don't have time. I'll write a nice card to go with it. . . ."

"They don't have lemon. You'll have to order something else."

"All right already," Nina said. She sat down at her desk and opened Ed Mills's file. A loose pile of dental X rays fell out, reminding her of the state of her unfortunate client's teeth. "Try Collier's office again, will you?"

"In due course," Sandy said, but she stood there. Nina remembered that line. Sandy's former boss, a local attorney named Jeff Riesner, used it all the time. She smiled, thinking that Sandy would be disgusted if she realized she had appropriated anything from him.

"Well?" Nina asked.

"How was it?"

"What?"

"Up there on the mountain."

"Awful."

"But you had to get to the top, didn't you? Did Collier Hallowell want to go to the top with you or did you badger him into it?"

"What are you getting at, Sandy?"

"It's always good to have influence with the county district attorney."

"He's not the county DA yet. He still has to win the election in November. Do you think I'm seeing Collier only so I'll have a good connection in the DA's office?"

"It wouldn't hurt."

"I'm only interested in his body, Sandy." It was hard to tell if Sandy enjoyed the joke. She left in a flurry of parrot greens and hot pinks, and Nina returned to the daily drudgery of small-town lawyering.

At two o'clock sharp Nina walked into the coroner's office, located just off Al Tahoe Boulevard in the familiar County Office Building, across the patio from the courthouse and jail.

In these two buildings she spent much of her working life. Modern, unassuming structures, the woody brown of their exteriors minimized their impact on the parkland in which they were located. Tall firs shot through with sunlight bordered the buildings. Working in Tahoe had its positive aspects—a splendid, almost spiritual setting, a remove from frenetic city life, the chance to live where many worked hard just to visit. But sometimes just these qualities made it hard to work there. Sitting indoors all day looking out at the beaming tourists at play could be a kind of torture.

Inside the waiting room, the dead man's family had already assembled. "Hi," Nina said inadequately to the solemn faces. "Mrs. de Beers, how are you?" She shook Sarah de Beers's hand.

Hardly recognizable as the tired woman Nina had seen on the mountain, Sarah de Beers sat in the chair nearest the door. She had clipped her dark curls at the nape of her neck. Her skin was still reddened from the wind and weather on the mountain, but her eyes weren't red or swollen, and the thought came unbidden to Nina that she hadn't cried for her husband. She had chosen a sober navy blue jacket and skirt with a white blouse and black stockings, much like the business suit Nina herself was wearing. The plain style and low-heeled shoes showed off the frail lines of her body.

"Thank you for coming," she said. "It's just a formality. You were a witness of sorts."

"No problem."

The young girl, Molly, said, "Did you see the lightning actually hit him?"

"Not exactly," Nina said.

"Not exactly? What's that mean?"

"Shush, honey, we'll talk about all that in a minute," her mother said. "Please." Mrs. de Beers patted the chair beside her, and her daughter plopped down, picking up a magazine with a picture of Smoky the Bear on the front, and began flipping through it.

Nina smiled tentatively at Molly's brother, who had taken a seat across the room. "You and Molly are twins, aren't you?" she said.

"Born thirteen minutes apart," Jason said. He was remarkably tall, about six feet five, but still had filling out to do, so he didn't seem as overwhelming as he surely would be later in life. He held his finger in the college catalog he had been reading.

"Columbia? Fine school," Nina said, indicating the catalog. "Not that I went there."

"My history teacher in high school was friends with a professor there," Jason said.

"Jason wanted to go to Columbia, and he had the grades and everything, but our father wanted him to go into the family business," Molly said to Nina. "At least he didn't try to push that on me."

"No," Jason said. "He decided you would marry a rich guy to get some money coming into the company. He had it all figured out."

"Jason, Molly," their mother said sharply. "These are family matters."

The door opened and the man in the blue and green

bandanna who had followed the emergency techs down the hill entered. Nina now knew his full name was Leo Tarrant. He looked much the same as he had on the mountain, ruddy and fit in jeans and a pin-striped cotton dress shirt. He had the callused hands and hard body she associated with the construction trades.

"Sarah," he said. "Hey, Molly."

"Hey yourself," Molly said brightly.

"You guys hanging in there?"

"Choking back the sobs."

"Molly!"

"I'm glad he's dead," Molly said defiantly. "I'm not going to pretend." Her mouth quivered.

"Come on over here and sit with me, Moll," her brother said gently, and she did, avoiding looking at anyone. Jason reached out a hand and smoothed her pale hair back, saying, "It's all right, Moll."

Her mother whispered, but they all heard, "Don't be disrespectful." Molly ignored her.

Leo continued his way around the room. "How's it going, Jason?"

"All right. Mom's sleeping better," Jason said. "Dr. Lee says she hurt her leg again on the mountain."

"I'll be fine in a few days, Leo."

Tarrant said, "What fools we were." Then, turning away and holding out his hand to Nina, he went on, "We met on the mountain." He gave a quiet laugh and said, "Sounds like a sad folk song, doesn't it?"

"Sorry to meet you all again under these circumstances," Nina said, shaking his hand.

"We should have gone down when the clouds came up, when we talked to you. Ray never could do anything halfway, though." The inner door had opened and a young woman in white was gesturing at them.

"He's ready," she said, and they all got up dutifully to troop into Dr. Clauson's office.

The coroner sat at a metal conference table, barricaded behind files and papers in a windowless room. They sat on folding metal chairs around the table, the family and Leo huddling close together as if that might create a little haven of warmth in a place with as much atmosphere as a bathroom in a filling station.

Nina was wondering if Collier would make it at all. She couldn't blame him for skipping this dreary meeting.

"Sorry for your loss," Clauson said to no one in particular in his terse accent. "Call me Doc. Meeting's called to order. Get their names and addresses."

While the secretary did this, Clauson's quick eyes darted around at the assembled parties. His job encompassed more than simply determining the facts of the matter. He needed to be on the lookout for anything off-kilter that might suggest something other than an accidental death. Under these circumstances, Nina knew he must be operating from habit. He couldn't expect to find anything other than an accident in Ray de Beers's death.

From her tussles with Clauson in court, Nina knew he was a good autopsy surgeon but prosecution-oriented. He had dispensed with his jacket, and his thin white polyester shirt displayed a more substantial undershirt and an honest-to-God plastic pocket protector for his pens.

A knock on the door announced Collier, who came in with a nod and took his seat, looking as crumpled as his clothes. Bags under his eyes signaled a lack of sleep.

He nodded at Nina, his expression pleasant and professional, as always.

"Both illustrious counselors here, but no case this time," Clauson said. "Hope we can agree on that right quick."

"Act of God," Collier said, "in the fullest meaning of the legal term."

"Okay." Clauson saw the secretary was finished, and went on: "We're here pursuant to California Government Code section 27491, which states in pertinent part as follows: 'It shall be the duty of the coroner to inquire into and determine the circumstances, manner, and cause of all violent, sudden, or unusual deaths; unattended deaths; deaths wherein the deceased has not been attended by a physician in the twenty days before death; deaths related to or following known or suspected self-induced or criminal abortion, known or suspected homicide, suicide, or accidental poisoning; deaths known or suspected as resulting in whole or in part from or related to accident or injury either old or recent; deaths due to drowning, fire, hanging, gunshot, stabbing, cutting, exposure, starvation, acute alcoholism, drug addiction, strangulation, aspiration,' etcetera etcetera." He passed out copies of the statute.

"This death requires at least a good look," he went on. "Violent, sudden, unusual; no physician in attendance; death related to accident or injury. Agreed?"

They all nodded.

"We're having an informal inquiry, not an inquest. Read along a few more paragraphs, you'll see it, and I quote: 'The coroner shall have discretion to determine the extent of inquiry to be made into any death occurring under natural circumstances and falling within the provisions of this section.' So. Mrs. de Beers, you don't want an autopsy, you want the body released—or so you told my secretary this morning."

Sarah de Beers said, "He's already been . . . injured enough. I don't see any point."

"He didn't have a regular physician?"

"He was healthy, didn't even get colds. And he didn't trust doctors." She obviously didn't mean this as an insult to Doc Clauson, who peered at her as if to assure himself of it before continuing.

"Anyone else want to comment on the autopsy question? I have a report on the incident here from the emergency medical techs. I took custody of the deceased and looked him over. Deceased was struck by lightning. Direct strike. Severe linear burns and lacerations at both the entry and exit sites of the current. Charring through the full thickness of the skin in places.

"The body exhibited lightning prints, reddish streaks that form a skin rash like a fern, on the trunk. The characteristic pattern is called Lichtenberg's flowers. Clothes burned or torn off, body hurled some distance. Body fluids ejected. Skin cyanotic. The body was banged up on the trip down the cliff, but there's no medical doubt as to cause of death. I'm not inclined to overrule the wife."

Nobody seemed to have any comments. Sarah de Beers showed no emotion at the listing of her husband's injuries. She was so abnormally serene under the circumstances that Nina decided she must be on some kind of tranquilizer.

"Okay. Next. Mr. Hallowell, you first. Tell us what you saw."

Collier reported in an unemotional voice how the storm came up suddenly, how they reached the summit just as it broke, how they saw de Beers's body flung off the summit, how he went down and found de Beers and tried mouth-to-mouth breathing and other resuscitation efforts for a long time, at least half an hour, and how he quit just before help arrived. He made no mention of his own physical condition or the mental confusion he had experienced. Jason's foot, resting on his knee, jerked up and down with what appeared to be impatience or boredom while Collier spoke, stopping suddenly as he arrived at the end.

"A laudable effort," Clauson said. "Electrocution victims often look dead but aren't. You did the right thing. And you, counselor. What did you see?"

Before speaking, Nina thought back to right before the lightning strike, recalling vividly that moment when all the passions of the atmosphere gathered themselves, the humming and the bang just before the bolt of lightning rent the skies and the man flew past.

"You heard a bang? A rock split, maybe," Clauson said. "He wasn't shot; he was electrocuted. Considerable trauma, naturally, from the fall, but he was dead already."

"I never thought of a shot," said Nina. "You can't imagine how wild it was out there. Maybe a tree cracked and fell in the wind."

"We were above the tree line," Collier said.

"What about the humming you mentioned?" asked Clauson.

Nina tried to shape the amorphous thought. "I *felt* humming more than heard humming. Like tension rising in the air or pressure building up. You know how you tingle just before you touch a live wire, like something invisible connects your finger to the wire before you ever touch it? That's how it felt. Static? Foreboding? I don't know anything about lightning—maybe I felt something other people have felt before a strike."

"Ominous," said Collier, abandoning his aloofness long enough to agree with her description.

"How many feet you reckon you were below the summit?" Clauson asked.

"Only about a hundred feet," Collier said, rubbing his forehead. "We were trying to make it to the nearest group of trees another hundred feet down."

"What made you think de Beers fell from the summit?"

"The angle and the direction of the . . . body," said Collier.

"Exactly," Nina added. "He was dropping, but also seemed to be blowing sideways. He came from the summit."

"He made the top," Sarah de Beers said. "He had time and he would never quit until he did."

"Okay, let's hear from the rest of you," Clauson said. "Mr. Tarrant. Were you with the rest of this group?"

"Oh, yes. We went up together. I'm . . . I was . . . a business partner of Ray's. Mrs. de Beers invited me to join them."

Nina remembered the way the group had re-formed as they stepped aside for her and Collier, dropping unconsciously into natural emotional alliances, Sarah with Leo, Molly with Jason, and Ray, all alone. Leo had kept an attentive eye on Sarah throughout the meeting. She seemed oblivious of his interest. Well, that was their business, not hers.

"After meeting up with Ms. Reilly and Mr. Hallowell we got separated," Leo Tarrant went on. "Or, to be more honest, we all were on the tired side, so we decided to split up."

How had Ray taken that decision? Or had Leo and Sarah simply dropped behind after agreeing to follow him?

"Ray went on alone—he was by far the best hiker," Tarrant continued. "I stayed behind to help Mrs. de Beers, who was feeling the effects of the elevation, and Molly and Jason continued up, but more slowly."

"How far below the summit are we talking here?" Clauson asked. The secretary took no notes but frequently checked a recorder running on the credenza next to her chair.

"Mmm, less than four hundred feet. We all wanted to try to finish at that point. We were so close. Dumb decision; I see that now. Anyway, Mrs. de Beers and I continued up to a little copse of fir trees. She couldn't go further and then the storm broke. We spent the worst of the downpour huddling under the trees. When things eased up, we looked for the others."

"How long before you found them?" Clauson asked.

"About half an hour. We found the kids and started wondering if Ray had been caught at the top. We were almost to the top, coming from the other side of the mountain, when I saw a clump of people down a slope of loose rocks. I called to Mrs. de Beers and the kids to stay put and I climbed down to see what was happening."

"So you never made it to the summit," Clauson said.

"No," Mrs. de Beers said. "Nobody made it to the top except Ray. We were evacuated—me, Ray, and

Ms. Reilly and Mr. Hallowell. You met us at Boulder Hospital. You know the rest."

"The kids and I came down in a second helicopter," Tarrant said. "I didn't realize I would be billed for the rescue. Anything we can do about that?"

"You can pay it in installments." Clauson took the non sequitur in stride.

"But it's a fortune!"

"Leo, don't worry about it," said Sarah. "I'll take care of it. You shouldn't have to pay. This was our fault."

"It wasn't our fault!" Molly said. "It was meant to be or it never would have happened." Sarah patted her on the arm, but Molly moved away, as if the touch stung. The experience had been traumatic for Molly, Nina thought. But she didn't seem grief-stricken, either, just nervous and moody. People handled such things so differently.

"Any of you see anybody else on the mountain near the summit?"

"We saw hikers at the lower elevations," Nina said. "Nobody else near the top. I guess they had more sense."

"We didn't see anybody else," Jason said. "Molly and I stuck together. We were trying to· get up the other side, but I doubt if we got within two or three hundred feet of the summit before the storm broke."

"Okay," Clauson said. "I'm going to use the discretion vested in me to certify this case as an accidental death due to a direct lightning strike. Statements you made today will be kept on file in case you get any hassles from insurance companies, ma'am. Many policies pay double if the death is accidental. Your husband have that kind of insurance?"

"I haven't looked into that," Sarah de Beers said.

"I'll expect a call from a claims adjuster, then. The deceased is hereby released into your custody. You picked a funeral home?"

"Chapel of Memories. Mr. Mooney."

"Nice fella," Clauson said. "Anything else?" He got up briskly, gathering his papers, his mind apparently already moving on to other matters, this one being such a no-brainer. "Okay, meeting's adjourned."

Out in the parking lot, Jason and Molly took off in a copper-colored, sparkle-painted Jeep, looking like movie stars in their sunglasses. Sarah de Beers and Leo Tarrant climbed into a cherry-red Nissan Pathfinder, with Tarrant driving.

By the time Nina caught up with Collier he was unlocking his own car, a nondescript beige model. "Will you just wait a minute?" she said. "I need to talk to you."

"Sorry. I need to get back to the office." He opened the door and got in, but at least he didn't slam it in her face.

"Are you embarrassed that you had a bad moment up there on the mountain in front of me? Is that it? Because I hope you know me better than that," Nina said. "Jesus, Collier, you were suffering from exposure, exhaustion. You'd been blowing air down a dead man's throat for half an hour!"

He didn't answer. He sat in his car, looking down, hands slack on his thighs.

"Come on. Let's get a cup of coffee," Nina said.

"I can't."

"Then talk to me."

"What do you want to know, Nina?"

His tone came too close to sounding hounded, even hostile. He was breaking off with her before they'd even started. She didn't want things to fall apart because he'd had a moment of ordinary human weakness.

"I want to know that we'll keep on seeing each other," she said, trying so hard to keep the pleading out of her words that they sounded almost businesslike.

"I don't know."

"Why? Because of the mountain?"

"Because of Anna," Collier said, looking straight ahead instead of at her. "Maybe I'll never be ready."

"You know," she said, her voice catching a little, "Jewish people have a ceremony I've always admired, the kaddish. One year after someone dies, the kaddish signifies the end of official mourning. I don't mean to sound hard, but life is too short to put on hold forever, Collier."

"She wanted to talk with me that night, but I was too busy," Collier repeated to himself as if he'd said it a thousand times already. "I let her go."

"How did it happen?" Nina asked. She didn't really want to know, but he obviously wanted to tell her.

"She went to the grocery store to buy bread and milk. Someone ran her down at Raley's and left her to bleed to death."

"You know I'm sorry. But—"

"Three years since she died," Collier said. "Three years following a cold trail. While her killer eats steak at the next table, stands in line in front of me at the post office . . . she lies in her grave. I'm a fucking prosecutor with all the right connections, and even I can't find the driver. Sometimes the rage, the feeling of loss, gets unbearable. I look at the defendants in court and think, this one might have done it. . . . No, no, it was that one . . . I dream about her several times a week."

"I didn't know," said Nina. "I thought . . . Whatever I thought, you can't keep on like this. It's not healthy. You need to see someone who can help you."

He laughed without humor. "A shrink? Now, there's a standard California solution. That won't help. Whether I accept her death or not doesn't matter. I can't let go until her killer pays for what he did to her. I owe her that, and that's who I am. That's what I'm all about."

Nina thought, then said, "Have you tried hiring a private investigator?"

"What for? Believe me, this investigation went beyond exhaustive before anyone would give up. Everyone here got involved, from the chief on down."

"Some people won't talk to the police."

"Little Miss Fix-It," Collier said, but he seemed to be thinking about what she had said.

"Remember Paul van Wagoner, the Carmel PI? He is a wonderful investigator."

"I remember you think he's wonderful."

"He's helped me on several cases. He used to work the homicide division in San Francisco and Monterey before he went out on his own. Can't hurt to give him a call, can it?"

"God, I am so sleepy," Collier said, covering a yawn with his hand. "Okay, since you insist. Give me his number."

"And go to bed early."

"I'm finishing up a three-defendant murder trial tomorrow against Jeff Riesner. I have to prepare my final rebuttal tonight and give it tomorrow. When it's finally over, I'll have to start some real electioneering. A speech at the Elks, then there's the League of Women Voters. . . ."

Nina said, "Well, bye, then," feeling forlorn. His words reminded her that she had a divorce trial that afternoon herself, opposite the bellicose Riesner, the most unpleasant lawyer she had met at Tahoe, and clients waiting back at the office.

"Look, I'll call you," Collier said. And she had to be content with that.

4

ON WEDNESDAY AFTERNOON, IN LIGHT RAIN, RAY-
mond de Beers went into the ground. The *Tahoe Mirror*
carried a late obituary on Thursday morning, which
Nina read with interest while waiting for her personal
injury case to come up on the Law and Motion docket
at court.

Nina always read the obituaries. These condensa-
tions of people's lives, showing how they ended up,
were revealing reports on the human condition. From
the obituaries you could tell whether the person had
been happy or unhappy, loved or unloved, deep in the
sea of life or beached and isolated. She found herself
paying closest attention to the women in their seventies
and eighties who had been lifelong members of their
churches, kept house, and raised a slew of children who
had gone on to have more children who had more
children, in exponential progression. From her death-
bed such a woman would see her personality and
physical characteristics extending down through the

generations, and know that in one sense, at least, she had become immortal.

Nina sometimes wondered what her own obituary might say. "Retired attorney Nina Reilly died today at the ripe old age of 99. In the eighties she attended the Monterey College of Law and in later years practiced law in San Francisco and Tahoe. She leaves behind a son, two grandchildren, and one great-grandchild." Even embellished with nonexistent generations of descendants, it was pretty plain. Someone would read between the lines and decide she had done her best, she hoped.

According to the newspaper, Raymond de Beers, age 48, a partner in De Beers Construction, had died in an accident during a storm while hiking on Mount Tallac. A civil engineer, he had built a number of homes in the area and handled the renovation of Prize's casino two years before. His funeral had been nondenominational and he had been interred in Tahoe's main cemetery. No church or other affiliation was mentioned.

He was survived by Sarah de Beers, his wife; his two children, Molly and Jason; his father and partner in the business, Quentin de Beers, and his other partner, Leo Tarrant.

De Beers Construction sounded like a company that was doing reasonably well. Nina had heard of Quentin de Beers. Who in Tahoe hadn't? A heavy contributor to politicians' campaigns, a former city councilman, a member of every service club you could name, Quentin de Beers was one of those upstanding citizens everybody loved to put on a committee. But Ray de Beers must have been a nonjoiner. The service clubs and professional organizations left unmentioned in the obituary would have welcomed Quentin de Beers's son.

She approved of the simple explanation given for de Beers's death. To say a man died after being struck by lightning diminished his life by playing up the sensational cause of his death. She could hear Molly's sardonic tone at the coroner's office again. "Choking back the tears," she had said.

Deputy Kimura opened the doors to the Superior Court courtroom, and she followed the crowd inside, holding the image of Ray de Beers's burned body splayed over gray granite, her mood somber. Even though he had revealed himself as a nasty character that day on the mountain it bothered her that no one in the family seemed to mourn de Beers's death. Like Willy Loman, he shouldn't fall into his grave like an old dog. Attention should be paid, but by the family, not by some stranger passing.

In the quaint and wildly prosperous little town of Carmel, some two hundred and fifty miles away on Monterey Bay, Paul van Wagoner invited Collier Hallowell to sit down. It was Thursday at six. Hallowell had made an appointment the day before and Paul had made room for him, because Nina had referred him and because Paul was curious as to why a deputy DA, with cops raring to jump through hoops for him, wanted a private investigator.

Hallowell had changed since Paul had last seen him. He was grayer, his square Irish face pale under a thin flush of sun. Tall, with dramatic black eyebrows over perpetually droopy eyes that were a sharp contrast to the fading, peppered hair, he clutched a thick folder on his lap. The Case, Paul thought, his pulse racing as it always did at the start of each new game. He leaned back in his three-thousand-dollar ergonomic chair, assuming an expression of polite inquiry.

"Good to see you again, Paul," Hallowell was saying.

"Out of the courtroom and not on opposite sides for once," Paul agreed. "Are you on vacation? Playing some golf down here? Del Monte's at its best in early autumn."

"Actually, I took a few days off because I wanted to come and see you. Maybe I can get a game in. You look like you're doing well."

"I work hard for the money," Paul said. "And as good as I am, I know that there are plenty of other hungry PI's between Carmel and Tahoe. So what brings you all this way to see me?"

"I wanted somebody from out of town. I want this kept very quiet. And I know you. Your work with Nina has given me one headache after another. That's a good recommendation in itself, but I also couldn't help noticing you have a way of charming information out of people who don't have much to say to the law."

"I have better luck now than I had as a cop, definitely," Paul said. "People were afraid of me. Half the world's running afoul of some law or another. Old traffic warrants, back child support, under-the-counter jobs, no green card, unsmogged cars—man, it's tough to stay straight in this society."

"You have another advantage over law enforcement. You don't have to go strictly by the book. The matter that I want to talk to you about has already been fully explored by the South Lake Tahoe police," Hallowell said. "In spite of an intensive, lengthy investigation, they got nowhere, but you and I both know there's always something or someone. An overlooked piece of evidence, a jilted girlfriend, a drinking buddy; there's someone out there who knows something and will talk to the right person."

Paul nodded. "Speaking of drinking buddies, want a beer? I laid in some Pilsner Urquells from Trader Joe's yesterday."

When he saw Hallowell's reaction, he said, "Hey, perk of being your own boss." He wouldn't have pulled one out back in the old days at the station house, true. Now he could while away his time dead drunk if he wanted to—not that he did. He just liked the feeling that he had the option.

"Sounds good," Hallowell answered.

Paul popped a couple of cold ones from his mini-fridge. Waiting until Hallowell had finished a good long pull, he said, "Let's hear it."

Hallowell set his bottle on the desk. "I want you to look into my wife's death."

"How did she die?"

"Hit and run, three years ago this month. August eighteenth."

"Go on."

"You'd think by now that would be easier to talk about. It's not."

"Take your time. I've got four more beers here, and there's plenty down below if we need longer."

With this encouragement, Hallowell picked up his bottle again and drank, nodded once, and said, "We met eight years ago, when I was just starting out in the DA's office. She was new too, had just graduated from UC Berkeley in criminology. She wanted to go into law enforcement and she ended up in the Tahoe probation department working as a case officer. We saw each

other in court because I was handling probation revo-
cation hearings back then. We were married about a
year and a half later. She kept her maiden name, Anna
Louise Meade."

He drew the name out, enjoying the words on his
tongue, obviously relishing the opportunity to talk
about a woman that still lived in his heart while others
had moved on and forgotten her.

"Do you have a picture?"

Hallowell pulled out a three-by-five glossy, handing
it over to Paul. The picture, taken outdoors in sunlight,
showed a woman's face. A tanned young woman with
neat dark brown hair smiled, but not too generously,
holding back some. Small, even teeth gleamed in a full-
lipped mouth. Because of the sun, half of her face was
shaded, and the strong, straight nose cast a shadow over
one glowing cheek. Dark eyes, intelligent-looking,
brown probably, crinkled up in the light. She had been
a pretty girl who wanted to be taken seriously, Paul
guessed.

"That picture was taken three weeks before she
died," Hallowell said.

"Bad luck," Paul said. "Makes you wonder whether
there's any justice in the world. Criminology was my
field too. Any kids?"

"She had a miscarriage the year before, and we were
trying again." He paused. "So, no."

"Other than her work, what did she like to do?"

"She loved to ride, ski, hike, skate, bike, camp. Anything outdoors. She loved to get out." As Hallowell
talked about his wife, the restraint that had been part of
him for as long as Paul had known him fell away, the
features on his face softening and looking more human.

"And although she had a solemn side, she could be funny as hell."

"Excuse me for saying so, and granted, I only see you between four walls, but you've never struck me as an outdoorsy type yourself. Your job doesn't lend itself to abundant free time."

"She got me out, when she could. She taught me about nature. I still hike whenever I get a chance."

"You brought the police reports?" Paul asked.

"Everything. Here." He passed over the file with a relieved sigh.

"Tell me what happened."

"I always think how normal it was, how comfortable it was that day when she got home. I was at my desk in the living room. I'd come home early to finish some work. I don't even remember what case I was working on. I did work at home sometimes, although she played a game about it with me. She would 'kidnap' me, take me to dinner or a movie. You think you have to do the work right then, that you can never make it up, but somehow the work always gets done. It's the rest of life that stays unfinished. . . .

"So that night, I was preoccupied. She told me she wanted to talk to me about something." His hands clenched and unclenched on his lap. "She liked to talk, so I didn't think much about it. But this time . . ." Hallowell stopped dead.

"Yes?" Paul prompted after a long moment.

"I figured whatever it was she wanted to talk about could wait for half an hour. I knew she planned to go to the grocery store that afternoon before dinner. I had been counting on that time to finish my work, so I told her to go on to the store and that we'd go for a walk after dinner and talk. She loved walking outside after dark, especially during the summer. She knew all the constellations and would point them out to me. What's that old Irish expression? 'May the seven summer stars shine on you, may heaven's brightest angels bless you'. . . . She was an angel, Paul. . . .''

As Hallowell continued, his expression alternately nostalgic and agitated, Paul saw that he was reliving those last moments, every word that had passed between them, every chance he had passed up to change his wife's destiny.

"I walked her to the door. She had this bright orange-colored dress on under her suit jacket; pretty, like a sunset. I pulled the jacket off her and hung it in the closet, telling her she wouldn't need it, it was so warm. At the door, we didn't kiss, just hugged. She had a way of collapsing in my arms when I held her, like it was the only place she could really relax, but in retrospect I realize that this time she didn't relax. There was something on her mind. And I'll never know what it was. Something small and silly? Or something that led to her death?"

"She was tense?" Paul asked, bringing him back.

"Yes. When I realized how upset she was, I said, okay, the food can wait; let's talk. But she was halfway out the door. She said she would hurry, but now she wanted to go and get it done.

"So I let her go." Hallowell's voice broke. He looked down at the floor. Paul could imagine how many sleepless nights that instant had cost him.

"She took the car down to Raley's at the state line. The air-conditioning was broken, so she must have parked at the far edge of the lot under the trees to keep the car cool.

"After shopping, she headed back to the car. About

fifty feet before she reached it, after she had already opened the locks with the remote on her key chain, a large light-colored car came across the lot and hit her from the left. She hit the windshield and fell off."

"Died immediately?"

"Massive brain damage, but she lived for two days."

"And the car?"

"No skid marks. Never slowed down."

"Terrible. But that's a busy corner. The lot must have been full of shoppers. Couldn't anyone describe the car better than that?"

"Nobody else had parked that far out. There was only one witness, a woman. She ran after the car to get the license plate number but she hurt her ankle and had to stop."

"You've talked to her yourself?"

"Of course. Kim Voss. Her statement is in the file. She'll talk to you."

"No trace of the car?"

"Permanently disappeared in somebody's garage, or driven to Mexico and parted out, but not repaired over a two-hundred-mile radius, I guarantee you that." Hallowell's jaw clenched, and Paul got a glimpse of the steely resolve that would not let him give up or let go.

"Sometimes the car leaves . . . traces on the victim," Paul said, choosing his words with care.

"She hit the bumper, then the windshield," Hallowell said. "No paint chips. The autopsy and lab reports are in the file." He polished off the beer, his head leaning back, his throat working as he swallowed it. Paul had another one open and waiting for him, which Hallowell took without comment, setting it neatly next to the empty.

"Even though they never found the car or the

driver, her death was ultimately ruled an accident, of course," Hallowell went on. "There was no evidence of premeditation."

"And she gave you no hint at all about what she wanted to discuss?"

"No. Later I talked with her boss, Marvin Gates. He couldn't think of anything unusual."

"None of her clients had threatened her? That happens to probation officers. Somebody goes back inside because she gives him a bad report. A relative blames her for not doing her job, or for doing it too well."

"There were no threats I had heard or that Gates knew about. He had nothing but praise for Anna. He said she had a rare rapport with offenders. Said her clients liked her, in fact."

"Did he know who she saw that day?"

"He had a list of her appointments, but that's next to useless. Anna wanted to help these people, and she tried to be accessible whenever possible. If someone came in before they were due, she always accommodated them, so some people she saw on that day might not show up on that list."

"Anyone else in the office who might know exactly who came in that day?"

"It's a busy place and each officer operates fairly independently. They had very heavy loads. I doubt anyone else was keeping track of Anna's clients other than Anna and her boss, but even he could only give her half an eye."

"Who was Anna supervising at that time?"

"She had sixty-two felons, mostly women but a few men, on her case list."

Paul whistled.

"Most of them were nonviolent, drugs and white-collar stuff. They checked in, they gave her the forms from whatever detox program or counseling thing they were in. She called the workplaces to make sure they were still there on the job and helped 'em when she could. You know the routine. She did what she had to do, but she tried to be compassionate."

"Still," Paul said.

"Still," Hallowell agreed. "It could be one of them."

"It's been three years," Paul said.

"For a long time, I expected the guy would come out of the woodwork if I was just patient," Hallowell said. "Somebody would get picked up on an unrelated charge and have some information to trade, or a wife would find out and have a crisis of conscience, I don't know. But it never happened."

"So why start this whole thing up again?"

"Because . . . I haven't been able to move on. It's affecting my work, my attempts to have a life outside work. I went for a hike a week ago—you may have heard about it from Nina. The damnedest thing happened. A terrific storm came up. Another hiker who had come up just behind us was struck by lightning and died. I had been thinking about Anna the whole way up the trail, about one time when we hiked that same trail. I don't know if it was the storm, exposure, the shock. . . . I didn't handle it very well. In fact, I had a little breakdown or something. I thought this dead guy I was giving CPR to was Anna. I realized I—I'm not much good for . . . anyone else. I have to know. Who killed her? Why did she die?"

"You were hiking with Nina, huh?" Paul said.

"Right."

Paul got up and went to his window, looking down

at the Hog's Breath Inn's outdoor courtyard, where the happy-hour crowd was sitting around in their casual California togs mellowing out on merlot or chardonnay from the little local vineyard where they'd gone wine-tasting that afternoon. In a little while they would meander down Ocean Boulevard to the main beach to watch the sunset, pleasantly fuzzy, just the way he intended to be in half an hour.

So Hallowell was the reason for his recent demotion by Nina to best buddy.

"I don't want revenge," Hallowell was saying. "I just want some peace. . . ."

"I oughta take her over my knee and spank her," Paul said to the heedless happy people.

"What?"

"Never mind," Paul said, turning back to face Hallowell. "I'm expensive."

"I haven't had much to spend my money on. This seems like a good buy."

"I'm based here. You'd have to cover my expenses at Tahoe."

"Fine," Hallowell said. "You'd have a free hand."

Paul thought, This might be a good time to go up there.

"Is there a problem?"

"Just going over my schedule mentally," Paul said. "I could get up there on Monday."

"Great."

"You staying over tonight?"

"I'm driving back in the morning."

"You like sushi?"

"My daddy was a samurai."

"Good, because I know a Japanese joint called the Robata with eel and squid and all that good squishy stuff. Let's go get a bite to eat, talk some more about your case. And mutual friends."

"Mutual friends? You mean Nina?" Hallowell said.

"Why, yes. I do mean Nina," said Paul.

5

IT'S YOUR OWN HOME, NOT TOO BIG TO HANDLE, with a fence and a gate, on a plot of land, your land. It's your fireplace in winter, in which you build fires from the woodpile outside, and your garden in summer, bursting with vegetables. Through tall windows what feels like your own sunlight pours in. Soft rugs caress your hardwood floors, a thick comforter protects your bed, oranges on the table welcome you home from the fray. . . .

Nina was dreaming. Her dream was so peaceful, so nice. She lived in a chalet under the pines, and no one knew her address. . . .

Someone was pounding on the door. She stuck her arm out from under the covers and looked groggily at her watch. Nine-fifteen. Saturday morning. Correction, someone was not pounding. Matt's new dog, a large slobbering hound named Hitchcock with a checkered past she didn't care to think about, wanted in. He liked Nina. He loved her. She rued the day Matt had taken in this mangy cur.

His scratching at the door was like fingernails on a blackboard. She knew what he wanted. He wanted a walk. Well, by God, somebody else could take him, this was her day off, and . . .

Hitchcock left her alone for a minute, then commenced a kind of keening, like a black, furry banshee. "No!" she commanded. Peace descended, and she felt the snoozes taking her down into that soft, delicious place. . . . The keening resumed, gaining in intensity, punctuated by occasional nerve-shattering scrapes on the door.

Cursing, she sat up and swung her feet over the side of the bed. Bob was still off in San Francisco visiting his father, and she could really use some time to herself, but she wasn't going to get it in Matt's household, with his two kids bouncing off the hallway walls and Hitchcock whining and Matt drilling in the garage.

She had been living with Matt and Andrea in Matt's house on Pony Express for almost two years, ever since her move to Tahoe from San Francisco and her divorce from Jack McIntyre. They had been as good as gold to her, helping with Bob, giving them both a warm and well-run household to live in. But the arrangement was supposed to be temporary.

Sometimes her work caused trouble for the family. Although Matt understood how much she loved her work, he hated what she did. He considered her legal work, as mundane as it usually was, riddled with potential violence. In those rare moments when things got out of hand, he had been too involved not to notice. Matt and Andrea must feel crowded at times, as crowded as she felt this morning.

A deep, loud bark came from the door.

"I'm going to get you, you dirty dog," Nina said, hobbling over to him, wrapping her robe around her.

When Nina finally made it to the kitchen for coffee, Andrea was already tossing dirty cereal bowls into a sinkful of suds, her red hair looking almost toned down above her brick-red shirt. "There's our big filthy beast," Andrea crooned, waving a bowl at the dog. "Ready for your kibble, boy?" Hitchcock perked up his floppy ears, trotting eagerly toward his food bowl, drool hanging from one flap of his jaws. While Andrea tenderly mashed canned dog food into the kibble, Nina made herself a bowl of Rice Krispies and a cup of coffee. She said, "I had to put him on a leash at the bottom of the hill. He was chasing the cars."

"He's not very bright," Andrea said. "But he does have a way about him." She smoothed his coat while Hitchcock crunched through an enormous bowl of kibble.

Matt slammed through the open back door, grabbed a cup from the shelf, poured himself coffee, and sat down, shooting a spray of fine sawdust in all directions.

"Has anyone else ever noticed that everything men do is noisy?" asked Nina. She didn't see much of Matt these days. He spent most of his spare time lately in the garage.

"And grungy," Andrea added, giving him a careful kiss on the forehead. She put a hand up to push back his hair. "You have to hunt for a clean spot."

"Good morning to you, too, ladies," said Matt, bending down to pet Hitchcock, who had appeared at his side and cocked his head at just the right height for an arm hanging at loose ends.

Matt had a frizzle of ash color over his ears these days. A dirty cap disguised the rest of his hair, but couldn't hide his mood. He looked like a man with a lot on his mind, a lot to do, as disturbed and lacking in peace as Nina was. The hand he rested on one knee jittered to the rhythm of his private thoughts.

"Matt, I've been thinking . . ." started Nina.

Matt stood up abruptly, holding tight to his cup, screeching the wooden legs of his chair over the floor and heading briskly for the back door. "Man, this morning's flying by. Well, I'll leave you ladies to your chat. . . ."

"Matt, sit down. This will only take a minute," said Nina firmly, "and it concerns you, too."

He sighed, and sat down.

"I've been thinking. You guys have been so great to us. Bob and me. You've put up with a lot."

"True," said Matt.

Andrea swatted at him with her hand.

"But when we came here, we only meant to stay until I knew what I would be doing. Now I'm settled here. I really want to know whether you guys are still happy with the arrangement. I mean, we could find a place of our own now. Bob's old enough to bike a few blocks to see his cousins, and I've been making some money. Maybe everyone's ready for that?"

Andrea came over and sat down by her at the table. She had a redhead's milky skin and freckles, and a no-nonsense way about her. A part-time director of the Tahoe Women's Shelter, she carried responsibility as if it weighed nothing. She cooked, she cleaned, she raised kids and held a responsible job. She was an affront to working women like Nina who could barely cope with half that.

"You could find a place close by," Matt said.

"Matt does have a use for the space," Andrea said at the same time.

So she had guessed right. It was time to move.

After Matt descended down the stairs into the cave of his garage workshop, Nina pushed back her chair, fending off Hitchcock, and said, "Well, no time like today. I'm going to start looking around."

"You know, Nina, we love you guys. You don't have to rush."

Nina was grimacing. She and Bob had overstayed their welcome. Sheer laziness and her own self-absorption had prevented her from recognizing what had clearly become an issue for Matt and Andrea.

Andrea said apologetically, "They're forecasting an early winter, with lots of snow. I know he's worrying about getting things in order. He's got two tow trucks now, and three more he wants to buy. It's turning into a good winter business. I hate to tell you this, but I have a feeling he's got his eye on your room for an office."

"Oh, it'll be fun," Nina said. "We'll buy a castle on the lake. You and Troy and Bree can come visit and zip around in our Boston Whaler without Matt until I find it in me to forgive him for throwing me out."

Andrea showed the dimple she usually kept sequestered in her right cheek. "We'll miss all the excitement," she said. "The break-ins, the kidnappings, the shootings . . . Find a place close by, okay? One with good security."

Before leaving the house, Nina called Bob in San Francisco.

She missed him. A week away from him, even in this

bustling household, made her aware how much she depended on him for company. An eleven-year-old boy said and did a number of unexpected things, she was finding out, and she'd only recently realized how much she enjoyed his spontaneity.

She had never married Bob's father, Kurt Scott, and the relationship had ended before Bob's birth. Bob was just getting to know Kurt, who lived in Germany but had been in the States for a long visit. Kurt had asked her to let him take Bob to San Francisco before he went back to Wiesbaden, and Nina had let Bob go with him, but she had been more lonely than she expected without Bob.

"How are you, honey?" she said when she heard Bob's voice.

"Great!" said Bob. "Yesterday we went to the Exploratorium. They have this exhibit there, where you stand in front of a blank wall, only you don't stand, you pose or something. So I jumped, and this light goes off, and guess what, Mom?"

"What?"

"Your shadow stays behind, frozen in a jump! Cool, huh?"

Frozen in a jump. Kind of how she felt, at the moment—suspended, transient, needing to land somewhere . . . "How's it going with your dad?"

"Does he have to go, Mom? Why can't he stay?"

"You'll have to talk to him about that, honey." She felt the familiar stab of guilt. Bob wasn't fated to have a pair of parents around the house. She just couldn't seem to get it right, unlike Andrea.

She went to see Mr. Muntz in his office a few blocks from her own. "What would be your financing options?" the dapper silver-haired realtor said twice before she heard him. Startled, she closed the multiple listing book with its pictures of homes all over Tahoe.

He handed her a long form full of financial minutiae. "Why don't you go ahead and fill this in?" he said. "It'll help me pick out some good properties for us to look at."

"I'd prefer to look first. Then, if I get interested in a house, we'll talk about that," Nina said.

Mr. Muntz remained outwardly cheerful, although she could sense that he had revised his initial good impression of her. At her request they went out to his car, a yellow Cadillac, a few years old, its waxed finish satiny. He said he would take her for a tour of the town, the "grand tour," he called it. She felt as if she were cruising on an ocean liner as she sat in the front seat flipping through the listings, fascinated as Mr. Muntz Berlitzed her through a whole new language. Where else would she learn that AEK meant "all-electric kitchen" or that *charm* was real-estate lingo for minuscule? Or that *fixer* was short for run for your life and *secure* stood for rotten, crime-ridden neighborhood?

They started down near the lake, in a neighborhood of crowded cottages, all alike in a rustic simplicity, and yet obviously put together by a hundred different people with a hundred different ideas about what constituted a home.

"This is the Bijou," he said. "A lot of rentals in this neighborhood." He turned his head slightly to observe her reaction. She didn't say anything, so he went on: "The prices are good, though. It's an excellent entry-level neighborhood, close to the casinos, if that's your style." Again he swung an eye her way.

"Small lots," she commented.

"You're looking for something large?" Almost imperceptibly, the edges of his mouth tipped up.

"Is there such a thing as property bordering on national forest or something? So that you have some privacy, but don't have to buy acres and acres of land?"

"Occasionally. Naturally, that adds to the price." The words rolled familiarly off his tongue. He navigated the big car around a corner, his tie flapping in the wind from the open window. The only thing lacking was a yachting cap.

"What I'd really love is lakefront," Nina went on.

"Wouldn't we all?"

"I don't suppose there are any fixer-uppers with their own little beach?"

"People who own lakefront property usually maintain it. But, of course, there's the Tahoe Keys," he said. "Most of the houses there have private docks. You're not on a beach, but it's water. Hop in your motorboat and let 'er rip."

He drove slowly through the Keys, which looked like a suburban neighborhood anywhere, with orderly dead-end streets lined with stucco-sided ranch houses on small lots with double garages. Grass huddled in scanty clumps as if waiting for the snow to come. Behind the houses, narrow man-made canals flowed out to the lake. The view toward the surrounding mountains was unobstructed.

The canals and view would be nice, but she would feel exposed out here, in the lake practically. She wanted sun, but filtered through tall trees. "Something more woodsy?" she said.

"Ah. Woodsy it is."

They drove through another neighborhood, close to

the city offices and court buildings, and past rustic cabins in an area called Tahoe Paradise, continuing from there along Pioneer Trail, stopping at a few vacant properties. Nina thought she liked Tahoe Paradise best, a heavily wooded area of A-frames and chalets, not too highfalutin. There were places nearby to walk and hike and the neighborhood was close enough to Matt's house that Bobby could ride his bike there. . . .

"Your price range?" Mr. Muntz was saying delicately but insistently, determined if possible to reduce her murmurs of approval to paperwork.

"I don't know much about real estate up here. It's hard to say."

That made him clutch his hands together tightly on the leather-wrapped wheel, the better to avoid rubbing them together with glee.

As they turned right on Highway 89 to head back up to the Y, Nina said, "Mr. Muntz, do you . . . did you know Ray de Beers?"

"De Beers Construction. They build houses. Oh, yes, I knew Ray. Why do you ask about him? You thinking about buying a lot and building yourself? That's one thing they do, build spec houses."

"No. But I recently . . . met Mr. de Beers. Right before his death."

"He stood up there on that mountain and he said one too many times 'May God strike me dead if I'm lying,' and God took him up on it," Mr. Muntz said with a malicious chuckle. "You heard he got killed by a lightning bolt?"

"I take it you didn't like him."

"You take it right, honey. I used to sell Ray's houses. His father, Quentin, had spent years building the business, but about ten years ago Ray moved in and started building the houses. And the houses were trashy junk. Ray worked his miracles with one-coat paint. I wouldn't even show you one of his places, everybody's so lawsuit-happy these days."

"Have you met his family?"

"His wife, once. Case in point: Ray took her out to one of his projects one fine day a few years back, and the damn thing fell down. Not really, just one of the joists came down because he wasn't using the right-size nails. Broke both her legs. Poetic justice."   ·

"Poetic justice would be if it broke both *his* legs, wouldn't you say?" Nina said. Once again she was back on the mountain, hearing Ray say, *Making sure I don't get to forget it even for one lousy minute.* So that was what he had meant.

They drove past the Y on 89, then turned left onto a wooded hill. "This is Gardner Mountain," Mr. Muntz said. "Some cozy places up here I think you might like. You say three bedrooms would do you. How big is your family?"

Looking out the window at the quiet neighborhood they were driving through, Nina said, "There are two of us, me and my son Bob. He's eleven."

"No one else?"

"I'm divorced." Don't be so prickly, Nina, she told herself. Half the world's divorced—maybe not as recently as you, but—

"You're one of those working mothers, then?"

"My office is just a few blocks down Highway Fifty, in the Starlake Building. You've probably seen my sign. I'm an attorney."

"Ah, yes," Mr. Muntz said, but he looked alarmed

instead of reassured. Nina thought, He hates lawyers, just my luck.

"I remember seeing some articles about you in the paper. The Patterson trial and the Scott thing. You do criminal defense work, right?"

"I'm a general practitioner. Wills, contracts, family law . . . and criminal law."

"You haven't been in town long?"

Who has, she thought. "Almost two years now."

"And . . . you're self-employed?"

"I can handle a reasonable down payment," Nina said. She had inherited a small cottage in Pacific Grove, which she rented out, and had a nest egg from her divorce settlement. "I can make the payments."

"I see." Mr. Muntz sounded disappointed. Dollar signs no longer shone in his eyes. The Caddy shimmied a little, as if preparing to eject her. "You haven't talked to your bank. Firmed up the, ah, loan situation?"

"You don't think I could get a mortgage? I'm making good money. I've been a lawyer for six years. My credit cards are paid up. What's the problem, Mr. Muntz?"

The realtor had all the sensitivity of a signpost. He piloted around another turn, the sun highlighting his carefully moussed hair and the lines in his infuriatingly smug face. "A single mother. Not long in the area. No employer."

"But I'm a lawyer!"

"This may surprise you, but being a lawyer isn't an advantage anymore. It's not a gentleman's profession since . . ." He paused delicately. "Plenty of 'em come up for the gambling or the skiing, like it, and rent a hole-in-the-wall office for a few months, after which they're gone and forgotten except for their bum accounts payable. Please don't take offense. It's the harsh reality of the business world. Those damn bankers, obsessed with stability, you know?" He looked at his watch. "I'm so sorry, I've got an appointment. Clients." Actual clients, his expression said, nuclear families headed by husbands with steady jobs.

"Clients, eh? You can't have too many of those," Nina said. "Not with your attitude."

"Now see here, honey—"

"I'm not your honey. And you just aced yourself out of a commission, pal."

"Well. Perhaps we should head back."

"You've got that right."

Head high, Nina jumped out of the Caddy and into her own dusty Ford Bronco at the realty office. An impromptu flea market had sprung up near the Y. Dusty cars and pickups clogged the factory outlet parking lots, turning Highway 50 into a ten-mile crawl toward the casinos. She opened the windows and resigned herself. High clouds drifted overhead, and the air felt mellow and warm. She was regretting her rudeness in spite of Mr. Muntz's provocations. Half the town would soon hear his version of their run-in. She lectured herself again about discretion, prudence, all those virtuous qualities she would probably never acquire.

Finally wending her way across the state line into Nevada, she parked in the lot behind Prize's and entered the casino, hoping to shake off the losses of the day.

Weekenders and locals alike smoked and drank and gambled and flirted on the blackjack stools and around the craps tables, their up-front greed for money looking like good clean fun after Mr. Muntz's tawdry business. As mindful of movement as hungry buzzards, black-suited pit bosses swiveled their eyes from table to table. Around the rooms that stretched from one perennial neon-lit night to another, bells rang and lights flashed, and the unlucky gathered to watch the lucky gather up their winnings. Over at the Tonga Bar, the alcoholics were getting an early start.

Why did she like it here so much? Was it the total acceptance (for as long as she had a quarter left to drop in the slots)? Shrugging, she gave a change person a twenty and started feeding quarters into the maw of a video poker machine.

After twenty minutes, three dollars up from her initial investment, she was getting carpal tunnel syndrome in her right index finger from punching the *play* and *hit* and *deal* buttons. Carrying her white plastic bucket with its scanty load of quarters, she got up and wandered over to the high-stakes room, where real gamblers playing stud poker sat at tables for eight headed by attentive dealers in green aprons.

Sometimes she caught a glimpse of Hollywood people or foreign dignitaries through the doorway. A bouncer trying not to look like one waited to toss out cash-poor curiosity-seekers like herself if they took it in mind to cross the threshold. Stepping out of his line of sight, Nina saw someone she recognized, a woman with sunglasses pushed up over curly black hair.

Although it was early afternoon, the woman was wearing a black cocktail dress, her long slim legs crossed at the ankles, tapping her lacquered fingernails on the side of her martini glass. She pushed a stack of chips to the middle of the table from several stockpiled neatly in front of her. While Nina considered whether she ought to say hello, the woman folded a dud hand, watching her hundred-dollar chips being raked away, her expression blank.

She wore black out of respect for her husband, of course, black to show her grief. It was Sarah de Beers, and next to her, not touching her but staying close by, sat Leo Tarrant.

She saw Nina watching and got up quickly, walking toward her. Brushing past the bouncer, she took Nina by the arm. "Why are you following me?"

"Mrs. de Beers, I'm here to have some fun on a Saturday afternoon, just like you. That's all."

"I don't believe it. It's Quentin, isn't it? What is he up to now? Are you going to photograph me having a moment of freedom? What does he want?"

"I don't know what you're talking about," said Nina. "Now, I can see you're upset, but I need my arm back."

She let go of Nina's arm and pulled a loose strap up over her own bare shoulder, staggering a little. "I'm sorry. It's Ray's father. He's going to take Ray's place, running my life, telling me and the kids what to do and how to do it. Criticizing everything. What's wrong with coming here to have a little fun? What's wrong with wanting to forget everything for a few hours?"

Leo appeared, naked adoration sandblasting the rough edges from his face as he looked at her. "Everything okay?" he asked her, his eyes turning on Nina with an entirely different expression.

"I want to go home, Leo. Let's go."

"Wait. Mrs. de Beers," said Nina quickly, "since you're here, there's something I've been meaning to ask."

"What?"

"Did our decision to continue on up to the summit

have anything at all to do with the rest of you trying to reach the top?"

"You feel guilty about that, don't you? You could tell Ray didn't like seeing you go ahead of us."

"I wondered."

"He's dead; that's the only thing that matters. Just like all of us, you had everything and nothing to do with it. I'm sorry . . . about what I said." She leaned a little on Leo as they walked away. Nina looked around. At the craps table nearby, the clamoring reached a crescendo as an elderly man blew on the dice, mumbled a prayer or something like it, and tossed the dice against the back wall of the table. Then there was jubilation from the winners, but now she registered, too, the moaning of the losers.

The fever had broken. She cashed in and went home.

6

PAUL LEFT BEFORE DAWN ON MONDAY MORNING and made it up to Tahoe from Carmel in four hours and thirty-seven minutes, arriving before ten, a personal best.

He checked into Caesars with one airline bag, one laptop Macintosh Powerbook, his cell phone, and his spanking-new Czech semiautomatic, purchased at a Cow Palace gun show just a few weeks before. Opening the bag on the bed, he laid out his swim suit, tennis racket, a pair of Dockers, and some polo shirts.

The leather toiletry bag he tossed into the bathroom, and the thick manila folder he laid on the table by the window, where he had already arranged the Powerbook and the phone. The gun went on the nightstand beside the bed, still in its holster.

Room service arrived with breakfast just as he finished unpacking, and he ate while he booted up the Powerbook. He was calling his investigation of Anna Meade's death the Windshield Case in his ClarisWorks file. He had already entered the notes he had made over the weekend from Hallowell's files. He had ideas and he had a list of people he wanted to meet.

Somebody in this town would know the name of the driver of the hit-and-run car. Even a tourist left a paper trail in this day and age. Hansel and Gretel wouldn't have needed to rely on bread crumbs to find their way out of the forest if they had lived at the end of the twentieth century; any number of things would have been tracking them, from satellites on down.

He clicked his mouse and looked at the accident-reconstruction expert's report.

No skid marks. Possibly the driver just didn't see her. Even if she was hit accidentally, the driver might not stop. Panic always headed the reasons, but the panicked innocent often showed up at the police station later to blab a weeping, guilt-stricken confession. The less innocent could choose from a thousand reasons not to come forward, ranging from trouble with the law to irresponsibility, immaturity, or sociopathy. Half the world had one of those problems, and the other half probably had them too.

For the purposes of his investigation, Paul decided to start with the idea that Anna Meade was killed deliberately. She had been happily married, if he believed Hallowell, which he did, so most likely he wouldn't have to look at any hanky-panky, although there was always the possibility of a psycho somewhere obsessed with her. He sighed. A world full of bad boys. *If I can't have her, nobody can!* How many times had he seen the bloody outcome of that kind of primitive emotion when he was a cop?

There was also the possibility of a revenge killing by one of the bad boys her husband the prosecutor had helped into jail. This, Paul found unlikely. Most criminals lacked subtlety. Collier would have been the one left to drain on the asphalt, not his wife, and Collier had not mentioned any intimidation or blackmail attempts.

Then there was the most likely possibility, that one of her clients had come after her. The cops had painstakingly checked and double-checked alibis on all sixty-two of the parolees and probationers assigned to her, but there was still the chance.

In her position, if she was good, she would have learned all the dirty family secrets. She would know what her parolees wanted and dreamed about at night, their weaknesses and strengths, who might stay out this time and who would be going down again. Had something she'd known about one of her clients gotten her killed?

According to the statement in the file by Marvin Gates, her supervisor, Anna was top-notch, one of those caring professional types who burn out after ten or fifteen years and move on to something less stressful. If she had lived, she and Collier would probably have had children. She might have changed to a part-time job or quit for a while to raise them, and Collier wouldn't have that achy-breaky look of a man who goes through the motions of life without enjoying its fruits.

Too much info, too many possibilities. He needed to start simple with a single end of the string and from there he could follow it through all its tangles, all the way home. He turned away from the Powerbook and picked up the pictures from the on-site police investigation. In sharp-focus black and white he studied Anna Meade lying on top of a white-painted parking stall stripe, her small shoe a couple of feet away.

Though the shadows were long on that August evening the photographer had managed to expose well for detail. Faceup on the asphalt, one of her eyes open and looking off shyly to the side, already comatose, she looked as if she felt slightly embarrassed to make such a mess. The left side of her head had been cracked open and the blood from that injury had pooled around the back of her head. Her legs had settled into impossible positions. The car had hit her broadside from her left while she was walking, and she might have gotten away with broken bones, except she'd apparently gone up over the hood on impact, hitting the windshield before sliding to the pavement.

Stroking his stubbly jaw, Paul thought about that. About ten years earlier he had handled a homicide investigation in San Francisco in which the victim had hit the windshield of the vehicle involved. The body had hit so hard, it had left an imprint of the face on the safety glass, a side view that showed the shape of the nose and an open mouth.

The massive contusion on the left side of Anna Meade's face looked similar to the injury on that victim. The cops were right. She had hit the windshield. He tried not to think about Hallowell seeing that face.

Find the end of the string that led to the car, and the rest would take care of itself. Even without broken glass or bits of chrome or paint to match from the scene, there might be marks on the front grillework or signs of replacement. And then there was the long shot, the remote possibility that, unless the windshield had been replaced or the car had been crushed for junk, the car might still carry some kind of an impression, a web of cracks, a slight indentation not worth fixing, an oh-so-slightly visible imprint, a memory of murder on glass.

He made some calls and opened a new file on the Powerbook. First, he would read it all, all three years of police work, again, taking notes on the computer. At three he would go to see Kim Voss, the eyewitness.

Kim Voss's home in Round Hill, on the Nevada side of Lake Tahoe, was an oddly shaped modern affair that started low and ended up more than two stories high, sheltered behind a solid eight-foot stucco wall with a security gate. Inside the gate, Paul found himself in a cactus forest, the tall cacti planted in massive pots beside a sandy walkway, in front of a white windowless house of the same stucco. The desolate effect was broken by a sun-colored door, which opened noiselessly to present the lady herself, late twenties, fluffy-haired, wearing paint-stained overalls and a wary look.

"Did you read the sign?" she asked, pointing to a discreet brass plate next to her door that said NO SOLICITORS.

"It doesn't apply."

She came closer, leaning a hip on the doorway and folding her arms as if settling in for a cozy talk. "Well, then. What does?"

"My name is Paul van Wagoner. Collier Hallowell hired me to investigate the death of his wife, Anna, three years ago. I understand you were a witness."

A fleeting look Paul couldn't identify passed over Kim Voss's face. She had strong classical features, a prominent nose, well-cut lips. Unlike so many women, she wore her body comfortably, as if she liked it.

"He'll never get over her, will he? I've already talked with Collier a number of times. Didn't he tell you? I didn't see anything."

"I really just have a few questions. . . ."

"This is pointless. I saw a car at a distance, no plate, not even a specific color."

Paul whipped out his notebook. "Okay, now we're getting somewhere. What else?"

"I'm busy . . ." she said, but he could see she was weakening. Good, he liked women who weakened.

Paul gestured through the door. "Any chance we could"—he paused and raised an eyebrow—"rake over the old coals just this one time"—his best imitation of Sean Connery in his heyday as James Bond—"someplace a bit more conducive?"

She smiled slightly, responding to the familiar Scottish burr, as Paul always hoped they would, and thought for a long moment.

"Let me see your ID."

He handed it over and she studied it. "You live in Carmel. That's a beautiful town," she said. "Lots of artists live there." She handed his card back, apparently satisfied.

Paul had seen the acknowledgment of being from a wealthy community defuse suspicion of him many times before. From salesmen at his favorite clothing store who jousted for an opportunity to become his personal shopper for the day, to cashiers at the Lucky Market who waved away his credit card proof-of-bucks-in-the-bank, they fell like supplicants at the magic word *Carmel*. Anyone who could afford to live there had to be okay, right?

"Great place for painting seascapes," he said, and when he saw the look on her face above the color-spattered clothing, added, "Of course, seascapes get so . . . so boring."

"How true." She stepped aside. "You can come in."

She led the way through a hallway decorated with

big terra-cotta pots and more cacti. Through the arched doorway most of the house seemed to consist of a twenty-foot-high studio, all glass on the back wall, providing indirect northern light. Stained cloth tarps served as carpeting. A conference table covered with another tarp held myriad jars and brushes, house paint, rollers, and all sorts of other equipment. Paintings and frames leaned in loose groups against the walls. Paul's eye was drawn to a disturbing canvas, slashed through with orange and green and white. The violent clash of colors attracted his attention. The thick brush strokes suggested an ordinary house painter's brush had been used in its execution, and he did mean execution. He walked over to examine it, but she stepped in front of him and threw a drape over it.

"I don't mean to be rude, but like any painter, I'm sensitive about my work. That's a really old one. I think I've improved. Let me show you some more recent work, if you're interested?"

He nodded. The longer they spent together on these unrelated topics, the more time she had to warm up to the pending topic, and to Paul.

She led him past a series displayed along a wall that ran the length of the room. Her main subject seemed to be needle-sharp cactus in extreme close-up, though the abstract splashes of paint made this debatable. They looked like tattooed cucumbers undergoing acupuncture, or portions of dead porcupines he would prefer not to think about.

"I really don't know much about art," he said finally, realizing that she was waiting for him to say something. "And I can't compare your work to the Expressionists or the Impressionists, because I only know enough to appear knowledgeable in a pinch. Is 'wow' going to do it for you?"

He didn't know what she had expected, but he guessed he had delivered when she threw her head back in a laugh. "That does me fine!" she said. "You've missed your calling as an art critic. You're a pretty refreshing character, aren't you?"

Paul was by now enjoying himself. Her finely cut lips pursed as she looked upon these paintings that had a crudeness he actually found rather powerful. She went over to one large painting, leaned over, and brushed a speck away. Sun glanced through the tall windows and made a halo of her hair. She had broad shoulders and a deep waist, a swaying walk that had an impact.

"Let's go out back," she went on. "That's my dining room, at least for another month until the weather's too cold."

Paul followed her rounded, denim-clad rump out the door. Why, oh why, were there so many foxy women in the world to tempt him? Like a cornucopia of luscious flesh, the world spilled them into his path, where there was no way to avoid them or step over them without taking a sample.

The backyard was like the front except more densely potted, a veritable Mojave Desert of spade-leafed cacti armed with prickers like tiny knives, faithful sentinels guarding the stone patio at center. A wooden table covered with a clean white cloth had been set up. Paul sat down in one of the two iron chairs. Behind him was a fireplace with a grill set up and a tall chimney, the whole thing made of white rocks.

"Let me make you a drink."

"No, thanks," Paul said.

"C'mon. If we've got to do this, let's make it fun. Be a sport. I make a mean martini. It's almost four o'clock, which makes it practically five."

"I'm not much for martinis . . ." he said, getting ready to make a little speech about how he hadn't given much thought to martinis since he last admired Myrna Loy as Nora Charles ordering five of them to keep pace with her inebriate husband back in the days when alcohol had flash and panache and a total Hollywood detachment from its evil effects, but by the time he thought all this up, she had drifted off back toward the house. A few moments later, she reappeared with a stainless steel martini shaker beaded with evaporation and two of those invitingly wide conical cocktail glasses.

"You know the right way to make one of these, don't you?" she asked, examining an empty glass in the sun, wiping an invisible speck with the immaculate white towel she had brought. She was conjuring up a show for him, Paul realized, pleased. "Shaken, not stirred?" he suggested, recalling his earlier success with Bond.

"No, no, no. Makes no difference whether it's shaken or stirred. That stuff about bruising the gin is just a lot of hooey. First, you swirl the driest of vermouths in a frosted glass, like this." She poured it out of a silver and green bottle from high up, lifting her breasts for him to notice.

"Then—and this is the fun part—you discard all excess." Keeping her eyes on Paul, she tossed all the vermouth in the glass over her shoulder, straight into a tumorous, twisted pear cactus barely supporting itself against the house, a real Elephant Man of cacti. "Finally, you pour perfectly frigid gin through cracked ice"—which she did, the gin flowing like diamonds from a jeweler's pouch—"into the now supremely primed vessel." She finished, popped an onion-stuffed olive inside, and handed him the glass, her hand touching his.

"Whew," said Paul. "That was great. You do make it sound luscious."

She made another for herself. "Chin-chin," she said, tapping his glass.

He drank out of politeness, to test his memory about how closely gin resembled battery acid.

"Don't the cacti die in the winter?" he asked after two sips. He didn't ask what the vermouth did to them in summer. If that prickly pear was any example, he already knew. Actually, the martini had a pleasant flavor, piquant almost, or was he merely seduced by the arrant sexuality of her little exhibition? He had some more of the drink.

"Most of these are imported from the low deserts of New Mexico, where I grew up. See the barrel cactus there? The Indians used those curved spines as fish-hooks. And near the back, I keep the jumping cholla," she said, pointing to a thorny, many-branched bush resembling a sea anemone. "It has a bad reputation for jumping people, but really only has weak branches that break off and cling to people and animals passing by. I haven't had much luck with the saguaro, or giant cactus, but there are a few out front that are surviving. Oh, and inside, later maybe, I'll show you the old man cactus."

"I saw it as we walked through," Paul said. "I even touched it; that white shaggy fur cover looked so soft. Fortunately, it didn't get me."

"It's thornless, that's why it works so well inside.

Anyway, the winters are cold and snowy in New Mexico, although drier. The sun is strong here, and the summers are hot and dry, just like in the desert. This patio has a winter cover, and I remove some of the plants to a greenhouse out back to keep them warm through the worst of the winter."

Paul's glass was empty. She poured him another from the stainless steel, praising the shaker's convenience and apologizing for its aesthetic failures. "I've read your statements from the accident," he said finally, promising himself not to drink another lick. He had work to do.

"I must have told the story a dozen times. Collier talked to me personally three times. I think he felt I was his last link to his wife. I felt so bad for him."

"He's not over it," Paul said.

"Maybe he never will be," she said, slipping an olive into her mouth and chewing thoughtfully. "Which would be very sad. Some people love only once. If you lose the one you love, you lose everything, your future as well as your present. You don't recover."

"Just bear with me. Try to remember what you can."

She nodded. "Too bad I was the witness. I have no interest in cars. I can't tell a Chevy from a Toyota. I don't notice most people, either. All I knew was that there was only one shadow in there. I was about two hundred feet away, and I couldn't pick up any details."

"You were shopping at the Raley's?"

"Yes. I picked up a few things. I guess I came out just after she did. The parking lot is huge—well, you've probably seen it, it's really for the whole shopping center. I spotted her heading for the far end of the lot, almost at the street. Nobody else was parked that far out."

"But her car was parked there?"

"I found out later it was her car parked under a tree in the last lane before the street. I saw it at the time, but it hardly registered. All I really noticed was her."

"You told Collier you noticed her because of her dress."

"Yes. The wind had come up a little and it was getting cooler, but she was wearing just a silk dress, a tangerine color, clingy, very full in the skirt, old-fashioned. A shirtwaist, I think it's called. The color caught my eye, so I watched her. Color is my thing."

"How close was she to her car when she was hit?"

"Very close. She was carrying a grocery bag in her left arm. Maybe that made it hard for her to see the car coming at her."

"When did you first see the car?"

"I don't know. All of a sudden, there was this car coming down the lane from the left." Kim pushed her chair back and rested her eyes on her cactus garden. "I heard a muffled thump. I saw it hit her at the same time. I saw her from the back, the car approaching from her left. She went up and over the hood. She hit the windshield. She never made a sound. The car had slowed down to a stop by then. She began to slide, and she slid off the car onto the ground just to the side of the car, while I stood rooted there like a tree. Then I heard the engine rev up. And the asshole took off straight ahead, curled out of the lot at the first exit to the right, and took off into the traffic past the movie theater."

"So you saw the whole thing."

"Apparently I'm the only one who saw anything.

Anyway, I ran after the car, yelling, but in my hurry, I twisted my ankle and I had to stop. Then I limped over to the girl to see if she was still alive. It was horrible. She was bleeding a lot. I suppose she was dying. Her dress was torn and spattered. I got down there and held her head. I had so much blood on me by the time the ambulance came they thought I was hit too."

"Did she say anything?"

"No, no. She didn't really seem to be there, as though her soul had fled at the impact."

Paul said, "Her death seems to have had a lasting effect on you."

"Oh yes, it did. To see another human being so hurt and not be able to help is . . . indelible. I don't take the newspaper, Paul. I don't watch TV. The suffering out there is too overwhelming. I try to stay in balance. I suppose you could call me an avoider. I stay home and paint my pictures."

He was touched by her earnestness and her obvious emotional reaction to the story she told. As the shade drifted across the patio, and the martinis did their work, he felt his attraction to her growing. Her lack of makeup could have made her plain, but clear tanned skin and intelligent eyes made a harmonious balance, full of character and liveliness. She was licking the rim of her glass, not caring that he was watching, the tongue flicking around it, her eyelids half lowered so the lashes shaded her cheeks, her expression still thoughtful.

He envied artists. He suspected they tapped in to tantalizing mysteries beyond his ken, mysteries he could only imagine in a special state of mind, such as right after drinking straight gin over vermouth vapor.

She was getting up. His time was over, but he wanted to stay.

"I wish I could have helped. Tell Collier I hope you catch the bastard."

"You live alone?" Paul asked as they walked back through her studio.

"Yes. And you?"

"Yes."

"Do you like it?" she said. They were at the door now, and outside the sandscape was blinding under the sky, as if he had suddenly been transported to Taos.

"Not much," Paul said.

"I do. I love it. My work means everything to me. I feel like I'm rushing toward a great future." She blushed slightly.

"You were married?"

"No. Just a long relationship."

"Your paintings. You've sold a lot?"

"Almost everything I've painted over the past four years. Several Asian collectors pay very good prices for almost everything I can bring myself to part with." She smiled. The thought of her success seemed to amuse her.

"I'd like to have dinner with you," Paul said. "To-night."

"I don't date."

"Okay." He started toward the door, and then, his eye caught by the drape on the painting he had seen when he first entered, he stumbled, knocking the drape off the picture.

Strong emotion had been layered onto it in the wide, thick brush strokes. "Sorry," he said. "Hmm. This is different from your other work." He stooped down to read Kim's signature. Above it, in italics, was the word *Anna*.

"It's the accident," Kim said. "I painted it after she died. I don't show it to strangers. It's hideous, but I can't bring myself to get rid of it."

The bending curve of orange on the right looked like a woman to him now, vulnerable, surprised by death in the middle of life. The car, white except for a hyphen of green in front, formless over the black streak of asphalt, surged across the canvas from left to right like a nightmare locomotive. The far left side of the picture broke into two red triangles, like a pair of following sharks.

"So the car was white?" he said.

"Maybe. Light-colored. I told Collier that." She tried to cover the painting again.

Paul held her hand gently. "And what about this— these triangular shapes on the left. What are they?"

"I don't know," she said. "Now, please. Let me cover this ugly thing. It makes me sad."

"Can I borrow it?"

"I knew you were going to ask me that."

"That's good. You're getting to know me."

"If you really want to, you can borrow it. But I want this one back. I want to decide what happens to this painting." She pulled the drape back over the painting, tucking it behind for safe measure, and handing the wrapped bundle to Paul. "You didn't really trip, did you?" she asked.

"No."

"You don't like people having secrets from you."

"That's right."

He turned to go, but she said suddenly, "We could eat here."

"I could build a fire in that stone fireplace you've got back there," said Paul, trying not to appear as eager as he felt.

"I could marinate some steaks."

"Would seven be a good time?"

"It would."

"See you then." He opened the gate and like magic was transported back into the forest of Tahoe.

Paul's Private Eye Rule #1: Always check the scene yourself. He drove his van back along the highway through the casino district. As he crossed the state line back into California the casinos and glitz ended abruptly and the quieter facades took over. He turned left again a block or so farther on, into the parking lot of the shopping center where Anna Meade had died. A line of clothing and kitsch stores surrounded the lot, anchored by the Raley's supermarket at the far end.

He started in front of the Raley's and cruised around the lot. The last lane before the street that ran in front of the center ran parallel to the Raley's. Locating the accident site from his pictures and photos, he parked a few feet away, then got out and leaned against the car, taking it all in.

One thing he had learned through hard experience: You can't expect to take in a scene from somebody else's description of it. Even photo locations and angles were chosen by somebody else for somebody else's eyes. The actuality was fresh to him, different from what he had already been led to expect.

For one thing, the pavement at this far edge of the lot was cracked and worn. Chances were the surface had not been re-covered since the accident.

For another, nobody else parked this far out. Why

had Anna Meade, going in for a bag of groceries, done so? Had she met someone secretly? But there was no cover; they would have been exposed to the street. And the explanation could be as simple as Collier's suggestion that she had wanted to keep the car cool by parking under a tree.

What if she had been meeting someone she didn't want to meet in a hidden place? The location was ideal, open and public.

A client, Paul thought, who had something to say that couldn't be said at her office. Could be, although Collier had said she wanted to talk when she got home. Maybe she had planned to talk quickly. Maybe that was why, once she was at the door, she decided to go in spite of his belated invitation to stay and talk. And the client was late, so, being a sensible, efficient type, she had run into the store to get her shopping over with first.

He reached into the back of the van and got out his hand-held vacuum. Clicking open the top of the vacuum, he dumped the vacuum bag into the thickly stuffed trash bag he kept in the front seat and put on a clean one, whistling "Bernadette" by the Four Tops.

Then, Dustbuster in one hand and a racquetball bag full of his favorite tools in the other, he walked over to the spot where, by all accounts, the car had hit the girl. Grass grew from cracks in the rough paving. A plastic cup lay crunched in the middle of the lane. Not surprisingly, three years after the accident, no special signs of blood or anything else significant leapt out of the aging asphalt. The lone pine still cast its shade over some of the spaces. Picking the largest crack, Paul lay down on the warm asphalt and peered into it.

The sun shone at a good, sharp angle. A small black-

ish spider crawled up and out, its legs making tiny acro-
batic movements like a synchronized swimming team.
He used a Swiss Army knife to delve amid the pine
needles and other detritus. About an inch down he saw
old asphalt from a previous paving job. He dug some of
that up and put it in a small plastic bag, along with all
the loose bits. Then he vacuumed what was left into
the clean bag. He did the same for all the other cracks
in the six-foot-square area he had chosen.

Private Eye Rule #2: There's always physical evidence. It might not be on a scale convenient to the
human eye, that was all. Certainly, if the police did the
kind of thorough investigation Hallowell seemed to
think they had, this little exercise would net him a dirty
bag full of junk and a bent knife. But what if they'd
missed something? You never knew.

When he had tidied and dug to his satisfaction and
had returned his kit to the van, he retraced Anna's steps
that August day, walking from the Raley's door straight
out through the parking lot until he came to the car
lane. He stood at the spot, imagining a car bearing
down on him from the left. She was left-handed, carrying the sack of groceries on the left side. Her view
would have been obscured by the sack, or she would
have had plenty of room to jump away.

Not a professional hit, he thought. The driver got
lucky with the groceries. Or not a hit at all, just some
clod not paying attention, driving too fast for a parking
lot, headed . . . where? According to Kim, the driver
had exited out the driveway that led to the Stateline
Movie Theater across the street to the right. Maybe he
had just taken a short cut.

★ ★ ★

He drove back to Caesars, letting the valet take care of the parking chore. Back at the table in his room, he gently pushed his computer aside and carefully emptied out the plastic bags he had collected in the parking lot. Holding his magnifying glass over each piece and his flashlight ready, he hunched over the table and began looking for something wrong.

An hour later, he had examined every particle from the bags, and found spider eggs, pine needles, basic dirt, and pieces of an ancient, unbiodegraded plastic cup, looking fresh as the day it left the factory. He also found traces of dried brownish liquid, which his testing kit showed was blood. He wasn't surprised—there had been plenty of blood seeping down and no way to clean it all up.

He leaned back, putting his hands on top of his head, and stretched his shoulders and neck. Then he opened the plastic bag where he had dumped the vacuum's contents, depositing his gleanings on the last clear area of laminate, and gave them the same treatment, trying not to breathe and blow the stuff away.

Some tiny speck hit the light just the right way. It shone out like a lighthouse for bacteria. He picked up the lamp and ran it across the collection of particles.

Lots of shining. Glass.

Funny thing about glass. Even when the particles were too small to permit a matching of fracture surfaces, it still might be possible to show a similarity of their physical properties to the glass from a suspected car. Values like specific gravity, refractive index, and dispersion could still be determined.

A cracked windshield? It didn't seem likely the glass would break into such small pieces.

He checked the list of the contents of Anna Meade's grocery bag.

No glass containers.

Could her belt buckle have dinged a headlight?

It wasn't much, but maybe it was better than nothing. Paul carefully pushed the dustlike particles into a plastic bag and made a call to a lab in Sacramento.

7

THE OLD MAN PUSHED OPEN THE DOOR TO THE second-floor courtroom where Nina was just finishing her hearing and sat down in the last aisle. Out of habit Nina looked over her shoulder at him. He was staring at her.

She had been afflicted with the compulsion to look behind her every time someone entered the courtroom ever since an ill-fated murder trial soon after her arrival in Tahoe. She didn't like having to sit at the counsel table facing the judge, with her back exposed. If she couldn't control that, at least she could take note of the audience sitting on the benches behind her.

Today there had been no audience, until now. The husband and wife trying to settle some of the financial issues that had wrecked their marriage hadn't wanted company. Other than Nina, opposing counsel, the clients, and the court personnel, the courtroom had been empty.

Judge Milne read the details of the settlement they had finally agreed on in chambers, putting it on the record. As he recited the lengthy list of debts and who would get stuck with what, she stole another glance back.

The man stared at her, a half-smile fixed on his deeply creased face, his head dipped a little, his eyes unblinking under bushy white brows. He had a lavish head of white hair that must have been his pride and joy, and a robust look under the brown tweed sport coat. She had never seen him before, and she found his steady regard unsettling. She turned her attention back to the case and tried to forget him.

When Milne had adjourned the hearing and the little group of litigants and lawyers made for the doors, he was waiting right outside in the hall. "Mrs. Reilly? I'm Quentin de Beers," he said, falling into step beside her.

"Yes?" She was holding several files in one arm, her briefcase in the other, and her purse strap in her teeth as they started down the stairs.

"Can't I take that for you?" he said, indicating the briefcase.

"I wish you could," Nina said. "But it's hard-wired to me." She finally got the strap back onto her shoulder.

"I'd like to talk to you."

"What about?"

"I'd like to retain your services."

At the foot of the stairway Nina stopped and said, "I'd be happy to talk to you, sir. Here's my card. Please call and set up an appointment. Unfortunately, I have to—"

"You saw my son die," Quentin de Beers said. He spoke without any heat. "Least you can do is make some time for me in your busy schedule."

"Oh, of course. I'm sorry. I'm just so busy, I wasn't thinking. You're Ray de Beers's father."

"Ray was my only child."

"I see." She did see the son in the father, the same vitality, the same mouth with its thin smile and the same fixed stare. Quentin de Beers must be nearly seventy, but he looked younger. "Is there some legal matter you want to consult me about, or did you want to ask me about—"

"Both." He held the outer door for her and they went out onto the patio in front of the court building. As soon as they were outside, he put on a tweed hat with a brown hat band. "I would like to know what you saw. And there is an urgent legal problem, otherwise I wouldn't have taken time out of my own busy day to hunt you down at the courthouse, now, would I?"

"Well," Nina said, stalling. She had planned to leave the office early, to take advantage of her precious time without Bob to do a little previewing of properties with a realtor named Mrs. Wendover who Sandy had found for her. She wanted to tell him to see her the following day, but she saw his hands were trembling. He was either nervous or ill. His son was dead. "Okay," she said. "Can you follow me back? I can free up a half hour in my office."

"Thank you. I will." His Mercedes was parked not far from her dusty Bronco. Nina drove, watching the sleek new car from her rearview mirror.

At the Starlake Building, de Beers followed her inside. In the outer office, Nina said, "Sandy, this is Mr. de Beers." De Beers appeared bemused at having the secretary introduced to him, but nodded politely. "We'll dispense with the usual forms for this initial consultation, Mr. de Beers," Nina said for Sandy's benefit. She led him into her office and pushed the door shut.

He paid no attention to the surroundings and attempted no small talk. "Sarah and the kids told me their story," he said. "But I can't help noticing how damn fast she had my boy in the ground and buried. I was in Singapore, getting over a bout of flu. Couldn't get back until the day after the funeral. I'm not satisfied with how this whole thing has been handled. I called the DA's office and got nowhere. Jeremy Stamp usually handles my legal work, but he's in L.A. at the moment. I hear you know how to get things done, and, of course, you were there when Ray died. I came looking for you."

"What do you want to know, Mr. de Beers?" So this was the father-in-law Sarah had talked about at the casino, moving in to take care of the family and its fortunes now that Ray was gone.

"For starters, why was Ray alone when he died?" de Beers said. "He hiked up with four other people."

"My understanding is that the rest of the group became separated from your son."

"So they say."

"Do you think they are lying?"

Ignoring her question, de Beers said, "And why didn't he take shelter? Ray could have taught mountaineering. He climbed in the Cascades, the Alps. He climbed Kilimanjaro last year. No way a hill like Tallac, which any kid in tennis shoes can go up, could catch him like that."

"I think I can help there," Nina said. "The storm blew up very quickly and caught everyone up there off guard."

De Beers shook his head. "If your son had died on that mountain, wouldn't you demand a better explanation than 'a storm blew up'? I'm not getting the full picture." He had the same flat delivery his son had. "Maybe you don't know this. Leo Tarrant, a partner in the business, was up on that mountain with them. Leo's infatuated with Sarah. Not only that, Ray and Leo have been on the outs for years because of it and some other things." He leaned closer. "Why did Leo go up there? For the fresh air?"

"I'm sorry for your loss. But lightning killed your son," Nina said. "I was there. I saw it. Sarah told the coroner that she and Leo waited out the storm below the summit—"

"Sarah's Leo's alibi? I'll get the truth out of her— I've been in business for many years. I know a fish story when I hear it. This one's rank. I wish I'd listened to Ray and gotten rid of Leo a long time ago, no matter how good he was at the business end. Leo won't get away with it."

"You know your son's body was examined by the coroner? There was nothing suspicious—"

"He rubber-stamped my son's death and Sarah had Ray in the ground before I was even informed. I want an autopsy."

"But it's too late for that!" He had provoked her into raising her voice.

"I want you to do whatever you have to do to exhume his body," de Beers said. "To come to the point."

Stunned, Nina sat back in her chair. Sandy knocked and came in with coffee, and Nina took advantage of the time she was in the room to gather her thoughts.

When Sandy had gone, she sampled her coffee and said, "What exactly do you think happened up there?"

"Obviously, I don't know," he said. "I'm just full of natural curiosity about why an experienced climber like my son was cut down in the prime of life by a so-called 'accident' that sounds entirely avoidable. So I want an autopsy. I want to have Ray's body fully examined. I want to see him myself. I don't think that's out of line. The coroner can do that, can't he?"

"Not without good reason. There is something in the, uh, Government Code about the coroner's duties." As she spoke, Nina dialed in to her Internet server on the computer. When the connection had been established, she used a bookmark to go straight to the California Codes, typing the word *autopsy* in the search box. "Just a minute," she said, displaying the Code sections on her desktop.

De Beers sat in front of her, his hat in his lap. *I do whatever it takes to win,* his jutting jaw and polished shoes said. He had the same combative and vigilant look as his son, as if the world were a shooting gallery where problems continually flew up in the air to be shot down one by one.

" 'For the purpose of inquiry, the coroner shall have the right to exhume the body of a deceased person when necessary to discharge the responsibilities set forth in this section,' " she read out loud. "The Code is vague. The responsibilities referred to are the general duties of the coroner in connection with determining the cause of death. Dr. Clauson already made an inquiry and closed the file on your son's death. He won't disinter the body without a strong showing of necessity."

"In other words, he won't do it just because we say do it."

Nina nodded. "And that's only the first problem of many."

"Keep going."

"He would probably require the permission of Mrs. de Beers."

"Leave that to me. What else?"

"You'll have to get another lawyer," Nina said. "I won't handle this for you. I saw the lightning. I saw your son falling through the air an instant later. I've read the coroner's report and I'm satisfied he died after being struck by lightning. In my opinion, trying to disinter your son's body is a waste of your time and money, to say nothing about the distress this is sure to cause the family."

"Don't forget, I'm part of the family too. What about my wishes? Don't my wishes mean anything?"

Nina was ready to give up on this conversation. De Beers was a grieving relative. Family members had come to her before, convinced there was foul play in perfectly natural deaths.

Many relatives now demanded an explanation for the inexplicable from their doctors, or told their lawyers to find somebody to blame. Nina sometimes wondered if the idea of accidental death was going to disappear from law altogether. An elderly person who slipped on the pavement, a man who set his bed on fire while smoking, a hiker who fell down a cliff—these accidents were often transmuted in American law into wrongful deaths attributable to somebody else's negligence.

The lawsuits that followed accidents and illnesses weren't about money in many cases. Americans who had lost the comfort of religious faith had to have some way of dealing with the mystery of death.

"If the coroner had seen any evidence of that, he would have performed a full autopsy," Nina said as considerately as she could. "It was an act of God, Mr. de Beers."

De Beers spread his hands on her desk, leaning in to her again, and she got a glimpse of the anger in his red face and red-veined eyes, hints as to how hard he was exerting himself to maintain control. "How could he find any evidence?" he shouted. "He didn't do the goddamn autopsy!"

"Keep your voice down," Nina said. "I understand your worry. You want to be absolutely sure. But if you think someone climbed several thousand feet to kill your son, and lightning conveniently covered traces of the murder, you're . . . Listen, I think you'd better go."

"Hang on a second here. Wait." He rubbed the back of his neck, grimacing as though the situation hurt him physically. "So you don't think we could get the coroner to do that, what did you call it . . ."

"Disinterment," Nina said. "The word *exhumation* isn't used in California law." She stood up. Usually clients took the cue and stood up with her. De Beers didn't budge.

"All right," he said. "Do just one more thing for me, and I promise to shut up or take my wacky suspicions elsewhere. Deal?"

"Mr. de Beers . . ."

"Please." It was an order.

She heard Sandy's chair scrape in the room beyond, and the squeak of rubber-soled shoes halting at her doorway.

Too inept to get de Beers out of her office through sheer force of personality, too small to deal with him physically, and unnerved by the image that popped into her mind of Sandy rushing to the rescue, tennies squeaking, her hands itching to heave the obstinate old man out the door, Nina sat back down at the still-open connection on her computer, saying loudly, "Okay. Five minutes."

The footsteps retreated.

"Look up the statute on grave robbing. No doubt they have some gobbledygook word for that too."

"Why?" Nina said.

"I'll tell you in a minute. Please."

Shaking her head, Nina entered the search words *grave* and *robbing* into the California Codes database. When that didn't work, she scratched her head and tried using free association: *graves, coffins, interment, theft.* She was about to give up and send de Beers on his way when she finally pulled up the obscure Health & Safety Code section she had been looking for.

"Okay," she said. "Disinterring or otherwise disturbing human remains in their place of interment could get you a year in jail. Also, Penal Code section 642 deals directly with the theft of articles of value from a dead human body. It's petty theft or grand theft, a felony, depending on the value of the items stolen. Another Code section makes it a crime to steal a body for the purpose of sale or dissection. And now, may I ask—why am I performing this morbid exercise?"

"Wait. So, is it a crime to dig up a body if the purpose is other than to rob it or steal it or harm it in some way?"

"Yep," Nina said. "It's a crime to dig up a body in a cemetery, period."

"Hmm. How about if the body is legally already aboveground? What's the penalty for borrowing it for an . . . some other reason?"

"I couldn't say for certain," Nina said. "Now we've entered Alfred Hitchcock country. You can't just keep your mother and stuff her after she dies and sit her in her rocker to keep you company. There are public health rules and notification rules."

"Would they put you in jail?"

"That depends," Nina said honestly. "Now you tell me something. What does this have to do with your son?"

"You've been very helpful," the old man said, with a smile close enough to a smirk to set off her internal alarm system. "I won't keep you any longer. I'll leave a check with your secretary for the consultation." He got up stiffly.

"Whatever you are thinking of doing, don't," Nina said.

"You don't need to worry. I won't tell anyone you're involved."

"I'm not covering myself, Mr. de Beers. I don't need to do that. But you came to me for advice, not to have me look up statutes and read them to you, so let me make myself perfectly clear. Don't do it. Even if you don't break the letter of the law, you may end up being charged with a crime. You also have to consider the possibility of a civil suit by another member of the family. Intentional infliction of emotional distress comes to mind. We didn't even have time to get into that—"

"And we won't," de Beers said. He put on his hat and said, "Good day."

When he had closed the outer door, Nina came out

and lowered herself into one of the new client chairs Sandy had ordered for the outer office.

Surely the Washoe tribe had not traditionally made chairs like this. They looked just like knockoffs from the Pottery Barn. "The tribe is diversifying," Sandy had told her as she brought them in. Large-seated, with slatted mission-style oak frames, they were so comfortable that Nina preferred them to her own leather highback. She leaned her head back and closed her eyes.

"You should have used the golf club on him," Sandy said, referring to the one-wood Nina kept in a corner of her office just in case.

"He wasn't threatening, Sandy. I just don't like it when somebody comes in and I don't manage to keep control. In a way I feel sorry for him."

Sandy shut down her computer, sharpened a few pencils with dedicated attention, and stacked her files at a right angle to the desk corner, saying nothing. That was one of the things Nina liked about her. She spoke only when there was something to say.

"Do you know anything about him?" Nina said finally.

"I know about the company. My nephew worked as a carpenter for them. They build all the expensive houses in town. They get approvals faster than anyone else."

"And how do they do that?"

Sandy was polishing away invisible motes of desk dust with the edge of her skirt. She stopped and cocked her head, looking for more. "How?" Nina said again.

Sandy rubbed her fingers against her thumb in the universal "money" gesture.

"He turned the company over to Ray a few years ago," she said. "And Ray started building pieces of shit. They were in court every other day for a while. Quentin finally had to pull Ray up short and bring in a real builder."

"Leo Tarrant?"

"That's right. He's been straightening it out."

"And I'll bet Ray was grateful to him for it, right?" Nina was beginning to get a picture of the three men: Quentin, who started the company; Ray, who took over and began running it into the ground; and Leo Tarrant, the fixer with his eye on his partner's wife.

The phone rang and Sandy, unmoving, regarded it with a jaundiced eye. After five o'clock, the machine could answer.

"Might as well," Nina said.

Sandy picked it up, saying, "Law office. Oh, it's you, Paul. Hang on." Heaving herself up, she gathered her things and let herself out. Nina sat down at her desk, resting her elbows.

"Hey, Paul, how's Carmel?" she said.

"Fog when I left this morning. I wouldn't know now."

"Where are you?"

"Tahoe. Caesars Palace, like always. I have a new employer up here."

"Anybody I know?"

"Your new boyfriend, Hallowell. The Anna Meade case. Thanks for the referral."

"He hasn't said a word to me," Nina said. "Of course, we've both been working our tails off, and he's got the election to worry about. I'm glad you're helping him, Paul."

"It's a challenge," Paul said. "But I'm developing leads here and there."

"He's not my boyfriend, you know. That's a silly word once you hit thirty, anyway."

Paul said, "Hey. You're a free agent. You insisted on that. Not my business."

"So what are we up to tonight?" Nina said brightly. It seemed to her that she had been working since dawn. She envisioned a nice dinner with good old Paul somewhere, a hot tub at Caesars, her own bed back at Matt's. Paul seemed to have accepted her interest in Collier. She and Paul had the perfect twenty-first-century man-woman relationship: colleagues and friends. "I'll buy the drinks."

"I'm sorry," Paul said. "I'm busy. Just called to say hello."

"You're busy? You can't work all the time."

"I don't. Unlike you."

"So what are you doing? Will it take the whole evening?"

"I sincerely hope so," Paul said, and something in his voice warned her not to ask any more questions. So he didn't just have plans. He had big plans.

"Well, how about lunch tomorrow, then?" Nina asked. "Oh, shoot, I can't. I have a noon meeting. . . ."

"I'll stay in touch," Paul said, and hung up.

Nina hung up the phone and leaned back in her chair. His call had left her feeling abandoned, which was ridiculous. She couldn't expect Paul to treat her like a lover without getting some love out of it, and she was focused on Collier.

She tried Collier's number at work and got his voice mail. She called his home and got another message. His voice was so kind, so soothing, but he was unreachable.

Was he? Unreachable? Wherever he was, did he dream about that kiss on the mountain the way she did, at night, alone in her bed, reliving it and wondering what it would have taken to keep him there with her that afternoon, away from the lightning and death that waited at the top?

Or did he dream of a dead woman?

She looked at her watch. She was fifteen minutes late for her appointment with the realtor, the usual situation. She grabbed her case full of homework, and ran out the door.

Paul arrived at the Voss house promptly at seven, bearing gifts. The florist's had been a problem, because Kim was artistic and he wanted something unconventional. He finally picked out some tall plants with complicated orange flowers that looked like birds' heads. Then he stopped at Cecil's for a bottle of British gin.

After much deliberation, staring at the clothes he had brought, he had opted for khakis and a white fleece shirt with an On the Beach logo. He had also showered, but hadn't shaved, because in his vision of art world fashion, facial hair was de rigueur.

On the way to Kim's, he had found himself thinking about Nina. He had asked her to marry him a few weeks before and she had turned him down flat, explaining that she was still too close to the divorce and wanted to live by herself for a while. Then she had said, let's be friends and colleagues, get together when we're in the same town. . . . Then she had called up Hallowell and asked him for a date, or so Hallowell had told him when he wormed the story out of him over smoked eel at the Robata. She was devious; they were all devious; they were so devilishly devious they didn't know, themselves, how devious they were.

She had been hurt when he turned her invitation down. He had to admit, he had enjoyed hearing the hurt tone in her voice. Maybe he had come to Tahoe to let her know that she had made a big mistake choosing Hallowell over him. Maybe his pride was ever so slightly bruised. Maybe he was slightly hurt at her rejection of him.

She might never recognize his ultradesirability over any other male who happened to cross her path. Fine. Let her lie in a bed heaped high with law books and talk torts with the melancholy Hallowell.

They would be colleagues and friends. But by God, she wasn't going to take him for granted.

At Kim's driveway, he paused to watch the last glowing light of sunset suspended in the west above the mountains as if reluctant to see the last of summer fading. A star emerged as he watched, and he made a fervent unspoken wish.

Kim waited for him behind the golden door.

She wore a gauzy skirt, showing slim, smooth brown calves and bare feet. A white cotton Mexican blouse with a lacy ruffle swung low above her breasts, and her earrings sparkled. She gave him a warm smile. Her white teeth gleamed in the porch light.

"For you," he said, handing her the flowers. "The gin's for martinis."

"The shaker is right this way." She led him through the tall studio into a small kitchen on the right. Paul got onto a bar stool and watched her put the flowers into a blue glass vase while he opened up the gin bottle. "Blue and orange," she said. "My favorite combination."

As she handed him his glass, she added, "You're quiet tonight. Everything okay?"

"Sorry," Paul said. "I'm just a little tongue-tied. When I saw you at the door this morning . . . I didn't realize how beautiful you actually are."

She lowered her eyes and bit her lip. "I'm not," she said. "Do you like artichokes, Paul? And Spanish rice? I made some to go with the steaks."

"I couldn't have picked better myself." He held up his glass. "To painters," he said.

"And to Anna. Let's go on out to the patio." They loaded the thick raw steaks onto a platter and went outside to candles in blue glass holders, the white tablecloth, and the silent and dignified forms standing around them. Cacti for friends, Paul thought. Kim had to be lonely, like he was; she just didn't know it. He relaxed into that other world he had glimpsed earlier, full of enigmatic potential. He still couldn't believe his luck, happening upon this lovely stranger in her candlelit courtyard.

The grill set in the fireplace put the steaks at just the right height. Paul lifted his own bare feet up onto the hearth, near his martini. When Kim returned from the kitchen with a steaming tray, she said, "Try this."

He bit into a puffy hors d'oeuvre. The red pepper was like fire, but there was something cool and creamy in there that converted the flames into rich warmth. He had two more. He had never tasted anything so sensational in his life. He finished off his glass, poured some more from the shaker, and looked for hers.

"You paint, you cook, you look like Demi Moore. Where is he?" Paul said.

"Who?"

"The man. There has to be one. The race of man

does not permit a woman like yourself to stay alone long."

"I told you, I don't date." She said this simply, without much emotion, as if it was perfectly normal.

He couldn't let it go. Why would a woman like this resign herself to a life without men?

"You're not used to the idea that a woman might choose to be celibate, I can see that."

"Goes against the instincts," Paul said. "Mating and maternal. A woman needs a man."

"'A man needs a maid,'" she said, quoting one of Neil Young's more unfortunate lines, her eyes twinkling. "These days, some of us women aren't as anxious as we used to be to commit suttee. But it isn't just that. I love men, I do. It's just that I love my work more, and those instincts—once they're awakened, they eat up your life."

"How old are you?" Paul asked her abruptly.

"Twenty-nine. And you?"

"Forty. It's time to change your ways, Kim."

She laughed. "Don't hesitate to say what's on your mind."

"Maybe I could find a way to tempt you."

"I don't think so. Although I do find you very attractive. There's a great deal of erotic heat coming from you. The color I feel around you is a hot orange-red. There's a poem I like. . . ."

"Tell me."

"It starts out, 'I blush for you, steaming man.' I don't remember the rest."

She was flirting, but warning him off at the same time. Never had he felt so confused. He leaned toward her, to get closer to the spell she cast.

"I see your aura too," he said. "It's half cool and half

hot, like that appetizer you brought in. You have a very ambivalent aura."

"The steaks," she said, smiling.

"Oh." He turned them over with the ice tongs.

"Love is too powerful for me. Do you know what I mean, Paul?"

"It's a powerful thing, all right." The word *love* coming from her lips had a whole new resonance to it. She made it sound like the sacred thing it should be.

They sat for a while, while night seeped across the wall, while the steaks hissed and spit and the heat in Paul grew and grew, until Paul smelled something burning and hastily put the sizzling meat on a platter. Kim got up and went inside, the muscles of her legs straight and firm in the flickering light, while he finished his third drink, letting it go straight to his head. He felt challenged, excited, aroused. He was so fired up he wanted to sweep her into his arms right then and there and find her bedroom, the hell with the dinner.

On the other hand, he didn't want to blow it this early. He would wait for the full message first. By the time she came back with her tray he was back under control.

They ate slowly, talking about Paul now, his work as a cop, his life in Carmel. He let her get to know him, her delicate probing questions like fingers caressing him, charming him. He dropped his guard too low to defend himself from her. She bloomed beside him like a tropical flower with a scent he couldn't quite identify and he lost himself in her dark-fringed eyes, her gravity and her laugh. . . .

They walked around the studio and she talked some more about her painting. This time Paul felt as attracted to her work as he was to her. Stopping in front of one with delicate splinters of yellow and white, which resembled a whimsically suggestive piece of the old man cactus, he said, "I want to buy this one."

"You're very nice. But—"

"But nothing. Wrap it for me, I'll pick it up tomorrow. I want to put it on my office wall."

"You mean it! But it's expensive—"

"I'm not asking for a special deal," Paul said. "I want to buy it."

She stood close to him and looked at it with him, her eyes lingering over the painting. Standing next to her, he realized with a shock that she was nearly as tall as he was. "Well now, that's an impetuous thought. Maybe you ought to think it over."

"You've never met such an impetuous man," Paul said. He couldn't stand it any longer. He took her by her shoulders and pulled her toward him.

Crushing her mouth against his, he felt the physical boundaries between them dissolve. Her hand slid down his chest, her touch forcing waves of pure sexual appetite through his body. He shivered as if he were sixteen, the newness of a stranger's touch as intimately shocking as the directness of it.

Then he heard her murmur, "Paul, no."

"Yes."

"No!" She pushed him away. She was strong.

He stood there, breathing hard.

"It's time for you to go, Paul."

"Yes. Okay. Sorry."

She led him as far as the gate, holding it open for him. "Thanks," she said. "I enjoyed it."

"What?"

"Enjoyed it. Good night, Paul." The gate bolt

clanked firmly into place, expelling him from her garden of earthly delights.

He returned swiftly to himself. "Don't let the door hit you in the butt on the way out, buddy," he muttered, searching for his car keys in the dark.

8

ON THE WAY TO WORK THE NEXT MORNING NINA
stopped at the cemetery where Ray de Beers's body
had been laid to rest.

The main Tahoe cemetery lay in a neatly wooded
square field near Truckee Marsh, not far from her office. She had never seen the cemetery up close before.

Iron gates stood open at the entrance and dew still
sat lightly upon the green grass beyond. She didn't
know what she had expected, maybe white crypts like
ones she had seen in a photo of a New Orleans cemetery, but like most California places, this one had little
feeling of history or event. Each grave had its own
modest little stone or brass marker set in the ground.
She went into the brick office building and asked for
help.

"Are you with the press?" the caretaker, who was
reading the paper, asked her.

"No."

"Who are you with, then?"

"Nobody. I'm just here to pay my respects," Nina said, bewildered.

"I guess it doesn't matter," the man said to himself. "Come on, I have to go out there and look at it anyway." They walked up a narrow path alongside the markers, Nina mulling over his attitude.

Next to the brick building and entrance were older graves, marked with larger stones and etched with a more floral style. They walked almost to the back and picked their way across the wet lawn, Nina avoiding markers when she came to them, until they arrived at a large burnished brass plate set well into the ground. Fresh grass grew beneath it. A large wreath of chrysanthemums obscured the inscription: RAYMOND CHARLES DE BEERS, 1949–1997.

That was all. No words of praise or pity.

Her guide was kicking at the compacted dirt. "I could have told them," he said. "You here to check on the condition of the grave?"

"What? Oh, it looks fine," said Nina heartily. "Perfectly adequate . . ."

"You see, right here." He squatted down. "The ants have made a nice trail from this plot to the one next door. Their trail hasn't been disturbed, so the site hasn't been disturbed either. The whole thing is a mistake, if you want my opinion, and you probably don't, since nobody right down to my daughter does. But this thing looks just like it did a couple of days ago when I smoothed it over. Nobody else has touched it."

"What on earth are you talking about?" Nina said, unable to puzzle it out.

"You ain't here from the City?"

"No."

"Well, see this paper here?" He pulled out several

folded sheets of paper from his pocket. "A deputy brought it. Somebody wants to dig this one up."

"May I see the papers?" Nina said.

"Why?"

"As it happens, I'm a lawyer. Maybe I could explain to you what's going on."

"My boss'll be here soon enough with his lawyer." But he handed her the papers. They walked over to the nearest bench while she scanned them.

Quentin de Beers had moved fast. Somehow, between late yesterday and this morning, he had persuaded the firm of Caplan, Stamp, Powell, and Riesner to work for him. Some frayed associate at the firm had undoubtedly stayed up all night drafting the paperwork in order to get the hearing set.

"Petition and Motion for Disinterment," the motion was entitled. The summons was directed at the coroner, the cemetery, and Sarah de Beers. Judge Milne had issued an Order Shortening Time to permit the hearing to be held on Thursday, only two days away.

Her compassion for Quentin evaporated. He'd misused the information he'd learned from her. He hadn't gone to Jeff Riesner's firm with his wild suspicions of foul play. No hints in this paperwork revealed that he thought his son had been murdered.

Instead, the basis of the motion was that Quentin had been offered Ray de Beers's gold wedding ring by some unspecified person who claimed to have purchased it from the deceased shortly before his death. However, Quentin claimed, the wedding ring was still on de Beers's finger during the viewing of the open casket, and had been buried with him. Accompanying the papers, a declaration signed by the mortician stated that de Beers had been wearing the ring at the burial.

The papers alleged that someone had disinterred the coffin and stolen the ring and other valuables buried with de Beers. The Court was respectfully requested to order a disinterment to ascertain the extent of loss and aid in a criminal investigation pursuant to assorted sections of the Penal Code and the Health & Safety Code.

The whole legal proceeding was Quentin's spurious attempt to get his son's body aboveground legally. He had never said anything about a ring to her; he must have dreamed that story up after he left the office, based on the information she had given him, and then pressured or bribed the mortician.

Nina read on, furious about the way the information she had provided had been used.

He had been clever, the scheming, shifty old reprobate. He might at least get the body aboveground.

Nina remembered his last questions to her, about whether there were penalties for taking a dead body already aboveground even if it wasn't for the purpose of sale or dissection.

How did he think he could steal the body from under Doc Clauson's watchful eye? What was he going to do, hire a pathologist to perform a secret examination in the dead of night in some motel room? Did he understand that even if any foul play was discovered the evidence couldn't be presented in a court of law?

Obviously, he didn't care. She had an unpleasant feeling that he would convince himself he'd found evidence of foul play, and then something might happen to Leo Tarrant.

He must have felt he had nothing to lose. With his connections, his age, and his status as a grieving family member, if he couldn't find anything at all, he would return the body and take his slap on the wrist.

Now she was worried. The old man was a menace. He had too much power and not a rational thought in his head. But what could she do about this wily hoax? She knew and the old man knew that the conversation they had had in her office couldn't be discussed with anyone, even if the result might be a fraud on the Court. The attorney-client privilege had to be guarded even in a bizarre situation like this.

She drove back to the office seething, trying to figure out how to stop the old man without getting her license revoked.

Sarah de Beers was waiting for her in the outer office. When Nina walked in she came over quickly and said, "I have to see you."

Sandy announced, "I told her to make an appointment. We like appointments."

"It's okay, Sandy."

"You have Law and Motion at ten." She handed Nina the introductory paperwork.

In the inner office, Sarah sank down into one of Nina's client chairs. The glamorous gambler had vanished. So had the hiker. Today she was a middle-class housewife in a gray running suit. She would blend into any crowd at the supermarket in this new disguise, except for the dark circles under her eyes and the troubled expression.

"I want to hire you," she said, wresting some familiar papers out of her purse and thrusting them at Nina.

Without looking at them, or acknowledging their existence, Nina said, "Why would you want to hire me, Mrs. de Beers? The last time we met, you seemed convinced I was part of some plot to persecute you."

"I'm sorry about that. I was confused and upset that night, and Leo thought going out to a club might cheer me up. The martinis I was drinking didn't help. I—I thought Quentin had gotten to you too. The whole town belongs to Quentin, I sometimes think."

Nina accepted this. Sarah de Beers didn't seem dishonest, just uncertain, as though her sense of self had gone underground during the Ray years. She seemed to Nina like a mole, buried for a long time, gamely digging toward dimly seen light.

"How are you doing now? And the twins?"

"We're all pretty unsteady. Wobbly. We need to find a new footing, but things keep happening that knock us off our feet. We all need more time—a chance to adjust to Ray's death. It changes so many things. I almost feel hopeful. Hopeful! I hardly dare say the word. I'm sorry. I'm not making much sense. These papers . . ."

"No offense, but I noticed Molly and Jason didn't seem to be overwhelmed by Ray's death."

"No, not the way you mean, anyway. But they *are* overwhelmed. I don't seem to be able to comfort them yet. They've drawn away from me instead of coming closer, yet I know they love me—I know they do. Molly locks herself in her room and won't talk to me. . . . I think she feels guilty. They didn't get along."

Nina nodded. "I saw that. On the mountain."

"And Jason has moved in with a friend of his from high school, Kenny Munger. He says he needs some space. He's always been so responsible, taken everything on his shoulders. It's not like him to run away when we need him. I suppose the atmosphere at home is too depressing for him. And he'll feel even worse when he hears about this move by Quentin."

"How did Leo take Ray's death?" asked Nina. She wasn't surprised to hear the casino jaunt had been Leo's idea. Leo the ever-helpful, always on hand to comfort the widow . . . Quentin de Beers's words about Leo's interest in Sarah came back to her.

"I can't really say he was devastated," Sarah said. "I'm trying to be honest with you. Please, read these court papers. I know Quentin came to see you yesterday and that you refused to help him. He told me. He's hired Jeremy Stamp's firm to . . . dig Ray up. Please, help us stop him before he has the chance to drag what's left of our family through hell with him."

Nina said reluctantly, "If you want to consult me regarding a matter in which Mr. de Beers consulted me yesterday, I probably won't be able to assist you. There may be a conflict of interest."

"But you know all about this whole thing! And if I read the papers right, we only have a day or two to do something! I don't know anyone else, except Jeremy Stamp from the business." Her eyes brimmed. "Try to imagine how I feel."

Nina offered her the always well-stocked box of tissue. Sarah was as vehemently against an exhumation as Quentin de Beers was vehement in wanting one. All this emotion over a dead body! For a moment Nina allowed herself to wonder—could someone have killed Ray? Then she thought back over the lightning strike and remembered Clauson's absolute certainty about cause of death. Ray had died from being struck by lightning, and no amount of struggling over his body was going to change that.

"I suppose I can talk to you long enough to see if

there is a conflict," she said. "Also, theoretically, even if there is, Mr. de Beers could agree to allow me to represent you."

"I have money," Sarah de Beers said. "The coroner was right about accidental death. Our policy paid double. I can pay you."

"Forgive me for saying this, but I thought De Beers Construction—"

"You thought we were well-off? No. Quentin and Ray tried to keep up appearances. But the company has been close to bankruptcy. Leo is turning it around now, though." She was looking out the window, toward Tallac. Nina turned to look at the mountain.

"It's cloudless at the summit today. Hard to believe we were up there," Nina said. "Look, see the final ridge there, at the top? I still see that lightning bolt at night before I go to sleep."

"Ray made me go," Sarah said with some bitterness. "I've been doing physical therapy—for my legs—for some time, and Dr. Lee recommended that I try some hiking. So Ray decided to take me on that trail. When Leo heard I was going, he decided to come, and talked Jason and Molly into it. I think Ray was surprised at how far I got."

"He wanted you to fail?"

"It's complicated. I was hurt at a job site. Leo and Jason thought it was Ray's fault. It caused quite a crisis in our family. Ray became angry at me, as though I had hurt myself on purpose to make him look bad. So he was—oh, I know this sounds very strange—he's been punishing me since then. Here I am talking non-sense again. Sorry." She laughed, painfully.

"Not at all. I understand."

She sat up straight, as if she had just remembered

why she had come. "What do you charge? Two hundred an hour? I'll pay it."

"Let's hold off on that for a minute, Mrs. de Beers."

"Call me Sarah."

Nina picked up the motion with its supporting papers. She read it more carefully this time, noting errors of law and fact that might be capitalized upon if she chose to teach Quentin de Beers a well-deserved lesson. De Beers wouldn't dare assert that she had a conflict of interest, because then she would be able to break confidentiality enough to alert the coroner and the police about his own damn perjury.

Really, the wife—or widow, as Sarah was now—was consulting her on a different matter, if you wanted to get technical about it, and Nina did want to get technical about it. Quentin had never mentioned a gold wedding ring, nor suspicions of grave robbing.

"What's this about your husband's wedding ring, Sarah?" Nina said.

"It's a lie, that's what it is. That ring was long gone before Ray was buried."

"And how do you know that?"

"Because I took the ring when I went to the coroner's office to identify him formally. They gave me a moment alone with him. When I got home, I put it into my lingerie drawer, thinking I'd decide whether to throw it down the toilet later."

"You have the ring?"

"Not anymore. Quentin came by yesterday, he said to look through some paperwork on Ray's desk upstairs. He must have sneaked into the master bedroom and stolen it out of my drawer."

"Hmm. You really think he would search your bedroom?"

"He's been acting strangely since he came back from Singapore. I know he's grieving for Ray, but his grief is expressed in this anger and irritation. . . . He's always been controlling, like Ray, but now he's worse than ever. He doesn't seem to trust us to be able to make any decisions. He comes to the house every day. He built it and gave it to Ray, so I suppose he still thinks it's his."

"Why did you take the ring? As a . . . remembrance?"

She blushed to the roots of her hair. "No. I didn't want Ray to go down in the ground linked like that to me. I'm ashamed to say it."

"Wouldn't the ring be yours for the asking? Why didn't you just ask for it?"

"Quentin bought the rings. I know him. He would have raised a stink."

Nina doodled rings on her pad, as mystified as ever about the family.

"He knows I can't admit I took it off Ray's finger!" she said. "I'm sorry, but it sounds so awful, like I was so greedy and heartless that I would remove a dead man's wedding ring."

"Just say it was a memento you wanted to keep."

"Everyone would know I was lying. A reporter from the *Mirror* called just before I left and tried to ask me some questions about these papers. I couldn't stand for that to be made public."

"Sarah, have you thought . . . I understand Mr. de Beers was out of town when Ray's death occurred. I . . . heard that he was unable to get back in time for the funeral."

"So?"

"Maybe he has developed some silly ideas about

Ray's death because he couldn't see the body. Sometimes that's important when a loved one dies," Nina said, treading carefully. "I understand your feelings. But I wonder—if he's going to obsess about this, come up with wild accusations and so on—maybe we should just let him have a look, and make sure the casket is buried again right away."

"No! That isn't what he wants, Nina! It won't satisfy him! I called him this morning and tried to talk to him, but he won't listen. He said some things—I couldn't believe what he was thinking."

"What did he say?"

"He wants to persuade the world that Leo killed Ray. He'll find someone who'll lie for him, someone who'll frame Leo. I don't know how he'll do it; I just know he will."

"Why would he think that, Sarah?"

"He thinks that Leo and I are having an affair," Sarah said in a choked voice.

"Are you?"

"No! Leo has been a tremendous help to me and the kids. He's a friend, one I don't want to lose because of Quentin's dirty mind. Besides, I was with Leo when Ray was killed. And how would Leo make lightning strike Ray? It's insane. . . ."

"Were you thinking of leaving Ray?"

Sarah stopped, her mouth open. "Yes," she whispered. "I suppose I was. I hadn't told him yet, but he knew it. I was . . . a little afraid of Ray."

"If your marriage was so unhappy, Sarah, I don't understand why Ray would object."

"Ray had his fears too," Sarah said. "Jason was his life. I think Ray knew that if I went, Jason would go with me. He wanted Jason to come into the business with him. If I was here with Molly, he knew he could keep Jason here, and there wouldn't be much else Jason could do in Tahoe.

"Or maybe Ray just couldn't bear to give up one possession, even an old one he hardly ever used anymore." She laughed again, a dry, hard sound that ended abruptly. "Maybe he remembered loving me once. Anyway, he's dead now.

"But you see, Quentin feels the same way about us. He wants us all here, close by. He has this need to keep us under his thumb, just like Ray had. He wants Jason to come into the business, just like Ray did. Jason's the heir to the de Beers name, you see. Quentin is very proud of the family name. He once told me he had the family traced back to Charlemagne."

A long silence. Sarah had run down, and Nina had to make a decision. It would be best not to get enmeshed in this messy family brawl, and there was the possible conflict of interest—but Sarah was really trying; she deserved to be able to move on, and Quentin was wrong. . . .

"Okay. I can deal with the conflict problem," Nina said. "As to the motion, I believe the cemetery caretaker might be able to state for the record that in his opinion the grave hasn't been disturbed. Let me ask you one more time. Are you willing to file a declaration stating that you removed the ring prior to your husband's burial?"

"No. I'm sorry, but you'll have to find another way."

"I don't know if I can, but I believe your wishes in this matter should carry a lot of weight anyway."

"I'm sorry—I know I'm not making it easy."

"You don't have to apologize all the time," Nina

said, "Even though, I admit, it's a nice change from what I usually hear."

"Oh! I'm sorry—I didn't know I was apologizing." Then she heard what she had just said and had the grace to smile. "I'll try to do better," she said.

"I might be able to get the hearing put over for a week or even two. I could use some extra time."

"No, no. Until this is over . . . Nina, my life is in shambles. And it's the same for Molly and Jason. We can't wait."

"All right. I'll help you, Sarah. I'll draft some responsive papers for you to sign. I'd like to get declarations from your son and daughter as well, opposing the exhumation. There isn't much time."

"Thank you. Thank you so much." This time her smile was relieved. "Molly gets home from the college about four. If you want to see her, it might be best to come by the house this afternoon after you leave work. We have a place near Regan Beach—400 Dartmouth Way."

"I'll drop by, if I can manage to get a draft put together by then," Nina said. "And Jason?"

"I can give you his address. Kenny's phone has been turned off. What about a retainer?"

"A thousand will get us started, I think. Billed against hours worked, of course."

Sarah wrote out the check. After she left, Nina, trying to make a picture out of all the colors and pieces Sarah had supplied, noticed the check number, 106. Sarah couldn't have had this account long. SARAH DE BEERS, read the top, 400 DARTMOUTH WAY. No sign of Ray's name.

Sarah was trying to shake Ray de Beers off like a nagging old cough.

★ ★ ★

Paul stopped by the Tahoe courthouse to catch Collier Hallowell just before noon. He found him in the law library, sitting at a scratched oak table and whispering to another attorney while other leather-dress-shoe types scribbled at other tables.

"Excuse the interruption," Paul said, keeping his voice down.

"No problem, Paul. Meet Jeremy Stamp. Jeremy is—"

"I know your firm, Mr. Stamp. I've been in court with Nina Reilly opposite Jeff Riesner." He pulled up a chair, and shook Stamp's hand at the same time.

Stamp had the lean body and calorie-deprived look of a fitness freak. Long-distance runner, Paul thought. He was about five-nine or thereabouts, so he probably didn't weigh more than one-forty. Paul felt like a rhino sitting next to him.

The suit, watch, shoes, and haircut all said major money. He had the easy smile of the man who has made it by fifty and only works because he enjoys it. "What a coincidence," Stamp said. "I received a phone call from Ms. Reilly's office this morning. Will you be working on the de Beers case?"

"Not that I know of," Paul said. "I'm up here on other business at the moment."

"Really." Stamp glanced at his watch. Paul had seen that heavy gold I.W.C. model in a catalog that also sold yachts and airplanes. "See you later, Collier. I'm afraid I'll be unavailable this afternoon. I'm playing golf at the Edgewood course." He rose, waving to Paul. "Don't you boys work too hard."

"Ah, get outta here," Collier said. Carrying his

briefcase as lightly as an empty file folder, Stamp
breezed out the open door.

"Nina better watch out," Paul observed. "He's the
type with a squadron of eager legal groupies laboring
away back at the office. He'll show up in court fresh
and rested after a round of golf."

"He's what we all aspire to," Collier said, back up to
his shirtsleeved elbows in law books. "Rich, respected,
and semiretired."

"Lunch?" Paul said.

"Can't. I have a trial resuming at one-thirty. Judge
Milne wants to meet the lawyers in chambers at one to
work out a couple of problems. I'm researching those
now." He didn't exactly sound impatient—that wasn't
his style—but there was a zone of high pressure around
him.

"It's past noon, man. You have to eat."

"I'll eat later. Anything to report, Paul? I can spare
five minutes." Other patrons of the law library had
taken Paul's side and gone to lunch, leaving behind
stacks of books and scraps of paper.

"I took some samples at the scene. It's a long shot,
but I have Ginger Hirabayashi in Sacramento doing
some lab work. I also put an ad in the paper. Reward
for information, and so on. Anonymous, of course."
Paul gave Hallowell a copy of the ad.

"I tried that three years ago."

"Let's try it again. We have to get the word out.
We're going to have to make our luck in this case."

"Yeah. You're right."

"And I talked to Kim Voss."

Hallowell looked up. "She's interesting, isn't she?
Could she add anything?"

"Hard to say. I'm still working on that. We had dinner last night." Paul warmed to this irresistible topic. "Collier, you remember that scene in *The Hustler* where Paul Newman is standing with Piper Laurie at her door? She's wearing a tight skirt and this little cardigan and pearls, and he's lost everything; he's finished; he's got nobody; and he's with this girl. She's just met him; she's a little afraid of him; and suddenly Newman moves in on her and they start kissing. Only he's so intense, it gets heavier and heavier until you know he's out of control. You remember that?"

"Not really," Hallowell said.

"And she breaks away. She looks at him. Her lips are swollen up and she's got these smoky eyes, and she says to him— You don't remember this?"

"Not ringing a bell yet, Paul."

"She says in this low voice that you have to strain your ears to hear, 'You're too hungry.' Amazing statement, isn't it? 'You're too hungry,' she says. And she runs through her door and locks it from the other side. You hear the latch and Newman's standing there with this hound-dog face staring at her door, like he's gonna burn holes through it with his hot eyes, and for a minute there you think he's gonna break the door down—"

"I take it you liked Kim," Hallowell said.

"That's how it went, no shit. She had to run from me. I haven't felt that way for a long, long time, buddy."

"I thought that you and Nina had something going," Hallowell said.

"Pure Plato from here on out," Paul said. "Nina dumped me. She used the 'friends and colleagues' speech. She's got something against me. You should be glad. You're the lucky fellow she dumped me for."

"I doubt that," Hallowell said, looking startled.

"Come on. I know you've taken at least one long look hello into those big brown eyes."

"Let's not talk about Nina again right this minute, okay, Paul? I'm in trial, and whatever else I've got left, I'm putting toward Anna. Remember her? You're working the case, aren't you, in addition to your other interests?"

"Yeah, I'm working."

"Good. Then I can relax and do the same." Hallowell hunched back over the books and papers on the table in front of him.

Paul returned to his van, hesitated, and decided to pick up the painting he wanted to buy from Kim, and any other lucky thing that came his way. The Eagle radio station from Sacramento was belting out classic rock from his quadraphonic sound system, the traffic was light, and he was Newman on his way to see a woman.

Meantime, he would do a little business. Picking up the cell phone with his free hand, he called the lab in Sacramento.

The long day passed like a dream. Nina talked to people until she was hoarse, zipped over to court for a sentencing hearing, signed things, dictated things, and went to her lunch meeting. Sandy finished typing up the responsive paperwork in the de Beers case just before five, and Nina took it out to the house.

An area of vacation houses hidden down a long street off Lake Tahoe Boulevard, Regan Beach had only a few large properties, most set at some distance from the lake in sparse woods. The de Beers home, a brand-new three-story edifice with oversize chimneys in the pseudo-Tudor style Nina loved to hate, must have replaced an older structure. From the street all that could be seen was a parking area and heavy foliage.

A walkway led to the side, where she pushed open an unlocked wooden gate. Fringed by trees, a large expanse of lawn and formal flower gardens speckled with cobbled pathways made up the generous back-yard, bordered at the far end by a white gazebo with a vista of the distant lake. A gardener in a straw cowboy hat was stooping over one of the flower beds.

Close to the gazebo, Sarah de Beers lay on a white wicker lawn chair shaded from the low late-afternoon sun by a canvas canopy. From all appearances she had been there for quite some time. Her shoes lay kicked aside and forgotten on the soft green tendrils of grass next to the table.

"Sit down," she said, patting the chair beside her. "Time for a nice cool drink." She sounded too re-laxed, and Nina thought again that she was probably medicating herself with something. Well, whether it was booze, tobacco, or caffeine, everybody else in America was doing it too.

"Thanks, but I have to drive—"

"Stay long enough to sober up, then." Taking a martini glass from a tray on the table, she asked Nina, "What's your preference? Seven to one, like publishers prefer their martinis? Or do you like your vermouth the way they say Winston Churchill took it, across the room, to be glanced at briefly?"

"You're going to laugh, but I don't think I've ever had a martini," Nina said, giving in to her curiosity. She couldn't imagine a life where you had an after-noon available to pour gin down your throat, but she had had a difficult day, and the thought held a certain appeal.

She stretched out on the padded chaise beside Sarah, letting her back de-kink. The afternoon breeze caressed her knees. Lake Tahoe was a twenty-six-mile-long glossy sheet under the blue North Shore mountains right in front of her, but her thoughts were still on the job.

A client of hers convicted of selling cocaine would be leaving for a stay in the joint in a few days. She had done the best she could for him, preaching about mitigating factors until she was purple in the face, but Milne had listened stonily and given him the middle term of years. A poor hardworking defense lawyer could hardly find a legal technicality to stand on anymore. The loopholes of the seventies were being firmly tied up, one by one, by appellate courts overstocked with ex-prosecutors.

"Is there any other drink?" Sarah was saying. "Hmm, in your case, we go with classic one-fifth vermouth." She poured vermouth over ice into a silver shaker and added chilled gin, measuring both with the finicky precision of a candy-store owner.

Nina's parents had drunk martinis. She remembered her father at the end of the day, offering her a gin-soaked olive. Nobody had drunk martinis for decades, but here they were, popping up again for some obscure reason.

"The olive is such a mysterious fruit," she said.

Sarah handed her the glass. *"Salud,"* she said. Nina took a small sip, and then another. Though it tasted like mercury in a thermometer on a freezing day, the drink was industrial-strength, and she liked the wallop.

It was exactly what she needed, another vice to substitute for a love life.

"I'm sorry," Sarah said, "if I seemed pushy in your office. I'm not used to being the one who has to get things done. I don't have a lot of style at it."

"You're apologizing again."

"So I am. It's an old habit. I wonder when I'll stop."

"When you're ready."

"Do you take that thing with you everywhere?" Sarah said, pointing at her briefcase.

"It's waterproof, so I can take it into the shower," Nina said almost gaily. "It's my albatross."

"What's in it?"

"Why, my wallet and cell phone, spare shoes, uh, my laptop computer, a big bottle of ibuprofen, an apple. And a file or two. Pretty boring. Oh, and my copy of *Smilla's Sense of Snow*. Got any more from that shaker?" Nina held out her glass, had some more, and said, "Mmm. You know, the fifties weren't such a bad era after all." Her father used to eat herring when he drank gin, she remembered suddenly, almost able to smell the vinegary fish. Now she could admire the reflections on the distant water, wondering what it would be like to spend her life at this house with this view and that shakerful of moonshine.

Of course, that picture would have to include drill-sergeant Ray, up until quite recently. This thought brought her back to business. "Is Molly here?" she asked. "I need to show her the draft I put together and get any changes and a signature tonight."

"She went in," Sarah said. At the mention of Molly, Sarah's mood had changed swiftly. Now she blurted out, "Molly doesn't like it when I sit out here like this. She says I'm zoning out. Maybe I'll be able to stop now. The martinis and the sleeping pills and the Xanax. I've been thinking a lot since I saw you this morning. I'm glad he's dead," she went on, in eerie imitation of Molly at the coroner's. "I often dreamed of the day when I'd be free of him. I thought if Ray was gone I could fix everything and . . . but I'm so afraid."

"Afraid of what?" Nina said. "Ray's dead."

"I'm so afraid it's too late, that we can't fix it."

There was a long pause. "It may be too late," Sarah repeated. The way she said the words, they sounded desperate.

Nina said, "I was shot. In the chest, almost two years ago now. For a long time after that I was afraid of just about everything. The wound was more than just a physical wound, you know? But Sarah, I got over it."

Sarah didn't answer. She set her drink on the tray carefully, and folded her arms around her body, as if clasping a familiar despair to herself.

Noticing, Nina went on. "I wrapped my fear around me like one of those blankets that gave the Native American people smallpox. It was making me sick. I couldn't do my job, raise my son, live again, until I gave it up."

Sarah got up, said, "I'll go get Molly and bring her out." She went into the house.

Nina watched the lake gulls flying low across the silver water. The sun dipped behind Tallac.

A scream cut through the air, shrill and high.

Nina knocked over her chair jumping up. The gardener was ahead of her. She ran after him through the great front door.

Northwestern lodge decor. A huge stone fireplace.

Pine paneling. A thick rug in greens and blues. A long, long staircase . . .

"Help me!" she heard. "Help me!" They ran up the staircase and into a bedroom at the end of the hall.

Heavy curtains covered the windows. In the center of the room Molly was hanging, squirming on a rope attached to the light fixture, her mother frantically trying to bring her down.

9

MOLLY SWUNG SILENTLY ON HER ROPE BETWEEN worlds, hovering between life and death, her toes only inches from the floor. Dropping the dull knife with a clang and a cry of frustration, Sarah clawed and jabbed at the rope with her fingernails, her struggles weirdly ineffective as if Molly were turning into a ghost she could not touch. Molly wore an astonished expression, as though she had not expected to suffer. Garbled noises came from her throat as she clutched at the rope around it.

The gardener pushed Sarah aside, ordering her and Nina to hold Molly up. Nina ran to grab a wildly flailing leg, and took a hard thump to her kidney before she was able, with Sarah's help, to lift Molly a few inches and take the pressure off her neck. Whipping a pair of clippers out of the tool bag he wore around his waist, the gardener cut the rope hanging from a hook in the ceiling beam that must usually hold the large Boston fern lying spilled on the rug beside them.

Molly collapsed onto them, causing Nina to stagger

and almost fall. They lowered her gently to the floor, where she continued to scrabble at her neck, her movements weaker, her bulging eyes beginning to glaze over. As Nina and Sarah jumped out of the way, in one swift movement the gardener severed the tightened necklace of rope.

Blue-lipped, gasping and coughing feebly, Molly lay on the floor, her eyes open but dull with shock. Very gently, as gracefully as choreographed dancers who had rehearsed together, the three adults lifted her up in one move, placing her on the bed.

Sarah bent over her, examining the girl's neck and listening to her breathing, talking gently to her while Molly sobbed hoarsely, "I'm sorry, Mom."

Down on her knees now, her arms wrapped around the girl, Sarah said, "It's all right, baby, it's all right. We'll get the doctor." The mother and daughter comforted each other with the heat of their bodies, pressing them together as if their closeness could erase the ugly tangle of rope on the floor and the marks coming up around Molly's neck. Sarah reached over to the tissue box by the bed with one hand, never letting Molly go, and began wiping the snot and tears off Molly's face.

Nina saw no sign of pills or drugs or bottles there or in the bathroom. Now certain she could control herself well enough to speak intelligibly, she picked up the phone to call 911, which seemed to have become her favorite number, but Molly saw her from the bed. "Don't," Molly said. Her voice sounded rolled in gravel. Nina held the phone but didn't go ahead. She had learned since her 911 call on the mountain that even punching in the first number might bring a callback or even a police car.

Molly spoke to her mother in a low voice. Nina couldn't hear what they were saying.

Sarah said finally, "She won't go in an ambulance. She doesn't want a fuss. Call Dr. Lee. He's the family physician. His number's downstairs, in the address book on the buffet in the entryway."

The gardener, who had watched quietly from a few feet away, now spoke up. "She needs to go to a hospital."

"I'm just fine now," Molly whispered loudly from the bed, obviously not fine but looking less awful as awareness and color returned to her face. "Mom, make them leave."

Nina looked around the room. It was far from the ruffled pastel room she might have expected of a girl still in her teens. Although it was upstairs it felt like a basement. The narrow bed with steel rails on which Molly lay, covered with a black sleeping bag, could have come straight on the bus from San Quentin, and the chest in the corner and the computer desk had been painted black. A thin indoor-outdoor rug in dark gray completed the stark postindustrial look.

But the most depressing thing about the cell Molly had made of her bedroom was the wall of photos torn out of magazines, all of the late rocker Kurt Cobain, a famous young suicide; Cobain smoking a cigarette, riding a skateboard, playing music, mugging for the camera, stringy blond hair hanging over his face to shield his lost and lonely eyes.

"Please, Nina, Joe, both of you, go downstairs. Call the doctor," Sarah said insistently.

Nina and Joe looked at each other. Joe's hands, so steady in the emergency, now shook like leaves in a gust of wind. "That was a close one," he said. "Are you sure you should—"

"Get going!" Sarah shouted.

The physician's answering service located Dr. Lee at the hospital. After quizzing Nina briefly on why an ambulance had not been called, he promised to arrive in ten minutes. Nina and the gardener sat down on a couch made of enormous pieces of burlwood covered with a thick, fluffy sheepskin, staring into the darkness of the fireplace, listening to the silence above. As evening came on, the house had gotten cold, even though September was still a few days away.

"That little girl, she's got big problems," Joe said eventually. He got up, stuffed papers and logs on the grate, and lit a match from a metal container on the hearth. Then he sat back on the edge of the couch, holding his baseball cap on his knees. He smelled of grass and sweat. "Her and her brother, both."

"She looked so . . . I'm amazed she can talk," said Nina.

"I saw it once before. I saw a man who died like that. My cousin killed himself."

"It's a hard way to die. I'm surprised she didn't use pills. You saved her life, you know."

He looked shocked, and Nina saw that his hands continued to shake, and his skin had developed a sickly pallor under its warm brown color. He had been as affected, or even more affected, as she had been by the sight of the girl.

"Not me! Her mother was already there. She would have found a way to get her down without me or you."

"Maybe," Nina said.

"Jason and Molly, they've been protecting their

mother like she was the kid. Now I guess she has to be the grown-up. That's good, at least."

"What do you mean, protecting?"

"I saw them try many times to stand between their mother and father. He never hit her, he just ran her down all the time, and raised his fist at her—you know—to keep her in line. The kids, they were afraid of him, but they were more afraid for their mother. Jason was starting to stand up to him, becoming a man."

"You know a lot about the family."

"They spend a lot of time outdoors. It's not like I listen at the window. And Molly talks to me sometimes."

"What about?"

"I don't know if I should talk to you about this."

"I'm Mrs. de Beers's attorney," Nina said. "I'm just trying to help."

"She wisecracks," Joe said, "but underneath she's not laughing. She has all the boys hanging around, but she doesn't care, she just hangs out with Jason and their friend Kenny. She and Jason are like this. . . ." The fingers on his hands intertwined. "Jason shouldn't have moved out like he did. She misses him a lot. She goes out on the lawn and sits on the phone with him so her mother can't hear."

"And what does she say on the phone?"

He looked at her sideways. "How am I supposed to know that?"

"You can't help overhearing," Nina said. "I mean, you're out there doing your job just a few feet away. Of course you hear things."

"It's true. She doesn't care what she says around me. I'm like that herb garden that's hidden behind the flowers, useful but they don't have to see me," he said. "Well, I heard her yesterday talking to her brother. She says she's tired of telling lies. Then Jason says something, and she says, don't worry, she'll keep her promise, but she's worried and can't sleep and why doesn't he come home."

The front door opened with a bang and a stocky Asian-American man with gray hair brushed straight back, holding a doctor's bag, strode in, Leo Tarrant close on his heels.

"I'm Dr. Lee. Where is she?" he said.

"Top of the stairs, to your right."

"I'm coming up," Tarrant said.

"Oh, no, you're not," Dr. Lee called, taking the stairs two at a time. "I'll be down as soon as I can. You just sit tight."

Tarrant turned to Nina and Joe, saying, "I just drove up and saw Dr. Lee getting out of his car. He told me about Molly on the way in. How is she?" He looked frightened.

"I really don't know," Nina said. "But she was awake and talking when we left the room. She wouldn't let us call an ambulance."

"May I be excused?" Joe said. "I have to finish the lawn." Tarrant's entrance had erased him. His intelligent face smoothed out into bland emptiness and he seemed to shrink a little as he slid back into the role of being just the gardener.

"I guess," Nina said. Joe went out and Tarrant walked over to the fireplace, where the logs crackled and burned, propping his arm on the mantel in an easy stance. He wore a tan sport coat and chinos over chukka boots. He had a face like an old boxer's, flat-nosed and battered, but his eyes were shrewd, and he had a gentle voice. Ugly-handsome, Nina decided.

"Thank God you people went in there in time. Poor Molly," he said, looking toward the top of the staircase. "How close was it?"

"Ask the doctor, Mr. Tarrant. She was talking to her mother, fully conscious. I don't know. She had a close call."

"What in the world made her do this? The shock of Ray's death? I don't believe it. I hate to say it, but she disliked Ray so much, I would have thought she'd . . ." Tarrant said. "Never mind. She's going downhill instead. Damn it! Poor little thing." He shook his head in disbelief.

"You came to see Sarah?"

"Yes. I thought she might like to go over to Harrah's for a bite to eat and a show."

"Do you see each other often?" Nina asked.

"Is that your business?"

"I just like to have a half-wit's understanding of what's going on when I take on a client," Nina said. "And I am deeply confused about this whole family."

"Don't get involved. Do what you're supposed to do," Tarrant said. "Get Quentin off our butts."

"Explain one thing to me. I'm curious about Quentin's relationship to his son. I understand you were in partnership with the two of them in De Beers Construction," Nina said.

"Quentin drummed up the business, Ray screwed up the construction, and I cleaned up the mess," Tarrant said. "Quentin had to bring somebody in after Ray almost drove the company into the ground. I'm making the company profitable again, in spite of Ray obstructing me at every turn. I'll say this for Quentin:

He's a smart enough businessman to keep me as general manager no matter what Ray says—said, I mean.

"Quentin forgave every crummy thing Ray did. He just couldn't see it. Quentin worked for thirty years to make a good reputation and Ray dragged it in the dirt, but Quentin just made excuses for him. They hunted, fished, gambled together. He took Ray's death hard. He needs somebody to blame. He missed seeing the body, that's the whole problem. He's a concrete thinker. He doesn't trust anybody else's opinion. He has to see things with his own eyes."

"Maybe we should just let the old man have a look," Nina said. "If it means that much to him. We could have the police do a civil standby, so he wouldn't have a chance to—wouldn't be alone with the body. Sarah doesn't agree, of course, or we wouldn't be handling this hearing the way we are. . . ."

She expected Tarrant to flare up at her suggestion, but his expression broke into one she was getting used to instead—the harassed look she had seen on the faces of both Sarah and Molly.

"Listen. This hearing is about much more than Quentin's fatherly need to see his son's body. It's about Quentin controlling Sarah and the kids. Sarah is trying to stand up to him for the first time. Her freedom, and Molly and Jason's freedom, depend on her breaking that control. She needs you to battle him, not compromise with him. Are you going to take care of the job or not? Or should I tell Sarah she should get a postponement and another lawyer?"

"Oh, I'll go to battle, Mr. Tarrant. But I won't go in blind," Nina said. "You and Sarah had better understand that."

Tarrant nodded, saying, "Thanks. I'm sure you'll do

your best." He glanced up toward the landing. "I'm going up there."

Dr. Lee appeared above them, brushing off his sleeves. "She's fine," he said, talking down the stairwell. "Just a few bruises. She'll be hoarse for a few days. That kind of rope stretches, so her weight when she stepped off the chair didn't break her neck. Her mother is staying with her. She said there's no reason for you to stay at this point."

"She's not going to the hospital?" Nina said in amazement.

"She'll be all right here," the doctor said flatly.

"She needs psychiatric help," Nina persisted. "Don't we have to report this to someone?"

"Excuse me," said the doctor, stepping rapidly down the stairs. "I don't believe we've met."

"I'm Mrs. de Beers's attorney, Nina Reilly."

"Well, then, Ms. Reilly, you'll understand why I suggest that you discuss any questions on medical treatment with your client, won't you?"

"Can I go up now?" Tarrant said.

"You can knock on the door and see," Dr. Lee said. "I'll let myself out."

Tarrant took to the stairs. "See you at the hearing, Ms. Reilly," he said.

"Please tell Sarah that I will be in touch," Nina said.

From below, Nina heard Tarrant's rapping and the door opening. The door to the bedroom shut again and the house fell silent except for the snapping of the fire. Outside, she heard Joe's leaf blower extirpating every wild thing that had had the temerity to fall upon the expensive grass. It was getting dark.

Apparently, the incident with Molly was closed. It seemed wrong that a human being could come so close to losing her life with so little official involvement. Nina had the sense that Molly's suicide attempt was being buried just as efficiently as Ray had been. She would bet she'd never hear another word about this, unless she brought it up herself.

And then she thought of something else. The declaration she had prepared for Molly to sign, opposing the motion for exhumation, might as well be thrown away. Molly wouldn't be available to sign it.

Could the declaration have had anything to do with Molly's attempted suicide? All it did was briefly reiterate her statement to the coroner's office about her father's death on the mountain, express the wish that her father not be disinterred, and state that she had not seen the ring on his finger at the open viewing at the mortuary.

Probably the situation—the mother and grandfather fighting about digging up her father, and her father's death—and maybe those Kurt Cobain memorials—had more to do with causing her despair.

Would de Beers change his mind when he learned about Molly? She thought about that. The county lawyers had told Nina she was free to handle the motion however Sarah wanted, so long as it didn't end up costing the county any money. In hand, she had the coroner's declaration, Sarah's declaration, and a declaration from the cemetery. Tomorrow she would be picking up another declaration from the police department. But to assure a win she needed at least one of the children to oppose the exhumation request in writing.

The papers had to be filed by tomorrow. She had to go ahead. If de Beers changed his mind, fine, but she wasn't going to jump to any optimistic conclusions.

The clock on the mantel said six o'clock. Time was running out. She needed to find Jason.

Stacks of phone books from San Francisco to Tahoe were piled on the table in the entry. The local Tahoe directory listed a Kenneth Munger. She wrote down the address, pulled the double walnut doors shut tightly behind her, and breathed a sigh of relief as she slid behind the wheel in the pleasant personal chaos of her Bronco. Here, at least, was a mess she understood.

Paul lay on the big hotel bed in his shorts, hands behind his head on the pillow, gazing at the painting that he had propped up against the wall: Kim's painting of the hit-and-run.

Outside his tenth-floor window, the neon lights of the casinos were starting to flare up as the daylight faded. He had just worked out in the weight room in the basement and sat in the spa with some jolly French golfers who had a few gems to offer about playing the Pebble Beach links. His body felt light and warm, the muscles of his shoulders pleasantly tired.

Ginger Hirabayashi had identified the glass bits as standard for auto headlights, and faxed him the dispersion and reflectivity indexes from Sacramento. The figures were useless without a car with which to make comparisons, but they might someday turn into evidence.

He had spent the afternoon double-checking the three-year-old police work. The local repair shops turned up nothing—all cars that could have been brought in for accident-based repairs checked out clean. The hospital records had listed weeks of accident victims, including patients with accident-consistent injuries, but revealed nothing. The tow-truck companies and junkyards and police departments for miles around had been advised to report cars disposed of over cliffs or in water or for junk—nothing.

The problem was, they lacked a decent description of the vehicle, much less the driver. Kim called herself a colorist and said details weren't her thing. If only she'd been from the photo-realist school of art, Paul thought sourly. Her painting contained only massive, barely differentiated forms, not much to hang a theory on. . . .

He stared at the two red triangles pushing the light streak he took to be the car, speeding toward its destiny. These triangles and the green streak constituted the only real details in the picture. Kim hadn't known why she put the triangles into the picture. He had thought perhaps they stood for a nearby sign, but another look at the photographs of the scene and a spin around the parking lot on the way home had left him unconvinced. Maybe they just stood for blood, or maybe she had simply added something red to balance the green. . . .

His eyes closed and he began drifting into a nap, his thoughts gradually giving way to hypnagogic images swirling like sharks in an asphalt sea, only their shiny fins showing above the water—

Waking with a start, he knew what to do next.

Kenny Munger lived in the run-down apartments on Ski Run Boulevard that housed many of Tahoe's poorest residents. Nina had dealt with the absentee landlord on several previous occasions and even called in the Department of Health on behalf of one young mother without heat or plumbing the previous winter.

She pulled into the full parking lot and pulled out

again, hunting for a spot on the street. Squeezing into a too-small space behind a camper, Nina passed quickly through the dimly lit concrete walkways, her eyes scanning doors for number 108. As she dodged cats and toys, passing by the windows of the apartments, the blue light of TVs flickered through the curtains, babies cried, children laughed, and men and women bickered.

At 108, Jason de Beers opened the door. Barefoot, he wore baggy shorts and an ironed cotton T-shirt. His expression was despondent. "What can I do for you?" he said, not moving out of the doorway. "I'm kind of busy."

"You talked to your mother?"

"Yes! You know about Molly?" He held the door open for her to enter. "I'm getting my clothes on to go over there."

"I came into the bedroom right after your mother found her. Molly stayed conscious throughout. The gardener cut her down right away. He had garden clippers in his belt. Dr. Lee says she'll be all right."

Jason sank down on the couch. "Why'd she do it? What did she say?" When he sat down, the broken springs just let him sink until he was only a few inches above the floor, his big feet planted firmly on the rug.

"Nothing, to me."

"You're sure she's not going to—"

"Not tonight, anyway. Your mother's not going to let her out of her sight."

"I shouldn't have left them! This isn't the kind of thing my mom can handle. Where's my shoes?" he went on as if she weren't there. He picked up a sneaker and pulled it on, sockless. Even sitting down, he took up most of the room, and Nina wondered how he could sleep in the makeshift bed in the corner.

Again, she was struck by the anomaly of reasonably ordinary-looking parents having two such knockouts for children. She let the silence lengthen while she studied the lines of his face, certain she had seen them before on a statue, the muscles chiseled in smooth marble, sinewy and definite like his. . . . Both he and Molly had the high forehead and fine features of their mother, and her wavy hair, reproduced in gold.

Jason looked sturdier than his sister, more athletic. Sarah had mentioned some of the sports Jason had been involved in over the years: tennis, swim team, hockey, baseball. And Molly played basketball. The twins were high achievers, even if they weren't happy. Many driven, compulsive achievers weren't.

While he fumbled with the other shoe, Nina looked around the neat living room. Against the inner wall, an oversize entertainment center/desk combination spilled out books and wires linked to extensive electronic equipment. Covering most of the surface of the desk, tiny animations turning and jumping on its screen, was a state-of-the-art computer with a hard-disk tower and two plastic holders stuffed with disks. Nina could see the Netscape headers and some text but couldn't read the monitor from where she stood.

Through the half-open door into the bedroom, she saw a table set up like her chemistry lab table in high school, piled with bundles of rods and tubes and cylindrical forms she couldn't identify. A book on pyrotechnics lay on the carpet. Her eye fell on the open page, which carried the title *Recipe for a Sugar Rocket*.

Jason finished putting on his shoes, and moved ahead of her, straightening the comforter on the bed, shutting down the computer and locking the bedroom door before turning to her. She approved of and understood this impulse to order. As he straightened up the outer room, his mind could also order itself.

He said, "Thank you for coming over to get me, but I'll take it from here. And thank you . . . for helping Molly. I have to go."

Nina hesitated.

Looking at him, she could easily erase the shadow of beard and picture him much younger, maybe Bob's age. But Bob had never felt, she hoped never would feel, the anguish on this young man's face. He didn't need any more trouble. But she was going to have to bring it to him anyway.

Briskly, she said, "I didn't come to get you. I know you need to go, but wait just a minute. Have you talked to your mother about your grandfather's lawsuit to exhume your father's body?"

Jason's reaction was worse than she had expected. He obviously hadn't heard a thing about the suit. His jaw dropped and his face went ashy. He had trouble finding his voice, and when he found it, it broke. "He wants—what?" he said.

She explained what Quentin de Beers was up to, and all the while he just cocked his head and watched her like a dog she had sneaked up on and kicked. "Look, I'm sorry. You didn't need another shock. Hasn't your mother talked to you in the last day or so?"

"No. I . . . went out hiking today. When I called her from the store, she was . . . we only talked about Molly."

"I have a declaration here"—Nina pulled it out of the briefcase—"that I need you to read. I wrote it for your sister to sign, so it has her name on it, but the information is the same. Read it, please. Talk to your mother. If you are willing to sign it I need you to bring it down to my office in the Starlake Building by to-morrow morning at the latest so we can put it in final form and submit it to the Court. At the latest, right?"

She walked over and gave him the draft declaration with her business card. He was more than a foot taller than she was. She seemed to be handing paper to an uncomprehending wall. "It's important, Jason."

His father had been killed, his sister had just tried to kill herself, and while he was still reeling, he had learned that his grandfather had sued his mother. She hoped he had a point of stability inside him. His mother and sister did not, and somebody had to try to keep them grounded.

"The hearing is on Thursday morning in the main Superior Court. Day after tomorrow, unless your grandfather and your mother settle it earlier. You can come if you want, but you don't have to be there."

He folded the papers up carefully and pushed them into his pocket. "I have to think," he said to himself. She wanted to calm him down before he got out on the road; so she asked, just trying to ratchet down the conversation a little, "Jason? What's a sugar rocket?"

"Oh, that's Kenny's book. He's a mad scientist. I'd introduce you, but he's out." He passed a hand over his eyes.

"Are you okay?" Nina asked. It was past eight, and she became aware that she was so tired and hungry, she wasn't even sure about driving home. "I'm going now."

He held the door open for her, car keys in his hand, his eyes somewhere else.

10

"YEAH, FINS. A BIG GAS-GUZZLER FROM THE FIFTIES, early sixties. Chrysler, Buick, Pontiac, maybe. White, with the big ones. What were the biggest years for the fins? Nineteen fifty-eight? Fifty-nine? You tell me."

Sitting cross-legged on the bed and munching on a toasted sourdough bagel with salmon and cream cheese, Paul was making his telephone rounds. At barely nine o'clock in the morning, some of the places on his list hadn't opened yet. He would get to them later.

"Fins. How many fins you get turned in as a trade-in each year? Maybe two? You can look for me. Oh, yes, you can. Come up with the car I want and there's a bonus in it for you . . . it's a private collector. Nothing to do with the cops or the DMV—just a minute, somebody's at the door."

A tacky suit stood at the door, with a beat-up car salesman in it. Paul could tell he was a salesman because he had the salesman's smile, big on teeth and small on warmth, under a black bristly mustache. Heavyset, he wore his hair combed straight back. In the buttonhole of his jacket a white rosebud sent out its own flowery greeting.

"Gotta go," Paul said.

Hanging up, he surveyed his visitor, who held out his hand and said, "Munir El-Barouki. How do you do? You are Mr. van Wagoner?"

"Come on in."

Inside the room, El-Barouki said, "Nice place to do business. You're a private investigator, right?"

"That's right."

"I always wanted to do that, but I'll never get a license now. Little problem down South. Wow, that's a nice semiauto you have on the table there."

"So what brings you to my humble hotel room?"

El-Barouki ignored this. He said, "I used to carry a custom forty-five when I worked executive protection. You know what they say: 'One shot stops, the bad guy drops.' Customized by Bill Wilson out of Arkansas. Had the feed ramp polished, had it throated, had the ejection port flared, added a Beavertail safety. A set of cocobolo grips by Kim Ahrends. A Wilson barrel and a Videcki trigger. And a set of Bo-Mar sights. I loved that gun."

"We all love our guns," Paul said. "What happened to it?"

"Lost my license to carry. Started selling used Caddys in Chico, Merced, other places, and ended up in Tahoe a few years ago. Gambled away my stake and got stuck here, actually. So, what you got there? Looks like a Sig P210."

"Close," Paul said. "CZ-75 nine millimeter. Fifteen rounds and one in the chamber. Almost as accurate as the Sig. One of the original wonder nines."

"Preban magazines, huh?" El-Barouki said, edging up toward the gun. Paul reached over to pick it up.

"Yeah. Straight from the factory in Brno."

"My brother-in-law had a CZ. I know the type. You can carry it cocked and locked."

"You got it," said Paul. He figured El-Barouki would get to the point soon enough. Besides, he liked having his gun admired. Other people had pets; he had a relationship with his gun. It was beautiful and sexy and fit his hand perfectly. He held it in his palm so El-Barouki could get a good look.

"Course, the nine millimeter doesn't have the stopping power of the forty-five," El-Barouki said.

"I use hollow points," Paul said. "Black Rhinos. Almost as effective as a forty-five and carries twice as many."

"Still, you can't beat a full metal jacket in a big bore. You know what they say: 'They all fall to hardball.' "

"If you shoot straight, they all fall, period," Paul said. He put the gun away, gently, in its holster. "So," he said.

El-Barouki took the hint. "You called my place of employment this morning, Sierra Cadillac. My boss told me about the call. He's new, and I was around three years ago."

"Go on. You're a car salesman?"

"That's what I do, move the metal. I may know the car you're looking for. How much is the bonus?"

"If it really is the car I'm looking for, and you give me the location, I'll give you a hundred bucks."

"Hundred bucks? Don't waste my time." El-Barouki headed for the door, turning his head to eye Paul and see how he was taking it. Paul watched him put his hand on the knob, hesitate, and turn back.

"There are special circumstances with this car," El-Barouki said.

"I'm listening."

"I handled the transaction privately. Not through Sierra."

"What transaction?"

"A guy paid me to get rid of it. I didn't want to run it through the lot, just in case, you know?"

"In case it was hot, yeah, I know."

El-Barouki shrugged. "Well, who knew? Anyway, I drove it home. If there was a problem, it wasn't my problem. I sold it to a tourist from Whittier, town outside Los Angeles, cheap."

"When exactly was this?" Paul said.

"Make it five hundred, we can get into the details."

"It's chilly out there. Close the door on your way out," Paul told him.

"Three hundred."

"Two-fifty. My final offer."

"I could get into trouble about this," El-Barouki complained, "Plus I had to take off work." Seeing Paul unmoved, he tried again. "Mr. van Wagoner, you're killing me, I've got expenses—"

"You've already collected from both the seller and the buyer," Paul interrupted. "You didn't report the income to the IRS. You sold cars off the job. That could get you fired. So let's say we need each other at this point. And unlike your clients at the car shop, I won't waste my time listening to you natter on in the hopes that you can shake another couple of bucks out of me. Two-fifty."

"And no trouble?"

"No trouble."

"Okay. There are always side deals to be made. One

condition. You let me hold the gun for a minute before we start."

Sighing, Paul worked the slide and ejected the bullet in the chamber into his hand, then pressed the magazine release and withdrew the clip. He handed the gun to El-Barouki, who weighed it, tested the grip, looked down the barrel and aligned the front sight at a bird pecking at seeds outside on the windowsill.

"Pow," he said, recoiling his hand. "He's history."

The bird took the hint and flew away. El-Barouki smiled, handing the gun back. "You've got a nice piece there."

Paul tucked the gun back into its holster.

"Okay. This all happened in September, three years ago. The car was a white 1959 Pontiac Catalina in good shape, clean, little crack in one of the headlights, coupla dings. That's it. The buyer paid one thousand for it, a great deal considering the blue book for a classic in that condition."

Paul had grabbed his notebook off the table and was making rapid notes.

"Who was the seller?" he said.

"We'll get to that in a minute. The buyer's name was Bryan Bright. He said his family had a Catalina in the sixties and he had always wanted another one. Here's his address." He handed over a dirty slip of paper.

Paul said again, "The seller?"

"No name."

"What about the registration?"

"I forgot what it said."

"You put any of the sale papers through the DMV?"

"No, I put the two dudes in touch and they handled the rest themselves."

"What did the seller look like?"

El-Barouki was shaking his head. "He was maybe forty, fifty. Not young. I'm not too clear on how he looked. This was three years ago, you know."

"How much did he pay you to forget his name and what he looked like?"

"A little extra," El-Barouki said. "And he also said he'd personally cut my nuts off if I told anyone else—so you know, I'm forgetful."

"I can relate. But you didn't promise not to describe the car he drove."

El-Barouki thought about this, and said, "He drove the Catalina in and left on foot. There's a 7-Eleven down the road. Maybe he called a taxi from there."

"What about the license plate?" Paul asked, but El-Barouki was already shaking his head. He wasn't going to ID the seller, period. Paul decided that if he could work backward from the trail of documents he might locate the seller. "What else can you tell me?"

"Just . . . I always felt funny about it. The car wasn't hot, that much I checked out, but the situation felt hot. Not long after, the dealership got a call from the cops. They were looking for a light-colored car that had been in an accident. I mean, that wasn't necessarily the Catalina. I can't even say it was in an accident. But I always wondered . . ."

"Yeah?"

"What'd the guy do?" El-Barouki said, almost in a whisper.

Paul gave him his money and a business card, saying, "I'll be in touch."

By one o'clock, Paul had caught the daily flight to Los Angeles from the Tahoe airport. Bryan Bright hadn't been listed in phone information, but El-

Barouki had given him a lead that was too good to sit on.

The small prop plane ripped in and out of the cloud banks, jolting its way out of the mountains. Down below, the foothills looked untouched, a sprawl of forest camouflaging the one-lane roads, pickup trucks, bars, and cabins.

The plane bumped again, but the three other passengers didn't seem to notice. The steward sat up front, reading a magazine. No movie, no peanuts, no lovely lady leaning over him with a drink.

His right knee gave him a warning twinge. Efficiency, compactness, and frugality were all very well for small, stingy robots, Paul thought, trying to find a new configuration for his long legs, which were being tortured by the seat in front. He could appreciate why Bryan Bright would buy an old car with fins that got about eight miles to the gallon. The Catalina would have leg room delightful to stretch out in, and a trunk roomy enough to carry the TV set down to the repair shop.

After an hour and a half and a stop somewhere in the Central Valley, Paul woke from a nap to the brown haze suspended over the L.A. basin. Traveling directly into the murky sunlight with its deceitful way of adding a healthy golden glow to everything it touched, they landed without incident and Paul followed the pilots out the corridor and into a blast of broiling-hot smog. City of fallen angels!

To honor the spirit of the occasion, Paul had decided to rent a big car, but all the agency offered was a Chrysler Le Baron convertible, a Lilliput to yesteryear's Brobdingnags. Consulting his map, he saw that East Whittier was just across town—about fifty miles, that would be. He slipped shades on his face, got in the car, and merged onto the clogged freeway. Hot wind and exhaust fumes blasted his face, causing his eyes to sting and water so badly he had to wipe the tears away with his sleeve.

He had thought a convertible would be cool, but in about five minutes he pulled over to raise the vinyl hood and turn on the air-conditioning. Unfortunately, the hood latch in front was broken. He drove on, watching with irritation as the other drivers in their tightly sealed air-conditioned cars sailed by.

As he made his way across the gargantuan, stifling city, with nothing but graffiti-blotched sound walls and dusty ice plant to distract him, he let go of the Case and thought about women, his favorite meditation topic, more engrossing even than guns or what to have for dinner.

He was tired of following Nina around like a love-starved puppy. By God, he'd prove it with Kim. The sheer cockiness of this mental pronouncement forced him to look at a possibility, one he didn't particularly care to see. Was Kim just a reaction to Nina?

Kim is sexy, he thought, classic. She's got a nose like the ones on Roman coins, and she exudes femaleness, serenity. She works at home. She likes being there, likes cooking there, likes me there. She's artistic, fascinating, and worth going after.

But what about the celibacy riff she had laid on him? What about "I don't date"? She was definitely hetero; he had seen the mist rise in her eyes when he kissed her. She wouldn't be worth going after if she didn't put up an obstacle or two.

He wondered if Nina would even notice. Let her

find out from Collier. Let her know he had somebody else.

Coming to a clear stretch of road, he whizzed past an eighteen-wheeler already doing seventy. Chinks in the sound walls offered a glimpse of block after block of dilapidated tract houses. According to the signs, he had passed through Hawthorne, Gardena, Watts, Lynwood, the edge of Compton, Paramount, and Bellflower.

He turned north on the 605. The traffic thickened and slowed, as if the heat had coagulated it. Norwalk, Downey, Santa Fe Springs . . . might as well get off here. He could drive out Telegraph Road and end up in East Whittier, his destination.

Dumpy ranch houses. Ritzy ranch houses. Dry concrete culverts and identical strip malls, each with its convenience store and fast-food outlet. At four o'clock it was still so hot he could smell the asphalt melting.

He found the sameness depressing. More than once he convinced himself that he had driven in circles. Surely the evil empire couldn't go on much farther. He was driving through the center of the postwar American dream, surrounded by fifty miles, maybe a hundred miles, of one-story three-bedroom two-bath two-car-garage gimcrack houses, with wall-to-wall carpeting and a barbecue pit out back.

At last he turned onto a cul-de-sac called Avalon Place and came to the home of Bryan Bright. Just like all the others, it was painted stucco, with an oil stain in the driveway and a jumble of bicycles on the porch. Paul pulled right into the wide driveway. He had planned a little covert surveillance before he approached the man, but it was too fucking hot.

At the front door, he knocked but got no answer. He thought he could guess exactly what time Bright would be pulling up from his job in the dying aerospace industry. Down the street he bought himself a six-pack of diet cola, then parked right in Bright's driveway, where a half-dead tree near the driveway shed a meager shade. There he passed the next hour, the hottest hour of his life.

With a thunderous roar and a cloud of oily exhaust, just after six, right to the minute according to Paul's projected schedule, Bryan Bright bumped into the driveway next to the Le Baron. Paul was just returning from the backyard, where he had been forced to take a whiz after downing the entire six-pack.

"Hey! What are you doing in my backyard!" the man said, climbing out of the big, sleek car. Not a car: an automobile. Twenty feet long, so heavy it scraped the bottom on the slight incline of the driveway, white-walled and blindingly chromed, it had been repainted a glimmering black. At the rear of the vehicle, sticking eight inches into the air, winking their twin red orbicular lights, the fins looked hilarious or hip, depending on the observer's point of view. To Paul they looked like red triangles in a painting.

A 1959 Pontiac Catalina, Paul thought with satisfaction.

"Sorry," he said. "I was just looking for you. Thought you might be out back." He walked over to the car, looked at the headlights. Not a ding. He looked at the windshield. Nothing he could see. "This is some car."

"Who are you?" the man demanded. He was about thirty, pink-faced, balding fast, wearing wraparound sunglasses and carrying a lunch box.

"My name's Paul van Wagoner. Are you Mr. Bright?"

"Yes."

"I'm a private investigator, Mr. Bright. May I talk to you for a minute?"

"What about?"

"Your car."

"What about my car? What's this about?"

"Don't be alarmed, Mr. Bright. I'm looking for a previous owner. It's got nothing to do with you."

"Oh. Well, I just drove thirty-five miles on the freeway, and I had a long day at the office. My wife and kids will be home soon. So why don't you come back after supper."

"I just flew five hundred miles and drove another fifty to see you as soon as I could, Mr. Bright. Give me a break. It's too hot to stand around out here. Let's go inside."

Bright looked at Paul's rental car, and said, "Never drive in a convertible around here in August. You'll get sunstroke. Only tourists drive convertibles. The sun's too strong to ride around like that. Wheel gets too hot to touch, and the vinyl seats on that thing, they'll—"

"You're telling me," Paul said.

"Oh, well. Come on out to the lanai."

Paul followed Bright out to the concrete patio he had already seen, passing through small boxy rooms, stepping over a Slinky and various stuffed animals. The backyard consisted of a tall red fence surrounding a treeless square of crabgrass. The barren patio was shaded by a roof of garden trellising. Paul sat down in one of the folding chairs, his stomach still sloshing from the sodas.

"Be right back," Bright said.

In no time he was back in a pair of plaid shorts, holding two tall glasses of ice water. He asked for Paul's license and scrutinized the picture. Then he leaned back in his chair and said, "I always thought buying the Catalina would come back to haunt me. The price was too cheap. I suppose it was stolen."

"What makes you think that?"

"There's no such thing as a bargain. I let myself be bamboozled, I guess. Do I have to give it back, or what? I've put a lot of money into it. I really love it. Is there any way I can keep it?"

"It's an interesting choice of vehicle," Paul said. "Why did you want it in the first place?"

"Yeah, it costs a bundle to operate," Bright said with a laugh. "My wife said I was crazy, but when we all get in the car and drive down to Huntington Beach on Saturdays, she loves it. Everybody on the street stares. At work, they all know Bryan's way-cool V8 with fins. I sit in a cubicle all day at a gray desk with a beige phone and a tan computer and a dipshit younger than me looking over my shoulder, and I live like everybody else." He motioned toward the house. "But my car, now, that's a whole other story."

Paul nodded sympathetically, thinking about his love affair with his own Dodge Ram van.

"This is L.A. You wouldn't believe how much time you spend in your car. At parties here they don't ask what do you do, they ask what do you drive.

"I've lived here in the 'burbs all my life," Bright went on, tinkling the ice in his glass. "All over Whittier, Pico Rivera, Norwalk, La Mirada, a few years in the San Fernando Valley, a year in Orange County. If they built a new tract, my parents wanted to move into it. They came from the South after the war and thought they'd found paradise. They couldn't wait to cut off their past. I grew up thinking everybody came

out of nowhere, and every year we'd move on to another suburb just like the one we'd left, a few miles
farther out where the orange groves used to be. All the
history and routines got lost in the moves, you know
what I mean?"

"Some people want that."

"Not me. It bothered me. I knew I lacked soul,
Paul." This was said with such lugubrious earnestness
that even Paul felt subdued.

"Why didn't you leave when you got older, if you
don't like it?" he asked.

"Who says I don't? It's a good place to raise kids.
You know they'll get lots of exercise, lots of time outdoors. I don't know any place better. They'll never see
a cockroach or see anybody dealing drugs on the corner, at least in this neighborhood. They're protected
here. They think going to the mall and watching
Baywatch is what life's all about. It's comfortable here.
But . . ."

"Safe and sanitary," Paul said. He let his eyes wander
over the yard. In the next yard, on the other side of the
fence, he could see a shower of water coming, then
going, then coming back, and hear the *whap whap whap
whap* of a mechanical lawn sprinkler. The day had finally begun to cool and the sky had cleared to a Tech-
nicolor blue.

He felt as if he knew Bryan Bright. He could have
been Bryan Bright, going off to work and coming
home again and raising his kids and golfing on Sundays
in weather that was always dry, always sunny, until he
dried up completely, and then he would take his last
drive in a hearse to Rose Lawn Cemetery and be taken
up to a heaven where a wizened God wears shorts over

his skinny legs and drinks ice water and putts better than any angel. . . .

Bryan, too, was waxing reflective. "Sometimes at night I would think, what am I doing here, what's unique about me? You know? Who is Bryan Bright, anyway? I'm not a religious type. I can't get into that New Age shit. I didn't know where to look. Finally, I looked inside myself. It was like a big TV set in there, Paul, lots of ads and brand names and my job and house and family, but no sign of me, you know, Paul?

"So one day I told my wife I was going up to Lake Tahoe by myself. She didn't understand that. 'Never mind, I'm going,' I said. 'That's that.' I was driving a Nissan Sentra with seventy thousand miles on it. I went up there and saw the trees and the mountains. On about the third day I was sitting on the rocks overlooking Emerald Bay, and something happened. Inside my head, I mean. I realized for the very first time that I was me. I became aware of myself. Anything like that ever happened to you? UFOs, mystical shit?"

"No such luck."

"When I came out of it, I knew something heavy had happened. I knew who Bryan Bright is. And I wanted to express who I am. So people would know I'm different from the next guy." He jabbed his thumb at his chest for emphasis. He had propped his legs on a low white plastic table. He flapped the bottoms of his rubber thongs against the soles of his feet for a time, in rhythm with the sprinkler next door.

Paul crunched ice cubes and let him be. Bright wanted to talk. Let him talk.

"I decided to buy a car," Bright said.

"So you went looking for a car up there at Tahoe?"

"I talked to a few salesmen, yeah, I did. I didn't

know what I was looking for at first. It couldn't cost too much; I've got the mortgage and the kids, even though Debs works too— Shoot, I hear the car out there, you took her parking space. . . ."

Paul got up and said, "I'll move it."

Bright got up too. "You're probably planning to eat at some fancy restaurant tonight," he said a little shyly.

"No. No, I didn't have any plans."

"You could eat with us. I have to get busy now. The kids will be hungry."

"Great." Paul moved his car, introduced himself to Mrs. Bright, and offered to lug a sack of groceries from her minivan back up the walkway to the house. Three kids galloped around him and he heard the TV sputter to life in the living room. Mrs. Bright gave him a harried smile from the kitchen, where her husband was already turning on the oven and getting out paper plates. They kissed and started the dinner, giving Paul the chore of scraping carrots.

Mrs. Bright had the slightly mad eyes of any woman with three small children who also holds down a full-time job. She had apparently decided that Paul was a golf buddy of Bryan's who had turned up to visit. She went into the bedroom, appearing shortly afterward in a flowered shift, barefoot. They sat down on the couch in front of the TV and watched *Jeopardy!* while the dinner cooked.

Then they ate fish sticks, carrot sticks, and french fries with a whole lot of ketchup while *Wheel of Fortune* was on.

When a cartoon show came on and Mrs. Bright, yawning, headed off to do laundry, Bryan said, "Paul and I are going out for a little spin in the Cat. Is that okay?"

"I forgot toilet tissue," she said.

"Yeah, okay, I'll pick some up."

"Oh, and eggs. And maybe some Popsicles for the kids for their bedtime snack."

"Okay."

The two men walked out to the car. Overbright streetlights shone down on the identical houses with their identical yards, on the empty streets. Bryan opened the door for Paul, and he got into the front seat.

The seats were a mile wide. Paul could sit straight without the top of his head brushing the ceiling, the expansive space and springy cushions combining to create the same comfort as a luxurious limo. The engine started up like a pride of lions sighting a plump zebra.

The big car cruised sedately down the block, emitting a steady stream of pollutants.

"The Cat, we call her."

"Mmm–hmm."

"The salesman, Mr. El-Barouki, took care of everything. The seller didn't want to have to deal directly with me, and didn't want to put it through the lot. So when I started asking around, saying I was looking for something different but not very expensive, Mr. El-Barouki took me out to his house. He has at least seven kids. Debs isn't real clear about the details, so I didn't want to get into this in front of her."

"Sure."

"The minute I saw it in his garage, I knew it was what I had been looking for. Different. Nobody else buys these things. He said I could have it for two thousand, but it would have to be on a salvage certificate. You know what that is?"

"Not exactly."

"Well, the seller sold it to a junkyard and told the DMV it was totaled. Then the junkyard sold it to me, only the junkyard was listed as owner and the registration process sort of starts over from scratch. What a chore. But I kept going back to the DMV down here, and finally I had the new registration."

"Do you still have your old paperwork?" Paul said.

"It's in here somewhere." Bryan dug around the glove compartment with one hand and came up with a grimy envelope.

Opening it, Paul found many repair slips, the new registration, and the salvage certificate, listing Gregory El-Barouki as the junkyard owner. "The salesman's brother?" Paul said.

"That's right. I forgot." None of the papers mentioned the name of the person who had delivered the "totaled" car to the junkyard. Paul, who had just called all the auto wrecking yards in the area, didn't recognize the name. The "junkyard" was probably a backyard.

"I'd like to make copies of these."

They pulled into a row of stores under strong parking lot lights. "The copy place is right over there," Bryan said. "I'll hit the store."

When they were back in the car and patrolling the boundlessly tedious neighborhoods once more, Paul said, "Did you ever see or talk to the seller?"

"Nope."

"Did El-Barouki ever mention his name, address, anything like that?"

"I don't think so."

"Didn't you ask him anything about why the car was being sold as salvage when it obviously wasn't totaled?"

"It was understood," Bryan said. "If I wanted the car, I wouldn't ask questions like that. Oh, I knew it would come back on me. I knew it was wrong. Who was it stolen from?"

"Nobody. But it may have been involved in a hit-and-run accident."

"Somebody die?"

"Yes."

"Oh, shoot. Shoot. Now I really feel bad."

"I'm going to need the car."

"What? You can't stroll in here and take my car!"

Paul told him about the police investigation, the death. Then he said, "Look, you can deal with me or you can deal with the police, because they're sure going to hear about it. But I'm sure you'll go for the better deal with me."

"But what about the money I put in?"

Paul said, "Tell you what. I need to have some tests run on the car. Maybe it's the wrong car. You'll have it back in a few weeks if it is."

"Did I break some law?" Bryan said. "I can't afford—you know, they're downsizing at work, any excuse—and Debs is pregnant again, she just told me last week."

"You didn't know about anything illegal," Paul said. "If anybody got taken, it was you. So don't worry. Look, I'll take the Catalina tonight, drive it upstate, and have it tested. I'll give you a receipt and my card. There's a chance it's not even the right car. You can drive the rental car I came in to work, and—"

"Debs can pick me up after work and we'll drop it off at the rental place," Bryan said mournfully. "Okay."

"If it turns out not to be the car, you'll get it back with a nice shine job. Scout's honor."

They parked out in front, leaving the motor running. The porch light cast a yellow glow out onto the crabgrass. Bright filled a box with personal things, stowing it on the porch next to the bikes. They traded car keys and Paul said, "Thanks for cooperating with me on this, Bryan. You could have made it a lot harder."

"I'll never find another one like the Cat." He adjusted the side mirror and stroked the hood.

"Probably not."

"I tell you my dad drove one kind of like this? Black, like I painted this one. Always overheated on the way to Vegas." Popping the lid, he peered into the engine compartment. He pulled out the oil dip stick, wiping it right on his pants, and checked the level.

"I'll be careful going up Interstate 5," Paul said.

"Don't worry, I had the radiator rebuilt." He unscrewed the radiator cap and peeked inside. Seeming satisfied at what he saw there, he slammed the hood down.

"The spare's good. You can find the jack."

"Sure I can, Bryan."

A deep sigh expanded Bright's slight potbelly. He let air out in a whoosh. "Who was I trying to kid, making out like I was something special? It was all a fake. The Cat was never really mine."

"It wasn't all a fake. Not the part at Emerald Bay."

"That was the fakest thing of all."

"People love you," Paul said. "Your wife, your kids. People who can achieve that, keep a family going in this day and age, they're special. A car's just a car, Bryan."

"Good-bye," Bright mumbled, patting the hood. Paul didn't answer. Bright hadn't been talking to him.

The last Paul saw of him was the rubber thong on his right foot, hooking the screen door and pulling it shut.

11

"ALL RISE," SAID DEPUTY KIMURA. "THE SUPERIOR Court of the County of El Dorado is now in session, the Honorable Curtis E. Milne presiding."

Nina stood up with everyone else in the bursting courtroom. Jeremy Stamp had not wanted to wait for a special setting of the hearing on Quentin de Beers's motion, so they would have to wait their turn.

Sarah de Beers had chosen not to come. She had left a message for Nina saying she wanted to stay with Molly. Jason hadn't made an appearance either, but he had come to Nina's office the day before to sign the declaration she had prepared.

Nina didn't mind their absences. When the clients weren't in court to worry and fret and drive her crazy, the pressure eased up. Motions were decided on the paperwork and the arguments of the attorneys, not on testimony of witnesses, anyway.

Quentin de Beers walked in, sitting down near the front of the courtroom with Jeremy Stamp, his grand old head of white hair unmistakable.

"You may be seated," said the clerk, setting off a general rustle and stir.

Judge Milne sat down behind the bench and poured himself a glass of water from his brown plastic pitcher. A fresh haircut revealed his satellite-dish ears. Wiping his specs on his robe, he announced, "It's going to be a long morning, ladies and gentlemen. We have a crowded docket. Therefore I am going to hold the attorneys strictly to the fifteen-minute rule. You have been warned. Case No. SLT 23748, *Bowker* versus *Sullivan*."

While the attorneys in the first case made their way to the counsel tables, Nina and several of the other lawyers went out. She didn't need to sit through the other cases. Out in the hall she could make some calls, review her notes for the argument again, and maybe catch Collier on his rounds.

She went to the pay phones near the law library and pulled out the sheaf of pink message slips that had accumulated since the previous afternoon.

"Ms. Reilly." Jeremy Stamp had followed her out, followed by his client. "Could I have a word with you?"

"All right."

"In the library?" He held the door for her.

Earlier, Sandy had spent a few minutes painting a picture of Stamp for her. She knew him from her three years as a file clerk in the firm of Caplan, Stamp, Powell, and Riesner, though Jeff Riesner had been her direct supervisor. "A damned sight more dangerous than Riesner," she had said. Stamp played golf with Milne and hobnobbed with the local Republican politicians. He had made his reputation representing insurance companies defending claims, a lucrative and stable specialty. He looked well-groomed and confident. De Beers, behind him, smiled at her, tilting his head faintly as if to remind her of their previous encounter, and that all's fair in war.

Nina waited for Stamp's opening gambit. She and Stamp had never appeared against each other in court. How would he approach her?

This early in the morning the clerks hadn't even turned on the lights. They sat down at one of the tables, and Stamp said, "A distressing situation," patting de Beers on the arm. "Hard on the whole family."

"Yes. Ray's wife and kids didn't need this," Nina said, her voice loaded with identical sympathy.

"Rest assured, Mr. de Beers is very upset about having to involve them. I understand he consulted with you. Naturally, that raises the issue of a potential conflict of interest in that you are now appearing against him." Stamp heaved a paternal sigh, meaning, My dear, you've let me down; you've disappointed a senior colleague; how embarrassed I am for you. But I'll forgive you if you rush to make amends.

That attitude would have to be adjusted. Nina accepted only one role from her opposing counsel, equal to equal. Stamp was trying to place her on the moral defensive and she had learned the hard way that you make points only on the attack. "He talked to me about other matters," she answered curtly. "Didn't you, Mr. de Beers? May I be candid with your attorney about our conversation?"

"Be my guest," de Beers rumbled.

"We talked about autopsies, and your client's suspicion that his son didn't die a natural death. And I had the clear impression that was the sole reason why Mr. de Beers wanted to disinter his son. So naturally when

Sarah de Beers brought me the motion you filed on completely different grounds, I felt free to assist her. There could be a conflict or confidentiality problem only if this motion is disingenuous, just a ploy to let Mr. de Beers have the body of his son disinterred for those other reasons. And of course, with your sterling reputation, Mr. Stamp, I know that you would never knowingly file inaccurate or, to be blunt, perjurious paperwork."

"Certainly not," Stamp said, his expression never varying from polite concern. "We do have the ring in question, and Ray de Beers was in fact wearing it during the open viewing at the mortuary. The mortician is quite sure he saw it."

"Oh, yes, the ring. I'm sure you do have it," Nina said. "The question is, where did your client get it?"

"I'm not here to rehearse the argument we may make in front of Milne. I want to convey to you Mr. de Beers's sincere desire to resolve this matter without going any further."

Nina sat back in her chair, crossed her legs, folded her arms, and said, "I'm listening."

De Beers gave Stamp an almost imperceptible nod of the head, and Nina thought, well, well, well. Look who's in charge. She had heard Stamp usually managed to keep his clients roped closely behind him.

"Well," Stamp said. "Let's step back from the, uh, personal differences within the family. Let's just look at the situation. When his son, his only child, died, Mr. de Beers was out of the country. He returned after suffering the terrible blow of the loss of his son, only to learn his son had been rushed into his grave. He had no opportunity to mourn or say good-bye. You can understand how he might feel?"

"If that's the true basis of this motion, why not come out and say so?"

"Because he wouldn't win with that argument, at least so long as the rest of the family is opposed. He only wants to see him one last time."

"And then what? He's made it clear that he is dissatisfied with the coroner's examination," Nina said. "Once the body is disinterred, it's my belief that he will find a way to have a medical examination performed. My client may not be aware of that. I can't tell her because Mr. de Beers's conversation with me was privileged. But I know it and you know it."

Stamp said, "The more they object, the more a medical exam does seem indicated. If there's nothing wrong, why don't we just have an independent exam?"

"Not for the reasons he's insinuating, that's for sure. Because there's no basis for an exam. Because my clients accept the coroner's ruling. Because they resent the insinuation. Because they don't like being pushed around."

Nina turned back to de Beers, who had been listening with his half-smile. "Mr. de Beers, Sarah and Jason and Molly do not want to disinter Ray's body. They need to put the past behind them. They need peace. Think about Molly. Think about how fragile she is right now. Please don't go forward with this. I told you I saw what happened. Your son was struck by lightning. But don't take my word for it, ask the expert, the coroner, Doc Clauson, who concluded the same thing. The cause of death was absolutely clear, do you understand?"

"Oh, I understand," de Beers said, contempt in his voice. "You're right in it with them. Leo's got you all flummoxed. You're covering up something. You think you can take me on."

"He doesn't mean that the way it sounds," Stamp said hurriedly, but Nina had already shouldered the briefcase strap.

"I'm getting rid of Leo tomorrow!" de Beers shouted. "I'll ruin him for making them fight me! Sarah would never do this on her own! Ray always said Leo was after her!"

"I'm sorry, Jeremy," Nina said, ignoring de Beers. "But I can't trust a man with an irrational obsession. After what you just heard, I think you and your client should have a talk about dropping the motion to exhume the body. I'll be out in the hall and glad to talk to you if that's what you want to do. But don't bother me for any other reason."

The door swung shut and she expelled the breath she had been holding.

Stamp and de Beers came out after half an hour, ignoring her presence down the hall, and Stamp went into the clerk's office while de Beers made a phone call. Then they both retired again to the library. For the next hour, while the judge waded through other cases, Nina made her calls and cooled her high heels. Finally Deputy Kimura came out and said, "Your case is next on the docket."

"Thanks." She went back to the library and said, "We're up next," to the two men, not at all happy to see the eagerness with which they took themselves back to the court.

"*De Beers* versus *de Beers* et al.," Milne announced as they walked in, so the two lawyers went straight up to the tables in front. Nina took her seat.

"Mr. Stamp?" Milne said. He gave the lawyer a

slight smile, an acknowledgment that outside court they were friends. Nina didn't like seeing it. She knew very well that she wasn't part of the small group of powerful men in Tahoe that welcomed Milne and Stamp and Quentin de Beers and would never welcome her.

But she had come to respect Milne. She had never caught him leaning unfairly toward one of his cronies. Milne had even helped her on occasion when she stumbled over evidentiary problems during trial. He was one reason she had been able to establish herself in a law practice at Tahoe. He was the only regularly sitting Superior Court judge, and he had always been fair to her.

Stamp was running through the facts of Ray's death. He had a fine, old-fashioned way of declaiming: his posture very erect, no notes, his well-manicured hands effecting a calculated series of graceful gestures. "As the Court will see, Penal Code section 642 makes it a felony willfully or maliciously to remove and appropriate for his own use articles of value from a human body. Mr. de Beers has filed a criminal complaint against persons unknown and requested that the South Lake Tahoe police department take immediate action to investigate.

"Therefore, we have a possibility of a crime involving Mr. de Beers's body. And if that body has been disturbed for the purpose of theft, who knows in what other respects it may have been disturbed? Have other items been taken? Has it been mutilated? Under the circumstances, Your Honor, my client felt that he had to do something. He begged Mrs. de Beers, his daughter-in-law, to have the body disinterred, but she inexplicably refuses to do anything to protect the body, while the South Lake Tahoe police department seems to think it has better things to do. This Court has discretion to order the disinterment when it will serve the ends of justice to do so.

"Mr. de Beers is already mourning the loss of his son, Your Honor. He shouldn't have to experience the dread that he now suffers in addition to his mourning. What harm will be done to anyone by allowing him to satisfy himself that his son is resting in peace, if that is the case? And if the worst has happened, isn't it in the interests of justice to determine that as soon as possible?"

Stamp sat down, smoothed his jacket and turned to de Beers, who sat behind him, patting his hand as he had done in the library.

Milne's brow had furrowed. Nina hoped that he was puzzled and thought something more was behind the motion. He was no slouch.

"Ms. Reilly?" he said.

Nina did a one-minute recap of her version of the facts, and then said, "The Court has our Points and Authorities. It's clear that a body should not be disinterred without some overriding public purpose. If this is such a red-hot criminal case, how come the Tahoe police aren't here requesting the disinterment? On the contrary, we have filed a declaration indicating the police haven't determined yet whether the ring actually was stolen. They're looking into it. Let them come to the Court to talk about enforcing the law. They are the authorities, not Mr. de Beers. He has no standing to be here requesting this relief.

"Counsel for Mr. de Beers keeps telling us about Mr. de Beers's grief, as if he's the only one who's lost a family member. What about Ray de Beers's children,

Molly and Jason? They've lost their father. What about Mrs. de Beers? As the surviving spouse she has the superior right here. She feels that the ring in question was previously removed and her husband was buried without it. The mortician who filed the declaration attesting otherwise is simply making a mistake. She doesn't think the situation warrants digging up her husband.

"The immediate family's desires take precedence here." Nina paused, then said very deliberately, "Perhaps Mrs. de Beers feels that there is more here than meets the eye, Your Honor. She has stated that she believes this motion is frivolous. Families become embroiled sometimes in strange games, Your Honor, particularly in times of stress. . . ." She caught the judge's eye, gave him a piercing look, trying to communicate that she knew much more she wanted to say but couldn't.

"I really have to protest the impropriety of this argument, Judge," Stamp said, not bothering to get up, using his voice to command attention. "Counsel has left the realm of legal argument and moved into the land of irrelevance. She has to confine herself to facts, not insinuations—"

"May I finish, Your Honor?" Nina said over Stamp's voice. Chalk one up for the clear, high female voice, she was thinking to herself as Milne's head swung back her way.

She opened her mouth to insinuate a few more things before being shut down, but then she felt a nudge at her elbow. Deputy Kimura, the courtroom bailiff, stood there with a note in his hand.

"May I have just a second, Your Honor?" she said, irritated. She was about to lose her momentum.

The note said "Call your client. She wants to drop her opposition."

The floor beneath her feet dissolved and she sank through it. Her arguments drained from her head. Weakly, she said, "Uh, excuse me, Your Honor. I, uh, need to consult briefly with my client. I wonder if we could trail this matter to the end of the docket."

Milne said, "Mr. Stamp? Would you be agreeable?"

Stamp said from his table, "Certainly. If counsel has some emergency, we're happy to accommodate."

And Nina turned to look at them both. De Beers's smile was mocking. She was absolutely sure that Stamp and de Beers had known the note would be coming.

Out in the hall, adrenaline pumping, she called the de Beers house. Sarah answered right away, as if she hadn't left the phone since she had called the courtroom. "Hi, Nina," she said in a strained voice.

"What's up?" Nina said as neutrally as she could.

"Oh, I've just been thinking. I've decided to let Quentin go ahead. He can have what he wants. I don't care any longer."

"This is kind of unusual, Sarah," Nina said. "I'm standing there in court in the final minutes of the argument and you suddenly—"

"Well, I changed my mind. I hired you. I'm your boss. You have to do what I say. You have to drop your opposition. Right now." The words sounded rehearsed.

"What do Molly and Jason think?"

"That really doesn't matter. I'm writing the checks."

"Is anyone else there with you, Sarah?"

"No."

"What's happened to make you change your mind? I understood that this was important to you. You've never shown the slightest doubt before."

"Just do what I say."

"Was it Quentin? Did he call you? What did he say?"

"Please. I'm sorry. I'm giving you a . . . an instruction," Sarah insisted.

"You came to me for help and advice. I'm trying to help you now, Sarah. I don't think you are quite yourself. Sometimes people say things when they're under a lot of stress and regret them later. You won't get another chance if you drop the matter now."

"I can't stand this! Not any of it!"

"It's almost over. Just hang in there with me, Sarah."

"No! I'm telling you what I want. Let Quentin have his fun."

She hung up. Nina called back, but there was no answer.

In the law library she took a breather, looking out at the trees pressed against the windows twenty feet above the ground, feeling as if she were in the middle of a jungle as thick and tangled as a tropical forest. She supposed that made her a monkey and that bonk on the head she had just taken must have been a coconut.

Then she went back into the courtroom, now emptying as other matters were heard and disposed of and the long parade of lawyers and scofflaws wended its way out the door. Two lawyers still at it were exchanging courteous invective in a breach of contract case. Stamp and de Beers sat near the front, listening. She sat down in the back and waited.

At ten minutes to twelve the case was called again, and Nina took her place at the defendant's table.

"Well, Ms. Reilly? You still have five more minutes," Milne said.

"I won't need that long, Your Honor. I'd just like to . . ." She looked directly at Stamp. "At this point I'd like to respectfully request that this matter be put over until next week."

"You want a continuance?" Milne said, his eyebrows raised. "Will it assist in resolution of this case?"

"I don't know, Your Honor. But we are appearing today without the usual notice period. We attempted to cooperate with Mr. Stamp by appearing and filing no objection to the short notice. However, I must now advise the Court that the notice period is inadequate to allow a proper response."

"You seem to be doing pretty well," Milne said dryly.

"She's waived any right to object to the notice period," Stamp interposed. "If Ms. Reilly has received some sort of communication from her client, perhaps indicating her desire not to go forward, then she should not be asking for a continuance, she should be dropping her opposition while we're on the record."

"Funny you should say that, Mr. Stamp," Nina said. "I don't recall saying that I received any such communication."

"You did receive a note."

"And you're pretty darn sure you know what's in it, aren't you, Mr. Stamp?"

"Address your arguments to the Court, not to each other," Milne snapped.

"There's no emergency, Your Honor," Nina said. "One week more or less will make no difference. New facts may arise that will allow the Court to rule on this matter with a clearer record."

"I have to tell you both that, with the record as it stands, I am inclined to defer to the wishes of the widow and not permit the disinterment," Milne said. "With that in mind, Ms. Reilly, what do you wish to do?"

Quentin de Beers had dropped the smile. Nina now knew that all she had to do was sit down and she would get what she knew Sarah de Beers really wanted.

But she couldn't do that. If she went on and won, she would be acting against an express instruction from her client.

On the other hand, after a few years of representing people in stressful circumstances, Nina had learned that a good lawyer knows when her client is blowing it and has to be protected from herself. She wasn't about to follow Sarah's instruction, either.

"I request a one-week continuance," she said.

Stamp rose to his feet. He told Milne how his client had put off a trip out of the state in order to appear in court that morning; that a continuance would only prolong his client's suffering; that Ray de Beers's body would be further decomposed and the viewing would be even more distressing; that Ms. Reilly had clearly been fully prepared for the hearing.

"In light of the Court's statement just now that the Court is inclined to rule in her favor, why in the world is Ms. Reilly suddenly asking for a continuance? Why doesn't she just let the Court rule?" Stamp said.

"In light of my inclination, Mr. Stamp, why do you want me to rule?" Milne said. "I confess I'm totally confused."

"Because," Stamp said, "there's only one reason she can't let the Court make a ruling here and now. Her client has instructed her to drop this opposition, and she isn't willing to follow that instruction, but she doesn't want to fly in the face of the instruction, either. She's weaseling, Judge."

"Is that true, counsel? Don't waste the Court's time if your client doesn't want to go forward."

"Mr. Stamp is trying to coerce me into going into more detail than I feel is appropriate at this time. I won't be coerced by him, and neither will my client. And I hope Mr. Stamp and his client understand that. I hope that the Court will also understand that."

A glimmer of understanding had indeed begun to flicker in Milne's keen eyes.

"True. Coercion will not be countenanced in my courtroom," he said, and Nina had to stifle a nervous laugh at the unconscious alliteration.

"Well, let's see what we have here," Milne went on. "Mr. Stamp wants the court to go ahead and rule, knowing that the ruling is likely to cost him his motion. Odd, very odd. And Ms. Reilly says she won't be coerced into winning. Also very odd. You folks should trade sides."

She had said as much as she dared, so she kept her mouth shut and waited.

"The matter will be put over for one week," Milne said. He closed the file and looked at the clock on the wall. "Court's adjourned until one-thirty," he said. Nina dropped her eyes and peeked sideways at de Beers.

He had a tight grip on Stamp's arm, preventing the angry lawyer from getting up to protest some more.

Looking past Stamp at Nina, de Beers locked eyes with her. The smile of triumph had faded; the weak scaffold of manners had tumbled; the businessman she had met in her office had evaporated.

His fury blew toward her like debris from an explosion. She turned away. Moving her own eyes to the table in front of her, she stacked and restacked papers in her briefcase until Stamp and de Beers had gone, leaving her alone in the court except for Deputy Kimura. The bailiff waited patiently as she slowly gathered up her notes and the pleadings still scattered around the table. As she left he escorted her out the door, and she saw him look both ways in the hall to make sure she would have a hassle-free passage to the outside. As he locked up in the hall, Nina said, "He's a good judge."

"A very good judge," Deputy Kimura agreed.

"About the phone message from my client that you took. . . ."

"I probably wrote it down wrong." But he knew he hadn't gotten it wrong.

"You seem to have been looking out for me since the shooting last year," Nina told him. "Thanks. Sometimes"—she stopped, able to resume only after a deep breath—"I find it hard to sit in that chair."

"Just want to make sure lightning doesn't strike twice." He looked so solid, standing there with his comforting girth and the holster hanging off his belt. All the air went out of her and she dropped her briefcase. Deputy Kimura picked it up and said, "I'll walk you out to your car."

"Oh, I—"

"No trouble," he said. "For a good lawyer. A very good lawyer."

Sarah de Beers's house was only a couple of miles away. Nina drove past the stores and restaurants in the

lunch-hour traffic, wondering what to say to Sarah.
Gnawing worry had replaced hunger in her stomach.

The de Beers family was flying apart. Ray had once
held them together, as Tito had once held Yugoslavia
together. But Ray was gone, and Yugoslavia was no
more.

The safest thing would be to keep a comfortable
emotional distance. At first it had been easy. She had
felt a distaste for the whole family. But now she felt a
stirring of sympathy for Sarah, as if she saw something
of herself in the woman. She felt Sarah had spent her
years with Ray embroiled in struggle; had done her
best for her children, raising them against grim odds,
and now, just when she might have a chance to grasp a
small piece of happiness, was failing. That sympathy
now extended to Jason and Molly. Poor Jason; poor
Molly, she thought.

Sarah was a single mother now, just like Nina.
Though her children were older, they were just as
needy, as if some crucial developmental phase still
hadn't taken place. There was no heavier responsibility
than being the sole parent. Nina could attest to that.

She parked behind the house. The grounds were
quiet, the drapes drawn. No one answered the bell.
She even tried the front door, but it was locked. She
wouldn't have a chance to talk to Sarah. Across the
sweep of lawn Lake Tahoe gleamed in the early afternoon. The martini shaker sat on its tray by the empty
chairs. Nina sat down in one of them and watched the
sailboats.

Sarah had said, "It's too late." But if any of us comes
across a drowning family, Nina thought, we have to do
something about it even if we feel inadequate, even if
the family has set out to drown itself. She and Bob had

come close to drowning a few times. And always, someone had helped them, as she wanted to help Sarah and the twins.

The lake was opaque, unknown, endlessly receptive, a live entity like the forest or the sky. Collier had said he hoped there existed some inhuman Justice that took care of the big problems human justice couldn't handle. If there was, Justice would be like the other natural forces, indifferent, unbiased, uncaring.

Nina thought, I don't want to be the instrument of that kind of Justice. Human justice is flawed, but there's room for mercy in it.

A paper boat floated by, already soggy, made by some kid farther down the beach. She set her troubled thoughts adrift on it, and watched them sink slowly into the secret depths.

12

PAUL TOOK THE INTERSTATE BACK FROM L.A., UP the long, dusty valley that was the spine of California. He had left Bright's house after dark on Thursday, but the new speed limit for most of the way was seventy miles per hour, so he flew through the night. Bryan had been right—the Cat attracted the attention of even the jaded truckers, who flashed their lights, giving him the thumbs-up sign as he roared by. He parked the Cat in the lot behind the lab of Ginger Hirabayashi, his lab expert in Sacramento, by two in the morning, not a bad time for four hundred miles of dodging eighteen-wheelers.

That this car had probably caused Anna Meade's death did not bother him. A car by itself was nothing more than a tool. The car and driver formed another entity altogether.

A short taxi ride took him to the Sacramento airport, where he found a car rental desk still open, but all the sleepy-eyed rep had to offer was a Geo Metro. Paul putt-putted up into the mountains, reduced to pulling over after several sports utility vehicles thundered up behind to chomp bites out of his tiny tail. He made the last forty miles of winding uphill driving bearable by swigging coffee and listening to a couple of football commentators talk about the upcoming season on AM radio.

At about five in the morning, dead beat, he reached the Caesars parking lot. Giddy with fatigue, he rode up the elevator to his room and, kicking off his shoes, collapsed on the neat blue quilt of his bed, conscious only long enough to make the sweet-smelling pillows into a feathery nest for his aching head.

The first thing Paul did on Friday morning was call his office in Carmel. The town had gone downhill since his departure. Several clients in ongoing cases wanted his personal juggling act back right away. He made a few calls and stalled them, maneuvering substitutes into place temporarily, but knew he'd have to get back by Sunday morning if he wanted to keep all the balls in the air.

He called Hallowell at the DA's office and left a message that he was back and would call again later. Then he called Ginger in Sacramento to goose her about the car.

All business, Ginger dispensed with a basic hello, reporting that the car had been repainted from white to black. That was easy, but she hadn't gotten much farther. Paul pinned her down to a time for a callback on Saturday.

He took the elevator down to the first floor of the building, into the carefully controlled pandemonium of the casino, where he couldn't resist pausing to make a twenty-dollar cash bet at one of the blackjack tables.

Although it was nine A.M. on a beautiful day, busload after busload of tourists was checking out the action.

A morose dealer who had substituted motor oil for shampoo flicked out the cards, Paul's first card facedown, the dealer's card up and showing a five. Paul's second card, dealt faceup, was a six. He lifted the corner of his hole card and found a seven. Thirteen. According to the rules he had learned from a canny card-counter named Al Otis, he should stand against the dealer's five and pray the dealer would bust.

But thirteen was such a crummy hand. He rapped the edge of his cards in front of him to indicate he wanted another card, and damned if the dealer didn't toss him a three. Now he had sixteen, the rottenest hand in the game of Twenty-one. The other players took their cards and busted, and now the dealer was back to Paul, the top card of the pack live in his hand.

He should definitely stand. There was still the chance the dealer would draw over twenty-one and bust. Paul bit his lip, his eyes trying to X-ray the top card in the deck, hovering in front him in the dealer's hand.

"Hit me," Paul said. "It's only a game."

And the card floated out on wings of fire, flipped in the air, and settled on the table in front of Paul.

"A six. Bust," said the dealer. "Sorry." He gathered up the cards. Paul skulked off to his car, his wallet lighter, his mood darker. He drove west along the bottom of Lake Tahoe toward the Y where Sierra Motors was located.

"Mr. El-Barouki is no longer with us," said the gum-snapping African American salesman who came to greet him. "But don't worry. I can do everything for you that he did, backward and in high heels." With a smile, he pulled a white handkerchief from his suit jacket and buffed an invisible mark on a nearby car.

"Where did he go? I talked to him yesterday."

"You're not going to believe this. He won the lottery!"

"You're right. I don't believe it."

"Not the big prize, he said, but enough."

"Enough for what?"

"To go back home."

"And where would home be?"

"Egypt."

Paul whistled. "Let's see. He won the lottery, so he packed up the wife and the kids and the whole house and caught an overseas flight all in the same day? No doubt his brother went too?"

The gum snapped furiously as the salesman nodded. "They left for San Francisco last night. I think they were going to catch the plane to Cairo this morning. So fill me in. What kind of car were you talking about with Munir?"

"Not one you could help me with."

"I've got some great deals today. Here's a '95 Olds with cruise, overdrive, antilocks—you name it. Coupla minor dents to make it a good deal. I've got the keys right here in my pocket, let's take the boy out for a ride— Hey, don't walk out on me, man! Gimme a break!"

Royally pissed, Paul drove to the address of the El-Barouki auto junkyard.

A vacant lot.

The phone book listed two addresses for El-Barouki, both shacks in the Bijou area of town. At both, a scatter of household goods lay hastily abandoned along the street. FREE said a sign propped against a ripped red couch. Paul thought about dredging around in the overflowing cans of refuse, but what was he going to find? An address in Cairo? He sat down on the sagging porch swing at the second shack and thought.

Only two things could have happened. El-Barouki had run down Anna Meade himself, and was so extraordinarily greedy he had put Paul on to the car for two hundred fifty bucks. Then he had come to his senses and fled. . . .

Scratch that. Nobody was that greedy. Okay, then, El-Barouki went straight from Paul to the guy who brought him the Catalina and blackmailed the living shit out of him. Or her.

He liked this better. The seller had access to enough money to enable two families to leave the country without scrambling for cheaper fourteen-day-advance-purchase reserved tickets. What else?

El-Barouki couldn't have made this deal on the phone and gotten the money so quickly, and he hadn't had time to leave the mountains to make the deal between talking to Paul and taking a long hike. That meant the seller might still be in Tahoe, but where?

The weight of his body strained the springs of the porch swing as he rocked. He creaked back and forth, like an old man taking a rest after a long day working his fields. Two little kids on bikes whizzed by the yard hollering, their faces a blur of gaping teeth. A pinecone dropped onto the roof with a noise like a shot, then rolled gently the long way down, landing with a thud in the dirt nearby. The wind whistled through the trash.

He looked up the street. A dead end, like the one he'd come to.

★   ★   ★

Marvin Gates, director of the Tahoe division of the El Dorado County Probation Department, proved to be a soft-spoken, portly bureaucrat with green eyes, freckles, and soft reddish hair that traveled down his jaw into muttonchops. He led Paul through a series of offices crowded with clients and caseworkers to an austere office in the back. Educational posters about AIDS and birth control and a map of Lake Tahoe, the All-Year Playland, had been tacked some time ago over fading green paint. The cost-cutting drabness overall had its compensation: a big window opening up to one of Tahoe's million-dollar views.

"I miss her," he said. "Anna was special. Her clients felt protective of her, and she went to bat for them. I was sick when I heard the news."

"I'm trying to find out if the hit-and-run might have been deliberate," Paul said. "Probation officers can't always be helpful. They're law enforcement, when you get down to it."

"Yes. Sometimes probation or parole has to be revoked."

"The defendant figures somebody has to pay, and it might as well be the son-of-a-gun probation officer who turned him in."

"You got that absolutely right. We get threatened a lot. Sometimes we get killed."

"How long have you been doing this?" Paul asked.

"Twenty-four years at this one gig. I'm out of here next year."

"What are you going to do then?"

"Move off the Hill. Sleep like a baby all night long, without the bad dreams. Slow down, like my doctor says. Make it up to my wife."

"Sounds like a plan."

"Three hundred forty-three days left and counting, baby."

"Did Anna ever mention any particular trouble with a client, especially around the time she died?"

"Ah, that's a hard one. All her clients were particular to her, and they all had trouble."

"Any threats at the time?"

"She made friends out of these people. If anything, that's what got her killed."

"How do you mean?"

"I don't know what I mean. I just know it's safer to keep your distance. Most of the people who come through here are repeat offenders. It's a shame, but that's the way it is. Anna was never a fool. She didn't trust them, and she was good at spotting the liars and con men. But she let them get too close."

"You found her naive?"

"Not really. Just . . . too willing to listen." He laughed. "People you'd be scared to give the time of day to, she gave all her time to, you know? She'd have them in there for hours sometimes, while the work piled up and the rest of us tore out our hair. She refused to give anyone short shrift. If they wanted her attention, they got it."

"That last day, she had eight appointments," Paul said. "Anything significant happen that day that you can recall?"

"Only one unusual thing, like I told the police. One of her parolees came in without an appointment during the lunch hour and she shut the door and sat with him for at least an hour. He appeared intoxicated when he came in, and the receptionist tried to send him home, but Anna came out on her way to lunch and he caught her. That meeting seemed significant after we learned about the parolee killing himself later on, about three o'clock in the afternoon. Anna was hit about three hours after that, I understand."

"Right. Ruben Lauria, that was the name of the parolee, wasn't it? I saw it in your statement."

"Mmm-hmm. So they were talking for an hour or so. The receptionist checked on them—I was at a training session in Palm Springs, so I didn't hear all this until later—and Lauria looked harmless, so she left them alone. Anna left a little early, about four. Next day Toni, the receptionist, called to tell me Anna was in a coma, not expected to live. I came right back."

"When did you find out Lauria had committed suicide a few hours before Anna was hit?"

"The next day. His wife—Lucy, her name is—called to tell Anna. I took the call."

"Two people talk to each other at noon, and they're both dead by sunset," Paul said.

"It's pretty clear to me that Lauria was considering suicide and Anna tried to talk him out of it. I sometimes think—could she have walked into the path of the car because she was distracted, thinking about his problems? In a sense, she would have died because of him. I never told Collier this, because I didn't want to raise the question that she might have been a little . . . well, not watching where she was going."

Paul said, "I just can't understand why there was no record at all of the meeting with Lauria, no notes, no doodles."

"Pure stupidity on our part. Somebody probably threw her notes into the trash. We could have recovered them if we'd been thinking. But you see, we were all so shocked, and we thought it was an accident. The trash went out."

"Okay. You have the list of people she was seeing for me?"

"The ones she was scheduled to see that day, and the rest, in two sections. Right here." He handed Paul a typed list.

For the next hour they went over the list, name by name. A few days after Anna's death, Gates had made extensive notes on them all. He wouldn't show Paul any paperwork, including his notes, but considered much of the information public record. By the end, Gates had an eye glued to his watch.

"I really have to go. I promised to drive my wife over to Grass Valley this afternoon to see her mother."

"I'm almost done. Let me just go over one or two things that stuck in my mind here."

Gates really had to go, his drumming fingers informed Paul.

"Who else could have wanted her dead?"

"I went through all her files, her notes, the phone messages, for the cops. Nothing out of the ordinary. Her replacement is an ex-marine who transferred in as a trainee from guard duty at Soledad. Off duty, he uses words like *coddle* and *scum*. He's the one who'll lead the department into the twenty-first century, because he likes it here. He'll outlast all of us."

"How about Anna and the other staff here? Any problems?"

"Nothing. Certainly nothing to make somebody run her down. She got along with everybody."

"Okay. Boyfriends, then. An attractive girl like her, her husband always at work. Two-hour lunches, long phone calls . . ."

Gates was shaking his head vigorously. "She kept the wedding picture right on her desk. She talked about how much they wanted a family. She talked to her husband every day. I believe they were very close."

"I do believe you're right," Paul said, putting away his notebook.

"She was a rare and radiant maiden," Gates said unexpectedly, with a sorrowful note in his voice.

"Darkness there forevermore," said Paul. "It's a damn shame."

"Wish I knew something more to tell you." Gates got up, consulted his watch again, and shook Paul's hand.

"So it goes. Sorry to keep you for so long. Blame me, if it does you any good. Mind if I make a call before I go?"

Gates let Paul make the call from his desk phone, then locked up the office behind him, scurrying off to his car and his wife.

Paul drove away too, wondering why Ruben Lauria killed himself. He felt frustrated. He felt as if he were being pushed around, but by some impersonal force, led by a nose-ring like a balky donkey from murky connection to obscure lead. He kept trying to do the straightforward police work that cracked cases like this, but nothing came of those efforts; the breaks happened when he stared at a painting or a gun-crazy Egyptian salesman appeared at his door. He might as well consult the oracle at Delphi and get the thing over with.

Would Mrs. Lauria prove to be the oracle?

13

WITH AN HOUR TO KILL, PAUL DROVE UP TO HEAVenly. The Gunbarrel, a fearsome mogul-run in winter, looked like a peaceful fire trail up the mountain. He parked the van in full sun on the street that ran partway up, facing the lakeview far away, then pushed his seat back and dozed off.

The car phone rang.

"Paul? Are you there?" Nina.

"Lemme think about that."

"I was just sitting here in the hall at court, and it struck me that you probably are at loose ends tonight. Bob's not due home until Sunday, and . . ."

She was asking him, in her oblique female way, to have dinner with her. This immersed Paul in a brief internal struggle. Any male on the make could see Hallowell was blowing his advantage by not paying attention to her. If she spent the evening with Paul, she might spend the night with him, as she had on a memorable evening a few months before, and he wanted that in a way.

But he thought Nina was pulling an old maneuver, even if it was unconscious. She was trying to pull him back because she'd noticed he had moved away. And if he surrendered, he would just be old Paul who came running when she didn't have anything else going. He didn't feel like seeing her on her terms anymore.

Besides, he had made a date, right after talking to El-Barouki, with the woman who didn't date. So he told Nina he was busy, sorry, and there was a great scraping sound as the tables turned. Nina put on an I-was-just-being-nice voice and said she had to go, the bailiff was calling her, and Paul said good luck, from one colleague and friend to another. He felt mean complacence, even if he was cutting off his nose to spite his face.

He picked up Highway 89 where the lake road turned north at the Y. The stores and restaurants thinned into the forest. Bicyclists paced him, but there were few cars on the road. Summer was about over, and Tahoe was emptying out. When the snow began to fall they would all be back, but for now Paul had the first flaming yellows of the quaking aspen along the road to himself.

At Camp Richardson he made a right and drove down through the forest past the occasional rustic cabin to the small marina on the lake. The hostess led him through the restaurant bar area to the outside deck and he sat down in a corner. Most of the tables were empty.

In front of him, across the narrow beach of dark sand, a small pier jutted out to a circle of white and yellow sailboats at their moorings. Except for them, the view was all blue, the lake dark blue on shimmering sapphire, the rim of mountains green-blue on the horizon, the sky pale and glowing. A breeze had come up, clearing the air of the smoke from the latest fire in the nearby national forest, so he could see all around the lake in exquisite detail.

Off to the right, the distant casinos were painted a rustic brown amid the trees, the town otherwise hidden. Farther north along the Nevada side he saw Cave Rock and Sand Harbor. To the left, on the west side, his eyes found the thick ponderosa pine forest rising toward the granite flanks of Tallac.

No sign of Mrs. Lauria. His call had caught her at home, and she'd agreed to his lunch invitation. He wasn't sure what she could contribute anyway, so he didn't worry about it, just let his eyes graze on the beauty surrounding him. The breeze blew steadily, cooling the air and ruffling the lake into wavelets. Up higher, above the eastern mountains, flat-bottomed clouds shaped like saucers glided toward the lake like stately UFOs. Several handsome wild geese waddled up to the deck, their heads dipping in hungry greeting. "Later," he told them.

The waiter was a blond dude with a thick yellow mustache, perfectly tanned like a displaced character from a Jimmy Buffett song and shivering in his shorts on this cool autumnlike day. Paul asked for a chicken quesadilla and sank back into his reverie. After lunch he would take a walk along the beach under the firs and sink his toes into the sand. He thought about Kim and how much she would like this, and half rose to his feet to call her, but then he saw a young Hispanic woman with two children in tow coming across the deck toward him.

"Mr. van Wagoner?"

"Yes. Mrs. Lauria?"

"Sorry it took me so long. I had to stop and pick up the children from day care. This is Agosto, and this is Lourdes."

"How do you do," Paul said. The little boy and girl gazed shyly at him. They all sat down, and Mrs. Lauria ordered sandwiches and drinks for all of them, while Paul rearranged his thoughts.

Mrs. Lauria seemed extraordinarily young, nineteen or twenty. She wore pressed slacks and a sweatshirt and carried a backpack. Her face was fresh and pretty and her glossy hair fell in a neat braid most of the way down her back.

"Excuse me for staring," Paul said. "But I was expecting someone a little different."

She smiled and said, "I married Ruben in our hometown in Mexico when I was fifteen. I'm twenty-one now." Then, earnestly, "I don't understand why the police want to talk to me again. It's been so long."

"I'm not exactly the police."

"Who are you?"

"When Ruben died, he was on probation, as I understand it. Well, I'm working for his probation officer's husband. She was killed by a hit-and-run driver the same day your husband died."

"Oh, yes. Mrs. Meade. I heard about it. That was so sad, wasn't it? But I had my own problems that day. . . . I don't know what I can tell you except that Ruben had nothing to do with that lady getting hit. He died that afternoon, hours before she did."

Milk arrived for the kids, and coffee for the girl. She was looking around, as Paul had done. She said, "This scenery makes it all worthwhile, the snow and ice, the job problems, the family so far away. I hope I stay here forever."

"When did you come to Tahoe?"

"Four years ago. Ruben's parents and cousin lived here at the time. We got green cards without any trouble. But then his parents went home, and Ruben lost his job. I couldn't help much. We had some hard times. Ruben got very discouraged. He couldn't stand to see the babies crying because we had no milk. He stole." She spoke nonjudgmentally, as if she had made peace with this period of her life long ago.

"And he got caught."

"He was no good at it. He had been in trouble before. This time, he knocked a lady down stealing her purse. He got three months and almost got deported but Mrs. Meade helped him."

Lunch arrived, and they dug right in. The quesadilla was melting with Monterey Jack cheese and mild green chilies and chunks of grilled chicken. Mrs. Lauria was a woman after his own heart, enjoying every bite of her meal. The kids jumped down and hit the sand, staying within twenty feet as though tethered to an invisible leash.

"What are you doing now?" Paul asked when the plates had been cleared away and they were both drinking coffee.

"I go to the community college. I'm studying early childhood education. I'm going to teach in a preschool."

"You like kids."

"I love them. At night I work at El Vaquero, the restaurant down in the basement at Harvey's. I'm a cook. I make good wages now."

"How do you . . . I mean, the children?"

"How do I take care of them? Ruben's cousin takes care of them at night."

"Ah. That must help a lot."

"Yes. He does help. We're getting married in December." She smiled again, a spirited and optimistic smile that made Paul realize those days would never come for him again. "We're going to be fine now."

"Good for you." Another nod and happy smile. She exuded youth and health.

"About Ruben," Paul said. "How did he get along with Mrs. Meade?"

"Very well. She came to our apartment twice trying to help us. She helped Ruben find a job but it was minimum wage and winter was coming. We needed warm clothes and some wood and a car. Even though she promised she could get us a car, he got low again. And when he was low, he drank."

"And when he drank?"

"He got into fights. He couldn't hold down a job."

"He ever hit you?"

"Never. He just burned off steam. That one guy he killed when he was a kid, that was really an accident. Ruben bragged about it to his friends, made himself look like a real criminal. But he wasn't really."

Mrs. Lauria's memories had hit the golden haze stage. Lauria was a thief, a drinker, and a brawler, but she found an excuse for everything. Paul said, "Tell me about how he died."

"That morning I could tell Ruben was sick with worry about us, how we were going to pay the rent. I was upset that he didn't go to work, and he was upset that I didn't trust him. He told me if I would only trust him, he would get the money we needed. He was talking big again. I guess he just wanted to make me feel better. But when I saw him like that, all excited and crazy, it made me feel worse. I took the kids to the park."

"Excited and crazy?"

"Scared-excited. He got that way sometimes right before he stole or got drunk or did something else he shouldn't do. He was basically an honest man. I think that was why he was so bad at crime. He only did the bad things because of his worry for us." She looked out at the shore where her children were playing. "I don't know why you want to know about this."

"I'm checking Mrs. Meade's clients, just to see if anyone knows anything at all. It's routine. How did you find out . . . about your husband?"

"The police. An officer called me. They had found him at Zephyr Cove. He was . . . he was hanging from a tree. He'd been drinking. He didn't know what he was doing."

"I'm sorry."

"Don't be. Ruben wasn't right for this hard world. Now he's at peace."

"And you?"

"Me? I am very tough, Mr. van Wagoner. I am going to make it. I am going to be happy. So will my children."

Paul paid the tab and they walked out together to the parking lot. Next to his van stood an aged Hyundai, the paint entirely gone to gray, the seats torn.

"About Mrs. Meade?" Mrs. Lauria said as she put the kids into their car seats in back. "Why did her husband hire you?"

"He still wants to know who hit his wife with the car. He wants to know if it was intentional, or just an accident. It might make him feel better, just to know why she died. If there was a reason."

She nodded her tidy little head. "Her husband's doing the right thing. You can't just accept the bad things, you have to keep up the struggle. I would never give up either. He ought to find that driver and *fttt*." A fingernail flashed across her neck.

"He's a prosecutor, a very upright citizen. He'll be calling the police if I learn anything."

"Ah. Well, where I come from, if you want justice, that's not the place you go. Trouble falls from the sky, or it comes in a letter from the government. It's like rain; it just comes, you don't have to deserve it. And you handle it yourself because the system is set up for the system, not for you."

"I've heard about the police in Mexico."

"Very corrupt. They commit more bank robberies than the regular criminals. You know, if you have no money for bribes, no position, no importance, you get no justice. You think it's better here?"

"It's better."

"Do you know when Ruben went in for ninety days just for purse snatching, the white guy in the next cell, who also stole a lady's purse and then beat her up just for the hell of it, got out in thirty days?"

Her brown eyes looked into his; then she held out a hand to shake, which he took. She held on, until the moment became awkward, and he looked down to where her small brown hand clung tenaciously to his large white one. Then she smiled, drawing her hand away slowly, in case he hadn't noticed the contrast in color, the difference she meant for him to see. "For you, it may be better. For me, for Ruben, no." She gathered up her children.

"Thanks for taking the time," said Paul, shutting the driver's door behind her.

"Thank you for lunch. Tell your client I am sorry. I understand. He's not alone." Her car let out an unmuffled blast of engine noise as she drove off confidently into her future.

Nina played a game of kick-yourself as she sat outside Milne's chambers listening for her turn. Collier was supposed to be around the courthouse somewhere but she hadn't been able to find him. So she had called Paul, who had turned her down flat, the troglodyte, with hardly a hesitation. He had no idea how to be friends with a woman and no interest in it, either. He couldn't be bothered with a woman unless she was part of the great chase.

She was just good old Nina now, always around if he happened to have a dull minute, and he hadn't had any of those on this trip. She possessed that precious thing for a mother, a free Friday night, and nobody was interested. She felt distinctly unpopular, and this thought added to the general aggravation of being in court on a loser case on a Friday afternoon.

Her client waited in the hallway, praying for a miracle.

Nina entered Milne's chambers with her opposing counsel, an offensive insurance lawyer so arrogant and so young that she knew this settlement conference was already a bust.

Milne had moved away from his desk by the window and was sitting in his high-backed chair, facing the door, files on the coffee table in front of him. His blue bag of golf clubs topped with merry red pompoms leaned against the desk, close to his hands so that he could stroke them between settlement conferences. On the other side of the table two smaller chairs sat next to each other. He beckoned them in without a word, not a good augury. Gingerly, Nina took a seat and awaited the blast.

"*Ng* versus *Yellow Cab.* How are you, Nina?"

"Fine, Your Honor. And you?"

"I'm waiting for a jury to come in with a verdict in a murder case. Been out a week. The bailiff says they're close but that could mean eight o'clock tonight. Have a golf game at Edgewood starting at six. Celebrity Pro-Am tournament all weekend, first time I ever got asked, and I'm paired with Johnny Miller. Wonderful golfer. Kevin Costner and Tiger Woods are playing as a pair, first time since the AT&T Tournament, right in front of us."

"If the jury's close, they'll want to get home early," Nina said comfortingly.

"Two months I've been looking forward to this golf game. I should have stayed in private practice, where Friday afternoon is sacrosanct. Except for you people, who get to join me in my misery. All right. Mr., ah, Bailey, you're from the insurance company for the taxi company?"

"Yessir. Drove up from San Francisco."

"How come you didn't associate local counsel and save yourself a trip? This isn't a big case, as I see it, anyway." Nina winced at this. Her client, a passenger in a cab that had rear-ended a bus on Lake Tahoe Boulevard the year before, thought it was a very big case.

"That's right, Your Honor. The damages are minimal, except her client's got some ludicrous inflated figure in his head—"

"Did you talk outside?"

"We've offered five thousand plus the specials just for the nuisance value, and she's rejected our offer. The only thing she's been talking about is a trial in this Court, which would be a waste of the Court's time. This is a small case that belongs in Municipal Court. Absurd—"

Milne said, "Five thousand in hand, Nina. Your statement of damages shows mostly chiropractic fees. It's a soft-tissue case. Nothing on the MRI. Lots of sound and fury . . ."

"The medical bills are already sixty-five hundred and my client will be in chiropractic therapy for another few months at least," said Nina. "He lost his job when his sick leave ran out. What kind of offer is five thousand for seventeen months of pain and suffering? The cabdriver told my client he had been driving for fourteen hours without a break. He had his girlfriend in the front seat, which is a blatant violation of the cab company's own rules, and was in the middle of a heated argument with her when he rear-ended the bus. His boss knew the driver rode around with this girl all day. We could up the ante and add in a count against the company for reckless endangerment, maybe start talking about punitive damages—"

"Oh, get real!" huffed Bailey. "That's imposs—"

"Don't interrupt me!" Nina interrupted.

"The truth is, Judge, she sees the deep pockets. She's on us like a wasp looking for bare skin to sting—"

"Typical, isn't it, Your Honor? Bog me down with paper and delays, make me try the case just to squeeze out a little help for a guy who has to live in a neck brace—"

Milne said, "Come in," looking beseechingly at the door for deliverance. Deputy Kimura, who had been knocking, stuck his head in and said, "The jury's back."

"Glory be," Milne said, jumping up and adjusting his robes. "You folks go down to the clerk's office before five and select a trial date together. Mr. Bailey, learn some manners before I see you again. Nina, if I were you I'd tell my client to adjust his expectations downward. I'd assess this case at this point at less than twenty-five thousand. You're going to end up in Muni Court if you don't settle it. You might even expose your client to payment of the insurance company's court costs."

"Twenty-five. Outrageous," announced her pompous young opponent.

"And you, Mr. Bailey. Talk to someone in your office with some experience and sage advice before you come back. You annoy me."

"I was just trying to—"

"Now get out of here! Both of you!"

Nina and Bailey wrangled the whole time they were waiting for the busy clerk to give them some trial dates. They finally settled on a date three months away, which would certainly be continued several times before any trial could actually take place. Bailey gave her a crocodile smile as he headed for the stairs.

Young Bailey might well show those big sharp teeth. He had cold-bloodedly confounded yet another simple case by doing exactly the job the company paid him to do—namely, postponing, hassling, and complicating matters until her client ran out of money and forced her to settle low. Nina went back to relay the bad news.

Her client's bench was empty. He must have gone into the main courtroom, the one Milne had headed for earlier, drooling with anticipation of a settlement. As she slipped through the door, spotting her client in the audience, the jurors Milne had been waiting for were filing back into the jury box, their faces unreadable.

With shock, Nina saw Collier sitting at one of the counsel tables, back rigorously straight, his face, what she could see of it in half-profile, dispassionate. His second chair, Barbara Banning, who had just transferred to Tahoe three months before, sat beside him, her usually wild dark hair twisted tightly into the sprayed French roll of a busy woman on a bad hair day.

This must be the big case he had been working on for the past year. At the other table, several extra chairs had been pulled up for the three male defendants and their lawyers, including the odious Jeffrey Riesner.

Nina whispered the bad news to her client. He listened, his eagerness fading, his face above the uncomfortable brace looking crestfallen. He had gotten his hopes up, even though she had warned him not to expect much.

After he left, Nina stayed. She wanted to hear the verdict. In spite of Collier's surface cool, he was sweating under the collar about this one, she knew. She could only imagine the all-nighters he'd pulled on this case. In addition to demonstrating his genuine sympathy for the family of the victim in this murder case, a win today would spiff up the invisible star he wore on his lapel, the star of a lawman. It might even win him the election for county district attorney.

She was vexed with herself. No wonder he had been so hard to reach. His jury had been out. How could she have been so busy with her own concerns not to know it?

He would get his convictions, as he usually did. Afterward, she would go up and congratulate him, and

invite him out for a celebratory drink. The dark air
that had hung around him since their hike would fly
away and they would laugh and talk as they had before. . . . She bore the hardness of the wooden bench
with a smile, thinking how much she wanted that.

Milne rocketed through the preliminaries, scanning
the verdict form handed to him with brusque efficiency. The bailiff handed the form to the clerk, who
handed it back to the jury forewoman. Relatives of the
defendants had come breathlessly in during this process, and Barbet Cain, the *Tahoe Mirror* reporter, sat in
the back with her photographer, but otherwise the
courtroom was empty. The lawyers and the defendants
were standing.

The forewoman, who Nina recognized as the local
community college's head librarian, stood up and,
stumbling over the unfamiliar names, read out the ver-
dicts as to each defendant.

"Not guilty. Not guilty. Not guilty." Screams of joy
from the relatives as each verdict was read. The defendants grabbed their lawyers and each other, one of
them crying from relief. The jury looked unhappy.
Collier—she couldn't see his face, but his shoulders
had hunched forward at each of the *not guilty*s, and she
could imagine well enough how he felt. Barbara Banning actually put an arm around his shoulder, as if to
steady him.

It was going to be a very bad night for Collier.
When Milne let them all go on the dot of five o'clock,
she tried to catch up with him, but he was talking in
the hall to several of the jurors. An expression of savage
pain and humiliation crossed his face when he saw that
she had been in the courtroom. His eyes went back to

the jurors, who were saying they felt bad but the State just hadn't beaten the reasonable doubt standard.

He didn't want to talk to her. She went down the stairs, worried about him.

By seven, back at Caesars, Paul had showered and brushed his hair for an extra minute or two. Downstairs at the florist's he had found a bunch of sunflowers from the valleys below, their huge heads languishing but still a luminous gold.

Greeting him at the gate, brown and barefoot in the warm dusk of evening, Kim wore only a pale cotton sheath. As she turned and walked in front of him toward the lantern-lit courtyard there was a loaded moment as Paul previewed her nakedness beneath the flimsy dress.

"How is your work coming?" she asked when they had settled behind a couple of martinis. Candles flickered around her face, their warm light playing along the brown throat with its necklace of amethysts.

"The fins helped. I may have found the car."

"I'm so glad. I feel stupid, not being able to describe things concretely. But the colors . . . I have all the colors right."

"There's one color left in the picture we haven't identified."

"Yes. The green. In front. You noticed that. The driver was . . . green. That's the only way I can put it."

"Wearing something green?"

"I don't remember the hair, or the face. Just the color. I don't think when I paint. I never said 'This is the car, this is the blacktop.' The blocks of color form themselves. What I painted was the emotion I felt. The white is tempered with grayish tones; the orange is shaded with blue; the green is an acid, almost metallic, green. The painting is violent and tragic in color. And yet some of the blocks obviously do represent what I saw, the car especially. So maybe the green does represent something real. I don't know. It's so frustrating!"

"You've done very well," Paul said soothingly. He drew her hand with its pale almond nails to him, and held it, examining a faint blue stain of color in the crook between her thumb and forefinger. "Nice hands," he said, kissing that place. She let him turn it over and kiss her palm. "What have you been painting? Can I see it after dinner?"

"A little picture of the cactus garden."

Paul sucked on his olive. "I admire people who are creative."

"It seems to me that your work can be quite creative."

"Yeah. Actually, it is," Paul said, surprised. "I never thought of it that way."

"You have to be willing to fail occasionally, to make a fool of yourself."

"No problem. I do that all the time."

She had a way of appreciating him with her eyes that he found extremely flattering. She was doing it to him again, hypnotizing him with her movements and eyes and scent. She wore a musing smile.

"I'd like to paint you, Paul. In the nude," she said.

He laughed, his mind springing involuntarily to her rendition of the old man cactus. He tried to imagine himself in the abstract, plunked down in those outlandish colors. He couldn't.

"I'm serious. Blond men are a challenge to paint, because the gradations in color are so subtle."

"Me subtle? That's a new one."

Her eyes moved up and down on him. "Your name is Dutch, but you have the build of a Swede or a Dane, big-boned and muscular."

Her objective attitude finally took hold of him. He listened to the soft words coming from her perfectly cut lips.

"I'd like to paint you sitting there drinking a martini from that crystal glass in candlelight. . . ."

"Stark naked?"

"Mmm-hmm. I wonder . . . would you mind removing your shirt?"

"Not at all," Paul said politely, and he had the polo shirt off his back so fast, he almost spilled his drink.

She got up and approached him, moving languidly, her voice dreamy. "See how the light glints off the blond hair on your chest," she murmured, running a professional finger across his nipple.

Paul's shirt fell forgotten from his hand.

"Please don't move—I like to . . . examine the effect."

She touched him with fingers like feathers, dusting them patiently over his cheek, his hair, his shoulders, over a heart that thudded so mightily it seemed to leap out of his skin. Suddenly, somewhere down around his tenderly cultivated washboard abs, she hesitated.

Scented hair floated around her head. He couldn't see her face.

"You know," she said, her voice faint as if she were far away, "it's a lot to ask, but I'd really like to see your legs. Do you think you could—here, let me help." And she pulled his slacks and BVDs down his legs and right off him. The fingers started up again, cruising along his calf, migrating up his thigh.

She knelt down in front of his colossal erection.

And then, she picked up his foot. She held it, as if weighing it, and turned it this way and that. "If you don't mind, Paul, lean back a little. That's good. Close your eyes and relax your muscles. Put your arms behind your head, that's very good . . . yes, I like that very much. . . ."

A long silence ensued. Paul's nerves strained for the touch of her velvety mouth. C'mon, baby, c'mon.

Titillated beyond endurance, he waited.

14

"SO THEN WHAT HAPPENED?" HALLOWELL SAID
first thing on Saturday morning in Paul's room at
Caesars. Paul sat cross-legged as usual on the bed with
his coffee, but Hallowell seemed unable to sit down.
He wandered from the window to the door, back and
forth.

Paul was shocked by Hallowell's appearance. He
seemed to be aging more every day. He hadn't bothered to comb his hair and his eyes had the glazed look
of the sleep-deprived.

Paul had been reporting on his progress in the
Meade case, but then he had veered onto something
that he thought might cheer Hallowell up.

"Nothing happened. I vogued like a Madonna
stand-in, quivering all over, until I had to have a quick
look. She had moved back to her seat without a sound
and was tasting her drink, smiling. She said, 'Shall we
have our salad?' "

"That's all that happened? You're not leaving something out?"

"That's it. 'Shall we have our salad,' she says, cool as a . . . an olive."

"What did you do?"

"We had our salad."

"You had your salad?"

"Lots of croutons. Fresh black pepper. Artichoke hearts. Tomatoes. Avocado. She wouldn't let me touch her all evening."

"She was teasing you."

"She was toying with me as no man has ever been toyed with before. Righteously. I was so turned on, and she hardly laid her soft little paws on me. Each little touch was like—oh, man, when it does happen, it's gonna be so good."

"If it happens. She left a message at my office this morning. She wants to review her statement. She says she's trying again to jog her memory."

"What do you mean, if it happens?"

"All I mean is—"

"You think she's just fooling around with me. Like you're fooling around with Nina."

"Nina? What has she got to do with this?"

"Well, the deeper you get into your wife's death, the less time you have for her. I hate seeing her hurt."

Hallowell turned to look at him, cocking his head. "Who are you, her brother from Montenegro?"

"Yeah, that's me. Her *big* brother," Paul said. "You're letting this wear you down, man. You're putting yourself under a monster strain. You're in court all day with the creeps and the criminals, and you spend your nights in bed with a dead woman. Am I right?"

Hallowell combed through his unruly mop with his fingers. He didn't answer, so Paul said, "I look at you, and I see what everybody else sees: this highly respected deputy DA who's got a lock on the next election for county district attorney—"

"Maybe yesterday before court I did."

"Something happened I should know about?"

"Nothing to do with your work."

"But now that I'm getting to know you, I also see you blowing it, living in the past."

"Don't psychoanalyze me, Paul. I don't like it."

"Have it your way."

"Let's get back to Anna."

Paul remembered that Hallowell was his employer, and straightened up. He told him about the flight of the El-Baroukis into Egypt and the conversations with Gates and Mrs. Lauria.

Hallowell said, "He's out there, and he knows we're looking. He won't get away this time."

"Could as easily be a she."

"What about El-Barouki's description of the man who sold the car?"

"Maybe he made it up on the spot. He wasn't going to give me any help on the seller at all. I think he already had it in his mind to collect what he could from me, then to go back to the seller and say, 'I'm going to give you up unless you buy me and my entire extended family tickets back to Egypt.' He knew all along he was just using me to set up a blackmail payment."

"There has to be something in the car. How long do we have to wait for some lab reports?"

"I'll be talking to Ginger today. I think it's still too early, though."

"I have to tell you I'm having a hard time believing what you've conjured up, all from Kim's painting. I looked at that picture and saw just meaningless blobs of

220   PERRI O'SHAUGHNESSY

paint. Let's hope you're on to something there. What else can you do to find the seller?"

"Call a friend at the DMV," Paul said. "I don't know if there could be a way to get a list of every Catalina registered to a Tahoe owner three years ago. The DMVs getting up to speed with its computers now, but three or four years ago—I just don't know. And other than that, I'll call all the garages again to see if any of them remember working on a Catalina. It's hard to believe a big car with fins could be cruising around here for a long time and no mechanic or gas station attendant would have noticed."

"What if you don't get a line that way?"

"We'll be deeply embedded in shit, buddy."

Hallowell started rubbing his eyes with his fists like a little kid trying to wake up from a nightmare. He was realizing that the leads were petering out on them, that they might not succeed this time around either. Paul caught a glimpse of the gold band he still wore on his left hand.

Paul thought about what he was going to say next, and decided there was no easy way to put it.

"I have to go back to Carmel tonight," he said. "One week was all I could give you full-time on short notice. I really thought I could break it for you in a week. It could break yet, but . . . anyway, I'm not sure when I can get back."

Hallowell said, "Law enforcement lost big when you went out on your own, Paul. Let me know if you ever decide to come back in." He was trying to smile, but the smile turned into something else. "I'll call Nina," he said.

"Do that. Love is like a gun, you know? Whole lotta power, but you've gotta pull the trigger first."

Collier had hardly gone when the hotel clerk called Paul to say he had an urgent message from Ms. Reilly to meet her at a certain address at a place called Happy Homestead. The name suggested a waitress in a gingham apron. Maybe she wanted to have a colleague-and-friend breakfast. He could manage that. He pulled on his shoes, whistling.

Framed by a glorious morning, Nina was waiting for Paul at the address, the main gate of a cemetery, wearing dark glasses and a frown, her voluptuous self sneakily accentuated by the severe cut of her suit. His heart went pit-a-pat at the sight of her and he reminded himself sternly that she was a workaholic, a thick-skinned mouthpiece who had had the audacity to turn down his proposal. She waved and came to meet him when she saw him. Steady now, boy, he thought, they all do that thing with their hips when they walk. Remember the overdeveloped brain in that pretty cranium, that brain that keeps the hormones in check when it ought to be the other way around. . . .

"You came," she said. "I've missed you." She rose up on her tiptoes to kiss his cheek, which commenced to burning as though singed by a flamethrower.

"I had to head this way anyway," he said. "So this is Happy Homestead. What are we doing here? What's the story with the patrol cars out front?"

"The caretaker got here at seven and noticed the ground in one of the plots had been disturbed. He called his boss and then the police."

"Disturbed?"

"Somebody dug up a grave. The casket's intact, except . . . it's open. And the body is gone."

"Whoa! Whose body?"

"A man named Ray de Beers."

"Ah. The guy who got struck by lightning the day you and Collier hiked Tallac."

"A lot has happened since then. Paul, I've been fighting a motion filed by Ray's father to exhume the body. We spent the day before yesterday in court haggling."

"Who won the motion?"

"Nobody. In the middle of the argument, my client fell apart and instructed me to drop the opposition, but I managed to get the whole thing postponed instead. Quentin de Beers, Ray's father, was furious at my maneuver."

"You think de Beers did this?"

"I don't know what to think. He was about to win, because my client wouldn't fight anymore. But he might have had to wait a few days for his order. Maybe he thought my client might change her mind again and so he decided to take matters into his own hands. I'm flabbergasted, I truly am. I thought it would be nice to have your cool head."

"Cool-headed colleague, that's me," Paul said. "Lead on."

They walked down the path together, Nina silent, apparently wrapped up in her thoughts.

"How's the house-hunting going?" he asked to bring her back. "Find anything that looks good?"

She raised her eyes to his, then dropped them again, as if she enjoyed the contact but needed to keep it brief. "I seem to be looking for the wrong thing. Nothing I see feels right."

"Keep looking," Paul advised. "One day you'll walk into a place and voilà! It'll sing to you."

"I'm going to wear out poor Mrs. Wendover's tires.

She's really trying, unlike the realtor I started out with."

They reached the clump of people at Ray de Beers's grave site. A patrol car had driven right up onto the lawn, the red lights flashing, the radio squawking. "Who's he?" Paul asked, pointing toward the gesticulating fellow who was helping them.

"The caretaker. They've found something," Nina said in a low voice. A few feet from the site, a small group of people had formed, kept from getting any closer to the grave by crime tape and a uniformed patrol officer. They were watching a police forensics technician bag some large tool near the grave site in plastic. On the other side, a photographer from the *Mirror* competed with a police photographer for the best angles into the pit.

A backhoe had been taped off-limits on the driveway, indicating how the digging had been accomplished. Paul slipped by the group when the patrolman's back was turned, stood at the edge of the pit, and looked in. Down there he saw a black casket, hinged on the left, yawning open and revealing a stained white satin lining. Soft clods of dirt had fallen or had been knocked in from above.

A man had lain there in what was supposed to be eternal darkness. It should have been raining or foggy or snowing, in keeping with the morbid scene, but this was California. The sun shone down into the pit, illuminating every crevice, pitiless, indecent.

"Creepy, isn't it?" the elderly man said. "I come to put flowers on my wife's grave this morning, and this is what I see. Like an episode from *Tales of the Crypt*. The guy's been buried alive, right, and he wakes up in the dark, he screams and screams, and then he tries to claw his way out—"

"And it cuts to a commercial," Paul said. "I hate that." Stepping back from the pit, he looked around for Nina, who was talking to a tall, skinny woman with a mane of black hair who had just come up the walk.

"Quentin did this," the woman told Nina.

Nina turned and said, "Paul, I'd like you to meet my client. Sarah de Beers. I was just telling her about you."

At first, the woman paid no attention to Paul. She raked the bushes with hypervigilant eyes as if she thought something lay in wait for her. Finally, she held out frosty fingers, grasped his hand, and released it with a jerk. "I called him. Quentin," she said. "His house-man said he didn't come home last night." She looked over at the grave site. "I want to see."

Stepping carefully over the fresh earth, she peered into the hole, bloodless hands clenched at her sides. After a few minutes, Nina and Paul joined her silent vigil.

"Are you Mrs. de Beers?" the patrolman said, coming over to them. He opened his leather notepad and said, "This is your husband's grave?"

"Yes."

"Any idea what happened?"

"Quentin dug him up. He said he would, and now he has."

"Quentin de Beers?" the young patrolman said, sounding intensely interested.

Nina said, "Her father-in-law. The dead man's father." She seemed to step between her client and the cop without moving a muscle, capturing his attention away from the quaking woman beside her. Paul took Mrs. de Beers's elbow and steered her a few feet away.

While she leaned her head against him, he listened as Nina calmly informed the patrolman about the court case that seemed to have led up to this debacle, and all she knew about Quentin de Beers, whom she had met at least once. The one in charge wrote it all down in a notebook. Finally Nina said, "Is that it? Because Mrs. de Beers needs to go home."

"That's all for *now*," he said to Nina, as though she were her own client. "Stay available."

While Nina walked her client back to her car, Paul went over to the lab tech, who was just pulling his gloves off. He closed his case with a snap.

"What was that garden tool you just bagged?" Paul said. "Looked like a shovel."

"Can't say at this time, sir. Excuse me." Toting the case, he walked rapidly toward the patrol car and loaded it into the back, where the big plastic bag was also being loaded. Paul followed him and had a good look, confirming his idea that the item was a shovel.

"The idea that Ray is out there somewhere wandering around in that blue suit, hating all of us because he's dead and we're still alive . . ." Mrs. de Beers was saying as Paul caught up. "What's Quentin doing with him? Why is he torturing us? What have we done to him?"

"Can I drive you home?" Nina asked, concern clouding her usually translucent brown eyes.

"No. That's not necessary. I'm going straight over to see Leo. I'm sure he's back from . . . well, wherever he was this morning when I called. He's been angry with me because I—I was going to let Quentin have his way. All Quentin had to do was wait! And the kids will have to hear about all this. They've been angry at me too, for the same reason. I guess I'll try to get them all over to the house this afternoon."

"By the way, Sarah. I stopped by your house briefly last night but no one answered the doorbell."

"Molly felt better. I thought it would be all right to leave her for a few minutes. I went for a drive. I—I didn't get back until very late."

"Molly went out too? By herself? Is that a good idea?"

"Oh, no! She wasn't planning to go anywhere. She probably just didn't feel like answering the door. The doctor started her on antidepressants yesterday. Those things wipe you out." She fiddled in a small red leather bag, eventually locating what she was hunting for, a silver key ring forming twin linking circles around the letters *M* and *J*.

"I know it's a bad time to ask a lot of questions, and I won't, but I need to know one thing," said Nina. "Why did you call me at court and instruct me to drop your opposition to Ray's exhumation? Maybe it's a bad time to talk about it, but you didn't call me back yesterday either."

"Quentin made me. He came to talk to me, and by the time he was done, he had what he wanted. I couldn't stand up to him when he was right there in front of me. He told me what to say.

"Then . . . I called the court to find out what happened. I was too ashamed to talk to you directly, Nina. And when I learned you had asked for a postponement instead, I was glad. Except now this has happened, and I can't help thinking that if you'd done what I said, Quentin would have had the exhumation done properly, and I would have been there with a policeman, and we would have been able to keep better control of the situation. . . . The thing is, Quentin has a different set of values from the rest of us. Ray was just like him. He got what he wanted, just like Quentin."

She beeped her Pathfinder and the locks popped up. "I'm sorry if I caused a lot of trouble for you," she said, lifting her legs into the truck, watching Paul's eyes rev up at the sight, and with a brisk slam shutting them down.   ∖

"Sarah," said Nina, but Sarah's car rolled slowly out of sight, leaving Paul and Nina in its dust.

"What in the world is going on?" Nina asked with real distress.

"I don't like it either," Paul said. "It's like some ancient drama. Lightning flashes, grieving widow, grave robbers . . . how come you never get involved in anything that makes sense?"

"What do you think happened?"

"She's probably right, from what you've told me. The grandfather's lost his grip on reality. It's a good example of how miserable a mentally ill person can make the people around him."

"He was pretty irrational, Paul, but he didn't seem mentally ill."

"I shudder to think what he's doing with the body. Too grotesque to contemplate."

"Maybe it wasn't him. Like Sarah said, all he had to do was wait a few days."

"Maybe he thought she'd change her mind again. And he is missing."

"I don't know. He was so sure of himself," Nina said.

"Then . . . you're saying it might have been one

of the three people she mentioned as being angry at her?"

"They were the ones who were about to lose, Paul. Leo Tarrant, Jason, Molly. Why is Ray's body so important? I knew on the mountain something was beginning, not ending. The power of that flash, taking away my sight and hearing and leaving me in terror, cowering on the ground . . . I felt that I was in the presence of some bright death-dealing spirit, not a lightning bolt."

"Who the hell knows what electricity is, anyway?" Paul said. "It's a mystery, like where we came from and where we're going. Like what sleep really is. Maybe God's a current. I'm having some of the same thoughts on the case I'm working. I'm having weird flashes of insight that don't even seem to come from me, like something out there wants the case solved and is leading me from clue to clue."

"I owe you breakfast. Come on. I'll drive and drop you back here later."

"It's getting late. Make it a grilled chicken sandwich at that restaurant on the beach."

She swung onto the highway, heading west.

"Bet whoever really was up to all those late-night graveyard shenanigans had a huge appetite this morning," Paul said. "We should check the restaurants, see who had the He-man Special with extra everything for breakfast."

"Brilliant," Nina said. "And you just know the police are going to overlook that telltale clue."

"Wait! I'm having a weird flash of insight right now! About the greasy spoon we just passed! Yes. Yes. I hear, oh, Master."

"What message have you received from on high?" Nina asked, getting into it.

Paul touched a forefinger to the spot between his closed eyes. "Steak and eggs," he intoned. "Steak and eggs."

15

A SHRILL RINGING. NINA'S OFFICE COMPUTER MON-
itor told her it was nearly three-thirty in the afternoon.
She held her place in the file she was plowing through
and picked up the phone with her other hand.

"It's Sarah. I have to talk to you about this morning."

"Have they found—"

"No. I'll come to you."

"All right."

"Ten minutes." Sarah hung up. Nina's thoughts had
been irretrievably interrupted. She walked down the
hall, empty because it was Saturday, to the bathroom,
fluffed her hair and washed her hands. When she came
back Sarah de Beers was sitting in the outer room.
Nina closed and locked the outer door and sat down in
the other chair, across from the desk where on week-
days Sandy held sway.

"He's gone!"

"Who?"

"Jason!"

"Where has he gone?"

"I don't know. I called the boy he's been staying with. He said Jason took his stuff and split."

"Sarah, calm down."

"Where could he be? I called all his other friends this morning. They haven't seen him since yesterday. Molly doesn't know either. Jason's Jeep is in our driveway, where he left it yesterday."

"I'm sure he'll turn up," Nina said. "He's having a hard time. He's lost a father, no matter how difficult the relationship was."

Sarah began to tremble, and the trembling changed into a nervous giggle, and the giggle became a laugh. The laugh escalated into a fit that Humphrey Bogart might stop with a slap, but Nina didn't think Sarah would take that too well from her, so she waited.

Sarah lifted her hands to her mouth, trying to stifle herself, but she laughed on. Her purse fell to the floor with a crash. She spread her arms out weakly toward the silver wallet and the cosmetics skidding over the floor, as if they were children she loved but couldn't control.

Nina got up and picked it all up, placing everything securely in the brass-chased Cartier bag, closing the latch firmly, placing it back into Sarah's hands, giving her a chance to come back.

"I'm . . . so . . . afraid," Sarah said, the words coming out in short gasps. "Ray has brought death on us. . . . I'm very afraid of death. . . . My mother died when I was a child. . . . It was horrible. . . . The worst does happen. . . ."

She wiped her eyes. "I apologize for that. But you must know by now how difficult Jason's relationship with his father really was. He hated him, but underneath he still loved him, too, the way a child loves a father no matter what. Jason talked me into opposing Quentin in the first place. He even gave me your name. He said you could go up against Quentin and win. He read about your cases in the newspaper. And I . . ."

"What reason did he give for opposing the motion?"

"He said that Quentin would find some way of accusing Leo of doing something to Ray up on that mountain. Quentin hasn't been normal. His personality seems totally different. Leo and Molly thought Jason was right, so I came to you."

"But you wouldn't let me win it for you."

"I'm sorry. I'm sorry." It was her mantra. Sarah had found herself in the middle again, Nina thought, and she moved in accordance with who was pushing her at the moment. "I should have talked to Leo and the children, but there was no time. Quentin said I had to tell you to stop right away." She hung her head, seeming to need reassurance, so Nina tried to offer some.

"I'm sure you did what you had to do."

"That's just it. I did what other people wanted me to do, just like I always did with Ray. I don't know my own mind. I'm going to try to stand up for my own thoughts on things. Like, when I was injured, my legs, you know. I would listen to Ray, and he'd have me thinking I pulled that beam down over myself. Then I'd listen to Jason, and he'd have me believing Ray pulled it down on me. The truth is, it was an accident, nobody's fault. We had been coping until then as a family, but a . . . hatred flared up and grew among us after I was hurt."

"When did you last speak to Jason?"

"On Thursday while you were still in court, I told

him I was withdrawing my opposition. Yesterday he came to the house to talk to me. Quentin was just leaving. They quarreled. Oh, I'm so afraid!"

"Why did they quarrel, Sarah? Go ahead, take a minute if you need to."

Sarah said, "I didn't hear all of it. Jason was asking him to drop the court proceeding. Quentin said something like 'Ever heard of the Furies, boy?' Who are the Furies, Nina?"

"I don't know," Nina said. "Something to do with Greek mythology. That's all you heard?"

"Yes. Quentin left. Jason left without saying good-bye. You see, what I am afraid of . . . I can't say it . . ."

"You're afraid Jason took Ray's body and Quentin followed him, and Jason's . . . in trouble? We should tell the police." Nina stood up.

"Tell them what?" Sarah crossed her arms. "He's nineteen. Not a kid. They aren't going to care. And Quentin and Jason—they have always cared deeply for each other, until this. I'm just overreacting, aren't I?"

"Sarah," Nina said. "This can't stay in the family. The police might be able to help."

"I can't even say he's done anything. It's just a feeling of dread. But I had to tell someone. And you stood up to Quentin. I feel that I can lean on you, Nina. Can you help me find Jason?"

"There is someone I could call," Nina said. "A private investigator, Paul van Wagoner."

"That tall man at the cemetery with you?"

"Yes. If I can reach him, and if he has some spare time."

"Call him and set it up."

"I'll try to help you, Sarah."

"I knew I could count on you."

"But you have to stop leaning on people, even me. You have to straighten up for the sake of the twins. I think you are stronger than you know, Sarah. I think you can take whatever comes."

"I know. I'll try. I love them so much."

She stood up, shaking out the soft material of her skirt. "Oh, one more thing. You should try talking with Jose."

"Jose?"

"Joe. The gardener. He might know where Jason's gone."

"Thanks, Sarah. I'll be in touch."

Nina's hand was on the phone as the door closed. She called Caesars. Paul wasn't in. She left a message. She called Collier, leaving stilted messages on his machines at both his home and his office.

Sarah had come to her for help, seeking a more decisive, even a more powerful person in Nina. But what could Nina do? Her only real asset was her mind, and right now, like Sarah's, it was befuddled by the incidents of the past week. So she shut off the computer at her desk, put her feet up, and reviewed all the small things she had heard about Quentin and the theft of Ray's body. The Starlake Building was quiet. In her hands, with her legal pad and sharp pencil, she drew quick sketches while she thought.

After some time, she looked down at the sketch. Lightning zigzagged across the top of the paper. Below were her doodles, outlined again and again with the pencil and cross-hatched into three dimensions: a coffin, Molly hanging from a rope, the empty grave, a body in the bushes.

Dreadful images.

Her heart beat faster. She had been stupidly shuffling papers and mouthing legal arguments while the situation opened up under her like Ray's grave.

Briefcase loaded with the paperwork she ought to be doing, she headed toward Regan Beach. Sarah had mentioned that Joe might know something. The least she could do was ask him.

Sarah's car wasn't in its parking spot. Joe was loading a bin full of grass clippings into a pickup marked JL GARDENING in the driveway behind the de Beers house, its engine idling.

"Joe?" The gardener was sweating through the blue denim work shirt, the muscles in the back of his shoulders and the thick neck twisted and straining. She noticed that his profile was noble, incised, with a jutting nose and strong brow under the straw cowboy hat. He turned toward her, and she realized she had never really looked at him when they talked in the house. He had made himself unimportant even while he talked to her.

At first he didn't seem to recognize her in her Saturday clothes of jeans and T-shirt. He was older than she had thought, in his thirties. Standing close to him, both of them about the same height, she felt the heat of his masculinity emitting from him, rapidly controlled as he saw who she was.

"Oh," he said. "The lady lawyer. How are you?"

"I'm in a hurry," Nina said. "Jason de Beers has disappeared."

"I told you."

"What? What did you tell me?"

"That he was causing problems."

"I think you know much more about this family's problems than you told me."

"I don't know anything. I'm just—"

"Yeah, just the gardener. Do me a favor, Joe. Don't give me that crap, okay?"

The smooth oval brown face broke into a sullen smile, quickly hidden. "What do you want from me?" he said. "I'm late myself. The dump closes at five."

"Where were you last night?"

"Last night? At home with my woman."

"That can be checked."

"Who would bother to check?"

"I would. The police will, when I finish talking to them. I think you helped to dig up the body of Ray de Beers last night. You've worked here a long time. I imagine you know how to use a backhoe. Was it Quentin de Beers? How much did he pay you?"

That blank stare again. She stared right back, through it.

Joe laughed. His posture relaxed, as if he were throwing off a disguise. Suddenly he took up space, and she felt the heat of his personality again. "You are a very beautiful woman," he said. He was very close to her now. His eyes with their long lashes looked aggressively into her own. "I sat next to you in the house, and I thought to myself, Man, she is a nice lady, she ought to be in the bed, not running around with her little briefcase causing problems. You don't have any husband, do you?" He reached out, ran his hand along her bare left arm appraisingly. "No ring."

Nina took a step back. "That's none of your business."

"Oh, I see. You can come here where I work, accuse me of bad things, ask me how much I got paid to dig up a body. You act like the landowner's wife, huh?

I'm not your servant. I don't answer that kind of talk. I have my own business, plenty of customers—"

"Okay. Okay. I didn't mean to jump on you."

"Anglo women are the worst. In Mexico women show respect to a man. Not in the U.S. The women are the head of the house in this crazy country." His mouth spread into a silly mocking simper. " 'Joe, you didn't clean up the dog doodoo over there by the bushes. Joe, the fuchsia looks bad, put down some fertilizer. Joe, you stink, don't you ever take a bath?' And dirty looks when it's time to pay me my money."

"Is she really so bad? Mrs. de Beers?"

His face softened somewhat. "She's not as bad as the others."

"Then let's give it a rest, Joe. I get the point. I apologize if I offended you."

"No more *padron* bullshit."

"Okay. And no more macho flexing."

"What do you want to know?"

"Did you help anyone dig up the body of Ray de Beers?"

"Huh? No."

"No? You give me your word?"

"You have my word."

Nina bit her lip. She believed him. She had been wrong.

Joe took off his heavy work gloves and stuffed them into his pocket, then slammed the back of the truck closed and climbed onto the back fender to tighten one of the lids on his trash cans. Nina watched him, thinking, he'll be a rich man someday. Now he was looking up and behind her. She turned in time to see a curtain being pulled shut on an upstairs floor, a white face disappearing.

"Joe," she said, "Sarah and Molly are very frightened that something has happened to Jason."

"There is a place at Wright's Lake—you know it?" Joe said. He put on a pair of sunglasses and opened the door to the truck.

"No."

"Take Highway 50 over Echo Summit. Just past Strawberry, you see the turnoff on the right. About half an hour. Then you climb a steep one-lane road high into the mountains. The lake is almost deserted at this time of year, and the summer cabins are empty. The grandfather has a friend who owns one of them." He described the exterior of the cabin and its exact location. "He has a key. He goes up there sometimes. I think he forgot he told me about it a long time ago. The family went up there once or twice, but not lately. If Quentin de Beers dug up the body, he might have gone there. Jason knows about the place too. He drove up to the house one day last summer with a big trout he said he got at Wright's Lake."

"Thank you. Thank you, Joe. Will you drive up to Wright's Lake with me?"

"I can't do that," Joe said. "That's not my business. I told you what I know. Now the rest is your business. You take care of it." He looked up again, toward the window.

Back in the Bronco, pulling her seat belt over her shoulders with impatient, clumsy movements, Nina waged a struggle with herself. From an objective viewpoint, what did she know that would cause the sheriff's office to go chasing off to Wright's Lake? That Quentin or even Jason might be there? She didn't really know that. That Sarah's dread colored her thoughts now, a feeling that something must urgently be done to prevent more tragedy? What would some hard-bitten sheriff's deputy make of that?

Not much. She would be patted on the head and told to go home.

She could tell Sarah. She could go up there with Sarah. But Sarah might add to whatever volatile emotions were at play.

She banged the steering wheel with her hand. Where was Paul! Paul, who had always been around when she needed him, had abandoned her! She picked up the cell phone and dialed Caesars again. The phone in his room rang again and again, until the phone operator came on the line to take a message, but Nina had already hung up. He was probably with that woman who was so talented and pretty, the witness Collier had told her about.

Jealousy blazed up at her core, a burning mix of wounded self-esteem, anger, longing, and needfulness. Her other side—the prudent, logical part of her, which had decided to back away from Paul—tried to reassert itself but was no match for this sudden conflagration. She was feeling very inadequate, thinking how very alone she was, how much she had given up—for what?

For this lousy profession, built on sleepless nights and anxiety-ridden days, at the nexus of trouble, failure, guilt, hatred, every human failing? She was so busy trying to prop up her clients that she was on the edge herself, and there was no one who cared to catch her— not Collier, farther out on the edge than she was, and not Paul—and that was her own fault.

A memory surfaced, of a legal services lawyer she had known in San Francisco, a young man committed from the beginning to righting injustices and saving his clients from their own mistakes. He had come from a poor family and worked his way through college and law school the hard way. In the rotunda of city hall she had met him one day, and he had said, "I'm burned out. I'm getting out."

"To where?" she had said.

"I'm going to drive a forklift at a warehouse in San Jose. Like I did in college."

"You can't do that!" she had said, aghast. "All your training, your ambition—"

"I'm looking forward to it. It beats lawyering all to hell. I'll pick up boxes and put them on pallets, and at the end of the day they'll still be sitting where I put them. I'll actually accomplish something positive."

"That's ridiculous."

"Not as ridiculous as rolling rocks up a mountain all day, only to find they roll back down as soon as you turn your back."

She never saw him again. He had been a casualty.

She thought, It's not my duty, I'm not going to put this on my shoulders, I'm not going to drive up to that cabin by myself, no matter what. . . . It isn't fair, no one could ask it of me. . . .

While all these thoughts born of fear caromed around in her head, she was already climbing the face of the granite cliff that led over Echo Summit and out of the Tahoe basin, keeping the Bronco in second gear, trying not to hit the sightseers gawking over the edge of the cliff at the turnouts. Clouds were gathering over the Carson range, just as they had on Tallac barely two weeks before.

And then, from nowhere, her doubts began to subside. Some hidden source of strength surged up and she said to herself, It may be too big to fight, but you have to get in the ring with it anyway. What else had she spent years developing her skills and her strength for? Was she going to cringe and run back to push some more papers after telling Sarah she'd help her?

The inner tumult continued to recede, like the backwash of a stream that has met the giant Amazon. The road left the cliff and turned west, toward Wright's Lake. She followed it.

16

"DO YOU WANT THE GOOD NEWS OR THE BAD news first?" Ginger asked Paul over the phone.

Having spent Saturday afternoon closing off leads one by one, Paul was calling from a pay phone on the street. His friend at the DMV had said the computers at the agency wouldn't be able to scrounge up all Catalina owners from a particular town years ago.

"Bad news first."

"The bad news is, this car's been washed and vacuumed inside and out. I pulled out the seats, the gear shift mechanism—stuff gets down in there sometimes. I vacuumed until I felt like the upstairs maid. I found enough dog hair to stuff a pillow—kid hair, grownup hair. You send me samples from the family down in L.A. My guess is it's all their hair."

"Any sign the car's ever been in the mountains?"

"A few pine needles under the floorboards. Might or might not confirm your man's story that he bought the car in the mountains."

"What else?"

"Chewing gum under the door handles. Skittles and M&M's. Cardboard holder that used to hold fried zucchini. Pepsi can under the right front seat. Cheap ballpoint pen. Loose change and an old eyebrow pencil, light brown."

"Any fingerprints?"

"Millions. I got the prints from the family. A million of those. Even a few of yours on the steering wheel and door handle. Lots more. I'm working on them, but you know you can't expect me to be able to identify all of them. No bloody prints at all.

"Beyond that, I found lots of sandy dirt. And, no, there's nothing special about the dirt, either. Even at the molecular level, it's just L.A. dirt. No obscure seeds or spores."

Disappointed, Paul said, "Rats."

"One interesting thing—semen stains on the backseat. You send me a semen sample from Bright, I can try for a match. Or do a straight DNA test on a blood sample if he doesn't want to send his jism through UPS. UPS has been losing my checks, and God knows where my last set of test tubes from the factory in New Jersey ended up."

"You do have your fun, analyzing secretions for a living," Paul said. Peculiar clunking sounds came over the phone line. Paul imagined Ginger, whom he had worked with through the computer and phone but never met in person, as one of those perfectly groomed petite Asian-American ladies who wore high heels shopping; the soul of efficiency, walking around the lab in her pristine whites, the phone glued to her ear with a shoulder, performing four other tasks at the same time.

"Are the mom and pop likely candidates for a little

romance in the backseat? It's a big, wide car. Even big, wide, middle-aged people might be tempted."

Paul thought back to Bryan Bright and his wife. It was hard to imagine Debs having the energy or time for a romp in the Cat, but you never knew. "Don't ask me."

"Ask Bright, then."

"I will."

"Because if they didn't do it, and the kids are too young, that leaves the previous owner."

"Or some member of the El-Barouki tribe. They had the car for a while. You wouldn't even need a partner."

"It's a long shot," Ginger said. "Pun intended."

"Good news?"

"The car was definitely in an accident. Since then, as I already mentioned, a nice paint job overlaid the original white color with black. The windshield has also been replaced. It's nonstandard for that type car in that year, jury-rigged to fit. Crummy work. The wind practically whistles through it. The radiator is new, new tires, and there's a new transmission. Other than that, the car's cherry. Bright maintained it very well."

"What about the glass I collected in the parking lot?"

"Meets the factory specs for this type car's windshield, but not for headlights. That's all I can say, because the old windshield is gone."

So Paul would never see the ghost of Anna's face in the windshield. "That's it?"

"I've saved the best for last. The really good news, if you can call it that, is that the sample you gave me for Anna Meade matched up with some blood I discovered gunked behind a dent in the bumper. Apparently, the bumper was just washed, not replaced. Those carwashes do such a piss-poor job."

Paul felt a maniacal grin break out on his face. Ginger had come through. Bright's Pontiac had to be the car.

"Well, you do like keeping people in suspense, don't you?" he said. "Good work, Ginger. Dammit! I have to get back to Carmel and take care of some other clients. I don't know how long it will take."

"What do I do about the car?"

"My client wants to send down an El Dorado County forensics tech to bring it back up here. It's still an open case. He's going to give what I've dug up to the police."

"He's sending a cop down here? What is he, the police chief?"

"Better."

"I guess that explains how you managed to get me samples from a woman who died three years ago. But what about the hair and semen samples? And continuing with the fingerprint work? I'd like to finish this job, Paul. Somebody else takes over now, there could be a screw-up."

"I'll have the client hold off picking up the car for a week or so, and call the guy in L.A. I'll try to get you the samples right away. You do the analysis and write up a report. Can you do it that fast?"

"Send me the samples, and I'll analyze them. But it's been three years and a lot of other people have been in the car. Don't expect anything."

"If you never expect anything, you never get anything. We've got the car. Our eyewitness couldn't ID it from my Polaroid, but maybe she'll have better luck when she sees the actual car."

"What else do you have?"

"Not a dad-blamed thing."

"Put an ad in the paper," Ginger said. "Offer a reward for anybody who saw the car or the accident. Attorney friend of mine always does that on his hit-and-runs."

"I just did that."

"Oh." Ginger had run out of suggestions. "Okay, then. I have to go babysit the centrifuge."

"Talk to you soon." Paul hung up, looking at the low-hanging clouds. He found a quarter and called Nina's office and house and car phone. Recordings and ringing.

Too bad he couldn't say good-bye in person. He felt a longing to talk to her. Shaking that uncomfortable feeling off, he called Kim and heard her recorded sultry alto telling the world that she would be out of town for a few days, leave a message.

Well, shit. His racquetball bag full of dirty clothes and his equipment were already loaded in the back of the van, and he had checked out of Caesars that morning. He shrugged and climbed in.

On the way out of town he stopped for an early dinner. At barely five-thirty, the heavy overcast had effectively ended the day. Up the highway past Echo Summit he started the seventy-mile, seven-thousand-foot descent toward Sacramento, where Interstate 5 would take him south toward the Pacheco Pass and home, hard jazz like ice cubes coming from the quad speakers, the heater on for the first time that season.

His jubilation had passed. The news from Ginger was a breakthrough, but there was too much unfinished business at Tahoe. He had taken the Meade case from cold to simmering, and he hated to leave it. And Nina worried him. Her case had a menacing, live-action quality he didn't like. She had called on him, and he hadn't done much to help. And Kim—also a hot situation.

He almost turned the van around and drove back, but if he did, he would lose at least two regular clients in Carmel, which would cramp his lifestyle for several months.

Still trying to make up his mind, he passed the sign for Wright's Lake, ten miles off the highway somewhere up in the mountains on his right, and from the edge of his rearview mirror even thought he caught a glimpse of Nina's weatherbeaten white Bronco heading up that road. Now he was seeing things. He drove on.

She drove up, up the narrow, twisting road hewn somehow from the side of the mountain. How could there be a lake up here? At the top the road leveled out and she entered dwarf Alpine forest, each bush neatly skirting its neighbors, and all the same height. She was on a high, beautiful meadow, about eight thousand feet in altitude, no more mountains above her, completely alone. She followed the cracked and potholed road a few miles farther, seeing no sign of man or animal, then went from overcast sky to dark trees as the road entered a well-forested hidden valley.

Signs of logging here and there: a truck loaded with tree trunks at a turnout, stumps and sawdust and debris across the road, but no people. The clouds had lowered to obscure the narrow road and she traveled at twenty miles per hour, even the motor sound hushed. It would be dark soon.

At last she reached a sign that said WRIGHT'S LAKE—

CAMPGROUND AND CABINS. Slowing to a crawl as the first cabin came into view, she spotted the small lake, gray and flat through the trees. As on many of the lakes that fringed Lake Tahoe basin, these cabins had been built right up to the edge of the lake, many with decks built out over the water. Almost all were boarded up for the winter. Each house had its propane tank and its outhouse, and, using the last light to see, she could glimpse no sign of electrical lines. The summer residents must enjoy returning to the nineteenth century. Their days would be spent fishing from canoes, scrambling among the boulders, and working jigsaw puzzles under Coleman lanterns at night.

The cabin she sought was set a little apart from the others, down its own dirt driveway and directly on the lake.

The shades had been pulled down, but she saw flickering light around the edges.

No car in the driveway. A sharp sense of relief came. No one home. But that light . . .

Her first knock was so tentative, they couldn't have heard it. Yet she heard an answering sound, furtive and soft, like the rustling of a curtain. Warmth leaked from the interior. She tapped again; a dry, official rap that meant business. No answer except for that faint rustle. She tried the latch.

She pushed the door open. The rustle was fire.

Fire darted from all sides, hot shadows moving in the corners. As she watched, rigid with astonishment, the curtains burst into flames. Over there, stretched out on the floor, adding the sweet, foul stench of a once living thing to the odor of gasoline, something wrapped in a blanket smoked, something large—oh, God, it was a person, it had to be the body of Ray de Beers. . . .

She was backing out when she saw Quentin de Beers lying on the smoking couch, his mouth sagging in the tanned, lined face as if to say something, his eyes wide and staring, his eyelashes singeing as she watched, his clothes smoking too. She couldn't tell what had killed him.

Gagging and choking, she ran across the room to him, feeling the vicious heat of the flames on the other side of the cabin intensify as she came closer. Quentin stared up at her as she seized his limp hand, feeling for his pulse above the wrist. The hand was warm, but then everything in the room was hot, getting hotter. . . . She couldn't feel the pulse. She reached under his shoulders and tried to lift him out, but he was too big, and he was dead, every bone in her body screamed it. . . .

The flames ran up the curtains and began to lick the ceiling. Bits of burning fabric peeled off and fell to the floor, starting their own tiny fires.

A pair of green Vuarnets lay on the floor. She scooped them up, knowing whose they were.

"Jason! Jason!"

She ran through the front door again as a spark attached itself to her shirt and began to grow. She ripped open the shirt, tossed it onto a flat rock, and ran for the truck. The crackling fire behind her clamored for fuel, whooshing up the side walls and piercing through the shingled roof to twist into its wild dance against a dark sky. . . .

She jumped in, threw the Bronco into reverse. . . .

And the front windows of the cabin exploded, the shards blasting twenty feet away, much too close. . . .

Then the peaked roof of the place seemed to lift off slowly like a rocket at Canaveral, landing askew with a *whump.* New tongues of fire lapped around new chinks and crannies. She had the impression that the whole place was bowing outward, enlarging as if in a cartoon.

The Bronco rolled backward as she wrestled the wheel to stay on the dirt, her eyes helplessly bonded to the cabin. She heard a terrible sucking noise.

The cabin burst apart, sending out blue and orange flames and a concussion of hot air against the Bronco. Burning wood crashed everywhere.

She was at the road. Prying her hands from the wheel, she pulled out the cell phone. No. She put it back and steered the Bronco to the campground, only a minute down the road, where she pulled up to the pay phone she had passed on the way in. Slamming a quarter into the slot, she pushed the numbers, all of them, 911. "Fire!" she yelled. "At Wright's Lake! Hurry!" As the questions came, the phone went back into its slot, and Nina took off for the highway.

Her eyes searched for him all the way down the mountain. She called his name into the vacant meadows and black forests. But Jason never answered. At Echo Summit she heard the sirens, then saw the red flashing lights, as the fire trucks from Tahoe came toward her.

It was only when she parked the truck in Matt's driveway, safe, and reached with trembling fingers into her pocket to find the house keys, that she picked them up again off the front seat.

A pair of green Vuarnet sunglasses, the lenses coated with soot.

Jason's sunglasses.

PART TWO

PART TWO

17

TWO WEEKS PASSED.

Jason had disappeared. He might be dead, or he might be on the run. The police were looking for him. Quentin de Beers's death had been ruled a homicide. Sarah and Molly had holed up in the house at Regan Beach and refused to talk to anyone. For the moment the situation had developed the kind of surface calm of a house teetering at the edge of a slippery hillside just before a severe winter storm.

Nina told no one about her visit to Wright's Lake. She needed some time to sort out why she had picked up a pair of sunglasses from the cabin floor, and why she had used a pay phone to make her 911 call untraceable.

She was obstructing the police investigation and concealing possible evidence in a homicide, offenses that could easily lead to disbarment and the loss of her law practice. Every day that she delayed telling the police what she had seen and done, she knew she exposed herself further. This frightened her very much. Yet she

still fought the tide of reasons to come forward, obsti-
nately and instinctively.

About a week after the fire, she woke up at three
A.M., her mind racing. She had been dreaming about
the waves at Asilomar.

When she was fifteen years old at Pacific Grove High
School, Nina had learned to surf. A boyfriend taught
her and helped her find a wetsuit and a board she could
handle. When they broke up, Nina kept surfing, from
Asilomar State Beach near Monterey to Steamer's
Landing at Santa Cruz sixty miles around Monterey
Bay. Most of the time she went alone, or with Matt.
For two years she lived for the cold clean waves, the
moment of truth when she pulled herself up on the
board and went for it.

Surfing made her aware of the complete indifference
of nature. The waves were powerful forces, predictable
sometimes, but utterly unconcerned with the small be-
ings in rubber suits trying to stay astride them. When
possible, she cooperated with the waves and enjoyed
their power, but sometimes she had to resist them. She
learned to watch them and see how they were running
before she went out, to pace herself and come in when
she was too tired, and to paddle out fast to get over the
ones that were too big and dangerous, or dive to avoid
them.

Now, in the middle of the night, in the silent sleeping house, at the hour when insights come, she realized
that she practiced law like that. She tried to assess the
dangers and be prudent, to ride whatever situation she
found herself in and save her energy, but sometimes
her instincts told her she had to fight, to intervene, to
paddle against the tide of events.

During the fire, and most strongly when she saw the

sunglasses on the cabin floor, she remembered sensing a force that seemed to her to be as aloof from human concerns as the moon pulling the tidal swell, catching her up and pulling her into the confusion. It had felt like her days in the ocean years before.

Instinctively, she had resisted. She had intervened to try to change the way things were going.

She got up and drank a glass of water in the bathroom, re-living that moment. She had not taken the sunglasses because she thought Jason had killed his grandfather and she wanted to cover up for him. She had intervened because she had instantly known that they would take Jason beyond any help, and that seemed inhuman to her. She had not identified herself to the 911 dispatcher because, as a witness, she would become powerless, just another piece of evidence, losing both her ability to stand outside the situation as a lawyer and her capacity to influence events.

Sure, she had done a risky thing, but when she took on Sarah as a client, she had agreed to become Sarah's ally in her central struggle, whatever that might be. The legal form the struggle took didn't matter. That was the kind of lawyer she was, for better or worse. She took on the person, not the case. As it turned out, Sarah's struggle was very much like her own—to protect the children, to learn how to survive alone, to find solid ground to stand on.

Back in bed, lying under the warm covers in the dark, Nina made one more discovery before she fell back into sleep. There was another, more obscure, reason why she had chosen not to do what the situation at Wright's Lake called for her to do.

During that one period in her life, day after day, winter and summer, she had plunged into the ocean to test herself against the waves and try her damnedest to make them serve human purposes. This situation felt just the same. She felt as if she were paddling out on a godawful day to test herself against the mysterious workings of the universe, trying to turn them to advantage.

She was playing this high-risk game because she had the chance, and because it was the only game she'd ever thought was worth playing.

Bob came back on the train to Truckee from San Francisco struggling, too, having left his father without knowing when he might see him again. She broke from everything to let him rebalance, go through a combative phase for a day or two while he blamed her for keeping him from his father, and, with the lovely inability of youth to hold a grudge for more than five minutes, return to his normal exuberance. The sixth-grade school year began and he settled into the drudgery of daily homework.

The calm broke almost three weeks after the fire, in the second week of September. Sandy beckoned Nina over to her desk with a finger, which meant there was big news.

"They found him," Sandy said in a discreet undertone. Her one o'clock, a litigious and hot-tempered fellow with a red beard who wanted her to take over a dubious suit against his employer, sat on the edge of a reception-area chair. Nina greeted him pleasantly, and said, "Excuse me just for a minute, Mr. Hogue."

"I have to be back at work."

"I'm sorry. I'll be right with you."

"I brought all the documents today. Every one. Like you said. This'll take a lot of time." Three cardboard boxes spilling out dog-eared handwritten papers lay on the floor beside him. Nina cast them an unhappy glance and tried to smile.

"Right with you," she repeated. She followed Sandy into her private office and shut the door. "Found who?" she asked Sandy, who had installed herself in one of the client chairs and was looking critically around the office.

"It's too hot in here again. You better talk to the landlord. I told you that," Sandy said, starting in on a familiar refrain.

"It's always too hot in here. I roast or I freeze. I'd rather roast. The landlord can't fix it. Now, who did they find?"

"Jason. He's alive and kicking, but he's sitting in the county jail. Sarah called half an hour ago."

Nina let this sink in. Jason wasn't dead. "Thank God," she said. "Sarah's been so anxious. But—he's been arrested?"

"You don't push him hard enough. The landlord."

"Tell you what, Sandy. You talk to the landlord. With my blessing." Sandy shook her head. Her long silver earrings caught the light.

"He wouldn't pay attention to me."

"Now, about Jason!"

"Also, I found a house for you, but you have to be willing to push the seller. A house for you to buy, if you don't blow it."

"We'll talk about that later! Jason—"

"Jason's in jail. He's not going anywhere. His appointments have all been canceled. This house is in Tahoe Paradise, the neighborhood you wanted."

"Which jail?"

"Right here in town. They picked him up in Las

Vegas. You could get this place for under market value. I know the seller. You should go over and look at it."

"Give me the message!" Nina read it, then picked up the phone. "Tell Mr. Hogue I'll need one more minute."

"You don't have time to go over to the jail this afternoon—"

"Sandy."

"You've got a deposition at Boulder Hospital at two. And you have four more client appointments this afternoon."

"Sarah? This is Nina." Nina listened on the phone for a few seconds, then said, "I'm really blocked up this afternoon. . . ." She listened a little longer. Sandy sat watching her, hands folded, lips compressed. Nina said, "Okay. I'll meet you at the jail in ten minutes." She hung up the phone and said to Sandy, "I have to go. I'll make the deposition and the late-afternoon appointments. But I have to cancel Mr. Hogue."

"He'll enjoy hearing that."

"Tell Mr. Hogue I had an emergency." She picked up her briefcase.

"There's no back way out," Sandy said. "I suppose you could climb out the window. Otherwise you'll have to tell him yourself." Nina remembered the boxes and the joyful anticipation on Mr. Hogue's face. She actually went to the window that looked out over the lake, trying the latch and finding it jammed.

"Which is why it's so hot in here," Sandy said. "I told you."

"Damn!"

"Here's the address of the house for sale. Stop by when you're done at the jail." She inserted it into the front pocket of Nina's briefcase.

"Sandy, you go out and get rid of him. I'll wait in here. Set it up for tomorrow."

"Oh, no," Sandy said. "He won't leave without hearing from you personally. He's a very stubborn man, and he's waited for two weeks for this appointment."

"This is one of the things I pay your salary for, Sandy."

"That pittance?"

Neither of them moved. Nina smelled negotiation in the air. "Out with it," she said.

"Wish could fix that window, if you set it up with the landlord," Sandy said immediately. "He would do it for twenty-five bucks." Wish, Sandy's son, already cleaned the office and delivered papers for the office.

"All right! I'll talk to the landlord! Now I have to go!"

"Just let me give Mr. Hogue one swift kick, and you're out of here." Sandy closed the door and Nina heard her breaking the bad news to Mr. Hogue. For a minute her voice and his mingled in a perverse duet, hers low and deep, his high and shrill. Then the outer door slammed shut and Sandy knocked on the door, saying, "It's safe now."

"Thanks. What did you say?"

"I told him you climbed out the window," Sandy said.

Nina, who was halfway out the door, said, "What? You're kidding."

"I told you before," Sandy said. "I never kid."

Sarah met her outside the jail building. "I've seen him," she said. "He's in rotten shape. We've got to do something right away to get him out of there." Her clothes, a blue raw silk blouse and matching pants, suited her, and her face and voice were resolute. But her legs seemed to be hurting her; she leaned against the wall and shifted from foot to foot.

"Come over here to my portable office, and we'll talk for a minute." Nina led her to a bench and helped her sit down.

"He's lost weight. He was staying at some cheap motel right off the Strip in Las Vegas, scrounging for meals. When he got down to his last fifty dollars, he decided to put it all on red on the roulette wheel at Circus Circus. Of course, he lost. Casino security noticed how young he looked and asked for his driver's license. When they saw he was just nineteen, they took him to a little office and checked him out instead of just eighty-sixing him. They found his face on some kind of computer notice system they have. He tried to run, but the security man knocked him down and arrested him."

"Oh, boy."

"They told him he could talk to a Nevada lawyer, but he said, 'No, just ship me back to Tahoe.' He says he was too tired to care anymore."

"Because of his age, the transfer may not have been valid. Or the arrest, possibly," Nina said. "He should have had an attorney's advice. What's the reason for the California hold on him?"

"Oh, God, Nina, didn't Sandy tell you? He's been booked for murdering his own grandfather. He asked me to call you."

Nina's mind jumped to the fast track.

"Did he say whether he made any statements to the police in Nevada or California?"

"He knows his rights. He's keeping his mouth shut until you come."

"Good. Very good. Unfortunately, I'm short on time. I'm going over there right now, and I'll call you about six at home. Okay?"

"Call earlier if you can. Call as soon as you can."

"I'll try."

"Molly—can she see him? She really wants to. She's been . . . she hasn't been well."

"Maybe tomorrow."

"Is he going to be all right? I mean, he's never been in a place like that. They won't mistreat him?"

"Don't worry. It's a well-supervised jail. I'll see if I can get him into a single. He's very young. He'll be watched."

"A single. It sounds like a cheap motel."

"Give me twenty dollars, if you have it. I'll pass it on to the guard in case there are commissary privileges today. And I'll let you know what personal things you can bring him tomorrow."

"Thank you, Nina. You know—"

"Don't worry about it. I'm going now. Can you be strong for Jason, Sarah? He's going to need you."

"I'll give it everything I have."

Nina buzzed at the inner door and stood patiently looking at the Police Association athletic trophies in their glass case, the only decoration in the jail ante-room. Why the police would want to display their trophies to inmates and their relatives and lawyers was beyond her. The inner door finally buzzed and she walked down the short, ill-lit hall to the guard at the final door.

Five minutes later she was facing Jason at the glass,

she on one side in her cubicle, he on the other. On her side, freedom; on his, captivity. His cubicle was glassed in all around so he could be watched, and she feared, overheard, although she had never been able to confirm her suspicions on that score.

He wore the regulation orange jumpsuit, too short in the legs and arms, his shoulders stretching the material awkwardly tight. His blond hair had grown out somewhat; his sensitive face with the startling dark eyebrows looked thinner than she remembered. Every time she saw Jason, she remembered that Bob might look like this in a few years, a boy peering out of a man's eyes.

But these blue eyes were wounded. He looked much different from other young men his age; his expression was grave. Nina had never seen him smile. Too heavy a weight had fallen on him too early. Picking up the phone that connected them, he said, "My mother was sure you'd come."

"I just got the message. How are they treating you?"

"Better than the Nevada cops."

"Any injuries?"

"Just to my pride."

"Well, Jason," Nina said. "You're in some trouble."

"You can say that again."

"You decided on the spur of the moment to take a two-week vacation in Vegas?"

"No. I was running. I admit that. But not because I killed my grandfather."

"Before we go any further, Jason: this conversation isn't privileged at this point. I'm not your attorney as to the charges that have put you here."

He ran his hand through his hair. His drawn face took on a suffering aspect that was becoming familiar.

"You want me to defend you on this murder charge?"

"Yes. I trust you to help me."

"Did you talk to your mother about it?"

"She'll pay you. She told me she would."

"Why me?" Nina said. "What do you know about me?" And to her astonishment Jason launched into a detailed synopsis of her professional history, about the five years in San Francisco pursuing criminal appeals, about the two sensational murder trials she'd been involved in at Tahoe in the past two years, about her other criminal and civil trial work.

"I did a search on you on the Internet. Some news stories came up."

"Really? I'll have to try that."

"That was why I told Mom she should come to you about the motion to exhume my father's body," he said. "I really look up to you. Before all this happened—I hoped that one day I could go to law school. That'll never happen now. I was crazy to think I'd ever get out of this town."

As he spoke he stroked his cheek gently with his free hand, looking away from her, comforting himself with his own hand, as if he'd been comfortless all his life.

"Have you been charged with illegally disinterring the body of your father?"

"Not that I know of."

"Okay. I can find out more on that."

"So you'll represent me?"

"I'm considering that now, Jason. Since we're contemplating an attorney-client relationship, our conversation has now become privileged."

"Okay."

"So let me ask you some questions. If I don't want

you to go on at any point, I'll stop you. Understand?"
The boy nodded but still stroked his cheek absently and
looked away.

"Where were you on the Friday night before you
disappeared?" Nina said, bracing herself.

"I can't tell you that."

Taken aback, Nina said, "Were you at Kenny Munger's?"

"I can't tell you that."

"Were you at the cemetery? Or a cabin at Wright's
Lake?"

"These aren't questions I can answer. I'm sorry."

"But Jason, I can't defend you unless you're willing
to tell me your story. Nothing you say to me can be
repeated unless we both decide we want it repeated.
Not even to your mother."

"You won't represent me?" he said. "Why not?"

"Because I can't work in the dark. Come on, now, I
know you're nervous, but you have to trust me."

Some lawyers didn't want to know. Some lawyers
didn't believe anything the client said. Some clients
were too disturbed to know what the truth was.

Nina had to hear it from the client. Truth or lie from
here on out, she had to hear it. She hoped to hear why
a pair of Vuarnets lay on the cabin floor in the fiery
room. But no matter what he said, this was the moment when she would decide whether or not she could
help him. She wanted to help him because of Sarah,
but she had to feel a connection with him too. A
murder defense took such a cruel toll on the defense
lawyer; it couldn't be done for money or for the experience. It had to be worth the hellish pressure.

"I do trust you," Jason was saying. "I just don't want
to talk about Friday night. Or Saturday. I'm sorry."

"You won't tell me anything about that time period?"

"I can't."

"Then I can't help you," Nina said. "Neither can any other lawyer." It was a simple, unsubtle bluff that usually brought people around. She got up.

"Okay," Jason mumbled. "Thanks for coming."

"What are you going to do?"

"Nothing."

"You have to do something."

"I'll get along without a lawyer."

"You can't do that."

"Whatever happens," Jason said.

"Even if you killed your grandfather, you need a lawyer's help to make sure you're treated fairly, Jason," Nina said, alarmed, sitting back down.

"I didn't kill my grandfather," Jason said. There was a long pause.

"Then talk to me!" Nina said, abandoning the pretense of walking out. She wanted to shake him. She was thinking about the feel of metal rims, the sooty lenses. . . .

"Can't you help me? They have to make a case against me, don't they? I don't have to testify, do I? Can't you sit with me, and make sure it's fair?"

She considered this. "It doesn't all happen at once," she said. "There's the arraignment and bail hearing, then a preliminary hearing, then other appearances, before there is a trial. Do you know when you're going to be arraigned?"

"Tomorrow at one-thirty. Municipal Court. The guard gave me a piece of paper." He held it up to the glass, and Nina read it carefully.

"All right. I'll be here at one to talk to you some

more and I'll make a special appearance at the hearing for you even if I don't end up representing you. Meantime, think about talking to me."

"Can I get bail?"

"Unlikely. Not after the trip to Las Vegas."

He closed his eyes and absorbed this blow.

"I hate being so useless to Molly and Mom. When can I see Molly?"

"Tomorrow at court, and then she can come for a visit in the afternoon. How are you doing in there?"

"It doesn't matter."

She looked at her watch. She had to go. She looked at him again. He gave her a small, encouraging smile this time. He was trying to be brave.

"Your mother and sister want to look out for you, Jason," she said. "You have to think about yourself for a while."

The kindness in her voice seemed to hurt him. Jason's throat worked, and he coughed, as if to prevent some other less welcome sound from escaping. "Thank you," he said. "I don't know why you're bothering with me. But thank you."

18

September is carmel's warmest month, high summer, the water at the white sand beach as warm as it gets, which is still wet suit temperature. The tourists are back buzzing in the hives of San Jose and the rest of Bay area. The locals can once again walk to the post office without having to push their way through the crowds; they can let their dogs run on the beach, and even shop at the boutiques and galleries that have been too full to walk into for months.

Paul had been paying attention to business since his return to Carmel, but he had also been cruising the art galleries in search of the perfect present for Kim.

Kim. The name evoked her fingertips tantalizing him in the firelight.

Since Tahoe he had been in an uneasy state, irritable, nervous even. Kim had done this to him, provoking him into a state of anticipation and arousal he hadn't felt since the years of suffering through the frenzy of adolescence. He cut himself shaving; he locked himself out of the van; he wrestled with the pillow at night and dreamed wet dreams of cheerleaders and stewardesses.

He felt had. He was disgusted at his complete capitulation to her, at how much he had enjoyed displaying himself for her like a slab of meat. And he wanted more, craved it. He wanted her to thrill and bewitch him some more.

While he was slurping down martinis, she had somehow gotten the upper hand. She had literally caught him with his pants down. He no longer wanted her; he needed her, needed to finish what had started, and soon. He had gone over the scene in his mind a thousand times, wondering what had prevented him that night from seizing her and making love to her, instead of sitting down like a perfect little gentleman to eat his salad.

He had always considered bedding a woman to be a simple and direct thing. He thought of himself as Ferdinand the Gentle Bull. He bulled his way gently past their defenses, and then it was missionary-style or doggie-style, or bouncy-bouncy on a chair.

Kim had expanded his horizons. Certain adventurous fantasies that he kept well-hidden had risen up that night with her and now devoured his every waking thought.

But before going any further he needed to make it clear that he was the boss. That was part of what was driving him crazy, that he hadn't had a chance to show her who was the boss.

Afterward she could tie him to the bed and screw him silly.

Underlying these half-frustrating, half-pleasurable contemplations was a lurking fear that she might not want to screw him silly. What if she wouldn't let him have her at all? What if she had just been making fun of him? Those possibilities made his blood boil with emotions too chaotic to sort out.

He had called to invite her to Carmel, and in her infuriatingly teasing manner she had sorta kinda promised to visit him over the weekend. That motivated a second call, to the cleaning lady for a special job on his Carmel Fields condo, a visit to Trader Joe's for Norwegian smoked salmon and frozen scallops for a *tête-à-tête* dinner, and a supply run for Sapphire gin and vermouth and no-sulfite organic wine—wouldn't want her to get a headache. He was ready, except for the present that would demonstrate how much he liked her.

He decided to buy her a painting, and he began looking around the hundred galleries within a half mile of his office.

He soon learned that very few of the galleries carried what Kim would call art. Kim liked brilliant color, new ideas. Carmel galleries were not exactly on the cutting edge of the art world. Over and over he saw the same old oceans at sunset, golf links at Pebble Beach, rainy Places Vendôme in an ersatz Paris, nudes with lopsided breasts. Occasionally he would happen upon a neon cactus or a gleaming abstract sculpture, but these didn't seem right either.

He was getting an education in upscale popular art, but not having much luck. Flavio's Art on Mission and Seventh had some small lithographs from Dalí's last years, pricey and degenerate. Paul liked Dalí because you could see what he meant, twisting and bending clocks and other objects to make his own warped sense out of prosaic things. He, at least, showed a sense of humor. He thought about buying one for a couple of days, but finally decided Kim didn't seem like a Dalí type, either.

As he went in and out of the art emporiums that week, Paul would mention Kim's name now and then, but her agent evidently hadn't cracked the Carmel market, because no one he spoke with had ever heard of her.

On his Friday lunch hour, after his regular char-broiled steak lunch at the Hog's Breath, Paul set forth again on his walking tour of downtown.

On Delores, three blocks from his office, he passed one of those quaint alcoves full of tiny shops that never seem to sell anything useful, and he turned into it. The first tiny gallery he saw was selling Henry Miller water-colors.

Henry Miller was more familiar territory than he'd been traveling. He was one of Paul's favorite writers. Paul had made the trek to Partington Ridge in Big Sur to see the shanty where Miller spent the seventies, and he had read everything Miller ever wrote, because he got a kick out of the warm, slapdash extravagance of the writing.

Miller was a heroic figure, much maligned, passion-ate to the last. He had written a line Paul had read long ago that had stayed with him: "The great artist is he who has conquered the romantic in himself." Miller had never been able to conquer the romantic, any more than Paul ever would. Paul knew that Miller had also painted in watercolor for most of his adult life, so he looked very curiously at the bright pictures on the walls, blotchy, sloppy, but brilliantly colored pictures of people and places.

Though the pictures weren't well drawn, they had a

joyous, youthful quality. Miller had been like that even as an old man. Paul could imagine Miller sitting outside at his table at Big Sur on a hot Sunday afternoon, half-crocked on sensimilla from the garden or a bottle of Pernod Fils sent by some faraway admirer, enjoying the breeze from the sea spread out below him, humming a ditty as he dotted blues and reds and oranges onto the damp paper.

The watercolors were grotesquely overpriced, but he was sure Kim would like one. He bought a small pic-ture of a boy in a blue cap and had it wrapped in silver paper with an orange bow. While the gallery owner, a lady in her sixties, patiently cut and folded the paper, Paul said pleasantly, "This is for a friend of mine who's an artist up at Tahoe."

"How nice."

"She's quite a well-known painter, I understand. Her agent sells a lot to foreign markets. Singapore and so forth."

"Mmm-hmm."

"Her name is Kim Voss. Ever seen any of her stuff?"

The lady lifted her head, considered, said, "Voss. Not that I recall."

"You know, I'd be curious to know if anything of hers is being sold around here," Paul said. "Do you have a catalog or something I could look at?"

"Sure." She pushed a huge book across the counter and said, "It's alphabetical. Look her up." She reached underneath for the ribbon and began constructing an outrageous, gardenia-shaped bow.

Paul thumbed through the catalog, which purported to be a kind of Who's Who of American artists. Voss, Voss . . .

No Voss was listed. He turned to the front and

looked at the date. The catalog was only a year old. "This is odd," he said. "She's not listed at all."

"Maybe she's just getting started."

"No, no. She's well established. She has a big studio, lots of works—"

"If she sells mostly in Asia and doesn't market her work here, she may not have been included," said the lady. "Or she may work under another name. It could be lots of things. Why don't you ask her?"

"I wouldn't want her to think I was checking up on her," Paul said. "I mean, I'm not. I'm just inquiring."

A beautiful Spanish-looking girl with long bleached-blond hair, wearing cutoffs and sandals, sashayed in, but Paul didn't even sneak a good look at her. He took the package off the counter, saying admiringly, "Great bow. Better than old Henry's picture." The saleswoman smiled for the first time. "I can't understand it," he went on. "How nobody around here knows who she is."

"As long as you know who she is."

"But I don't. That's the problem. She's this wonderful, successful artist and nobody's heard of her."

"You sound besotted," said the woman, squinting at him through Coke-bottle lenses. She shooed him out.

Back at the office, Paul set the package carefully on top of his computer hutch. The answering machine blinked. He pressed the *rewind* button.

"Paul?" Kim's throaty voice on the machine. "I can't make it this weekend. I have this important commission I'm working on. A big picture. Poor Paul."

Poor Paul saw himself in the little mirror on the door, a snarling, wolflike expression on his face. She was driving him insane!

"I'm wearing my overalls to paint in, but it's such a

hot day I didn't bother with a shirt or anything. I hope no one comes to the door, because I look really indecent," Kim was saying. "I wish you were here, Paul. If only you were here. It makes me feel warm just thinking about you."

He picked up the answer phone, squeezed it with terrible strength. . . .

"I do wish I could come," Kim's voice went on. "Think of me, will you? What a shame our work keeps us apart. Well, see you soon, I hope."

A click. Paul was panting, the little machine raised above his head, about to be hurled at the mirror—

"Paul?" Nina's voice now, clear and businesslike. He paused, hands high.

"I've got a new homicide case. Jason de Beers. Charged with killing his grandfather. Remember the man whose body disappeared from the cemetery? That was Jason's father, and you met his mother there, remember? I'm hoping you'd be able to take charge of the investigation. I want to put on a defense at the preliminary hearing. He was arraigned an hour ago. I just got back from court. We have only ten days. You'd have to start Monday. Uh, sorry to miss you. Let me know. Thanks."

A beep. As the machine began to reset, Paul punched in Nina's number. "I'm there," he told her. "Monday at eleven."

"Same hourly fees as usual?" Nina sounded like usual: brisk, smart as hell, and busy. He heard people talking in the background.

"Right. See you Monday." He couldn't keep the impatient note out of his voice. He wanted to call Kim. She thought she was safe, calling him like that, and—

taunting him, that was what she had been doing—frustration made him grit his teeth.

"I'll have Sandy put a file together for you. Paul . . ."

"Yeah."

"Don't you have any questions about it?"

"I'll find out more on Monday. Call Ginger Hirabayashi in Sac if you need a good all-around physical evidence expert. She'll know what other experts you might need."

"Okay." Paul thought he detected a melancholy note in her voice. "Did Bob get back from San Francisco all right?" he asked belatedly.

"Yes, he's back in school. He had a great time. His father's gone home to Wiesbaden. Bob wants to fly there at Christmas for a visit. He's only eleven, Paul. I just can't imagine letting him go. What do you think?"

"Keep him with you. You'd miss him too much," Paul said a little too brusquely. "You need him around so you'll do the tree thing and the presents thing."

"Hey, I've got a life, too, you know. I'd be fine. I just think—"

"You'd be at the office working on Christmas morning."

"I don't work all the time. And you don't have to sound so doggone scornful. Anyway, I'm going to try to get this case dismissed at the prelim stage. I don't think Collier has the evidence to take it to trial—"

Paul exploded. "Get real," he said. "It's a murder case. You can kiss life as we know it good-bye for the next six months. And then you'll take the next case, and the next. That's all you do, work. It's okay, it's your choice. I'd want you for my lawyer if I got busted on a felony."

"Thanks for the vote of confidence," Nina answered crisply, "but I'm way too fussy about my clients to take on an ill-tempered ex-cop with a chip on his shoulder the size of Gibraltar."

He was silent.

"What's the matter with you, Paul? You're jumping all over me!"

"You wish," Paul said cruelly and succinctly. There was a silence.

In the steely tone she usually reserved for not-very-credible witnesses, Nina said, "Take the burr out of your ass before you walk into my office, or don't come at all." The phone went down hard.

Paul looked inquiringly at his phone, as if it might tip him off about why in the world he had lit into Nina. He was completely over her. He had found somebody else. Nina deserved his pity, working all the time, nursing along this love fantasy of Hallowell, a half-man in love with work and a dead woman, in that order. He, Paul, had a life.

Kim didn't answer the phone. He snarled again, hanging up to save himself the final insult, the infernal sound of that damned beep.

19

MONDAY MORNING AT EIGHT A.M., AMID THE SMELL of Kona coffee rising from five mugs, Jason's defense team assembled for the first time in Nina's crowded office. She surveyed Paul propped in the corner chair, reading the *Tahoe Mirror*'s front-page account of Jason's arrest, a cranky expression on his face; Sandy, just now rolling in her steno chair, a pen clenched in her teeth; Sandy's gangly son Wish Whitefeather, who would serve as gofer and apprentice investigator, and Dr. Ginger Hirabayashi, who would handle forensic science and medical issues.

A cool breeze from the newly unjammed window cut the central heating, which never turned off. Outside, the aspens and a sycamore or two blended their yellows and oranges into the pine forest that stretched down to the lake.

"Folks, meet Dr. Hirabayashi," Nina said from behind her desk.

"Ginger, please." The consultant smiled. Wish and Sandy were looking her over. Paul, who had just met her in person after several long-distance associations with her, said, "Welcome to Tahoe."

"Let me tell you all about this lady," Nina went on. "Ginger has a Ph.D. in biochemistry, an M.D. from Johns Hopkins, and advanced training in forensic sciences from the FBI Intelligence Center at Langley. She left the FBI five years ago and went out on her own. She has sifted the ashes at Waco on behalf of some of the victims' families, and she helped dismantle the ATF cover-up at Ruby Ridge.

"Ginger is an expert on forensic pathology and works with a group of other consultants in the Sacramento area. Through her, we have access to expert help and testimony, if need be, on just about every branch of forensic science and medicine you can imagine. She is the scourge of the law enforcement community in northern California. We are lucky to have her."

Ginger wore jeans, a houndstooth-check sport jacket, and a white shirt with a Waterman fountain pen firmly affixed to the pocket. On her feet were a pair of black Doc Martens with soles as thick as small tires. Each earlobe was pierced three times and contained various small, unidentifiable objects. She wore no makeup, and her black hair was precision cut into a kind of military flattop. She sat just across from Nina's desk, skimming through the box of police reports Sandy had just given her, projecting awesome cool.

"I look forward to working with you guys," she said. She had a deep, confident voice that would be a big advantage on a witness stand. "It's a juicy murder case. Nina's pulled off some major upsets since she came to Tahoe. I hope we can make this another one."

She crossed one leg over the other at the ankle and gulped coffee.

"Well, let's get started," Nina said. "We are going for a dismissal at the preliminary hearing stage. Jason de Beers is nineteen years old and isn't going to fare very well in a jail cell for the many months it will take to get this case to trial. He's been denied bail because he fled the state. His family is in disarray. His mother and sister need his help.

"Here's how I see it. I think the district attorney's office has filed the murder charge prematurely. Collier Hallowell is banking on the fact that preliminary hearings are almost always continued by stipulation for weeks or months, giving everybody time to prepare. But the law still says the defendant has a right to the hearing within ten days. I've advised the Court and counsel that we won't agree to a continuance."

"So we have . . . seven days," Sandy said. "Until next Monday. That's why I Fed Exed a box of reports to each of you on Friday, Paul and Ginger."

"That's not very much time to figure this out, is it?" Wish asked.

"The advantage we have is that the burden is on the prosecution. True, it isn't a heavy burden they carry at this stage. All they have to do is show probable cause that there was a murder, and that Jason was the perpetrator. But they have to build their edifice, and all we have to do is—"

"Lay one pipe bomb at a weak point," Wish said, his eyes gleaming.

"Well, I don't know if I'd put it that way. We can only find the weak points by testing every fact they're relying on. It's a matter of hard work. Paul, you're awfully quiet today. I hope you're not sulking." This last just slipped out of Nina's mouth. She had been aware from the moment he slouched into the office of the tension between them. She was still smarting from his crack on the phone, and he was evidently still mad at her.

Paul said from his corner, "Oh, I'm happy as a clam." Ginger looked back and forth at the two of them, and Nina felt slightly embarrassed.

"Ginger, now that you've looked over the paper-work we had as of Friday, what are your thoughts?" she said quickly.

"The autopsy report is so half-assed I don't see how you can cross-examine from it," Ginger said. "What you'd expect from a cow town like this. Good old Doc Clauson. I know him. He has good hands, but he can't write for shit."

"Why don't you explain for all of us Doc Clauson's conclusion as to the cause of death of Quentin de Beers, and anything else you think is significant about the report," Nina said.

"Sure. It's an episode right out of *I Love Lucy*. Quentin de Beers was the man who wouldn't die. According to the report, first he was struck with a shovel. This blow didn't fracture his skull.

"But—and this was supposedly the second event— Quentin had a problem, a six-millimeter aneurysm located deep in the brain. The conclusion is that the trauma of the blow ruptured the aneurysm. Massive subarachnoid hemorrhaging followed. He died within about twenty minutes.

"According to Clauson, he could have died en route to Wright's Lake or at the cabin. But there's a third event—he also was burned in the fire at the cabin.

Clauson concludes that the fire didn't contribute to or cause the death, and I do agree with that.

"But cause of death is still a weak point in the report. I can't follow what Clauson's saying. I want to do some quick research on the aneurysm business. Clauson almost missed the aneurysm altogether due to the massive blood clots he found when he opened up the skull. I'm not satisfied that he has the sequence of events right."

"What's an aneurysm?" Wish asked.

"A dilated blood vessel, often found in the brain," Ginger said. "A little part of the wall of a blood vessel has ballooned out for whatever reason, and the wall stretches and gets thinner and thinner. And one day the wall breaks and blood goes pouring out into the rest of the brain. A burst aneurysm is often fatal."

"How do you get one in the first place, though?" Wish persisted.

"Some people are born with a predisposition to developing an aneurysm. About one out of twenty people walk around with an aneurysm their whole life, die of old age, and it's only found on autopsy. Or a blood vessel may become blocked with atherosclerotic deposits and balloon into an aneurysm. Quentin had advanced atherosclerosis. His heart could have used a triple bypass. From what I gather in this shit report."

"Okay," Nina said. "So: Issue One. Can we dismantle the autopsy report, show that the death couldn't have happened the way Doc Clauson says it did? Ginger and I have that one."

Ginger said, "The other big problem I see in the forensics area is the fingerprints. Let's call that Issue Two. Clauson has the shovel with prints from our guy on it. Sandy, where's the lab reports? Blood, blood, hmm. Here we go. Blood on the head of the shovel was Quentin's blood type. The perp didn't get hurt, looks like. They'll have to run a PCR on the blood to definitely link it to the body.

"The point is, there's no blood evidence linking Jason. The key is going to be the fingerprint evidence. They have two good prints of what they say is Jason's right thumb and forefinger on the handle of the shovel. Along with bunches of partials they haven't identified. I'll work with my fingerprint consultant in Sacramento on that problem."

"That doesn't sound good," Wish said. "The fingerprints on the shovel."

"It never sounds good at first, Wish," Ginger said. "If it sounded good, the client wouldn't have been arrested. Get it? Our job is much simpler than theirs. They have to build the case. As to our role, if I may quote Nechaev, the immortal nihilist: 'Our task is terrible, total, universal and pitiless destruction.' It's so much easier to destroy than to build, and so much more fun." She turned to Nina. "That's all I've got at the moment."

"Thanks, Ginger. Paul, you're in charge of the investigation. What are your thoughts?" Nina said, turning a neutral face to him. Gratefully, she saw that Paul had shaken himself out of his funk. While he talked, she watched the sharp hazel eyes that never missed a thing. It seemed as though she hadn't really looked at him for a long time. He had a new stubble on his face, which she associated with the new girlfriend. He had taken off his windbreaker and his muscular body looked as if it had been receiving regular workouts.

Paul said, "I've been reading through some of the

statements taken by police the next morning. The mother—Sarah de Beers—says Jason didn't spend the night at home. He was supposedly living in town with a kid named Kenny Munger. Kenny says he spent the night elsewhere and can't alibi Jason. Wish and I will talk to the mother, the sister, the business associate, Leo whatshisname, and Kenny to start with." A smidgen of enthusiasm had crept into his voice. He seemed to be perking up a little.

They were all sitting up. Ginger's nonchalant confidence had a positive impact on them. It seemed inconceivable that she could ever lose a case. And Paul gave them a method to tame the disorder and make it less overwhelming.

Paul went on: "Which means Issue Three is alibis. Jason's lack of one, and everybody else's alibi. Now, I know we're not supposed to ask the client if he's guilty. And if he says anything, we pay him no mind. That's the good old American way. Don't ask, don't tell. However, I need to know if I'm supposed to be concentrating on getting this kid off. If you're planning to plead him out, Nina, get him a manslaughter conviction or something, I need to know that so I can ask the right questions."

Nina said, "I'm going to tell you what he told me. This is to be kept one hundred percent confidential. Jason denies that he killed his grandfather. I believe him."

"All right! It's so much more enjoyable to try to win a case, not just finesse it," Ginger said.

"But there's a problem. He won't tell me anything about his activities from Friday night to Sunday morning."

"And you still took the case?" Paul said incredulously. "That leaves us nothing to work with!"

"It leaves us the issues we've just gone over. I've agreed to take Jason as far as the prelim. After that, if he still won't talk to me, I'm going to have to get out."

Nobody spoke for a minute. Then Wish said excitedly, "This is so totally weird."

"Has he made any statements to the police? His mother? Anybody else?" Paul said.

Nina said, "Not a word. He handled himself well, Paul. He's only nineteen, Wish's age, but he's quite sophisticated, I think."

"The police are tearing the countryside apart looking for Quentin's car," Paul said. "However Jason, I mean the perp, got to the cemetery, he must have driven Quentin's car up to the cabin, because Quentin's car is gone. There will be evidence in that car. There will be something to identify the perp."

"Paul is right. Bodily fluids may have leaked through the blanket into the trunk," Ginger said. "There will be soil from the grave site. In the driver's seat, on the steering wheel, in the trunk, there will be fibers, hair, fingerprints, something that may identify the driver."

Nina said, "Why do you think I insisted on having the hearing within ten days? The idea is to rush the police so much, they don't have time to find the car. Just in case."

"That's a cheap tactic," Paul said.

"If we're too cheap for you, the door's right there."

Sandy had been scribbling notes in her obscure shorthand. She raised her arm and put her hand in a stop sign, saying "Knock it off, you two." She looked back and forth from Paul to Nina. "Well?" she said. "Can I say something now?"

Nina stopped glaring at Paul, and said, "Please. Go ahead," with elaborate courtesy.

"Who made the 911 call?" Sandy said.

A huge, pregnant silence.

"Out of the mouths of babes . . ." Paul said, grinning, his eyebrows going up and down like Groucho Marx's. The corner of Sandy's mouth went up very slightly. She kicked his chair, almost knocking him off it.

"Anytime, big boy," she said. "I'll be your babe."

"You know, Sandy, that 911 call had not even crossed my mind. It just goes to show how easy it is to get lost in details," Paul said. "The perp was a woman. It all makes sense. Jason's protecting someone. His mother or his sister. I'm going to get on that."

"That's it, Mom," Wish said. "You solved the case! And Jason's not guilty!"

"So what's the defense?" Paul persisted. *"Cherchez la femme?"*

They all looked at Nina. She hoped they weren't looking through her. "Let's just do our work," she said. "We don't have to decide that yet. Let's just keep in mind that there is a lot we don't know. He says he didn't do it. I'm taking those words at face value for now. Remember who we are. We've taken on the heavy burden of saving his liberty, maybe his life. We are the only part of the justice system that believes in him. Powerful forces are arrayed against him. We're all he has."

"Don't worry, Nina. We'll save him," Wish said. Nina saw that he had been moved by her words.

But Paul, tough ex-cop that he was, just looked out the window, his face carefully blank.

"Er, Paul," Nina said after the rest of them had left

the office, "I need to talk to you so you won't go off looking in the wrong direction. About the 911 call."

Paul gave her a quizzical look, and said, "Shoot."

So she told him everything, because she had to. Everything except the sunglasses.

20

TACKED CROOKEDLY TO KENNY MUNGER'S APART-
ment door, a note read *Catch you later*.

Wish ignored it, pounding loudly and futilely.
"What do we do now?" he asked Paul. Paul's answer
was to sit down on the floor against the door in the
only sliver of sunlight piercing the squalid hallway.
Wish joined him.

An hour or so passed. Paul meditated upon many
things: the price of gas at Tahoe (high), the glance
Nina had shot him that morning (covert), Ginger Hirabayashi's hair (a dyke 'do if he'd ever seen one), Kim
(more four-poster-bed fantasies). Settling restively into
the last, he closed his eyes and sank into a light doze.

Now and then another resident of the building
squeezed by them, pushing a stroller or a walker. The
rug in the hall was brown; the walls were blue. Kim
was squirming.

"Uh, Paul."

He tried to ignore the voice. Nina was squirming,
and her clothing was awry, revealing—

"Paul?"

"What!"

"You want to play hearts or something?" Wish displayed a pack of cards with a hole punched through the middle, a casino castoff.

"No!"

Another epoch went by. Paul's left foot fell asleep. He opened one eye, warily. Wish, sitting on the opposite side of the hall, was staring unblinkingly at him.

"What do you think you're doing?" Paul barked.

"I've been here before," Wish said. "That's not a problem, right? So please don't fire me." This brought both of Paul's eyes into focus.

"Fire you? What are you talking about?"

"Well, see, I know Kenny. I know Molly and Jason too. One time I came to Kenny's apartment. Last year, when we were seniors. But it was just a party. So, you know, I can keep a clear head. Don't worry about me."

Paul straightened himself up, pushing the small of his back against the door, saying, "What're you talking about?"

"We all went to Kit Carson High together," Wish said. "I didn't want to say anything, because you might think I'm prejudiced and can't do my investigative duties."

"Don't be an idiot," Paul said. "Why would that matter? If you know these kids, it's a plus." He studied Wish, whose spidery legs in the pegged pants stretched across the hallway, wondering what in the world Wish had in common with people like Molly and Jason de Beers. "You're nineteen, too, aren't you? So you were in the same graduating class at school."

"So it's okay?"

"I just said so, didn't I?"

"Yeah, but you sounded mad."

"I'm not mad!"

"Then how come you're yelling?" Wish used the same phlegmatic gaze on Paul that his mother often used on Nina. Was this a special Washoe thing, this you-bug-on-a-pin, me-scientist-cataloging-outlandish-critter attitude? If so, it was no wonder the settlers had tried to wipe them out.

"Let's start over."

"Okay."

"You know the client?"

"Jason, Molly, and Kenny. Jason and Molly were in my class in high school all four years."

"Then I'd like to interview you."

Without changing his expression, Wish communicated his liking for this idea by saluting and saying, "Fire away, sir."

"Why didn't you tell me this before?"

"Because you might think I was prejudiced."

"Prejudiced for or against Jason?"

"Oh, for. Jason is totally a great person."

"Is he, now? Tell me about your school, Wish."

While Wish talked, Paul remembered his own high school years, his father dead and his mother trying to hold his family together on the dark side of San Francisco. He had been a poor kid like Wish; and high school seemed still to be the same rude awakening as to what really counts in American society: money to buy the right clothes. Money to take your friends home to a house that will impress them. Money to take girls places. Money for a car.

Wish, without money, had gotten along by becoming one of those shambling, good-natured guys who hang around the fringes and don't have any opinions, tolerated because they cultivate the persona of the completely harmless. He'd gone to work at fourteen, opening up a convenience store in town for the owner at six-thirty A.M., and he had never tried for the unreachable rings of popularity and respect. He hung around, always forbearing when the jocks and the social types made the same old stupid jokes about Indians.

Jason and Molly had been in the same class but as distant from him as the stars. "They always had a crowd around them, their group," he told Paul. "Jason played football. He was a quarterback. He set a state record for passing yardage in his senior year. Everybody thought he would take off for some East Coast college. Molly was always the girl lead in the school play, the head cheerleader, whatever. They both got good grades without even trying. I had to work so hard."

"Smart people study, Wish. Some just don't admit it." Paul had known people like Jason. His old friend and climbing buddy Jack, Nina's ex, used to be a little like that, coming from privilege, making everything look easy. He knew things weren't always as easy as they looked from the outside. "People must have envied them," Paul said.

"Some people you might envy," Wish said, "but everybody liked Jason and Molly. They didn't sink to a level you could envy. They were above it all."

"Hmm," Paul said again. "And Kenny? How does he fit in?"

"Nobody talked to Kenny when he started out. He was a junior when he came, I think. He was even lower on the totem pole than me. He played his reggae music and hung out with the losers. Then word got around that Kenny was some kind of genius. He was supposed to have an IQ so high, the school didn't believe it."

"And after that? He became more popular?"

"Oh, no. Being a brain is the kiss of death," Wish said. "That just made him more of an outcast. That was when he started pretending he was a comedian. Then Jason and Molly both, you know, talked to him, so other people did too. But he's not funny—that's the problem. Really, he's . . ."

"He's what?"

"One of those guys who acts stupid but power-trips in the background. He invents stuff; he hacks. He got admitted to Cal Tech, but he didn't go."

"Why not?"

Wish rubbed his fingers together, gave Paul a significant look.

"No money? He couldn't get a scholarship?"

"He got his tuition paid, but what good is that if you can't afford the dorm fees? His mom doesn't have any extra money but looks okay on paper. And he can't work; the program's too hard, and besides, he'd have trouble being a waiter or something."

"Why is that?"

"You'll see when you meet him."

"So you went to a party in this apartment last year?"

"Yeah. Last time I saw Jason and Molly. Right before graduation. Lots of weed and beer. Kenny'd been living on his own most of the year. Since the rest of us still lived with our parents, his place became a party pad, a good place to be bad. Half the senior class came. Kenny had a bunch of dry ice from somewhere, and he kept the drinks smoking in the bedroom. This band played really loud while he shot off some homemade fireworks in the parking lot. That night, Kenny was drunk. He didn't usually drink, so it hit him hard. He and Molly were hanging with each other."

"She was his girlfriend?"

"Oh, no. Not Molly. She's nobody's girlfriend. She dated but never stuck with anyone, kind of like Jason. And Kenny's a loser. You'll see. But she liked Kenny, I don't know why. Jason and Molly put up with him— Uh-oh. Speak of the devil."

Along the hallway limped a little guy built like a barrel on two peg legs, carrying a deli bag. Wish jumped up and went down the hall to meet him, while Paul massaged his foot, which had reached the hideous painful-tickle stage. They came up together, Wish now toting Kenny's bag. "This is Kenny," he said to Paul.

"Hi." Paul got up to lean nonchalantly against the door, wishing he could hop around and scream a little.

"Yo, massa," Kenny Munger said. Short and burly and blond, he wore a sleeveless Santa Cruz T-shirt that hung almost to his knees. Big round shoulders and long arms made a strange contrast to his gnarled legs. He wore a brace on his bad foot. An embroidered Jamaican cap striped with red, yellow, and green covered the top of his head. The heavy head with its big nose looked up at Paul; the eyes, where the dreads didn't cover them, were bright and sardonic.

"Yo, yourself," Paul said. "Thanks for seeing us on short notice."

"I brought lunch. Molly stopped by to tell me the lawyer's office was sending you over. What's her name again?"

"Nina Reilly."

"Attorney with tits," Kenny said. "Babe with a briefcase. Saw her in the paper. Jason sure can pick 'em." He started unlocking the door. He had a dead bolt as well as a Yale lock, custom devices that had not come with the apartment. Eventually the door swung open and Kenny limped in first, followed by Paul, also limping, feeling as if he had fallen into a *Monty Python* skit. Kenny said, "Chief, just set the bag on the counter there. Good boy. For that, I'll leave your squaw alone today."

"Uh, Kenny . . ."

"Yeah, Chief?" Kenny turned on the lights, then went across the living room to a large aquarium and knocked on the glass. "It's me, sweetness," he said to the fish within.

"This isn't a joke. Jason's really in trouble."

"Don't I know it. But you people are going to get him off, right? It's not like he actually killed his grandpa. Hey, it's crunchtime. Let's eat." He limped back to Wish and upended his sack, pouring out a package of pastrami, some French bread, and a two-liter bottle of ginger ale. "You'll join me, won't you?" he said with an affected British accent. "Just let me get the Grey Poupon."

While Kenny slathered mustard on the bread, keeping up a non-stop flow of patter, Paul had a look around. He could feel Kenny's eyes on him, but Kenny never missed a beat. He and Wish were talking about some scatological event that had occurred at the party Wish had mentioned.

The living room Nina had described to him no longer existed. A neat green-and-black Baja throw blanketed the couch. A large-screen TV sat primly angled in the corner. Girlie magazines were stacked tidily on a coffee table next to the bubbling lava lamp. A beanbag chair encircled by a stained rug faced the TV. A Bob Marley concert poster had been tacked to the wall, next to a flag with green, yellow, and red stripes. Wandering around, Paul tried, as unobtrusively as possible, the door to the bedroom, finding it locked.

During her visit after Molly's suicide attempt, Nina had described seeing tools, chemical equipment, and all kinds of gear that she couldn't identify, so Kenny Munger must have cleaned house since then, leaving this simulacrum of a living room, devoid even of the computer.

"Lunchy-wunchy, Dad," Kenny called out from across the room. They sat down on bar stools at the kitchen counter and Kenny, adopting the gracious air of a host at a formal dinner, showed them the label on the plastic bottle, poured an ounce or so of ginger ale into a paper cup, sniffed and tasted it, swishing the stuff around in his mouth. "An excellent year, 1997, IMHO," he said, pouring out paper cupfuls for all.

Paul must have shown his lack of comprehension, since Wish filled him in while Kenny drank it down, watching them with a smile.

"Computerese for 'in my humble opinion,' " Wish said. "Don't you ever visit the on-line chat rooms?"

Kenny took one of the pile of sandwiches, parted the hair that fell over his face, and dug in, gesturing for them to follow, which they did, lighting into pastrami as slippery and delicious as Paul remembered from Manhattan.

While they ate, Kenny chattered on. Paul couldn't tell whether he was impelled by nerves or just a monumental ego kindled by an audience. Kenny was Robin Williams without the talent, jumping from character to character and never landing a funny line. Humor had probably worked as a longtime compensation for his ugliness, but he desperately needed a new shtick.

"Lived here long?" Paul asked between bites.

"The interview starts . . . now!" Kenny said in an announcer's voice through a mouthful of pastrami. He wiped his mouth with his hand.

Licking his lips, he made a face, and in a declamatory tone said, "Ossifer, I declare as follows: I moved here when my mother moved to Walnut Creek two years ago to live with her new boyfriend. Who could turn down an opportunity like this: a country estate with a pool, service in the form of quaint old Mr. La Soeur, our beloved landlord, and the occasional scintillating visitor such as yourself. The rent is high, naturally, but who can put a price on such quality?" He gestured at the kitchen cubicle. "A man like me, well, you can probably tell women tend to fawn. I needed a grand setting in which to quench my insatiable lusts, so I've been here ever since."

"Didn't you get in trouble with the school authorities? I mean, you were only seventeen."

"Ve haff our vays and mine vas to be eighteen at the time. Next question."

"How long have you known Jason de Beers?" Paul asked him, controlling his irritation. Kenny had gobbled up his first sandwich and was starting on his second. Wish chewed slowly, turning his head back and forth between the two of them like a spectator at a tennis match.

Kenny said, "Since I came here. Seems like all my life. Seems like we grew up together. Correction. He grew up. I grew in various directions. My foot grew this way, my back went thataway. Ar ar ar."

"You're friends?"

"Bosom buddies. Besom baddies. Rubber baby

buggy bumpers. Say it three times fast and you get another sandwich."

"No, thanks, but let me pay for this," Paul said. He held out a twenty-dollar bill, which Kenny tucked away. "Your buddy is in trouble," Paul said. "Isn't that worth a little straight talk?"

"Straight talk, straight walk. I'm bad at both."

"Yet you scored a perfect sixteen hundred on your SATs, Wish tells me."

"Big Chief have-um big mouth."

"Kenny—" Wish said.

"Fifteen-ninety. Not worth bragging about."

"Where were you on the Saturday night Quentin de Beers was killed?" Paul said.

Kenny sighed loudly. "Ask me a hard one. I was in Walnut Creek at my mother's latest wedding. I was the best man. I'll leave you to imagine what the groom looked like. Ar ar ar."

"What's your mother's phone number?" Paul said, failing to understand how Jason could move in with this geek, even temporarily. Kenny gave him the mother's number after some more encouragement. "Jason stayed with you for several days, until that Saturday. Why?"

"Just pursuing peace after Pater perished. Like some Abba Zabbas?"

"No," Paul said. "How did Jason feel about his father?"

Kenny's eyes flew to Paul's. He quickly dropped them again, but momentarily pulled forcefully from his fancies, he looked uncomfortable for the first time. "The details escape me."

Wish leaned over and poked Kenny in the chest.

Kenny jumped back, giving a little shriek. "You tell Paul, now," Wish said.

"So sorry. I just can't remember. There were so many delightful moments with Pater. Like the time he almost killed his wife. Accident, or Memorex?"

"When was that?" Paul interposed.

"Three years ago. Poor Sarah. Poor, poor Sarah."

"You think he set up that accident deliberately?" said Paul, not sure if he could believe anything Kenny said.

"Uh-hunh. Uh-hunh uh-hunh." He was doing a Goofy imitation now, nodding his head with an idiotic expression, the blond dreads flopping around him. Paul had just about had enough. "Jason told me about it," Kenny went on. "Ask him. Jason's a good boy. Everybody loves Jason."

Wish said, "I remember you used to call Jason some other name. Phoebus, right? And you called Molly another name the night of the party."

"Artemis. Virgin huntress."

"They had a name for you too."

"No, they didn't," Kenny said, and sweat sprang out on his forehead. Wish had succeeded in cutting through the crap somehow. Paul lay low, starting another pastrami sandwich.

"You ought to watch eating too much of that . . ." Wish said, giving all his attention to Paul and directing Kenny's that way too, blowing wide open Paul's attempt to fade into the background. "That stuff can be lethal." To Kenny, he said, "Yeah, they did. Heff or something. Because you make stuff. You told me about it at the party."

"I would never tell you anything, Chief."

"You were drunk," Wish said, leaning in to close

the gap between them. "You can tease me if you want. But I don't like you clowning around when Jason needs help," he said.

"So sue me." But Kenny shied back, shaking his unkempt locks with his hands as if agitating their spirit might ward off Wish. All attitude aside, Paul thought Wish exercised some power over Kenny. Maybe Kenny found Wish physically intimidating. Wish was large, Paul would give him that. On the intimidation scale, Paul would rate Wish at about the same level as a goldfish, but he wasn't five feet tall like Kenny, either.

"What about Molly? You still ready to die for her?" Wish persisted.

"Total and absolute denial," said Kenny. "Molly and I are just such good friends."

"As if," Wish said, but he seemed to have run out of steam.

Kenny rapidly drained what remained of his soda, emitted a long rumbling belch, which seemed to have a calming effect on him, and said, "Good Lord, I'm teddibly late. I must be off to the manicurist. You'll excuse me, gentlemen?"

"One more thing, Kenny," Paul said. "Where's all the equipment that was sitting around here when Ms. Reilly came to the apartment? What are you working on now?"

Kenny waved his finger like a metronome at Paul, saying, "You cheated. That was two questions. One. Two. Session terminates . . . now." Paul estimated the distance of Kenny's finger from his teeth, contemplating whether to bite it off.

"What he means is, can we go in the back room where you keep all the fireworks and stuff, Kenny?" Wish said. Now Kenny couldn't sit still any longer. He slid off the chair, shaking his locks in a violent negative, and hopped around the scarred counter, rattling out more of his jive.

"Kenny, what's a sugar rocket?" Paul said, cutting in. Kenny stopped dead in the middle of a sentence.

"A sugar rocket?" he said. The mannerisms fell away and Paul was facing a homely, scared young man. "Why do you want to know?" Kenny asked.

"Ms. Reilly saw it in one of your books, before you hid the book," Paul said. "What is it?"

"She did? A book of mine? I don't recall that."

"Well, what is a sugar rocket? You're obviously familiar with that term. I'm curious."

"You have to go away," Kenny said. "I'm tired now." The frenetic mood had lifted from him as fast as it had come. He sat back down on a barstool, slowly, and rested his head in his hands.

"Tired," he said. "Oh, so tired. Go away now."

Paul gave up, and motioned his head toward the door. As soon as the door closed he heard the locks clicking and the dead bolt shoot into place behind them.

"Dreadlocks and deadlocks. What's he on?" Paul asked as they walked out to the parking lot.

"It's just his way," Wish said. "He doesn't use any hard drugs that I know of. You gotta feel sorry for him. He's so smart, but he's so incredibly fucked up."

"I wonder what's wrong with him. Medically, I mean. A clubfoot that wasn't fully correctable, I'd say. And maybe some kind of bone or growth hormone disorder. And he seems to have some sort of psychiatric problem. So why would Jason have anything to do with him? Why did Molly come to his party?"

"I think he did something for them," Wish said.

"Made them something. I wish I could remember what Molly called him that night."

"I liked the way you picked up the slack in there, Wish."

"I did good?"

"You did good. So what did we learn?"

"Jason really doesn't have anybody who can say he was at the apartment that night."

"That's right. I'm going to call Kenny's mother, though, make sure he checks out. That's the rule. Confirm everything. What else?"

"More about how Jason wasn't too thrilled with his father. But he's not under arrest for killing his father." They got in the van. "Where to next?"

"Prize's. Leo Tarrant is remodeling the casino. He's next on the list. Interesting, how modest Kenny was about the stuff in the back room."

"Some of the stuff he does might be illegal," Wish said, and his voice held just the tiniest note of boyish thrill. "Like the fireworks. He'll probably get evicted or something."

"So how does he support himself? He's not in college. His family doesn't have money to spare. He must be making money somehow, not that he's exactly flush."

"You got me there," Wish said. "Oh, now I remember. He called himself Hephaestus. It was some kind of game between the three of them. We were studying Greek mythology in our lit class. Phoebus, Artemis, and Hephaestus."

Prize's casino hadn't closed for its second round of remodeling in as many years, but in the oblivious way of casino habitués, its clientele seemed unfazed and just as eager as ever to stand around its blackjack tables, tripping blithely over ripped-out rugs and tossing money around like confetti to add to the general disorder. Paul and Wish muscled their way through the crowds, past the rows of noisy slots and the roulette table with its natty croupier, Wish taking it in pie-eyed. The kid wasn't even twenty-one. He'd obviously never been inside a casino.

Partitions ringed the Tonga Bar, screening the saws that shrilled inside. They ducked under a drop cloth hanging from the ceiling.

The bar, which for years was sheltered under a pseudo-Polynesian thatched roof and housed an immense tropical fish aquarium near the bottles, had been stripped of its magic. The fish tanks, glass walls streaked with gray scum, and the roof, thatches lying in piles on the floor, had gone, and so had the liquor. Two workers ran a sander, busily moving it over the left half of the wooden floor's newly dull and dusty finish. Another one, a girl, Paul noted, was measuring the shelf area.

They found Leo Tarrant leaning over some blueprints piled on a makeshift table in the place where the bartender usually stood. When he saw the two men, he straightened up and came over, hand outstretched. "You're from Nina Reilly's office?" he said.

Paul introduced himself and Wish. He had come to meet the sole surviving partner in De Beers Construction and the man Nina suspected was Sarah de Beers's lover. Leo Tarrant had come out of the deaths with very good prospects, and Paul was as suspicious of his good fortune as Nina was.

Yet his first impression was favorable. The hand Paul shook was strong and heavily callused. Close-cut hair light with sawdust looked practical and unaffected. A heavy tool bag hung from Tarrant's belt. His face was lean and cracked from years of building outside, and he had the sort of forearm that is shaped by a hammer. He was a working man, not a person born to boss. "Can we talk here?" he said, a little breathlessly. "I have a meeting with the manager coming up in a few minutes. The whole renovation Ray did a couple years ago is coming apart. It's not safe. We'll have to work on the roof, shore up the fire escapes. . . ."

"Sure, this is fine. I know the manager," Paul said. "He won't mind if we run a little late."

"You know Steve?"

"How's his wife? And the baby? I haven't seen them in a while."

"Oh, Michelle is fine. I saw her last night. Ivan's a tough little guy. Blond like his mother. He looks like he'll be up and walking any day now. How do you come to know Steve and Michelle? Oh, of course, you must have worked on the Patterson case. . . ."

"Seems like a long time ago," Paul said. "Now, to move forward in time a little here, Nina has a few things she's trying to clear up before Jason's preliminary hearing."

"Like I told her. Anything I can do."

Tarrant's face seemed open and honest, but you never knew. Paul decided to dive right in. "You've known the de Beers family for a long time. If we read it right, you're interested in Sarah de Beers."

"That's true. I do love Sarah. I've cared for her a long time. But I want one thing to be clear." He took a step closer. "She's never encouraged me. She was Ray's wife and she stayed his wife, right up to the end."

"I hear you," Paul said. "I take it that since Ray's death you have worked something out between the two of you?"

"No. She's half crazed worrying about Jason. I'm worried about him too. I've known him since he was twelve years old, and I just want to say, the police are nuts accusing him of murder. Jason is a wonderful kid. Maybe something happened, a fight or something, I don't know. They both had strong tempers. But murder . . ."

Tarrant's voice had faded. He raised so many questions in Paul's mind that it took a minute to sort them out. Finally, Paul said, "Let's assume Jason was in fact at the cemetery that night, and did in fact dig up his father's body. None of that is proven yet."

"But Jason's fingerprints were on the shovel that was used . . . on Quentin," Tarrant said. "I read it in the paper."

"Reading it in the paper doesn't make it so," Paul said. "There were also some partial prints yet to be identified. But assuming it was true for the moment—a kid who would pull a bizarre trick like that could do almost anything. Couldn't he?"

"Not Jason. Hurt Quentin deliberately? I can't believe that."

"He's not a happy kid, though, is he? What drives him?"

"Ray was a taskmaster. His kids had to be perfect, you know? Attractive, smart, popular, the whole thing. He was always riding them. The thing was, they were damn near perfect, but he couldn't see that. They are both great kids, and it burns me to see how unhappy their lives have been. Ray always found some nitpicking way to criticize them. He was never satisfied.

"He wouldn't let them grow wings and fly away like kids naturally do. He did what he could to prevent it. That kind of parent gets in more and more trouble as his kids get older. They start to challenge him."

"Ray probably had the same kind of upbringing," Paul said. "It runs through the generations."

"I imagine he did," Tarrant said, smiling a little. "Quentin was a fearsome old man, I can vouch for that. Anyway, this went on for a long time, and it was hard on Sarah. She was trying to be supportive of Ray."

"Meaning, she didn't love her husband?"

"She tried her best to be a good wife to him, don't get me wrong; but, no, she didn't love him. Ray was too overbearing. You've heard about Sarah's accident three years ago? Both the kids blamed Ray for not reinforcing that beam properly and then bringing Sarah out there."

"Were they right to blame him? You're the builder," Paul said.

Tarrant said, "Sure they were. But I don't think it was anything deliberate. Ray was negligent on most of his construction jobs. The worst thing was, Ray never took responsibility. He always acted like Sarah brought the whole thing on herself. Anyway, the twins had borne up under the yoke until then, you might say, but then they started acting like they hated him. It really got to him, being treated that way. He got harsher and harsher, but that only made things worse."

"And you? What about your feelings?"

"I had a fight with Ray after Sarah's accident. I was furious. It was the first time I'd realized—I had strong feelings for her. I think Ray knew it, but try as he might, he couldn't talk Quentin into getting rid of me.

Quentin kept the peace, and put Ray on a close leash after that. I stayed in the business because of Sarah."

"I don't understand why she stayed with Ray after that," Paul said. "It seems like the height of masochism."

"She wanted to keep the family together," Tarrant said. "But the twins were growing up. She wouldn't have stayed with him forever."

"Okay. How did Molly get along with Ray, by the way?"

"Poorly," Tarrant said. "She has a sharp tongue and she turned it on her father. He couldn't fight that way, so he dug in his heels and got tough on both of them. I'd never seen him hit her before that day on Tallac though."

"You were going to tell me your theory about why Jason might dig—"

"Yeah, right. Sarah made a mistake. She wanted to get the funeral over with, keep it small and private. That's what we did, and it was over. But Quentin couldn't get back from Singapore. He had dysentery or food poisoning or something, and he was laid up. Sarah couldn't wait forever. We couldn't wait for him. We went ahead.

"Quentin came back, and he had it in his head that something fishy had happened to Ray. I tried to talk to him, but I told you . . ."

"He was stubborn. Yeah, I got that."

"He wouldn't listen. By God, he was going to see Ray for himself. Jason and Molly told Sarah it was now or never. She had to take a stand against Quentin or he'd never let up on her until the day he died. She'd have a new slave driver. If she let him dig Ray up, she'd never make an independent decision again. They convinced her that this was the only way to show Quentin who was going to run Sarah's life from here on out. So Sarah fought the exhumation request."

"Seems like I heard something about you being against the exhumation."

"I was. I never trusted the old man much. I thought there was a good chance he'd work up some cock-amamy BS about Ray and drag the thing on for years. I tell you, I think he believed I had something to do with Ray's death. Probably because Ray hated me so much. I'm surprised Ray didn't put out a contract on me."

Paul decided to set that suggestive comment aside for later. "What happened after Quentin heard Sarah and the kids wanted to oppose the exhumation? Why did Sarah change her mind?"

"Quentin applied the old stranglehold and she gave in. Nagged her until she couldn't stand it anymore. And here's where I start guessing. I start thinking how Jason would have reacted to that. He would have been angry. He would have decided to defy his grandfather.

"Like I said, that's a daunting thought, because Jason almost never openly defied Ray or Quentin. He just worked around them as best he could. But Jason's young and strong and stubborn and proud. He might have decided Quentin wasn't going to get what he wanted, period. And went to the cemetery and took the body."

"He dug up his father's body to piss off his grandfather? And then fought with him?" Paul said. "I don't buy it."

"I hate to imagine them fighting. I don't even mean the physical part of it. I mean, the grandson fighting his grandfather over the body of his father. It's sick."

"So you see it."

"If Quentin surprised Jason, and Jason somehow got the upper hand, I guess they would fight. It's hard to accept. Jason admired the old guy. You know, grandparents are always easier to take than parents." Tarrant's shoulders slumped. "I like Jason. I've always liked him. We've gone fishing together, hunted together. This is bad enough for him, but what about his sister? And Sarah . . . it's bad."

Paul shook himself mentally. Tarrant's resignation almost had him convinced that Jason had dug up his father and killed his grandfather. He had to remember, the case was young yet. Tarrant stood patiently, his next appointment apparently gone out of his mind for the moment, his arms hanging loosely, waiting for Paul to take the lead.

Wish had listened without saying a word.

"Be that as it may . . ." Paul said. "No offense, but the de Beers men dying off so precipitously has left you with a clear field in the business, hasn't it?"

Tarrant's mouth firmed up, and he said, "It's ironic, all right. I was practically out on my ass a few weeks ago, and now I'm the only partner left."

"Business differences?"

"Call it that." Paul waited for more, but Tarrant wasn't in the mood for a discussion of his business differences with the de Beerses. He kept his mouth shut.

"What happens to the company now?" Paul asked him.

"Well, Ray left his share to Sarah, and I've already talked to her about buying her out over a couple of years if . . . if things don't work out. There's never been a public stock offering. It's an S Corporation under the tax laws, private offerings only."

"How about Quentin's share?" Paul said. "He was the founder. How many shares did he own?"

"Fifty-one percent. Ray owned thirty percent, and I owned the rest. Quentin hadn't changed a will he made years ago leaving most of his estate to Ray. If Ray died before Quentin the property was supposed to go to Jason and Molly equally. So things are messy right now. Sarah's opened probate proceedings and been appointed executrix of both wills. I'm managing the business until all this gets sorted out."

"Sarah didn't use Nina to help with the probate?"

"She thinks Nina has her hands full already," Tarrant said with a lopsided smile. "So my hope would be to buy out Quentin's heirs, Molly and Jason, and Quentin's lady friend—"

"Who's this lady friend?" Paul said.

"She only got one percent. She was pretty peeved about it, too. I could probably buy her out for fifteen thousand. I've made the offer, and she's thinking it over."

"So Quentin had a girlfriend."

"Oh, yes. The one time I met her, she seemed like an intelligent young woman, but some women aren't that interested in a career. The two of them were quite discreet. Quentin was careful to keep the relationship quiet, even though he'd been a widower for many years and could do whatever he wanted. We all knew about her, of course. Her name's Kim. Kim Voss. Wait a minute, I have her number here. I figured you'd want to talk to her—well, do you or don't you?"

Leo tried several times to hand the piece of paper to Paul, whose fingers had momentarily turned to rubber. Paul didn't need the number. The outlines of its inscription began to form delicate scars over his heart.

He managed to get a grip on the paper. *I don't date,* she'd said in that husky voice. And he'd believed every word. . . .

It was a punch in the gut, and he couldn't breathe—

"You look like you need to sit down," Tarrant said. He pulled up a bar stool covered with a drop cloth. "Here."

"I told you to go easy on that pastrami!" Wish said. "Here, let me get you some water." He took off, leaving Paul feeling cold and queasy, caught with his pants down again.

21

"HELLO, KIM."

She put her arms around his neck and kissed him, a deep, thrilling kiss. "The Henry Miller was exquisite. How sweet of you. I've put it in a place of honor. Come see." Again they passed through the desert inside the wall to the main studio, and again Paul looked at the paintings. The small, colorful Miller watercolor he had sent had the white wall leading to the courtyard all to itself. He remembered bitterly what it had cost.

Her paintings, observed for the first time out from behind his rose-colored glasses, suddenly looked wildly self-indulgent. Was she a decent artist or not? He didn't know anymore. His feelings, without the magic, had also degraded. What was left was commonplace lust. Kim was a liar and a phony and maybe some other things as well.

He, himself, was feeling rather crude and self-indulgent at the moment. Kim was part of both his cases and he still needed to deal with that, but before he did, he wanted his due.

Smelling as sweet and desirable as a field of gardenias, she wore a long yellow cotton shift that accentuated the positive, the lean legs and the dainty bare feet. Her teeth and eyes practically blazed from their settings in the deep tan of her face. He drew her down on the rug near the sofa, and she let him stroke her length, nuzzle her neck. Her hands began moving on him, well-practiced, he thought now. He pulled the shift up roughly and ran his hand between her soft thighs—

And they clamped shut like Scylla and Charybdis. "It's early yet, my love," she whispered.

He kept his hand on her legs and said, "Let's go to bed. Now."

She said, "We'll see. Let's have a drink first." He made another move on her, also rough, but she wriggled out of his grasp, saying, "Bad boy. Come on." She jumped up lightly and held out her hand to him, but he stayed where he was, thinking: She's never going to come through; she's making a fool of me. He still wanted her, but in a new, nasty way.

The thought crossed his mind: I am stronger than she is. He knew he had to leave before he did something he'd regret.

The expression on his face must have alerted her that he had had enough. She moved away from him, smiling the great smile that had dazzled him, allowing him to get some control back over his feelings.

"I told you I'm celibate, Paul."

"Like hell."

"It's true. I like men, but I don't do that anymore. I've chosen freedom over passion."

"What's that supposed to mean?"

"I don't think you'd understand."

"Pretentious bullshit from a cheap little slut," Paul said. She bit her lip, looking wounded.

"Quentin de Beers," Paul said. "Well?"

"Oh." The look she turned on him now was calm, amused, showing no trace of surprise. "Is that what this is about?" She was one hell of a self-possessed woman. "This calls for a cigar," she said. "Come on, Paul, don't be such a baby. Let's go outside. Or leave. Take your pick."

He sat down in the courtyard, and she went through the martini routine as gracefully as she had the first time, but the performance left him cold and the drink tasted just as it always had before he met her, like drain cleaner. After a token tapping of glasses, Kim lit up a short stogie and sat puffing away, a pensive expression on her face.

Her lack of response and his rising curiosity had cooled his heat. If the object was to civilize him, it was working. Beyond the candles it was a moonless night, so the stars seemed to crowd in. A wisp of air silently carried warmth from the charcoal in the grill.

"You disappoint me," he said. "You lied. About not being with someone, and about your art."

"Do you have any idea how hard it is to break into the art world, Paul?" Kim said. "Especially for a woman with no credentials, no connections? It's almost impossible. But I am trying. I am a very good artist, Paul. I know it. I will be famous one day."

"Have you ever sold a painting? Even one?"

"To Quentin. To you. How did you find out about Quentin?"

"I'm working the defense for Jason de Beers."

"Oh. Of course. There would be an investigator."

"What about all the nonsense you gave me about galleries, and the Singapore collectors? I checked. None of the art dealers I talked to ever heard of you."

Kim laughed, a warm, uncomplicated laugh. "I gave you the story Quentin gave me."

"What are you talking about?"

"I met Quentin about four years ago, when I came to Tahoe. I was living in a tiny cabin with bad plumbing and bad light, spending all my time painting. One fine summer day I met him at an art fair in Tahoe City. He admired my work, then invited me to dinner."

"What did you find in each other?"

"He was lonely. He wanted the company of a woman he could talk to. My motives were simple. I was down to thirty-five dollars in my checking account."

"So you became his mistress."

"Mistress," Kim mused. "After his wife died, Quentin did want a mistress, but he couldn't find one. He liked young women, but they only wanted his money and didn't know how to take care of a man like him. The trouble is, the profession of mistress has disappeared. Quentin was looking for an anachronism."

"He found you."

"He scammed me," Kim said. "He decided he liked my company, and he saw I was broke. He wanted to give me money, but he was afraid I would be insulted if he suggested that he support me in exchange for my exclusive company. So the next time he went to Singapore, he told me he took some of my paintings with him. He had a gallery owner there make up some fake receipts showing the paintings had been sold to a wealthy Chinese collector. He gave me the money. I was very grateful." She laughed her special laugh, a low, husky sound that filled the courtyard with its amusement. "I was getting very good prices.

"For two years he kept it up. Then one day I got a call from the local dump. A collector—a garbage collector! Funny, isn't it?—had picked up one of my paintings in Quentin's trash, and he thought there might be a mistake. My name was written in the corner, so he looked me up in the phone book. The funny old bastard didn't know what to do with the paintings, so he was just throwing them away."

"Is this another story, Kim?" Paul said. "Because—"

"It's true. Cross my heart. Every bit. Well, I had to decide what to do. Quentin was a swine, but I had gotten used to living nicely. I could have just told him I knew, and continued to take his money, but he didn't deserve to get off that easily. So I never told him about the call. He kept giving me the money, and I painted my Singapore man at least a dozen more pictures. I had a lot of fun with them. I would throw a bunch of colors, different each time, on big canvases on the floor with dirt, needles, leaves, anything I could find in the garden that day. I pushed it around with a broom and told Quentin I was doing a series I called 'Synchronous Variations.' Each one took about five minutes. He kept up his charade and I kept up mine. Meantime, I kept painting my serious work, and I started trying to market it in San Francisco. We were both happy."

"You scammed each other," Paul said.

"I played, Paul. A sense of playfulness is important for a creative person. Also, being the one in control in a relationship," she said. "I have a feeling you know a lot about how important that is to some people." She poured him another martini and regarded the now hot grill.

"I thought you might like to try swordfish tonight," she said. "It's so good with kim chee and lots of lemon. You will stay, won't you?"

"I wouldn't miss the rest of this tale for the world." Tamed, at least temporarily, he put the fish steaks on the grill and let her feed him another dinner that was sheer ambrosia, and she told him about her early life on a hardscrabble ranch near Albuquerque. Her physicality was still overwhelming, but Paul realized he was now seeing the rest of her, the part that he had been blind to before. She was probably used to men coming on to her for the sex only. Maybe that was why she had hung up her spurs.

They finished off the meal with port and cheese. Then Kim brought her chair over to his and leaned her head against him.

"Are you wondering what Quentin and I did together if I'm so interested in celibacy?" she said. "We had dinner. He would tell me about his day, the union problems and lawsuits and slow subcontractors. Then he would give me a bath, and I massaged him. I posed for him sometimes, and he took pictures. He posed for me. I have several paintings of him. He took a great deal of pleasure in showing himself off." Paul felt a stab of embarrassment.

"Quentin was impotent. He was the quintessential man in the raincoat, able to get it up for a woman to see but unable to do anything with it. We played some very silly games. We had some fun."

"Did you talk to him about his son's death?"

"Only once, right after it happened. Quentin was shaken right down to the roots. He was so angry. And he wanted revenge. He thought his business partner had something to do with it."

"Leo Tarrant?"

"Yes. Leo. I couldn't talk him out of it. He said he couldn't come to see me for a while. Then—it was only a matter of a few days—I read in the paper about his death."

Her expression had sobered. "I was fond of him," she said. "Poor Quentin. He didn't die well."

"Did you kill him?" Paul said.

"I was wondering when you would ask that, Paul. The fact is, I did kill him."

Paul jumped up, knocking the chair over. She never moved.

"I killed him to clear the way for you. He was an obstacle to our love, and—"

"Damn it, Kim! Did you have a fight with him? Was he leaving you, withdrawing his support? Did you hate him for trashing your pictures?"

"No. Quentin was my patron. A friend." She turned her chair so she could face him. "I'm sorry he died. For him, and for me. Because now I'm in trouble. Quentin left me a little money, enough for a few months. I need a new patron."

"So that's what you called him. A patron, eh? How are you going to find another guy who will take care of you and not demand the dirty deed?"

"It may not be easy." She dabbed a finger in some sauce left on her plate and put it to her lips, lapping the lemon juice with a slow, sensual tongue. "I don't suppose you'd be interested, Paul?"

Paul cocked his head and rubbed his chin. He had to smile. She had surprised him again. "Me? You want me to be your sugar daddy? You'd have to be a little more specific."

"I can make it on about three thousand a month."

"And in return? What do I get?"

"That's negotiable."

"Baths, massages, dinner, lots of peeking and fooling around?"

"And my company. You seem to enjoy it."

"I do. But that ain't enough."

"I don't want to be possessed."

"Too abstract. Try being representational."

"Look. The mating instinct would emerge and take us over. We'd fall in love. We'd be jealous about each other. We'd try to make each other over. I'd be miserable when you were away. You'd want to get married. We would argue about everything. You'd think you owned me. I'd sleep with someone else to prove you didn't. That's modern love in America, isn't it?"

"Not to me, it isn't."

"You kid yourself. I can't do that. I won't do that."

"You're cynical beyond belief," Paul said. "I don't understand you, and that bothers me."

"I'm not cynical, Paul. I just stand outside all that. I can't help it. I was made that way. It's the flip side of the talent I've been given. I can transform the instinct into art, use the bodily energy for creative purposes. Celibacy is the source of the passion I put into my work. You still don't understand, do you?"

"Sounds like bullshit to me, but I understand that you're in earnest," Paul said. "You think you have a talent so important that you're willing to sacrifice everything to it, the good opinion of others, normal relationships, everything the rest of us consider crucial. But here's my problem. You're the only one who sees this gift inside you. What if no one else ever sees it? What if you're wrong about it?"

"Recognition would be nice," Kim said. "But I will

keep on, with or without it." She looked away, toward the cactus, her feet drawn up comfortably in the chair, her crystal glass beside her. In the dim flickering light she was like a woman out of a Gauguin, utterly and mysteriously complete, monumental in her completeness. Paul understood only one thing: She wasn't available to him or any man in the only way he thought mattered.

"Well, I hate to disappoint you, but I don't think I can afford you," Paul said. "Something tells me you'll get along fine. Sell the Miller I gave you."

"I wouldn't dream of it. Just a couple more years, Paul."

"No can do."

"Too bad," she said.

"The Miller was a good choice for you. You remind me of him," Paul said. "He lived off Anaïs Nin for a long time."

"That's right. He might never have been published without her support."

"But he was worth it. He loved her, and he fucked her. You're not worth it."

"Oh, really? I thought you liked me and my art."

"I was just trying to get into your pants."

She giggled at that. He didn't seem to be able to offend her.

"You're just a great big phallus, Paul," Kim said. She tossed down the last of her port.

"A private dick carrying a subpoena," Paul said. "Be at court on September eighteenth. I can't really say if you'll be a witness or not, but I think I'd better nail you down." He handed it to her, and she read the bold-print summons with interest.

"Honestly, I didn't kill Quentin. I don't have an alibi, of course. . . ."

"Of course. Nobody in the de Beers case has an alibi. Join the club."

"It must seem very odd to you that I should be a witness in Anna's case and so close to Quentin too. It has to be a case of synchronicity. A synchronous variation! Maybe my made-up phrase means something after all."

That's more than I can say for your paintings, Paul thought. He got up. He knew when he was beat up, down, and sideways. "Thanks for the dinner," he said.

"You don't have to stop coming. At least for a while."

"I do, though. I really do. You're business now. And you can't give me what I want."

"What *do* you want?"

"The real thing. I want to be loved," Paul said. "That's what I want. I'll show myself out."

"I hope you find what you need, Paul."

Paul nodded. "And I hope for your sake the next guy that comes knocking is loaded and has had his balls frozen off."

He looked back at the white-walled house as he drove down the road. In his many years of interviewing people and living his life, he had met only a few he couldn't see through. Kim was impenetrable to him. She was linked to both cases, but he didn't think she had killed anyone. She talked freely to him, but he understood less and less the more she talked.

Was she a liar and a phony or not? Was she involved in de Beers's death somehow? He wasn't sure anymore, but one thing he was sure of: she was not for him. He had said, "I want to be loved." It was such a simple desire. After two divorces and a dozen other relationships, he still hadn't found what he needed. He was surprised at the sadness he was finding down there where he seldom ventured, where his deepest feelings roved.

He drove back to Caesars about ten, pulled on his shorts, and went down to the basement to work out on the weights. Forty-five minutes later, his legs buckling and his bad shoulder sending twinges down his back, he tottered into his room again. The workout had restored his usual buoyancy, dispelling the moments of sadness. When in doubt, work out, he thought. The rhyme reminded him of El-Barouki and his way with gun rhymes.

He went into the bathroom, tossed the shorts into his laundry bag, turned on the shower, and climbed in, succumbing to the hot flooding spray on his shoulders, still trying to decide why Kim was part of both cases.

He couldn't make her for either death. Her only connection with Anna Meade was as a witness. And if her story checked out, she had lost her goose with the golden dollars when Quentin died. Even more important, she had only one passion in her life—to make it as a painter. Other than that, she was passionless, her viewpoint cynical and amused like some stereotypical Gauloise-puffing French intellectual.

He believed she meant what she said, and he admired her in a way because she knew what she wanted and was going for it, but her ambition still seemed pathetic. How many great women artists were there? Morisot? O'Keeffe? Kollwitz? He couldn't think of any others. What chance did she have, anyway? Close to zero. He soaped and rinsed his hair, thinking again about his bad luck, wishing he had been born fifty years earlier when women in general didn't suddenly twist their heads all the way around and stick their forked tongues out at him when he was least ready for it.

When he came out, still naked, he noticed the red light on the phone was flashing. He pressed the button and heard Hallowell's voice message from earlier in the afternoon overlying the sounds of a busy office. "About Anna's case. Sergeant Cheney managed to get something from the DMV on the Catalina," Hallowell said. "Three years ago, it was registered to a man named Jose Marquez. He's long gone from the address on the old registration, and he doesn't have a car registered in his name as an individual. We're still checking. Our own lab guys are working the car over now. Thanks, Paul. We're going to get him this time."

Paul was already at the table by the balcony, pulling out the police reports on Quentin de Beers's death. He felt a sense of compression as the two cases crashed hugely into each other, a pair of galaxies distorting space and time. . . .

He pulled out the witness statement he had been looking for. The gardener at the de Beers estate, who had seen Quentin de Beers talking to Sarah de Beers on the lawn the day before his death. Joe Marquez.

It was late, but so what? Hallowell never slept anyway. Still standing there, his hair dripping down his neck, he punched Hallowell's number.

"Hallowell."

"This is Paul van Wagoner. I just got your message."

"Good news, eh?" Hallowell sounded sleepy.

"I'll say. Especially since we both know this guy. You may not know it yet. Listen carefully. This Marquez guy is the gardener for Sarah de Beers, the mother of Jason de Beers. Has been for years. You sent us a witness statement from him."

"No shit?"

"No shit."

"Just goes to show you how behind I am, getting ready for the prelim next week. Don't even know my own witnesses. Is his home address on the statement?"

"Sure 'nuff."

"It's a small world."

"You going to bring him in?" Paul said.

"Let me think." In the pause that followed, Paul heard a woman's voice asking Hallowell something.

"Is that Nina?" he said.

"As a matter of fact, it is."

"Tell her I'll see her tomorrow."

"Sure. Paul, as soon as we bring him in he'll shut up and get a lawyer, and we may never learn anything more about Anna. I think we'll check him out further first." Paul thought, He's still talking about Anna in the present tense. Nina won't like that.

"I'm tied up for this week at least, with the de Beers defense. I can't do much at this point. You ought to know," Paul said.

"Since the de Beers prosecution got handed to me, I have the same problem," Hallowell said. "It's all right, Paul. Cheney's back on it. You've given us the break, but now it's up to law enforcement."

"You're cutting me loose?"

"I have to."

"This is not a good time for the cops to get back in. Somebody paid El-Barouki to leave the country. Marquez might do the same, if there's a leak. And there usually is a leak."

"I can't run the case privately any longer, Paul."

Paul understood. In his old life as a homicide detective he would have greatly resented interference by a private detective at this point. But he had revived the case, and he wanted to finish it. He wanted to know why Anna Meade had died, and the only person he trusted to handle it right was himself.

Carefully, he said, "I might run into Marquez in the course of the other investigation."

"You might at that," Hallowell said. It was a tacit approval, all Paul needed.

"Don't keep Nina up too late," he said. "She's got work to do." He hung up, congratulating himself on his cool. But right before sleep, as he went over the day in his head, Nina's attachment to Hallowell was the thing he found himself regretting, not the starlit white-walled courtyard with its Circean occupant.

22

HITCHCOCK STAGED HIS FAVORITE MAJOR WAKE-UP call with Nina on Friday morning, jumping on the bed and licking her face several times before she could get her hands up to defend herself. His ripe, liverish breath opened her eyes and her gag reflex at the same moment. While she brushed her teeth in the bathroom Bob came in to tell her he had the day off.

Another teacher-training day, he reported with glee.

The teachers of America had resigned themselves to being grossly underpaid, but were retaliating through their unions by teaching only the legally required 180 days a year. She had counted them herself on the school calendar.

She would have to bring him to the office or take time off. Andrea worked Fridays, and Nina wanted to rely on Andrea and Matt less and less anyway.

The longer she took to find a house, the more tightly wound they all had become. It was all her fault. Even Sandy had taken the low road with her the other day, accusing her of sheer lazy stubborn willfulness when she hadn't gotten around to checking out the house Sandy had gone to a lot of trouble to unearth for her.

Speaking of unearthing things, she had mounds of paper on her desk that would require archeological excavation if she didn't get to them soon, and at least six appointments, and the de Beers prelim coming up on Monday—and Bob was asking if they could go bowling.

"Okay," she said. "We'll rent a movie for you to watch in the library at the office this morning, and then I'll bring my work home in the afternoon so you can get out on your scooter. And maybe we can go bowl a game or two tonight." She would spread the files out on her bed and get to them again after Bob went to bed. What was it Graham Greene had titled his autobiography? *A Sort of Life,* that was it. . . .

Of course, she reflected as she struggled into her pantyhose, she actually had gone out the previous evening. She had gone to Collier's apartment. A sort of evening . . .

She had called Collier, for once finding him at home, and shaken an invitation out of him. Once there, she found the floors covered with papers and books, the corners grimy with rapidly reproducing dust bunnies, and a sink grim and grayed with coffee grounds and mold. She had to restrain herself from getting out the vacuum and sprucing up the place.

They sat down on the couch together, and she laid it all out, interrupted two times by phone calls from a police officer and Collier's secretary: how she had hoped the hike up Tallac would lead to something for them, how she thought they had a lot in common and could really understand each other; how much she enjoyed his sense of humor and their talks about law and life; and how all that hope and interest was starting to fizzle due to mutual neglect. She heard herself talking like a lawyer, making her pitch, choosing her words with care, not at all happy with the calculated technique of her delivery. He sat there so remotely. What else could she do?

They were both so guarded, that was the problem. She couldn't show him her spontaneous feelings until he chose to open up emotionally too. "Do you have anything to drink?" she asked him, thinking the unworthy thought that if they both got smashed they would get along much better.

Actually, though she couldn't possibly have told him directly, what she desired was to be swept up drunkenly and carried off to bed, and then in the morning they could talk about law and it would be fantastic, because underneath they would then have established the physical connection that was still lacking.

"Oh, Jesus, sorry," Collier had said, going to the kitchen for two cold bottles of Calistoga water. And that was how the talk went after that, cold and sober and fizzling every second.

Collier started off well, telling her how he'd like to have a love life too, and how he was sick of being lonesome, but as the conversation edged over to his campaign for DA, which was in trouble, it became more impassioned. He had lost the big case he should have won and feared he would probably lose the election as a result. And he was working closely with Sergeant Cheney and Paul on his wife's case. He really thought he might be able to find the driver. And training the new deputy in the office, Barbara Banning. And now he had the de Beers murder case . . .

Which brought them to silence, and the uncomfortable fact that they remained adversaries at work and would have to watch their tongues all the time. Collier desperately needed the de Beers prelim to go off without a hitch, and her job was to make it so chaotic that the judge would throw up his hands and throw the case out.

And for Nina, there was the additional problem that she knew something Collier didn't know, something she should tell him about the case if she was going to be as honest and aboveboard as she would expect him to be with her under the same circumstances, something she should tell him and the police. And the fact of the matter was, she intended to tell him nothing, the police nothing, and the world nothing about the sunglasses unless she was sworn under penalty of perjury.

"Nothing more is going to happen between us," Nina said at last, "is it? Two briefcases passing in the hall, and all that."

"Things will calm down around Christmas."

"It's only September! For Christ's sake, Collier, let's place the blame where it really belongs. If I don't attract you, just say so."

"But you do attract me. You do." As if to emphasize this, he finally touched her, running his hand along her hair, then down her back.

"I'm not asking to live with you or marry you, Collier. I just want to—"

"I know, Nina." He sighed, and she saw he was very tired. "I don't know how I got so lucky as to awaken your interest in me," he said. "I don't deserve it. I'm just an old workhorse, Nina. You're interested in the image of me you see in court. Look at me now. Look at this place. I'm ashamed, but I still don't have the steam to pull myself together and court you. My attention is absorbed by so many things. It wouldn't be fair for me to start up with you."

"Did it ever occur to you," Nina said, "that love is energizing? We could make time for that, and build up our strength for all those other things."

"You're very sweet and nice," Collier said, still stroking her hair, but his eyes had that faraway glaze and his voice held on to an infuriating detachment. Nina arrived at a sudden decision. She began unbuttoning her blouse, then pulled it off. Leaning toward Collier, she snaked an arm around his shaggy head and pulled him gently toward her.

"Remember kissing me on the mountain?" she said in a low voice. Responding like a man entranced, he put his arms around her. He began kissing her breasts and she closed her eyes, commanding her brain to shut down. They lay down on the couch side by side, kissing tender kisses. His eyes closed. His body warmed itself against hers. His warm, rhythmic breath exhaled softly over her cheek.

"Collier. Collier?" she whispered. His mouth had fallen slightly open.

He was asleep.

She was tiptoeing out when the phone rang again, jerking him awake. He began talking to Paul, gesturing with his hand for her to come back to the couch, an abashed look on his face.

She mumbled something and left anyway. Cutting her losses—that was something she understood.

By eight-thirty A.M., Nina sat before the glassed visiting cubicle waiting for Jason. The whole jail smelled like doughnuts. Behind the guard who had checked her bar card she had seen some of the inmates sitting on benches and chatting casually in the main room lined with cells. Even in jail, daily life had to go on.

Jason was led in a few minutes later, ducking his head to get in the low door, filling the small room with his height. Somehow, and she thought it probably hadn't been easy, he had managed to comb his hair and clean up. She seemed to remember the prisoners could shower twice a week. Maybe this morning had been one of those times.

Anyway, although his face was pale and careworn, he was not the fearful boy she had expected. He projected such calmness and maturity that Nina felt a great weight come off her shoulders. She didn't have to feel that she was defending a child. He was clearly over the line into manhood. She realized she liked him enormously.

He had brought a pad of paper just like hers, and for half an hour they talked over details of the upcoming preliminary hearing. Jason understood that he wouldn't be testifying.

"Who is the judge?" he said.

"A Municipal Court judge from Alpine County. Our regular sitting Municipal Court judge, Judge Flaherty, disqualified himself because he knew your grandfather."

"He'll give the new judge an earful."

"No. That's not allowed."

"I'm young, but I know a few things. And I know that the whole town is sure I did it. There's something in the paper every day about it. My grandfather knew everybody with any money here. Even the judge from Alpine will have heard something."

The only time Jason lost his calm was when Nina

mentioned his family. He didn't want to put his mother and sister on the stand, but Nina couldn't promise him that wouldn't happen. "This is a reactive situation," she told him. "We have to find out as much as we can about the prosecution's case. If the chance arises to refute an important point, we take it, even if it's Sarah or Molly who has to do it. Besides, they've both been subpoenaed by the prosecution. That doesn't mean they will definitely be called, but they may be."

"They don't know anything!" Jason said. If he had been behind bars, he would have grabbed and shaken them. All he could do was ball his hands into fists and push them against the window between them.

"We don't have a choice about that," Nina said. "Now settle down. Control yourself. I have to talk to you about something you're not going to like."

Jason put his hands down. He put his head back to breathe deeply for a minute. Then he opened his intense blue eyes, saying, "I'm ready."

"I want to defend you, but given what little you have told me, I can't do much. I need more, Jason. If you're protecting someone, I want you to tell me. You may be hoping that I'll win the prelim without that information and you won't ever have to tell me, but it doesn't work that way."

"I didn't kill my grandfather. What more do you have to know?"

"Maybe you can help me with one little piece of physical evidence that may convict you all by itself. Your prints were on the shovel at the grave."

"Oh, no." Jason moaned and buried his face in his hands. "Oh, God."

"Without the fingerprints, Jason, there isn't much of

a case against you. But the head of the shovel had blood on it. Your grandfather's blood."

"I never touched him!"

"You were there? You were the one digging? Why, Jason? Why?"

"I can't tell you!" he cried. "Don't ask me to!"

Flaring, Nina said, "You're not the only one with a stake in this thing! Who do you think called in the 911 from Wright's Lake the night of the fire?"

"How would I know?"

"I did!"

"You?" His look of horror only reflected back what she herself felt whenever she considered that night, her actions, and in particular, the item she had picked up from the floor of the cabin.

"I went looking for you." She wanted to tell the bare bones of the story, so that, if he really couldn't help her with what happened from personal knowledge, he might just be able to engage his mind in the ongoing battle she was fighting. "Your mother was worried about you when she learned you hadn't spent the night at Kenny's. She called me. I found out that you might have gone to the cabin."

"Oh, my God! She sent you after me?"

"She didn't know where you were. She thought Joe Marquez might know. I found out from Joe."

"Did Joe say I was up there?"

"He said you might be, so I went looking for you. The fire was just beginning."

"What did you see?" Jason demanded.

"I went inside the cabin, but the fire was too much. I made it back out just in time. Your grandfather was already dead. Whoever set the fire—I didn't see."

"But—but that makes you a witness, doesn't it?"

"Yes. And I probably will be, if this goes to trial, because I'm withholding evidence in a criminal proceeding. I'm obstructing justice."

"The police have no idea?"

"No. I'm going to see you through this prelim. The police are soon going to stumble onto the fact that I'm the one that discovered the body. When they take my sworn statement, I can't perjure myself. I'll have to say I was there. I have to tell them everything I know. Just like I'm telling you."

Jason, who had been tapping on the table in front of him with his fingers, speeded up the beat.

"I haven't told the police I went up there, because I found something in the cabin that I took with me. I'd rather not turn it over to them just yet," Nina went on.

"What?"

"A pair of green sunglasses. Vuarnets."

The tapping paused, then resumed. Jason's face was stricken. "Anyone could wear sunglasses, though. You can't know whose sunglasses they are." He thought hard, his second hand joining the frenetic thumping, and then, noticing the psychic maelstrom he had unleashed, he pressed them together to shut them up. "It's possible I left them up there visiting the cabin this summer."

"I'm told by your mother that the owner of the cabin says it wasn't used at all this summer. You've been wearing shades like those since at least the day I saw you on Tallac. Or do you have another pair you can show me to convince the world these sunglasses aren't yours?"

Jason didn't answer.

Nina said, "You've had those all through high school, your mother says. You hardly go anywhere

without them. Can you remember when you saw them
last?"

"No idea."

"Jason, please. Help me."

"I don't know what to say. I'm in so much trouble,
and I'm so confused. But . . . you haven't told anyone?"

"No one knows but me," said Nina.

"I'm in shock."

"That's enough for today. I have to go," Nina said.
"I had to tell you, Jason, even though it exposes me."

"That was brave," Jason said. "You're protecting me,
even though it puts you at risk. For family, I would do
it, too, no matter how bad a thing had happened. But
it's not like I was your own son, or your father, or
something. A stranger, doing that for me . . . I can
give you something back. Nina . . ."

"Mmm-hmm?"

"I loved my grandfather. I didn't kill him. I didn't
kill my grandfather. I swear!"

"I believe you," Nina said, and she did.

At the office, Sandy was having her breakfast, a
scrambled-egg burrito from across the street. Sandy
lived on burritos. "Looks good," Nina said.

"Did you eat yet?"

"They were having doughnuts at the jail. I couldn't
stand it. After I left, I stopped at Winchell's and had a
couple."

"You need protein."

"I need a miracle." She went into her office and
began returning the sheaf of phone messages. Sarah de
Beers had called twice that morning. Her messages
were marked urgent.

Molly answered the phone. "Is your mother home?" Nina asked her. "She's been trying to reach me."

"She wants to talk to you. She was wondering if you could come out to the house at twelve." Twelve to one was Nina's only free time left in the day, and she had promised herself a walk along the lake, but she said immediately, "Okay. I'll be there."

"Did you see Jason this morning? Your secretary said you were at the jail."

"Yes."

"How is he?" Her voice was tight and anxious.

"His spirits are good," Nina said. She always answered that sort of question that way, and it had its hoped-for effect, seeming to soothe Molly.

The rest of the morning passed in a blur of meetings, so she made little progress toward lowering the tower of files on her desk before she had to leave.

The de Beerses' house and gardens looked as formal as if a wedding party was planned, all laid out in pastels mixed with white and black. Joe must have been working hard. He had stowed his gardening implements away, and there was no sign of him outside.

Molly came to the door. Her hair was pulled back in a ponytail, and she wore jeans and a short white shirt that showed her navel and small, high breasts. She was so slim that her height didn't seem excessive. It was only when she walked beside her that Nina realized Molly must be almost six feet tall. She and Jason must stop traffic when they were together. "You look like a skier," Nina said.

"Snowboards," Molly said politely. "Jason and I go a lot in the winter."

"How are you doing?"

"Me? Better than Jason, I imagine. I'm taking the

medicine Dr. Lee gave me. I feel better. I'm sorry you saw all that. I didn't know you were out there."

"You gave us all quite a shock. Especially your mother."

"It was stupid. I won't let myself get that down again." Molly was looking away. She had the same radiant smile and natural ease as Jason, but she seemed younger and more vulnerable than her brother. "I'm really sorry about trying to kill myself, now. Jason told me afterward that it was the lowest moment of his life. And of course, if I'd died, he wouldn't have me around now, when he needs me so much."

"Why did you do it, Molly?"

"I just—I didn't see how I could live through any more."

"Any more what?"

Molly didn't answer.

They climbed the wide and winding staircase to the second floor and entered a small den with a couple of comfortable sofas and a wide-screen TV.

Sarah stood staring across the landscape at the distant lake through the casement window. She looked much as Nina had first seen her on the mountain, dressed casually, wearing no makeup.

"Thanks for coming," she said, and the two women sat down. Molly leaned against the hallway door. She was there for her mother's sake, her presence said, but the eyes that followed a flock of birds out the window also told Nina that Molly wanted to maintain her distance from both of them.

"I suppose you want to talk about the subpoena you received. It's just as well; we can get to this today instead of over the weekend," Nina said.

"What do they want from me?" Sarah asked.

"You gave a statement to the police that included information about the exhumation proceeding," Nina said. "Jason's motive to kill his grandfather isn't an essential element that has to be proven, and could even be left out at the preliminary hearing.

"However, in this case the prosecutor evidently wants to give the judge some evidence of motive. Your testimony will make it clear that Jason and his grandfather differed strongly regarding the exhumation proceeding."

"But they can get that from the court papers!"

"Yes, but real live testimony is often preferable to flesh out the paperwork and answer questions that may come up."

"I'm not going to testify against my son! I'm not going to let them drag me into court to hurt Jason. That's the bottom line."

Nina nodded. She hadn't thought about the reaction Sarah would naturally have to being subpoenaed. The problem wasn't legal, it was emotional, and she hadn't had time to think beyond the legal side. "I see what you're saying," she said. "Let me tell you three things that may help you. First, they may not call you. In general, the idea is to put on a minimal case, just enough to skate past the probable cause standard. This is a hearing, not a full-scale trial. If the judge seems to get the gist of the prosecution theory from the court papers, they may not bother you."

Sarah listened, frowning.

"Second, you don't really have a choice."

"I could get sick."

"That might alert them that there is something you're avoiding saying and draw more attention to you. They can just continue the hearing if a witness is sick.

That would work against the strategy I've already outlined to you, of catching the prosecution before it is
fully prepared."

"Ah," said Sarah.

"And third, I will be cross-examining you. When
the prosecutor asks you whether Jason was angry at his
grandfather, you have to answer carefully and truth-
fully. But I can then ask you questions that put your
answer in a proper perspective. For instance: Did Jason
ever make any threat against his grandfather that you
know of?"

"Never. Jason and Quentin liked each other. They
had always gotten along. Quentin often intervened between him and Ray."

"As far as you know, did Jason and his grandfather
ever engage in any physical altercation of any sort?"

"Of course not."

"Jason suggested to you that this matter might be
settled in a court proceeding, didn't he?"

"Yes. That was his idea."

"He and his grandfather were on speaking terms?"

"Yes, much more than that. Quentin's birthday was
last month, and Jason bought him a present, a new
hat."

"You see?" Nina said.

Sarah nodded again. "We can turn this around to
help Jason."

"Read over your statement with care, and make very
sure you don't contradict anything you have said previously," Nina said. "Review your calendar and have the
events straight in your head, so you don't get confused.
Answer the question directly, and explain your answer
if you need to, but don't say anything unnecessary.
Molly, are you listening carefully? You've been subpoe-

naed too, although I think it's even less likely that you'll be called."

"What if he says 'Just answer yes or no'?" Molly put in.

"I'll object," Nina said. "A witness has the right to finish an answer completely. Don't worry, I'll be there to make sure."

"I guess I'll have to handle this then," Sarah said.

Nina liked that statement. She said encouragingly, "You'll do fine."

"Can they ask me about anything else? I mean, things about Jason that aren't related to this case?"

"Like what?"

Molly was holding her hand up. "Don't tell her these things, Mother," she said.

"But honey, if I don't tell Nina she might be surprised by what comes out—"

"Nothing has to come out, Mom, unless you let it."

"But what if the police do know, Molly? About the fight with his dad—"

"It wasn't a fight! Dad hit him, and Jason was only trying to defend himself!"

"I'm sorry for bringing it up, Molly. Come here." Sarah held her arms out, but Molly stayed by the door, her face white, her voice trembling.

"No. You listen! Don't talk about Jason and Dad, because that's got nothing to do with Grandpa dying and it just makes Jason look bad. Don't pretend to know what you're talking about, because you don't, especially when it comes to Jason and me. You've been trying so hard not to know anything. You've been busy with your drinking and your boyfriend and your game of making this family look normal. And last of all, don't try to kiss me and make it all better. Because you can't! It's too late!" Molly yelled out the words, and ran out of the room.

Sarah jumped up to follow her, but Nina said, "Wait, Sarah. Just a minute."

"She's right," Sarah said, slumping in the doorway. "It does seem too late."

"It's never—"

"I can't help them. Why didn't I leave Ray? I feel so guilty."

"Someday they will understand."

"How sad," Sarah said. "I think I was finally growing up myself the past couple of years, getting stronger." She fell silent.

"Sarah, is there something important you haven't told me?"

"No."

"Do you believe Jason killed his grandfather, Sarah?" It was a risky question, but Nina had to ask it before someone else did.

"Sometimes I think—who else could it be?"

"Do you have any facts I ought to know that would indicate he did?"

"Nothing you don't know," Sarah said. "If only you can get him off, Nina. We'd start fresh, learn how to be a family. But it's like fate is against us."

"We can't lie down and let the situation roll over us. We have to open it up, find the chance. You've been trying hard, Sarah. Don't quit on me."

"I appreciate your coming," Sarah said. "You've been a great help to us."

"Not yet, but I'm trying. If you want to help— No offense, but don't let yourself get down. Stay out of the martini shaker. No more pills. Get your sleep. Stay calm with Molly. You'll pass through this whether you want to or not and come out the other side. So you might as well quit wasting your energy wishing it were otherwise."

To her surprise, Sarah embraced her. There were tears in her eyes. Nina could feel the bones as she pressed against her.

"You're my hero," she said. "I'd better go to Molly. You can find the door."

23

NEXT STOP, JOE MARQUEZ. COOL RAIN HAD started in just after noon.

From her car phone, Nina called Paul at Caesars. "Joe probably went home for lunch," she said. "Sandy says you haven't talked to him yet. I'm tired of pussy-footing around. I want to look him in the eye when he tells me he sent me off into the fire and brimstone up at that cabin by some unplanned fluke."

"Meet you there in ten minutes."

"You know where Joe lives?"

"Oh, yes," Paul said. "In fact, if you don't mind, I'd like to kill two birds." He told her about the Pontiac Catalina and how it had been registered to Joe at the time of Anna's death.

"There can't be a connection," Nina said.

"It could be coincidence," Paul agreed.

Nina slipped to the right of a car turning left off the highway, then moved back into the left lane. "Or it's synchronicity," she said into the phone.

"What exactly is that? I know the word. Title of a

great old song by the Police. Let's see . . . 'Many miles away, something crawls through the mud . . .' "

"Jung coined the word, I think."

"But what's it mean? I always just listened to the beat. Great tune too although 'Roxanne' is still my favorite."

"It means a series of events or objects that aren't connected in any logical or causal fashion," Nina said into the phone. "But they're connected."

The car just ahead of her in the left lane suddenly decided to change to the right lane, just as a little pickup, almost invisible in the right lane beside her, suddenly decided to put on a burst of speed. An accident was about to happen. Nina swerved left and the Bronco's tires jumped the curb of the center divider. The pickup driver slowed to watch her crazy maneuver, just long enough so that the car changing lanes could pull in front without hitting the pickup. The pickup slowed even more and honked angrily, but both vehicles were safe.

Nina bounced back into the street and continued on her way. "Lousy drivers," she muttered.

"Give me an example," Paul was saying. "How can they be connected some other way?"

"I can't think of anything right now. I'm too busy driving in the rain to think that hard. But the connection isn't random."

"Then what is the connection?"

"I don't know! It's mysterious! The connection is at a level beyond human understanding!"

"Sounds like a cop-out to me. There's a logical reason, or it's random. That's it. Of course, I don't read Jung right before I go to sleep. I read gun catalogs."

"It's how the gods do their work. So let's just put it

this way: What's crawling through the mud? Besides me out here?"

"Joe knows. Drive past and park down the block. I'll be there."

Twenty minutes later Nina wound her way in semi-darkness down a deserted road in Christmas Valley. The midday mimicked dusk because of thick pine forest that pressed in from the sides of the road, the branches overhanging like tangled black beards. Rain splattered in thick droplets onto the street and over the Bronco. Luckily for her, she was following the only road into the valley, and could not get lost.

She passed the Marquez mailbox and drove on for a few hundred feet. A neighbor's dachshund set up a howl and managed to keep pace with her on its stumpy legs. Paul's Dodge Ram van met her and her canine companion from head-on, smooth and silent as a detective vehicle should be, easily avoiding the small brown animal that followed, splashing at her bumper. Paul pulled over. Nina swung around and parked behind him.

"Hop in," Paul said, opening his door. "And tell your admirer there to pipe down. We're supposed to be sneaking up on our friend." He reached over to unlock the door. "Suitcase first."

"You mean my briefcase."

"You always look ready for a weekend getaway to Napa or somewhere really glam, as if you're about to jump into a Hertz Rent-a-Car," Paul said, placing her case on the floor behind his seat.

Before she could get her legs tucked safely away, the dog reached her, still barking frantically, its wiry tail upright and alert. She talked calmly to it for a moment, and then reached down to pet it, stroking the wet silky fur behind the ears and accepting a friendly lick before closing the door. "I'd have trouble getting away for a weekend with nothing but paper to wear," Nina said, "and not even tape to hold it on."

"Hmm. As you probably realize, that thought has a certain amount of appeal to a certain type of person."

"Certainly not you, though," said Nina. "Not if the vicious gossip I hear is accurate."

"Oh?" Paul raised a brow. "Which gossip would that be?"

"I can't repeat gossip."

"Then we're left with this case," he said, too eager, Nina thought, to let go of the game.

While Paul peered through the murk up the street, she looked at the height and breadth and weight of him, her heart sinking. He was a stranger again. He had another woman.

"What do you think? Anybody home?" Paul asked. A porch light burned dimly through the tree-induced gloom at the Marquez house.

"I went past the house first," Nina said. "I think Joe's home. Somebody is."

Paul's favorite tape, John Coltrane's *A Love Supreme,* sent soft sax through the cab. The van smelled like fresh coffee, Paul's aftershave, and damp leather. The wipers flapped, and she saw the reason for the leather smell. His old brown bomber jacket was tossed over the fake fur blanket and the pillows in the fold-down backseat, right next to the locked case he called his toolbox, which she had often wondered about.

Unlike his hotel rooms or even his condo, Paul's van revealed something intimate about him, his mix of whimsy and masculinity. He rode California's freeways with the same rousing sense of adventure as a cowboy of old once rode the West's ranges on his horse.

"Let's talk a minute before we go in," he said, setting the parking brake. The dachshund, apparently mollified by Nina's fondling, trotted off toward a doggie door in the side of the house next door and disappeared. "The Meade case and the de Beers case are starting to crash into each other. It's happening too fast for me to get a handle on it. Joe Marquez owned the car that killed Anna Meade. And Joe Marquez told you to go to Wright's Lake the night of the fire. You still haven't told the police that you were the one who went up there and made the 911 call?"

"Not yet."

"You're taking a major risk. You know that. They could tag you with an obstruction of justice charge. Even if you had a lot of friends in this town who would go easy on you—and you really don't, but that's another topic—why take chances? And if you don't tell them Joe sent you to Wright's Lake, nobody looks at Joe as a potential bad guy."

"If I give a statement now, any statement, I'm going to have to tell the whole truth, and I'm not prepared to do that quite yet."

"Hey," Paul said, placing his hands on her shoulders and turning her toward him so she had to look him in the eye. "What do you know that you haven't told me? Don't you trust me by now?"

"I don't see why I should get you charged, too, except maybe for the pleasure of your company in the slammer."

He sat on that thought for an instant, then said, "You know something else that could implicate Jason."

"I'm sorry, Paul. Even if I do know something

more, I can't tell you about it. I'm not sure it would be privileged information."

"Which leaves me bumbling around in the dark. Oh, you stubborn, stubborn woman. All right. Tell me this much. Are we the only people who know Joe has some connection, however tenuous, to both crimes?"

"Yes. But I can't say he knew what was happening at Wright's Lake, Paul. He said Jason might be up there. That's all."

"Joe could have dug up the body and set the fire, no matter how Quentin died. The only thing is, I can't imagine why," Paul said.

"Joe couldn't have set the fire. I went straight up there after I saw him at Sarah's house. He couldn't have beat me there."

"He could have gone up there before you saw him and set a slow-burning fire, couldn't he? It could have been smoldering for some time before you got there. Have you thought about that?"

"No," Nina said in a small voice. She thought about Joe loading lawn clippings into his truck that night, his slow deliberate movements, his flash of anger. . . .

"I suppose it's possible. I think I would have noticed something in his demeanor though, Paul. I think at most Joe might know who set the fire."

"What if he does know? What if he tells us it was Jason?" Paul said. "Do we really want to cajole the story out of him? Shouldn't we let sleeping gardeners lie?"

"I'll take the chance, Paul. I don't believe Jason killed his grandfather."

"You've been around the block, baby. Admit for once you might be wrong!"

His vehemence shook her confidence, which brought up her defenses. "Don't call me baby."

"Sorry, b—"

"And don't call me boss." She reached up, removing his hand from her shoulder.

Paul held his hands up in a gesture of conciliation. "Okay. So what's the plan of action?" he said.

"Play it by ear?"

"Not exactly a plan, but it'll have to do. Now, before we go in, I have to tell you about this other woman. Kim Voss."

"The woman who saw the car hit Collier's wife."

"Right. Well, she admits Quentin was supporting her for the past four years. They had a kinky thing going. That's what I mean by cases colliding."

Startled, Nina tried to absorb this information.

"She claims she was on good terms with him and lost her income when she lost him. According to Leo Tarrant, de Beers's will left her a share of the business worth about fifteen grand, but I doubt if she'd kill the old man for that. The fact is, I doubt she did have anything to do with it, or with Anna's death, but there she is, smack-dab in the middle of both cases, just like Joe Marquez."

"What's she like?" Nina said.

"A struggling artist. Very dedicated. No other interest in life. Smart and attractive."

Nina did not like the tone of fake disinterest. So Kim Voss was the one Paul was so hot on. An artist. Why did she have to be an artist? A creative type who probably cooked beautifully, with long flowing hair and dangling earrings, smelling of patchouli, her mind lazy and free, able to discuss Picasso, Hockney, and Judy Chicago in the same breath. As someone totally out of Paul's usual run of acquaintances, she would have special allure.

It was idiotic, but Nina experienced a pang. "Maybe Kim and Joe know each other," Nina said. "Maybe she and Anna and Joe and Quentin all used to play poker at Prize's on Thursday nights. Kim killed Anna because Anna had a real job and Quentin because he made fun of her art."

Paul looked amused. "As good a theory as any."

"You know, if she's another connection between the two cases, we should consider her, shouldn't we?"

"Let's see how things go before we start blaming Kim for everything, okay?" Paul said, and the double meaning of his comment didn't escape her, even if it did escape him. "Get ready for our grand entrance." Paul drove boldly into the rutted driveway amid yelps of protest from another dog, this one large and vigilant, who stopped a few feet from the van, its lip curled just like Elvis used to curl his, then charged forward and bounded riotously around the van, spraying water.

"More of your admirers. Dogs have a thing for you. Shall I shoot it?" Paul inquired, but just then a small boy, barefoot, came down the ramshackle porch, jumping nimbly over the puddles to grab the dog's collar, cuffing it and choking it. The dog subsided, and the boy piped, "Private property."

"Hi, there," Nina said. "We would like to speak to Mr. Marquez."

"He's working."

"We might have a job for him," Paul said.

The boy, who had black hair and a solemn expression on his face, said, "Wait a minute." He ran into the house, and they waited expectantly for a mom to appear behind him, but he reemerged alone, carrying a beeper. "I called him," he said in his stern little voice. The phone in the house rang. The boy left again to answer, returned and said, "Come in," directing them into the living room.

Though even darker than the overgrown clearing in which it was set, the house was not unpleasant inside. A large TV dominated the threadbare room, glowing orange and green and blue as silent ads flickered swiftly over its face. Pictures of Jesus, Mary, and unidentifiable saints were matted and framed in gold-painted wood. A sofa in worn white chenille faced the TV. "Rex the Wonder Horse," a rocking horse on a metal frame, and an air-resistance exercycle crowded into one corner. Nina took the phone.

"This is Nina Reilly. Mr. Marquez?"

"I recognized you from the description. What do you think you're doing at my house?"

"I need to talk to you."

"I'm busy. I don't have time."

"Is this your son? He's been very polite."

A silence, then Joe said grudgingly, "He's a good boy. But listen, lady, you shouldn't be there. That's my home."

"Is your boy all alone here?"

"Are you going to call Child Welfare or something? He's out sick, getting over the flu, so don't bother, okay? Now, what do you want?"

"Just a few words, Joe. We can wait."

"No you can't. I don't let people wait at my home."

"Tell me where I can meet you. Or are you afraid to talk to me?"

"I'm not afraid."

"Then what's the big deal?"

"Come on over," said Joe finally. "I'll be here another half hour." He gave an address back in town, which Nina memorized.

"We'll be there."

"Put my boy on." The boy took the phone. As they left they could still hear Joe's scolding voice through the receiver and see the child nodding as if his father faced him in person, saying, "*Sí, sí,* Papa," over and over.

They parted on the road. On the way back to town Nina called her office, where Bob was marooned with Sandy. "Bobby?"

"Hi, Mom."

"What are you doing?"

"Wish is teaching me how to fix a radio. He's got one all taken apart on the conference table. And Sandy brought us tacos."

"I'm sorry, honey, but I've been held up. It'll be another hour or maybe even longer."

"What else is new?" Bob said cheerfully.

"Put Wish on." Wish came on the line, and Nina said, "Wish? Do you mind keeping Bob occupied for a while longer? I'm running late."

"We'll be here," Wish said. "Gotta get this thing working again. There must be a million pieces."

"That's neat. You found an old radio to take apart?"

"Right in the front office."

"My radio from college? The one I keep on the shelf by the door? You better put that back together!"

"That's what we're doing," Wish said in a tone of injured innocence.

Not too far from Kenny Munger's apartment building, on Black Bart Road, Nina spied Joe's truck with its now-familiar logo parked in front of a cottage with a front yard scattered with leaves from a large central maple tree. She waited for Paul to arrive, thinking to herself about the snow that would be on its way in a month or so, wondering how she and Bob would manage with a steep driveway like this in the dead of winter.

Paul pulled in behind her this time and they walked rapidly up wet wooden stairs. The rain had let up and the pine needles on the trees and maple leaves on the ground glistened.

A girl with long hair drawn back in a braid opened the door. "Mr. van Wagoner!" she said with a gasp.

"What the . . . Mrs. Lauria?"

Paul and the woman stared at each other until Nina said, "May we come in?"

"I guess so," young Mrs. Lauria said, continuing to eye Paul.

After wiping their feet carefully on the mat, they entered the cottage. Inside, the house was dark like Joe's, but it smelled like onions and refried beans, and a fire burned in the stone fireplace. Two toddlers hid behind the girl, clinging to her jeans. Joe sat in a tattered recliner in front of the fire, his feet up, looking like the man of the house, holding a small boy in his lap.

"Sorry I can't get up, but I slipped off a roof this morning and hurt my back some. Who are you?" he said to Paul, setting the child on the floor beside him.

"This is the man who bought me lunch, Joe," Mrs. Lauria said. "He wanted to talk about Ruben and Mrs. Meade." She turned back to Paul. "I'm surprised to see you here."

"It's a shock to see you too. Nina, this young lady is

Lucy Lauria. She used to be married to Ruben Lauria, the parolee who saw Anna Meade the day she died."

"I'm Nina Reilly," Nina said to Mrs. Lauria, who said, "Pleased to meet you." She gestured toward the couch and Paul and Nina sat down.

Seeing this pleasant family circle made Nina think of the boy all alone at Joe's cottage. He was older. Maybe he didn't like playing with the little kids, and enjoyed a little peace and quiet. Or maybe he really was sick. They were probably worried he would pass his illness along to the other kids.

"What's this about?" Joe said to Nina. "Why did you bring him along?"

"He's working for me on Jason's defense. He's also working on the Anna Meade case," Nina said. "We'd like to talk to you—about both cases."

"I don't have anything to hide," Joe said, dangling a red ball in his hand and letting the little boy snatch at it. He looked relaxed. "Is my boy okay? I'm heading home in a few minutes."

"He seemed fine," Nina said.

"Well, then. Let's get this over with."

"Mrs. Lauria?" Paul said. "How do you come to know Joe?"

Mrs. Lauria looked at Joe. He nodded, and she said, "Joe and I are going to be married soon. Remember, I told you when we had lunch?"

"Congratulations. But how did you meet?"

"I can answer that for you," Joe said. "I see what you're trying to figure out. Through Ruben. Ruben was my cousin."

Something should have clicked into place, but nothing did. Again, Nina had the dizzy feeling of facts linked to each other, yet seemingly randomly.

"We fell in love after Ruben died, and we're getting married." Mrs. Lauria went over to the recliner and put her arm around the top of it as if it were an outgrowth of Joe. She seemed to Nina to be the stronger of the two. Joe patted her hand, never taking his eyes off Paul and Nina.

Paul said, "Nina tells me that you had an idea Jason might have been up at Wright's Lake the night Quentin de Beers was killed."

"It was just a thought. Did you go up there?" Joe said to Nina.

Ignoring him, Paul went on, "What I'm trying to figure out is, why did you think Jason might have gone there?"

"Because you said he was after his grandfather. And that was his grandfather's hideout, you know? The kid knew where it was. He came back with a six-pound trout from there last summer."

"His mother didn't mention it to me," Nina put in. "She was very worried about him. Why wouldn't she mention that Jason might have gone to the cabin?"

"How should I know? Maybe she didn't want to tell you herself."

Nina considered this. Was it possible? Sarah had in fact told her in an indirect sense, by sending her to Joe, who immediately had thought of the cabin. That way it wouldn't appear that Sarah knew where the bodies were.

Could Sarah have pretended concern for Jason, sent Nina up to the cabin to find the bodies and left Jason's sunglasses there to complete the picture? Sarah didn't want Ray's body exhumed either, and she must have resented whatever pressure Quentin had brought to bear. But did she know how to use a backhoe, a big, clumsy digging machine? And what kind of person would dig up a dead spouse or, worse, frame her own child!

Unless she had help and a lot of pressure on her from someone else. Leo?

Paul's eyebrows were raised practically to his hairline, and even Joe and Mrs. Lauria were watching her with puzzled expressions, but all she could think was: Leo, for the company; Sarah, for the final freedom from control by the de Beers men.

Or give them the benefit of not committing a cold-blooded murder. Quentin was digging up his son's body, the backhoe still warm and dropping bits of dirt from the grave, the hard breath as he shoveled with gloved hands . . . and Leo and Sarah following. A fight . . .

She thought coldly, if Sarah left the Vuarnets to frame Jason and picked me to find them, she must be furious that I haven't turned them over to the police.

"I have a copy of the statement you gave the police," Paul went on when Nina didn't continue. "You say you were at home when—"

"Yeah, with my boy."

"Any other witnesses?"

Joe started to laugh. He ruffled the little boy's hair, and said, "Why would I kill the old man?"

"Have you deposited any large sums of money in any bank account in the last couple of months?" Joe thought about this, but Mrs. Lauria understood first.

"Joe is not a killer!" she cried.

"Now, hold on," Joe said. "You think we'd be eating beans and rice every day like we do if I had money stashed away? You think I'd be out there busting my butt mowing lawns for you rich Anglos if I could stay home and live off my bank account? You must be desperate, man. You have anything else to say before little Lucy here kicks you out the door?"

"I'm looking for the owner of a '59 Pontiac Catalina, white or cream-colored, license number JOK6SSG. Ever owned anything like that?"

Joe's smile faded. Mrs. Lauria looked pretty unhappy all of a sudden too. Nina, who had been lost in her own thoughts for the past few minutes, started paying attention again.

"I had a car like that, a long time ago. I don't remember the license plate," Joe answered cautiously.

"How long ago?"

"Years."

"Three years?"

"Maybe."

"Where is it now?"

"It got stolen. I was working at the de Beers house that day. I left my keys in the car, parked in the driveway. When I went there after work, the car was gone."

"Did you report the theft?"

"It was just an old clunker. I mean, that car was almost thirty years old, falling apart. It wasn't worth reporting. I didn't have insurance on it either. I would have just bought a lot of headaches reporting it."

"You have to do better than that, Joe," Paul said.

"It's the truth! It would just get me in trouble somehow. I don't mix with the government."

"Don't talk to him like that," Mrs. Lauria commanded. "I thought you were a nice person, a smart one. Now I see you're just out to screw the Latinos too."

"Hold your horses, Lucy," Joe said, picking up the

little boy again. "Why are you asking about that old clunker?" he asked Paul.

"That old clunker killed Anna Meade."

A long silence followed, broken only by the children's various queries and activities and the sound of the trees dripping onto the roof. The fire had burned down and the room had grown chilly. Mrs. Lauria picked up a pine log and threw it onto the coals. Then she picked up her daughter, who had begun to complain.

Joe pushed the recliner up, and sat forward in the chair, wincing, handing her the younger child as soon as she finished getting the fire going again. Mrs. Lauria was so diminutive herself that Nina could hardly believe she could hold both of the chubby little bodies, but she didn't even seem to notice she had them. She held one on each hip, her face hostile.

"Don't talk to them anymore, Joe," she said.

"I didn't do it," Joe said. "It doesn't make sense. How could my car kill Ruben's probation officer?"

"If you weren't driving, someone else was," said Paul.

"Could Ruben have taken the car, Lucy?" asked Joe. "I brought him over to the de Beers place that one time to try to help him get some work. He knew where to find it. I remember asking you at the time—"

"Do you hear what you're saying? That Ruben ran that woman down! But it's impossible! He killed himself not two hours before she died!"

"That's right," Joe said, reassured. "Ruben was in bad trouble, but he would never do anything like that." He stretched in the chair and closed his eyes, wincing again.

Mrs. Lauria said, "Listen, Jose. In case you are having some doubts, I didn't take the car. I borrowed it a few times, yes, I see in your eyes that you remember that. But I never took it. Why would I harm Anna anyway? Ruben said—remember what he said about her? He said she had a heart. My God, it's enough to make you cry, all this mistrust and bad feeling in here."

Joe shook his head. "I never thought of you, Lucy. Never."

"Tell me about Ruben's trouble," Nina said, anticipating the question she could tell was fermenting in Paul's mind.

"Well, I don't get what this is about," Joe said. "I can't see how I am involved at all. Lucy and I haven't done anything wrong, so I'm glad to tell you what I know.

"Ruben and I were sophomores in high school when he started taking things, just little things. Everybody all around us had so much more, you know. I didn't let it bother me, but Ruben watched the commercials on television like those people who had all those expensive things were real people like us. He knew what was the right shoes, the right jacket, all that. He got caught lifting a watch at Mervyn's and was sent to a youth detention camp for six months.

"After that he changed. One night a few months later, he stabbed a guy outside a bar. He was lucky they tried him as a juvenile. He went to a detention center for a year that time.

"Right after he was released, we all moved up to Tahoe. My dad had a job with the forest service. Ruben wanted to get on with them more than anything. He had just gotten married to Lucy on a trip to Mexico and he wanted to better himself, but he had this record by then for this and that. There was no way the U.S. of A. was about to hire him. So he started hanging out with the wrong people again, drinking and partying. He was caught purse snatching and put in jail."

Mrs. Lauria said, "He cleaned up in jail. He wanted to take better care of us, but when he got out, nobody would hire him because of his record and because he had a history of being unreliable, of drinking. He lost heart. Jose was just getting started with the gardening and trying to help him, but Ruben . . . he never showed up for the jobs. I'll never forget you stopping by with dinner all the time like you did," she went on, turning to Joe. She was perched on the arm of his chair, and she leaned into him, joining her body to his as if to complete herself.

He smiled back and their smiles met somewhere between them in a hopeful splash, or so it seemed to Nina. She saw how much in love they were, and marveled at the connection between man and woman she was witnessing.

"Ruben was a good man," Mrs. Lauria said. "Don't think anything else. Unhappy, yes, drinking, yes. That changes you. You do foolish things you would never have done. But he was young, and he was not someone to give up on. He went to Mass once a week with me. He did everything Mrs. Meade told him to do. He praised her. He listened to her advice."

"I think we should tell them, Lucy," Joe said. "In case it would help Mrs. Meade."

"Fine," she said. "If you think it will help."

Paul asked, "Tell us what?"

"Right before he died Ruben told me he had come into some money," Joe said. "He never said where he got it. He had had a few beers and he was talking big. The last time I saw him was the morning he died—"

"The same day Mrs. Meade died," Mrs. Lauria put in.

"He was down, very far down. He said he was in trouble and he was going to see Mrs. Meade and ask her what to do. That's all he would say. I told him, 'Cousin, whatever it is, I'm your family, you can talk to me, or talk to Lucy, come on,' but he acted—he acted like he was either too big a man to tell us or he was too ashamed. The two feelings looked the same on him, you know? Then after he died, the next day, Lucy was folding up his jacket and she finds this big wad of cash."

Paul said, "How much?"

"Ten thousand dollars," he said sadly.

That had to be a fortune to Ruben Lauria.

"I kept it," Mrs. Lauria said, "for the funeral expenses. And his father was sick. My second pregnancy went very hard. I couldn't work. The rest of Ruben's money kept us going for six months after he died." Keeping her eyes on the burning logs, she said, "I would have given anything just to talk to him for five minutes before he— I could have stopped him.

"That was Ruben's money," she went on. "He paid for it with his life. I'm not ashamed for taking it, however he got it."

"Who found his body?" Paul asked.

"Some kids from the neighborhood. He wasn't far off the path at Zephyr Cove, near the beach. It's a busy place sometimes."

"What did he use, rope?"

Nina remembered Molly gasping at the end of a

rope at the de Beers house, the awful sound of her voice.

"Cable, like from a stereo."

"Was there an autopsy?"

"What difference does it make?" Joe asked, tightening the arm he had laced around Mrs. Lauria a little tighter.

Paul seemed to consider his next words. Outside, the rain had briefly resumed its beating on the roof.

Nina watched him frame an answer and discard it. Finally, Paul said simply, "Did you ever consider the possibility that Ruben was murdered?"

"He hung himself," said Mrs. Lauria firmly, as the words alone ought to be convincing enough.

"Sometimes, rarely, I'll admit it, but sometimes murder is disguised as suicide."

She put her hands on her hips and smiled, a hurt, frozen smile that didn't fit her age. "So. You think my husband might have been murdered. And all this time his murderer might have been walking around loose while I cried like a fool for Ruben's immortal soul that I thought was burning in hell. If that's true, I can't believe my own stupidity."

"Lucy," Joe said, warning her.

"You better go now," she said to Nina and Paul. "But let me tell you this. If anyone killed Ruben, I am going to find out, and I'm going to kill them. Not just for Ruben. For me and the children. For the hungry nights, and all the crying." Her mouth trembled, but her eyes were like chips of ice.

In those glittering eyes Nina saw the key to her character. The past three years must have been a living hell for her. She had survived, but only by living in the place in which men make war and women make inhu-

man sacrifices for their children, a place so cold and
merciless it had left freezer burns on her soul.

Outside on the road, the shower was ending as rapidly as it had begun. A luminous vapor enveloped the
street and trees. The asphalt steamed where the hidden
sun's rays managed to slip through, adding an unreal
aspect to the misty scene. At the turnout down the
street where they had parked, Nina and Paul leaned on
the wet hood of the Bronco. Paul said, "It was time to
regroup anyway. I was concerned about alerting him,
but . . ."

"He's got too much to stick around for. I don't
think he would run."

"He must have done something. He's close to everything. I'm going to try to find out if Joe had any reason
to kill Quentin. Motive is the problem."

"What about Lucy?" Nina said. "She's formidable.
She wouldn't hesitate to kill anybody who threatened
her kids, for instance."

"They didn't have the marks of people lying," Paul
said. "No blinking or body language or stumbles or
hesitations. But I really want to make Joe for the killing. Or killings."

Nina said, "Let's step back. How many deaths have
we got here?"

"Where's 'here'?"

"Floating around. You know." She drew out her
yellow pad from the briefcase, which she had propped
gingerly on the wet hood, and drew four circles, one in
each quadrant of the page. Holding the pen cap in her
teeth, she labeled them *Anna, Ruben, Ray,* and *Quentin.*

"Oh, no," groaned Paul. "Not another one of your metaphysical diagrams."

"Sorry, but I think best with a pen in my hand." She began writing names radiating out from each circle, ignoring Paul, who had turned his back and was conspicuously taking in the view.

"Paul, take a look; it won't kill you. See? Anna is connected to Ruben, who is connected to Mrs. Lauria and Joe Marquez. She's also connected to Kim Voss, who is connected to Quentin."

"The problem is that word *connected*. Kim saw her die, but so what? It's a random connection."

"A random connection?"

"Accidental! A coincidence!"

"Ah. Coincidence. Now, Quentin is connected to Joe and Kim, on the Anna side. But he's also connected to Sarah, Molly, Jason, and Ray. Now, get this. If you just follow the lines, the deaths all connect."

"Wait. I got lost before that, at the place you decided to make Ray and Ruben part of this thing."

"They're dead," Nina said simply. "That's a connection. And the deaths came in pairs. Ruben died the same day as Anna, three years ago. Ray died just a few days before Quentin, and Ray's body disappeared that night."

"But they all died different ways! Ray was struck by lightning, Quentin was killed by a shovel, Ruben killed himself, and Anna was hit by a car!"

"So?" Nina said. "The way they died isn't connected. I admit that. The question is, Why did they die? Why? What is at the center of this page?"

Nina stuck out her lower lip, pondering her piece of paper, which was rapidly wilting in the damp.

"It's not your fault," Paul said. "It's the New Age

Celestine Prophecy trendoid way of thinking. You have to be very strong-minded to not sink into it. This idea that everything that happens is somehow related."

Nina said softly. "The ancient Greek concept of fate. Synchronicity. The Buddhist idea of auspicious coincidence."

Paul opened his mouth and jabbed his forefinger toward it, making a gagging sound. "Hot tub philosophy."

"It has its points, like hot tub sex," Nina said dryly.

"No. This situation is more like that game they play on the Internet—the Kevin Bacon game. The object is to relate everyone to Kevin Bacon within a certain number of connections, or degrees. See, Kevin Bacon was in this movie with Leslie Nielsen, who was in a movie with Kirk Douglas, who was married to, I don't know, Bette Davis in 1940. Presto, Kevin Bacon is related to Bette Davis. I'd call it specious coincidence, not auspicious coincidence."

Nina folded up her paper. "Kirk Douglas never married Bette Davis," she said. "I have to get back to the office. I'll be working at home for the rest of the afternoon. I'll be working through the weekend. I'll be working when the human race dies out and the ants take over. Stop by the office tomorrow and let me know what's new."

"Do you know what you're doing, Nina?" Paul said, so seriously that she looked at him in surprise.

"Of course. I'm filling my head with information, and I'm waiting for it to gel. Bob made this fabulous science project at the end of last year. He had this plastic mold of a brain, and he filled it with raspberry gelatin and some extra ingredients. It looked wonderful unmolded on a platter."

"Your head quivering on a platter," Paul said. "That's where it's gonna be, all right, once the cops figure out what you've been up to."

"Paul? Do me a favor. Get hold of a copy of the police report on Ruben Lauria for me."

24

By Saturday night, Nina had a new record for materials amassed after ten days of hard work. One box of pleadings and legal research on her chest of drawers; two boxes of reports, statements, evidence lists, and desiderata regarding Quentin's death in the bathroom; another box of her copies of case opinions, pertinent statutes, and legal summaries on every aspect of evidence and criminal law that might come up at the prelim on the floor by the bed; and an impromptu law and medical library stacked next to the nightstand.

She sat on the bed in her aquamarine silk night-gown, making notes and looking for angles among the papers scattered everywhere. The phone rang and she grabbed it fast, as though she had been waiting for it. "Paul?" she said.

"Sorry to disappoint you. It's me, Ginger."

"Well, hi."

"Saturday night is my favorite time to get work done too," Ginger said in her deep, jovial voice. "The one night of the week with no pressure. The rest of the world runs out to pollute their brains with one thing and another, while we the cognoscenti sit in our austere garrets and think great thoughts."

"I take it that you have a great thought that you want to share with me."

"Oh yes," Ginger said. "Listen up, Nina: This makes your case."

"I'm listening, Ginger."

"The primary cause of death, in my opinion, was the aneurysm. Quentin de Beers died of natural causes. In my opinion, the aneurysm was bleeding before he came into contact with the head of the shovel, not after."

"What? Are you sure? How can you tell that?"

"I did a lot of follow-up research on the findings in the autopsy report. The location of the aneurysm and the type of aneurysm are the crucial findings. It's called a berry aneurysm, from its shape. This type of aneurysm occurs, sometimes in clusters, in a structure at the base of the brain called the circle of Willis, and is very resistant to trauma. From my research, I'm able to testify that those berries are highly unlikely to burst in connection with any outside trauma. Other aneurysms, maybe, but not berries."

"Wait. Let me try to assimilate this. Quentin had a stroke—"

"That's not the right word. He suffered a ruptured aneurysm."

"Which made him dizzy?"

"Sure. Or unconscious."

"He was hit by the shovel after becoming unconscious?"

"Doesn't prove anybody hit him. He came into contact with it. That's all that anyone can say. That's my

opinion as an officer and a gentleman. And a pathologist."

"What about the fingerprints on the shovel?"

"To be finessed."

"If it's so all-fired simple, I ought to be able to go in
there Monday morning and get the case dismissed,
then."

"Not so fast. Great minds may differ. Doc Clauson
and I, for instance. Doc Clauson is of the opinion that
the aneurysm burst as a result of the trauma. Medical
opinion in the literature is somewhat divided. Of
course, all the second-raters are on the other side."

"So we concentrate on my cross-examination of
Clauson," Nina said thoughtfully. "All the rest is just
filigree. The case gets dismissed as long as we can convince the judge that it's just as likely as not that Quentin died of natural causes. When are you coming up? I
want to prepare with you so I ask the right questions."

"Tomorrow afternoon be okay? I'll bring the research to show you."

"Great. My office at two. Great work, Ginger!"

She hung up the phone, bounced off the bed, and
danced around the bedroom. Hard-nosed medical testimony in Jason's favor! Judge Amagosian would love
its simplicity!

She would sleep tonight. That by itself was a re-
markable concept. She usually was so tired by the time
a hearing like this started that she sometimes crawled
into the Bronco during the lunch break to nap in private for a precious few minutes. Ginger had given her a
monster break!

As she sank thankfully back into her pillow, closing
her scratchy eyes at last, all the surrounding circumstances came at her in a rush. She still could not imag-

ine what happened at the cemetery. How could she finesse Jason's fingerprints? What about the sunglasses? He must have been there. But what had happened? How had Quentin ended up in the burning cabin with Ray's body? Why burn a cabin containing the bodies of two men who had died natural deaths? Why dig up Ray's body?

Did Jason do all that? His fingerprints on the shovel said that he did. His sunglasses from the cabin said that he did.

She could face those probabilities now. Assuming he had done all that, what crimes had he really committed? Disturbed a grave and a body? He was a family member, distraught, a shrink could be encouraged to say. No problem there. Burned down the cabin? That was harder. He was very, very distraught, Nina thought cynically.

She could see it all, like a tall white termite hill rising from the moiling facts, the complex construction that would free Jason so that his family could begin to heal at last. And she would be free from the guilt and fear and doubt that had been plaguing her. . . .

Plead him out, put him in counseling, put the Vuarnets in her jewelry box to remind herself that every once in a while a human being can intervene and thwart the will of the gods. . . .

She reached her arm down the side of the bed and slipped it under the mattress, where she had hidden the sunglasses in a plastic bag. They had been right there a foot from her head every night, but now they had lost their power to ruin her sleep and poison her dreams—

They must have slipped away. She slid off the bed to her knees and reached under the mattress, rooting all around, her breath coming in and out in short bursts as fright took hold of her with clammy hands. She ripped off the down comforter, the sheets, slid the mattress off the springs. . . .

The sunglasses were gone. Someone had taken them.

25

"*PEOPLE* VERSUS *JASON THOMAS DE BEERS*," JUDGE
Amagosian said in a pleasant and temperate tone. Nina
shifted to attention in her seat at the defense table next
to Jason. Through the tall windows at their left, amber
sunlight sifted into the downstairs courtroom, illuminating motes of dust. The drizzle of the past few days
had surrendered to a day of Indian summer, golden and
dusty, and today would be a hot one.

Amagosian always began pleasantly and temperately,
but often progressed from there along a predictable
spectrum to peeved, irked, aggravated, exasperated,
frazzled, incensed, outraged, and maddened. The trick
was to watch his face, which was of the skin tone once
called apoplectic, as it flushed from pale to purple.
Many defense attorneys used their peremptory disqual-
ification to avoid getting in front of him, even though
he had once been a public defender, appointed by Jerry
Brown in California's last liberal era, and his leanings
were left. Amagosian's leanings didn't matter to a lawyer being chewed out in front of a client.

Nina liked Amagosian, even if he had the temper of a turkey just before Thanksgiving, even though he couldn't help looking at her legs, even though he addressed her as Mrs. Reilly rather than Ms. She sensed the innate lack of bias that overshadowed his peccadilloes.

The courtroom was unusually crowded for a prelim. The press was out because the de Beers family was prominent at Tahoe, and because of the uncommonly provocative body-snatching angle. The witnesses under subpoena would have to wait outside in the hall so that they couldn't hear each other's testimony, with the exception of Collier's primary investigating officer, Dan "Suntan" Beatty, so called because he spent most of his days off trolling for beach bunnies from his trimaran in the lake. Paul, decked out in a cream-colored sport coat and brown slacks, had taken his seat next to Jason at the defendant's table.

Nina had chosen a white suit and gray silk blouse from the only store she enjoyed shopping at, Nordstrom's. As usual, the shoulder pads looked a little aggressive on her small frame. And how come all the nice suits had hems four inches above the knee? Was this a new plot to keep women so distracted by worrying about what might be showing that they couldn't think?

Ginger was on call, ready to come up from Sac on two hours' notice. The ducks were in line.

Jason sat there straight-backed and handsome. His mother had brought him a blue suit and red tie to wear, which contrasted well with his sunblasted California hair.

A few minutes before, in the anteroom where prisoners waited for their cases to be called, Nina had told him Ginger's good news very quickly, then had said,

"Jason, one more time, can you explain your finger-prints on the shovel?" He had shaken his head.

"Okay, but tell me this much," Nina had continued. Leaning close to him to avoid Deputy Kimura's big ears, she said, "Who did you tell about the sunglasses?"

"Huh?"

"You know. The sunglasses I—"

"I didn't tell anybody. Who would I tell?" He sprang up and Deputy Kimura, standing near, put his hand on his holster and gave Jason a warning look.

"Watch out, kid," he said. Jason sat back down.

"Someone found out about them. They're gone."

"Gone!"

"Come on! This is no time to hold out on me! Was it your mom? Or Molly?"

"I—I can't tell you."

"What happened? Did you tell Molly? Did she tell you she took them from my house?"

"Please." His face was so agonized that she didn't have the heart to press him. It was clear he was sur-prised that the sunglasses had been taken, and equally clear he knew who had taken them but wouldn't tell.

"Okay," Nina had said. "Okay, calm down. We'll talk more about this later."

Now, listening to Amagosian give his standard speech about the purposes of the preliminary hearing, she tried to thrust away the gnawing fear she felt for Jason and for herself, but it filled all the gaps in her thinking. She had no idea what to do about the missing sunglasses. The additional burden of having them stolen from her room was too much. Every minute that went by, she fought a desperate impulse to corner the nearest person and confess.

"The preliminary examination is not to be used by

either side for discovery purposes," Amagosian was saying, adjusting his black robes. "We're here only to determine whether there is probable cause to believe that the defendant has committed a felony. What I want to hear in the plainest and most efficient manner, Mr. Hallowell, is that there is reason to believe a felony has been committed and that the defendant here is the person who committed the crime.

"I remind you both that the Best Evidence Rule does not apply in these proceedings and that the investigating officer may use police reports and other law enforcement information that would normally be inadmissible as hearsay. How long is this going to take, Mr. Hallowell?"

"Two days on our side, Your Honor," Collier replied. "But I understand the defense may ask to put on some witnesses at the close of my examination of witnesses. If so, I request that Ms. Reilly first make an offer of proof as to the testimony expected from each witness and that such testimony be limited to the specific purposes outlined in Penal Code section 866(b)."

Amagosian said, "You expect to put on a case, Mrs. Reilly? That's unusual."

Nina said from her seat, "I do have at least one expert witness, and there may be others, Your Honor, depending on how the prosecution's case goes."

"See if you can squeeze it all into two days," Amagosian told them. "I need to be back in Markleeville for a trial on Wednesday. I'll do my best to help." Since the court day ran about six hours, excluding breaks, this was very little time, and Collier was grimacing. On the other hand, since there was no jury and the rules of evidence and regarding the burden of proof were relaxed, they could chug right along.

"Call your first witness," Amagosian said, and Collier said, "Sergeant Russ Balsam." Deputy Kimura went out to the hall and came back with a crewcut South Lake Tahoe policeman, hat in hand, middle-aged and pudgy in his uniform. Sergeant Balsam had been with the force for years, but Paul had told Nina he had a gambling problem that had kept him from moving up as high as he would otherwise have gone. Balsam had a permanent glare that said to all it touched upon, Blow it and go to jail.

After the preliminaries, Collier asked, "Were you called to the Happy Homestead Cemetery on Johnson Boulevard on Sunday, August twenty-third of this year, at about seven o'clock in the morning?"

"I was." A growl in the voice. He opened his notebook and said, "At 0706 hours. The caretaker, John Eggers, called and said one of the graves had been disturbed. I took Officer Black out there, arriving at 0718 hours."

"Who, if anyone, did you meet there?"

"The caretaker was waiting, and just as we arrived in the squad car, the manager, Mr. Ricapito, got there too. Mr. Eggers advised he had started his usual shift at 0702 hours. You could see the disturbance from the machine storage shed, which is where he took us first. Eggers then took us to a grave site."

"And what, if anything, did you observe?"

"The grave site of Raymond de Beers was located close to the eastern edge of the cemetery, where new sites are mostly located, to the left of the driveway. Next to one of the plaques, whatever you call those things with the decedent's name on it, a backhoe had been drawn up. The carrier section still contained dirt and the keys were in the ignition. Lying on the ground not far from the backhoe we located a large pointed-edged shovel with a wooden handle. The area in front of the plaque had been dug up. The hole was quite deep. At the bottom of it we could see the top of a casket. All around the grave there were piles of dirt. It wasn't a neat job." He consulted the report he had filed on the incident. Nina followed along on her heavily underlined copy.

"Was the casket lid open or shut?"

"Shut. Eggers got down in there and opened it. He told me they aren't locked shut during the burial process. That's an old tradition. A superstition kind of thing, just in case somebody isn't really dead. When he pulled it open we saw it was empty."

"Did someone identify to you the name of the decedent who was supposed to be in that casket?"

"Yes, sir. Raymond de Beers. He had been buried in that casket only a few days before."

"What signs, if any, did you note of a disturbance around the grave site area?" Collier was moving along at a pace that would be dizzying in a jury trial.

"The sun hadn't burned off the dew yet, and there were footprints in the grass near the grave and on some of the dirt, but they were trampled and not much use for identification purposes. No footprints led in from the driveway, which makes sense if the person doing the digging drove in on the backhoe over the grass. Also, the plaques are close together. You could just step from one plaque to another.

"We also noted a small granite boulder about four feet to the rear of the grave. Officer Black called me over and upon examination I saw an area of discoloration that appeared to be dried blood. I then examined the shovel lying near the rock and noticed the same type discoloration. The backhoe didn't show any such signs."

"Did you take samples and were those samples subsequently tested?"

"Yes, sir. Both samples were human blood, Type A-negative. Uncommon type. Only around fifteen percent of people have it."

"And did you subsequently learn the blood type of Quentin de Beers?"

"According to samples taken at the time of autopsy, A-negative." At trial, if there was a trial, it would take several witnesses and at least a day to get this information in, but Balsam had the advantage of being able to relay from reports of all the other law enforcement personnel involved.

The California legislature had abridged the usual evidence rules for these hearings to make sure they didn't turn into minitrials. As with all the recent changes, this generally worked to the disadvantage of the defense. Though there were technical objections to be made, Sergeant Balsam was experienced and getting his story out efficiently, which was what Amagosian wanted. The judge was taking rapid notes. Nina saw no point in provoking him.

"I proceeded to the shed and noted that the lock was a simple combination lock and appeared to have been broken. Upon entry to the shed I determined that it did not appear that anything else had been taken or disturbed.

"I questioned the caretaker regarding the backhoe. . . . may I continue?"

"Go right ahead."

"He advised the keys were usually left in the vehicle during the night in the locked shed. They have never had a previous break-in. They had gotten a little lax there." The eyes looked witheringly around as if searching for those responsible.

"What, if anything, did you do as a follow-up regarding the stains you found on the shovel?"

"We wrapped the shovel in a clean paper evidence bag and placed it into the trunk of the squad car, where it was transported directly to the evidence locker at the station."

"Did you observe anything else at the scene indicating signs of a struggle?"

"Objection. Lack of foundation," Nina said curtly. "There hasn't been any prior evidence of a struggle. Some footprints, some dried blood. That doesn't have to add up to a struggle."

Amagosian said, "Rephrase the question."

"Did you observe anything else at the scene?" Collier said.

"The eastern boundary of the cemetery was close by the grave, as I've stated. The fence separating the cemetery from open marshland behind is just a boundary marker, really. Just on the other side there are bushes about four feet high where a person could hide. Officer Black had a look and found more marks in the soft ground behind those bushes. They were fresh. The grass was pressed down but was already coming back up."

Collier got out the photographs and established the locations of grave, shovel, driveway, boundaries, and backhoe. Then he showed Sergeant Balsam photos of the marks behind the bushes and, after some more objections from Nina, established that Balsam thought the marks behind the bushes were knee prints.

OBSTRUCTION OF JUSTICE 377

"And what were the weather conditions in the early hours of Sunday morning, prior to your arrival?"

"Objection," Nina said. "I understand the officer can relay hearsay statements, but I'd like to know where this information is coming from, the ten o'clock news on his TV the night before, or something a little more direct. I know we're trying to move along here, but—"

"I can represent to the court that I took my dog out at about two A.M. the night before," Sergeant Balsam said, twisting in his seat to tell it to the judge. "I live within two miles of the cemetery. I took note of the weather conditions at that time."

Amagosian said, "Well, counselor? Do we have to subpoena the weatherman?"

"I'll withdraw the objection based on that foundational statement," Nina said.

At Amagosian's nod, Sergeant Balsam resumed. "The moon was directly overhead, just past crescent. Even though I saw plenty of stars, it wasn't a really bright night, just clear and still. No precipitation or anything like that."

"So a person installed behind the bushes would have been able to watch the goings-on?" Collier said.

"Yes, sir."

"Did you locate any signs of Raymond de Beers's body at the cemetery?"

"No, sir. The body was gone."

"Did you note any drag marks in the grass or dirt area?"

Balsam said, "Yes, sir, two sets." Amagosian looked up, and Nina felt Jason stiffen in the seat beside her.

"You say there were two sets of drag marks?" Amagosian said. "Draw us a diagram. I want to have a

better picture of this scene." Balsam got down from the
witness stand and went to the big easel with its large
sketch tablet in the corner by Collier's table, and began
drawing laboriously with a piece of charcoal. While
they waited, Paul passed her a note of encouragement
behind Jason's back that said *Chin up*.

Now Balsam dragged the easel in front of the judge's
bench and angled it so the lawyers at the counsel tables
could also see it. The diagram showed the rectangular
cemetery and the driveway bisecting it, the toolshed in
back to the right of the driveway, and the grave site to
the left of the driveway near the back boundary. Small
circles indicated bushes just past the boundary line on
the left.

"These squiggles behind the bushes indicate the areas of disturbance," Balsam said, pointing at the marks
on the diagram. "These heavy black lines illustrate the
drag marks. I've labeled them drag marks One and
Two."

"Okay," Collier said. "Describe what you noticed
in connection with drag mark One."

"Right. The marks commenced at the side of the
grave, about here." He pointed. "They go around this
large pile of dirt, here, and then head due south about
twenty feet to the driveway. Considerable dirt was
picked up during the process, and some of it was deposited on the asphalt of the driveway. Those deposits
end in about the middle of the driveway."

"What were the approximate dimensions of the
Number One drag mark?"

"About forty feet to the edge of the driveway. In
width, pretty consistently two to three feet. Whatever
was being dragged pulled along a lot of soil. As I've

pointed out, the drag marks are very obvious. This object must have been quite heavy."

"Indicating what, if anything, to you . . ." Collier glanced at Nina, saw her opening her mouth to object, and said ". . . as an investigating officer with seventeen years in law enforcement who assists in training other officers in crime scene investigation?"

"Indicating it was a human body being dragged from the grave to a vehicle parked in the driveway."

"Objection. There's no information about a vehicle. Lack of foundation."

"Well, it didn't disappear into thin air," Judge Amagosian said.

"The object could have been dragged to a—a wheelbarrow or something," Nina said.

"No. There would have been scrape marks on the asphalt," said the witness. "The asphalt showed faint tire marks—"

"Which could have been made anytime. Maybe someone just picked up the body!" Nina said.

Balsam pinched his nose shut with his fingers, and said, "A body dead for a week? I don't think so."

"All right," Amagosian said. "I'll take the answer with a grain of salt, and you can get into this on cross-examination, Mrs. Reilly. But right now, I want to know what this witness thinks happened. He was there. He's an experienced investigator. Sergeant Balsam? You think it was the body of Raymond de Beers?"

"Yes, Your Honor. The body wasn't in the grave, and there was a human-size drag mark away from the grave into the driveway. It was heavy enough that the person or persons pulling the body had to go around the main dirt pile. It was the body from the grave."

"And your preliminary theory is that the body was then placed into a vehicle?"

"That's right, Your Honor."

"Go ahead, Mr. Hallowell."

"Tell us about drag mark Two, Sergeant," Collier said.

Balsam took up his pointer again, like a high-school geometry teacher, saying, "This drag mark, as you can see, extends from a rock, this dark triangle here on the other side of the grave, all the way around the grave, around the same pile of dirt on the other side, and in a line almost parallel to drag mark One, in a southerly direction to the edge of the driveway. The width is also about two to three feet."

"Indicating?"

"A second body. Dragged from the area by the rock, around the grave site, to the driveway and the same vehicle, or at least one parked in the same spot. Also, since it was dragged around the pile of dirt, it must have been dragged after the grave was dug up."

"Could you say which body was dragged first?" Collier asked.

"No. The lines never cross. I can only say that both of the marks occurred after the digging."

"Now, you have some marks indicating the areas of trampled footprints."

"Yes, sir."

"Were there footprints between the bushy area just beyond the fence, and the rock?"

"Yes, sir. Mostly around the rock, but some partial footprints leading from the bushes. Also, there was the double round impression behind the bushes, which I took to be knee prints."

"How do you know the footprints were leading from the bushes, not toward the bushes?"

"We saw a couple of toe marks leading toward the rock. Men's shoes, I'd say."

"Objection!"

"Would you like to explain that statement that they were men's shoes, Officer?" Judge Amagosian said.

"Round-toed. Larger than my feet, and I wear a men's eleven. On a woman those would be some jumbo feet."

"I'll withdraw my objection, with that clarification," Nina said with dignity, though Collier was smiling.

"And the footprints became more disturbed near the rock?"

"Yes. I'd say so. A great many deep heel marks showed up somewhat randomly, here and there as if somebody was off balance. But the land is mostly grass there and the dew hadn't fallen when all this was going on, so we couldn't get photos or casts that would do us any good."

"You're referring now to the subsequent forensics work undertaken by other law enforcement personnel?"

"Yes, sir."

"Okay, let's put this together. As to the footprints between the bushes, the knee prints behind the bushes, and numerous footprints around the rock, do you have any preliminary theory as to how those foot marks occurred?"

"Objection. Lack of foundation," Nina said. "Calls for speculation. Calls for a conclusion."

"Overruled," Amagosian said. "Let's hear what he thinks."

"I can answer?" Balsam said. The judge nodded, and Balsam went on: "As I see it, someone was kneeling behind the bushes, watching while somebody else dug up the body in the grave. Then the first person was discovered, or came out, and went toward the grave. Right at the rock area a struggle occurred, and one of them hit the other with a shovel. The one who was hit went down within a foot or two of the rock. The winner dragged both bodies into a vehicle in the driveway and drove off."

Nina was chewing on Balsam's reconstruction.

Collier paused to let Amagosian catch up with his notes. A court reporter was taking it all down, but a transcript took time to prepare, and the judge's notes would highlight the evidence he found most important.

"All right. Now, Sergeant . . ." Sergeant Balsam had been looking down at his reports. With his fuzzy bullet-shaped head and lined face he looked like a grizzled marine, not a gambling addict in constant danger of suspension. "You have in front of you a report regarding fingerprint testing prepared by forensics technicians of the South Lake Tahoe police department?"

"I take it you have a copy of the report referred to?" Judge Amagosian said to Nina.

"Yes, Your Honor."

"Any problem putting it into evidence? I'd like to be able to refer to it if need be," Amagosian said.

Nina hesitated. The judge was leaning on her. It was bad enough that Balsam could testify about his colleagues' conclusions. To let Amagosian have the report without being able to cross-examine the technicians who had written it would be stupid.

She got up and said in the most humble tone she

could muster, "I'm sorry, Your Honor. But I'm not comfortable stipulating to putting in this hearsay report without having the chance to examine the lab techs who were involved." Her reward was a change in the weather of Amagosian's complexion, a slight darkening noticeable only to those watching for it.

"Bring the techs in yourself later, if you really want to," the judge said. "You said you wanted to put on witnesses, anyway."

"But I don't want to bring in police employees as hostile witnesses in the defense case, Your Honor," Nina said. "Last time I checked, I had control over which witnesses I choose to put on, even in this somewhat informal proceeding."

"You object to the Court taking into evidence the pertinent reports? I always take them home and read them. I find them helpful."

"I would have to object to that, Your Honor. The relaxation of the hearsay rule in a preliminary hearing doesn't mean every scrap of paper connected with the case can go into evidence."

In the complete silence that followed, the courtroom watched Amagosian's face boil into deep crimson and his eyes bulge slightly. Paul lifted his shoulders and seemed to duck his head inside them like a turtle. Collier, too, fell into a defensive pose, putting one hand up as if to shield himself, shading his eyes. Jason stared at her, the panic confined to his eyes all the more intense by being so concentrated.

Amagosian put his pencil down very slowly. The sound of it rolling across the wooden surface toward the edge was like the sound of a tree falling in the forest with the whole wide world listening anxiously for its dreadful and thundering final moment. With a clatter, the pencil fell onto the floor beside the judge's bench.

"We will now take our midmorning break," the judge said in a velvety tone, reserving an intent and baleful look for Nina alone. "Mrs. Reilly, I'd suggest you reconsider your position during the break."

As the courtroom cleared for the fifteen-minute break, Deputy Kimura came up to take Jason into the holding area, and Jason said to Nina, "That didn't take long."

"Ah, well," Paul said. "I've heard that when you're bitten by a big white shark, for instance, you don't feel a thing. You just keep swimming with that leg you don't even have anymore."

Jason disappeared into the holding room, and they walked outside into the mellow autumn sunlight.

Nina burst out, "It's never the problem you expect, Paul. How come I have to get in a fight with the judge on this extraneous BS right at the beginning? He leaned on me. I mean, all judges lean, but I can't just let Collier hand him all the police reports to take home tonight. Those things are full of junk, hearsay upon hearsay, speculations and so on. . . . What's the point of Jason having a lawyer if all the judge is going to do is read the reports and say, bang, there appears to be probable cause?"

"I think you're right. The written word outweighs the spoken word in the minds of you legal people. And there are a lot of reports. You give him this one, you give him all of them. Want some coffee?"

"I need to look over some notes."

"I'll bring it to you. It's the least I can do. I'm not much help in there. Milk, no sugar, right?"

Paul went down the stairs and Nina went into the women's bathroom.

In the cubicle, the final refuge of female lawyers, she composed her clothes and her expression. Then she washed her hands and brushed her long hair before the mirror. These small domestic acts, mindlessly performed, soothed her. She was worried about many things, though, and they all showed up in her eyes.

Collier would be feeling the pressure just as heavily. If she had her way he'd never get past the prelim, and after the resultant publicity, he could kiss the district attorney position good-bye. He'd be slaving away in the trial trenches for several more years at least. He'd tell her it was all right, but it wouldn't be. He would blame her. How could he not? She'd win one battle, and lose another equally important one.

"Before you worry about all you're going to lose if your long shot pays off, better get out there and win," she murmured to herself, then stepped outside to the *Mirror*'s reporter and Paul's hot coffee.

"Mrs. Reilly? Your position as to the admission of the fingerprint reports into evidence?" Amagosian said, starting right in as soon as he took the bench.

"Your Honor," Nina said, "think about it this way. I don't have any reports to give you. I don't have a police department and a set of experts on salary back at my office. I haven't talked to the officer who prepared the reports, because Mr. Hallowell didn't subpoena him and I knew he would not be a witness.

"With Sergeant Balsam here, Mr. Hallowell and I are on a level playing field. He gives the gist of the hearsay report, and the court gives it the proper weight, which is that it is a report of a hearsay document. But if the Court accepts and studies the written report, that report will naturally have a weightier impact.

"This is a matter of fundamental fairness, Your Honor. Of course my client and I both know we can expect the utmost fairness from this Court, but if Mr. Hallowell plans to make his case based on fingerprint evidence, then he needs to bring in the fingerprint witnesses, Your Honor. If my client's immediate and distant future depend on Mr. Hallowell's fingerprint witnesses, then let me examine the witnesses. That would be fair."

She knew that Amagosian prided himself on his reputation for fairness, so she had used the word over and over. He listened impatiently at first, but at some point the words took hold and began to carry him along with her.

"Mr. Hallowell?" he said. "Why didn't you subpoena the forensic lab technician who prepared the fingerprint report?"

"Because we are only looking at probable cause, Your Honor," Collier said smoothly. "Ms. Reilly would love to have me bring in everyone involved in the investigation so she can dig around looking for mistakes, but I don't have to do that. Unlike her, I trust this Court to be able to assess the report critically, understanding that it is a hearsay document—"

"On the other hand, I suppose that something I read right before I turn off the light at night might assume a little more importance than it should," Amagosian said, as if to himself. "I think I will . . . yes, as a matter of fairness, the Court will get along without the report. Proceed, Mr. Hallowell."

Nina let herself breathe again, Paul smiled, and Jason leaned his head close to hers and said, "Good, Nina."

Sergeant Balsam had taken the stand again, and Collier shrugged, saying, "Okay, Sergeant, you have the forensics report on fingerprints taken at the crime scene and analyzed by technicians associated with the South Lake Tahoe police department?"

"I have the report here."

"What, if any, fingerprints were recovered at the crime scene, based on that report?"

"Fingerprinting was done on the backhoe controls, the shovel handle, and the lock on the shed. The lock on the shed did not yield anything identifiable, and it was an outdoor scene, without any other good surfaces for taking prints."

"And was an expedited analysis of any fingerprints lifted from the backhoe and the shovel made by the department?"

"Yes, sir. There are still some partials that they haven't had time to try to match, but they have a clear thumb and forefinger on the shovel. No luck with the backhoe—too much dirt and rubbing on the controls. No blood on the fingerprints on the shovel, by the way."

"Were any of these prints identified?"

"Yes, sir. They were matched against the prints of the defendant, Jason de Beers, on file at the Department of Motor Vehicles. He applied for a driver's license the day he turned sixteen and his prints were taken at that time." Jason muttered something and Nina put a warning hand on his arm.

"How long did this process of identifying the defendant's prints take?"

"It says here within two days. We were in a hurry. The sheriff's office had found the bodies of Quentin de Beers and Raymond de Beers in a burning cabin at Wright's Lake. . . ."

"We'll get more into that with the next witness," Collier said.

"What was the next step taken by the South Lake Tahoe police department?" The question was vague, but Nina owed Amagosian, and she knew it. She would object now only if it was absolutely necessary. She kept her mouth shut.

"I was contacted with that information, and I attempted to locate the defendant. I went to the address listed on his application for the license and talked to his mother, Sarah de Beers. She informed me that Jason was staying with a friend by the name of Kenny Munger. I located Mr. Munger's address and talked to him, but he indicated he had not seen the defendant since the day just preceding the incident at the cemetery.

"Nobody seemed to know where the defendant was. Quentin de Beers's car was missing. I sent out bulletins on the car and on the defendant. The defendant was picked up by Las Vegas police while trying to play a slot machine on September second. He waived his right to counsel in Nevada and waived an extradition hearing. He was transferred into the custody of the County of El Dorado on a warrant of arrest."

"All right, Sergeant, thank you very much. I have no further questions."

"Mrs. Reilly?"

Nina looked up from her notes and said, "No questions at this time."

Clearly pleased that she was passing, Judge Amagosian gave both Balsam and Nina a big smile and said, "Well, then, Officer, I think you may go."

Paul passed a note to Nina that said *You are now*

officially rehabilitated. Nina scrawled at the bottom, for both Paul and Jason's benefit, *The next guy is ours*.

"Call Deputy Daniel Beatty," Collier said, and as Suntan Beatty uncurled from his chair next to Collier and strode up to the witness stand, Nina glanced over the notes she had made from Balsam's testimony, and wrote rapidly: "1. Footprints and trampling. One large man. 2. Two parallel drag marks of bodies to driveway. 3. Quentin's blood on shovel handle. 4. Jason's fingerprints on shovel handle."

All that raw material came down to so few physical facts. She shuffled and reshuffled them in her mind, then set them out one by one without the obvious linkages, and waited like the rest of them for the next witness to unfold the rest of the story.

26

"STATE YOUR FULL NAME AND OCCUPATION FOR the record," Collier said.

"Daniel Allen Beatty. Deputy sheriff assigned to the Placerville Station of the El Dorado County sheriff's office."

Collier elicited over the next few minutes that Suntan had received special training in investigation of crime scenes over his twelve years with the sheriff's office and that he was an arson specialist. Suntan had a low-key, ingratiating look. He was very young-looking, with deep-set eyes, a sharp jaw, and white teeth when he smiled, which was frequently. When he wasn't sailing on Lake Tahoe he was running Iron Man triathlons in Hawaii. According to Paul, he had dated every good-looking woman at the sheriff's office and somehow managed to keep them all happy.

He might be a great runner, but Paul had told Nina he was an uninspired, plodding investigator. His involvement was another good reason to rush the preliminary hearing. Suntan had been greatly stressed preparing any report of his investigation at all in the short time frame. Nina had received her copy only on Saturday, and recognized it as her favorite kind of police report, a sloppy job.

Now she listened with strained attention to every word, her mind searching for gaps and errors. Suntan had come to the fire.

"Two thirty-five A.M., a 911 call was received from a pay station at the Wright's Lake camp. A woman. We tape all 911's, so we have it." Nina's silk blouse stuck to her underarms as sweat surged from every pore. How in the world could she have overlooked the fact that she would be examining an officer who had listened to her voice on the phone over and over?

"Did the caller identify herself?"

"She hung up before the dispatcher could find out who she was. The caller was very excited. I have the tape with me. Or I can just read a transcript."

Collier started to say, "Well, let's go ahead and hear the—"

"As the court stated," Nina interrupted, "the Best Evidence Rule doesn't apply. There's no necessity here today to get all that equipment going, and—"

"It's really no problem," Suntan said, looking at her with a gleam that could mean something very bad for Nina or might just reveal a Boy Scout excitement over his preparations. He whipped out a retro-style tape player in red plastic. "It's already loaded up," he said.

"Let's not waste time on this, Your Honor," Nina said quickly. "The transcript will be sufficient."

Suntan continued to look at her, and she didn't like the look in his eye. But she didn't dare look away, and for a long moment he held on to her eyes until his steady gaze broke through her fear and she recognized with relief that the look in his eye was a look she had seen before quite recently in the doting eyes of her doggy admirers. Suntan must think she was cute. If she was really lucky, he might be half as stupid as she was. "Why don't we just get it read and move on?" she entreated the judge.

"No, I'd like to hear it," Amagosian said. "It won't take long." If she kept breathing this hard for another minute, she'd need a paper bag.

Paul reached out one of his long legs and kicked her ankle under the table. On the folded note he passed her he had scrawled the words *Shut up*. Nina leaned back in her chair, trying to get a little more air and rubbing her ankle.

Suntan turned on the tape.

"This is the emergency operator," a vaguely familiar voice said.

"Fire," a woman yelled. "At Wright's Lake. Two people are in the cabin! Hurry!" The woman had a much higher voice than Nina's, a bit of a screech really, and she sounded hysterical. This must be another 911 call. Nina had been perfectly rational at all times. . . .

"Give me your name, please—"

"No! I can't! I can see it from here! It's burning down!" A distant crash washed over the background. "Oh my God!"

It was her, all right. Nina looked fearfully around.

"We need your name."

"Wright's Lake! Wright's Lake!"

"The caller has disconnected. We've placed that call as coming from the Wright's Lake pay station," said the detached voice of the emergency dispatcher. Nina pried her fingers from their deathly grip on the table and forced them to lie perfectly still on the papers in front of her. "Placerville Fire, come in," the tape said. "Report of a burning building at Wright's Lake."

"Call the Lake for an extra unit, Dispatch," said a new voice.

"Calling now. Could result in a forest fire; it's been very dry up there. Shall I contact the Forest Service?"

"Ten-four, Dispatch, have them send a helicopter so we can see if there are any flamers starting up."

"Ten-four. Over and out."

"That's it," Suntan said, clicking the button and returning the recorder to his pocket.

"Did everybody hear that all right?" Amagosian said. Jason's head touched hers, and he muttered, "It's you, all right."

"Shhh," Nina said.

"Has the woman making the call been identified to this date?" Collier said, resuming his questioning while seated at the counsel table.

"Not yet, but we're working on it. We have some prints from the pay phone station. We're still sorting them out."

"What occurred after the 911 call?"

"Two fire units went up to Wright's Lake. It's kind of a shared responsibility area because it's almost equidistant from Placerville and Tahoe. The Placerville unit arrived at 0257, followed by the Tahoe unit at 0303 hours. The chopper was already circling the building. I have the reports here in front of me."

"Go on."

"The firefighters from the first unit went in and removed two adult male bodies from the living room area. Both had been severely burned. With a fire still burning, obviously they couldn't take photos of the placement of the bodies *in situ*. Emergency efforts to resuscitate one of the men failed to bring a response. The other body appeared to be partially decomposed and smelled of embalming fluid. It had clearly been dead for some days. Both bodies were taken to the Lake Tahoe morgue on Doc Clauson's instructions. The firefighters continued efforts to fight the fire and had it under control in under an hour. There were no subsidiary fires."

"Thank you, Deputy. Now, at some point were you called in to investigate the circumstances of this fire?"

"Yes. I was hauled out of bed at 0415 hours and reported for duty at the fire site along with my partner at 0500 hours. It took us thirty minutes from Placerville predawn. One of the Placerville fire units was still there, but the chopper and the Tahoe unit had already taken off. I suited up and went in."

"And what did you personally observe at the fire site?"

"I have my report right here." While Suntan looked it over, Judge Amagosian said pointedly, "Far be it from me to ask for it." Nina managed a sickly smile.

"This was a typical summer cabin with two bedrooms, a bathroom, kitchen area with a long counter, and a living area with a fieldstone fireplace, which remained intact. The walls and ceiling of the living area sustained the worst damage. Wallpaper on one wall hung off in shreds. The roof had burned through near the kitchen area to the point where you could see sky. Although the bedroom walls were blackened with soot and smoke, the fire never made it through the closed doors. In an area about four feet by four feet near the kitchen, the wooden floor had burned through, revealing the crawl space. I got down in there and found this." He held up a large, charred can of lighter fluid.

"Was there any fluid in the can?"

"No, sir. And I can tell you the can was empty before the fire started, because otherwise the heat would have caused it to explode. Instead, only the outside showed burning and it was intact."

"Indicating?"

"Indicating the floor burned through early and the can fell down there early in the fire. I could smell lighter fluid on what was left of the floorboards all around the living room and on the bodies."

"And based on this evidence did you arrive at any conclusion regarding the cause of the fire?"

"I concluded that the lighter fluid was spread around the bodies and the living area, then lit. I found no trace of a lighter or matches, but pocket matches would likely have burned up. We do have a number of samples from the flooring area that we are still analyzing."

"Could the fire have started by accident?"

"No, sir. An accidental lighter fluid spill would have occurred in a much more circumscribed area."

"What did you do next in the course of your investigation, Deputy?" Collier said. He had hit his pace, relaxed and confident, the pace that comes only from years of evidentiary hearings. He was bringing out the important points and leaving the morass of data for trial, where it could all be picked over for weeks or months. Nina felt mingled envy and admiration, watching him move so self-assuredly around the witness, hearing him never stutter, never ask a question she could object to unless he intended it. How could he be such a paragon in his job and such a wreck outside it? With an effort, she concentrated again on the testimony.

"My partner and I made an inventory of all the objects in the house and their condition. When it got light enough we examined the area for traces of vehicles. We found a lot of tire tracks in the drive. It's all woods behind the cabin, and there's only one road."

"You also photographed and diagramed the tire tracks?"

"Exactly. We sent the info to a tire tracks expert out of Cameron Park who works with us now and then."

"And do you have any report from this expert?"

"No, sir. He says he's just getting started. He did mention that one of the sets was light-duty truck tires like you would find on an SUV—a sports utility vehicle, like a Ford Explorer or something."

Or a Bronco, Nina corrected him silently.

"Did you recover any fingerprints?" Yikes! Nina thought. She would make a terrible burglar. She dug her nails into her palms.

"The soot was a major problem. We do have prints from the two bedrooms that were relatively undamaged, and we have a preliminary report. They include prints made by Quentin de Beers. Several more are still unidentified."

"Any prints on the can of lighter fluid?"

"No such luck," Suntan said regretfully, shifting his weight back and forth on the hard wooden seat. They were all getting hungry, but until the clock on the wall hit the exact moment of twelve, Nina knew Amagosian would not dismiss them, and that was still eighteen minutes away.

Collier plowed on. "Have you since made any determination as to the owner of the cabin?"

"The sole owner for the last twenty years, a man named Noel Gant, was interviewed and indicated the place was a fishing cabin, and that he had told Mr. de

Beers to use it whenever he wanted to. We also talked to several neighbors, none of whom were at their cabins that night.

"They say Mr. de Beers came up frequently during the summer to go fishing, using the canoe we found beside the house. He occasionally brought up friends and family over the years, including the youngest Mr. de Beers there." Suntan indicated Jason, who sat up straight in his seat. It was the first connection between Jason and the cabin, but it wasn't very persuasive. So Jason had been up there once or twice as a kid. So what?

"Over the last couple years, the defendant would go up there alone sometimes, the neighbors said. His grandfather gave him a key, introduced him around."

"Did you at some point learn that the South Lake Tahoe police had identified the two bodies taken from the burning house?"

"Yes, I learned sometime earlier that night that the body of a . . . a deceased person named Raymond de Beers had been removed from a grave in town. Quentin de Beers's body was initially identified by a representative of De Beers Construction Company, and later by family members."

"And did you have access to the reports of the South Lake Tahoe investigation of the incident at the Happy Homestead cemetery on that night?"

"They were provided to me by Sergeant Balsam. I've had a chance to read them."

"Now let me ask you . . ." Collier said, and Nina recognized the phrase with which he always introduced important testimony. "You, as a highly experienced sheriff's department investigator, have reviewed each and every report available as of this morning with regard to this case? All of which have been provided to counsel for the defense?"

"Well, I don't know if they've been provided—"

"They have."

"Yes, I believe I have all the reports except the autopsy report. Your office has also provided me with an account of a civil case to exhume the body of Raymond de Beers, in which Jason de Beers and his grandfather were apparently on opposite sides."

"The civil pleadings in that case are in evidence by stipulation and are available for the Court's bedtime reading," Collier said to Amagosian, who blinked his eyes and said, "Very well."

"Are you able at this time, based on your experience and the reports in question, to reconstruct what occurred at the cemetery in question and subsequently at the cabin at Wright's Lake on the night of August twenty-second?"

"Objection!" Nina called out. "Calls for speculation and a conclusion. Vague, ambiguous, and unintelligible. Lack of foundation. Leading. The whole thing is based on second- and third-hand reports. It's one thing to bring in the facts that way, because the hearing is preliminary. It's another to draw conclusions as to the ultimate facts in a case."

Collier said, "Let's take those objections one at a time." He then proceeded to dismember her objections, mostly on the basis that Suntan was an expert allowed to give his opinions, up to and including reconstruction of a crime scene. After Nina had her chance to speak again, Amagosian made Collier try again twice more until he was satisfied with the form of the question. The clock edged toward twelve, as implacable as Collier, who was now asking again what Suntan made of it all.

"I would also have to assume that the coroner has found that Quentin de Beers died of foul play," Suntan said.

"I will represent to the witness and the Court that exactly such a finding has been made and will be discussed when Dr. Clauson is called," Collier said. "Now go ahead."

"Ask me again. Sorry," Suntan said.

"Can you at this time, based on your experience in investigation of crimes and your review of the reports and information we have just discussed, reconstruct what occurred at the cemetery, in your professional opinion?"

"Here's what I think," Suntan said. "The defendant here was digging up the body of his father at the cemetery. He wasn't going to let his grandfather get hold of it. I don't know too much about the family situation, but evidently the family was pitted against the grandfather on this. It was a control thing, some kind of symbol as to whether the grandfather was going to take over for the father who had just died—"

"Your Honor," Nina said. "Move to strike all the testimony after the word *cemetery*, even if the witness has hearsay third-hand reports of Sigmund Freud. He's a policeman, not a psychiatrist."

"Let's get this over with," Amagosian said. "The witness thinks the defendant was the one doing the digging. Move on."

"The defendant was doing the digging, and the grandfather was watching from the bushes," Suntan continued. "How the grandfather knew this was going on has not been established. The defendant had almost completed his task when the grandfather came over and tried to stop him. In the struggle that followed, the defendant grabbed the shovel and hit his grandfather with it. Quentin de Beers was unconscious or dead at that point, I don't know.

"Then the defendant dragged both bodies into the trunk of the grandfather's car and drove to the cabin at Wright's Lake. He must have been flustered at this turn of events and he felt safe there, or maybe he had planned to go there all along. He got the two bodies into the living room of the cabin and decided to set the place on fire as a cover-up. That's it in a nutshell."

"What about the woman who called 911?" Collier said.

"I don't think a man could sound that shrill. I do believe it was a woman, so it wasn't the defendant calling it in. So there was a woman there. A witness or maybe a coconspirator. The defendant might have called somebody to help him. But I don't believe anyone else was at the grave site, based on the footprints and other evidence."

"Thank you, Deputy Beatty. I have nothing further," Collier said, and Suntan stepped down, smiling at everyone.

The minute hand on the clock clicked into its place, exactly on twelve.

"Come with me," Paul said, and then, whispering into Nina's ear, he added, "you shrill thing." In a normal voice he said, "We've got an hour and a half. We'll catch a sandwich on the way back. Here, hand me that." He took the briefcase and tossed it in the back of the van.

"I don't know."

"If you stare at the paperwork anymore, you won't be able to think this afternoon. Let's go." He tucked her into the seat belt and zoomed off, taking a left at Al Tahoe Boulevard, then a right onto Pioneer Trail.

"Where are we going?"

"Close by." They passed Black Bart and Golden Bear and Jicarilla, quiet streets off to their right. To the left was national forest, thick and fragrant. On this afternoon of oranges and yellows, sun fell onto her tired eyes; they closed, and next thing she knew they were parking in the driveway of a chalet-style house in some quiet neighborhood somewhere. A small blue painted sign said 90 KULOW. She frowned, trying to remember where she'd heard that street name before.

"What's this?" she said.

"The house Sandy's been trying to get you to go and see." He held a key in his palm. "The realtor loaned it to me for the afternoon. I told her you were a hotshot attorney in the middle of a trial who could steal a few minutes to look at it at lunch. Gullible, isn't she?"

"You and Sandy cooked this up?"

Blameless, wide eyes. "We just thought you ought to have a look."

Her little lapse into unconsciousness had left Nina groggy and all the more finely attuned to her overwhelming fatigue. She shook her head and looked around, at the deep lot with its hundred-foot high ponderosas, at the peaceful street with a few houses here and there, not too close together, not too grand, not too mean, each one different. And this one—oh, it was beautiful with its pointed gable and warm brown color. . . .

"Come on."

She followed him up a few porch steps to the solid carved front door, but he took her arm and steered her around to the back. A pine deck about four feet above the ground, of the same warm color, encircled most of the house, extending out into the yard about thirty feet in back. The forest beyond was undeveloped. Native shrubs, tall trees, and a soft mat of pine needles preserved the wilderness feeling. They walked down a few steps into the yard, and found at the far boundary a dip near the fence where a creek would run in the spring.

Nina hadn't said a word. She just followed Paul around as he went to the front door and opened it to an entry with curved wooden hooks protruding from its walls.

"For skis, see?" Paul said, demonstrating how they would be hung. "Here's where you take your winter woolies off." But she had moved on, venturing onward into the living room. This room rose all the way to the exposed ceiling rafters. Past the wood stove, a picture window at least fifteen feet high overlooked the deck and backyard forest beyond.

"The kitchen," Paul said. Off to the right of the living room, the small and well-equipped room featured the ideal window over the sink opening onto yet another view. She stood at the window for a moment, arms folded, gazing out at the sunlight on the trees, taking in the clarity of the air, which let each leaf and pine needle quiver individually in the breeze, and the tranquil perfection of this artwork composed by nature.

Then he led her down the hall to a large bathroom with a claw-foot tub, sun pouring through the dust in the air, and two bedrooms beyond, lit from one angle like a Vermeer, still, suggestive, and enticing.

"It's beautiful," she breathed.

"Last but not least." A staircase rose from the entry, and up they went quickly, Paul pushing Nina from behind as if she couldn't make it on her own. A sort of balcony or loft extended out over part of the living room, opening onto another bathroom and another door. She pushed the door, opening it into a spacious pine-paneled attic room, all eaves, with a small casement window hanging like a European window over the street. While she stood riveted, looking up and down the street at the neighboring cabins and the white-and-blue swirl of the Tahoe sky, Paul went back downstairs.

When she finally came down, she found him cross-legged on the floor taking in sun by the big window. She sat down next to him.

"Not too easy in a skirt like that," Paul said. "You do it very well." He leaned his back against the wall, looking drowsy.

"Bob could have one of the downstairs bedrooms," she said. "And the other one would make a little office. I have so many books in boxes in Matt's garage."

"Bob'll want the attic."

"Not a chance," Nina said. "How much are they asking?"

He named a figure within her budget, underpriced according to most California standards, as so many Tahoe homes were.

"Not bad," she said.

"You'd have to pay three times that in Carmel," Paul said.

"Who's the realtor?"

"Well, how's this for a coincidence? It's one of Sandy's aunts, a hawk-nosed lady with pointy glasses."

"And we'll eventually find out Sandy owns the place." They both started laughing. Nina laughed and laughed, and couldn't stop, and the pressure of the laughter brought tears at last. She let them flow.

Paul hadn't bothered her. He still sat against the wall, looking away, but there was a watchful stillness in him.

"Paul," she said. "I'm scared. I've done something."

"I know."

"I love the house, but I can't have it. I can't make any plans."

"Okay. I've been patient with you. I've watched you eating yourself up. You ready to tell me now what's going on? What the heck did you do?"

"When I went into that cabin, it was already on fire. I saw a pair of green Vuarnet sunglasses lying on the floor. I picked them up. I didn't have more than an instant to think, Paul, but I knew they were Jason's. I took them."

"You took evidence from a crime scene?"

"I didn't know anybody had been murdered. I didn't know it was a crime scene. His mother was my client. I felt that he was too, because the case involved the whole family. I mean, it was just too obvious the way they were lying there planted, just waiting to be found!"

"Not that obvious," Paul said. "If they were going to burn in the fire, they couldn't make much of a plant."

"Now I know that. If only I'd left them there to burn . . ."

"What did you do with them? Throw them out in the woods on your way out?"

Nina sighed. "I thought I should hold on to them,

Paul. I couldn't destroy evidence—I didn't want to compound it."

"So where are they now?"

"I stuck them in a plastic bag and slipped them under my mattress."

"Oh-ho. The first place the cops would look."

"Not just the cops. Anyone. I tried to find them over the weekend. They're gone. Someone came and got them. I thought I could handle what I'd done, Paul. I even felt brave about it, like I could tempt fate and get away with it. But then the sunglasses were gone, out of my control, and in such a stealthy way. . . ."

Paul had sat up. "One of the kids?"

"No, I asked them all. Someone broke in."

"I could swear you told me Matt insisted on an alarm after your last case. . . ."

"Oh, we have an alarm system now, but with three kids running in and out and three adults, the house isn't always secure. I'm sure someone went through my dresser drawers too."

He stared at her. She had jolted him.

"Did you tell Matt?" he asked a moment later.

"No."

"Oh, Nina."

"He's been trying to get me to move out, Paul. At first he was really patient, but I guess once the idea was planted he wanted to see progress. He sees I'm not looking, and he's getting antsy. I tried to talk to him about it over the weekend, and explain about this case. He said there's always a case. I just couldn't tell him someone had broken in. I'm afraid he'd physically throw me out, which is probably exactly what I deserve. Matt's been such an angel to me and Bob, but

he's the devil when anything threatens his family. He
has a right to view me as a major risk factor."

"But you told Jason, didn't you? Mistake number
two."

"I wanted to know if he had an explanation. I asked
him not to tell anyone I had the sunglasses. He swears
he didn't."

"You might have been overheard accidentally on
purpose at the jail."

"That's illegal."

"So?"

"I don't buy that the police broke into Matt's house.
I don't buy that they taped me illegally. Collier would
know, and he would find a way to let me know. But
someone knew about the sunglasses and that means
someone besides Jason and me knows what I did."

"You're in trouble, Nina."

She nodded. "You heard that 911 call today and so
did Collier. I'm amazed I wasn't made right there in
front of Judge Amagosian and that reporter for the
Tahoe Mirror who's always yipping at my heels. And at
this very moment, they may have somebody working
out the tire tracks and the prints on the phone. My
time's running out. Collier's going to recognize my
voice or the tire tracks and wonder if I was there that
night and made that call. When he asks me, I won't
lie."

"If he's got any balls, he'll let you go."

"I just didn't want to see an innocent person convicted. But how innocent is Jason really? I can't help
wondering. Did he dig up his father's grave? Did he set
the cabin on fire?"

"You're convinced, for whatever reasons, he didn't
kill his grandfather. That's all you have to worry about

right now. He gets charged with something else, you can farm it out."

She couldn't let it go. The relief of telling Paul and not having the sky fall on her felt tremendous. "My heart went out to Sarah and to her son. I had to step in. I guess . . . I still don't regret it. Jason was drowning, Paul."

Paul leaned across the floor and took both of her hands, rubbing them between his. "You're cold," he said.

She let the sun's warmth and his hands do their work on her.

Paul was patting her knee, awkwardly. It was so warm there on the floor. Exhausted by the effort her confession had cost her, she laid her head on his shoulder and closed her eyes.

"You're closer to a basket case than I realized," he said. "You shouldn't have intervened. You may go to jail. It could happen."

"It was arrogance, Paul. I had started thinking I could save everybody. What do you think I should do?"

. . . If she lived here, she would light a fire in the stone fireplace, pulling up a chair right in this sunny spot, with down cushions and a footstool. She would put a table right next to the new chair, piled with newspapers and a cup of coffee. And then, equipped for perfect leisure, she would doze like Hitchcock, mindless and happy, with music just like this music she was hearing now, playing in the background, soft voices singing.

She must have fallen asleep then, because she heard Paul's voice over the song, obtrusive as boots on gravel, saying, "Don't you worry about a thing now, Nina. Paul's on the case. First thing, I'll tell Sandy you'll be making an offer. Second thing . . ." But she didn't hear the second thing.

27

"DEPUTY BEATTY." NINA INCLINED HER HEAD. AN hour ago, Paul had let her sleep for ten minutes, and she felt like a new person.

"Ms. Reilly."

Nina consulted her notes. In spite of the warm courtroom, Amagosian looked frisky and energized. His hair was wet, as if he had been swimming. Everyone else seemed to drag, especially Jason, who had barely said a word to her in the five minutes they had had before the afternoon session began.

She charged ahead. "Deputy Beatty, did you find any fingerprints of Jason de Beers at the site of the fire at Wright's Lake?"

"All the results aren't in."

"I thought you said the only prints you found were in the bedrooms and belonged to Quentin de Beers."

"That's not what I said. I said that Quentin de Beers's prints were among those we lifted. There are a number, still unidentified, from the bedrooms. What we don't have is prints from the living room due to the almost complete destruction of the walls and furnishings by scorching or smoke damage or actual burning. We also have a few we can't identify from the front door."

Could he hear her heart pounding?

"Do you have two base sets of Jason de Beers's fingerprints, taken as a result of his application for a driver's license and from the booking process?"

"Yes."

"Have you compared those prints with the unidentified prints from the bedroom and doorway?"

"Yes."

"And?"

"No match."

"The defendant's prints are not there?"

"They are not there." He sure lucked out with the prints, Suntan's face said.

"Thank you." She consulted her notes, to give that point a chance to sink in with the judge. "You spoke with some neighbors who indicated they had seen Jason de Beers at the Wright's Lake cabin. How about a time frame on those sightings?"

"They were pretty vague. During the summers."

"During which summers?"

"They weren't clear on that."

"Possibly ten years ago, then?"

"On several occasions during the summer."

"He could have been a child of five?"

"Definitely more recent than that."

"Within the last month?"

"Not specifically. The summer season was over on Labor Day, and the cabins have been pretty much unoccupied since then."

"So no one has seen the defendant at that cabin within the last month?"

"Not specifically."

"Help me here, Deputy. What exactly is the physical evidence that shows Jason de Beers was present at any time on August twenty-second at the cabin on Wright's Lake?"

Suntan thought. The heel of his expensive shoe rubbed up and down against his chair while he thought.

"It's a logical deduction," he said. "The defendant was present at the grave site, if the fingerprints on the shovel are any indication. He got involved in a fight with his grandfather. His grandfather's body ended up in the cabin. Now, it didn't walk there by itself."

"Oh? How do you know that?"

"Because Quentin de Beers was knocked unconscious."

"He may or may not have been knocked unconscious. But how do you know he didn't recover and drive his car up to Wright's Lake on his own, with the body of his son in the trunk?" Nina said.

"If he drove up there, where's his car now? And if he wanted to burn his son's body, why burn himself? It doesn't make sense."

"Where is Quentin de Beers's car?"

"We're still looking for it."

"Is it your theory that Jason de Beers drove in that car to the cabin?"

"Since it's missing, it could well be, but I don't know for sure. We know he didn't take the Jeep he shares with his sister."

"Lots of theories," Nina said. "Where's the beef?"

"I beg your pardon?"

"Where's some solid evidence that Jason de Beers was at the cabin?"

"I believe the primary physical evidence connecting the defendant with Quentin de Beers's death was found at the grave site."

"In other words, there is no physical evidence at all that Jason de Beers was at the cabin that night. Right?"

"Not at this time." Just say no, Nina thought. She felt like a dentist extracting molars from an especially stubborn jaw. Her poor neglected dental-malpractice client, Ed Mills, flashed into her mind. She crossed off that segment of her notes, and said, "Let's talk about the physical evidence located at the grave site. Let's talk about the fingerprints on the shovel. You were present, sitting at the counsel table with Mr. Hallowell, when Sergeant Balsam testified this morning?"

"Yes."

"And you have read the reports of Sergeant Balsam concerning his investigation of the scene at the Happy Homestead Cemetery?"

"I have copies, yes."

"Are you aware that the defendant's father, Raymond de Beers, died the previous week and was buried at that cemetery?"

"Yes, based on the reports."

"And that there was a funeral and that the burial was attended by his family?"

"I presume that would happen. But I have no personal knowledge—"

Collier, who had been following her questions with a frown, said, "Objection. Deputy Beatty is being asked to read between the lines of Sergeant Balsam's report. Why didn't Counsel question Sergeant Balsam on these points?"

"I'm saving time in the interests of judicial economy, Your Honor," Nina said. "I'm permitted to question this officer concerning the reports of other officers even though it's hearsay, under Penal Code section 872(b). I know the district attorney's office feels that section was enacted just for them, but—"

"But Sergeant Balsam was right here!" Collier said.

"Mr. Hallowell had no problem using Sergeant Balsam to talk about the fingerprint expert's report, Your Honor, when it suited his convenience. I'm merely doing the same thing," Nina said. What she really was doing was making a stink, getting Amagosian involved, to drive her next point home.

"What are you trying to get at here, Mrs. Reilly?" Amagosian asked.

Nina walked around the counsel table, aware of all the eyes on her, especially Amagosian's. She bent over in front of the judge and made a shoveling motion. "This, Your Honor," she said. "At the burial service a shovelful of dirt is often thrown on the grave by a family member."

"But this witness can't testify as to whether that actually happened!" Collier protested.

"Exactly," Nina said. She leaned on her nonexistent shovel, looking back and forth from Collier, whose mouth remained open, to Amagosian.

"Now defense counsel is trying to testify, Your Honor! There's no evidence the defendant touched that shovel the week before!"

"There's no evidence he didn't," Nina said. "The obvious explanation, that the defendant did touch the shovel at the funeral just a few days before, hasn't been ruled out by the prosecution. The police don't know when the fingerprints were made on the shovel. How can they try to pass that off as evidence?" She walked back to her chair and sat down, satisfied. She had made the point in Amagosian's mind, and she didn't care how.

Amagosian said, "Deputy Beatty, to your knowledge has any investigation been made as to whether the defendant might have touched the shovel during his father's burial?"

Suntan raised his eyebrows at Collier, who gave him a stony nod. "Your Honor," he answered, "we haven't had time to complete all aspects of the investigation. If the Court will recall, the defendant has insisted on his right to hold a preliminary hearing within ten days. We are still in the evidence-gathering phase."

"Well, you still have to cover your probable cause bases," Amagosian said. "Mrs. Reilly?"

"Thank you, Your Honor," she said, meaning it for once. "Now, Deputy Beatty, what has law enforcement got in the way of physical evidence, other than fingerprints, which connect the defendant to any alleged crime at the grave site?"

"Other than fingerprints? There's the fact he fled the jurisdiction. The fact he wasn't home that night, and nobody saw him. The motive evidence."

"You're purposely misunderstanding me, aren't you, Deputy?"

Suntan was blinking. "Misunderstanding?"

"None of that is physical evidence. None of that is direct evidence. Other than the fingerprints, you don't have any direct link at all between the defendant and—"

"Objection. Argumentative. Asked and answered."

"Sustained."

Again Nina studied her notes, using the few seconds

to calm down. It seemed to her that the atmosphere of the courtroom had changed. She had control of the moment, and she mustn't let it go.

"All right. You say the defendant fled the jurisdiction."

"He was arrested in Las Vegas. I have the report of the Las Vegas police department."

"I have it too," Nina said. "Isn't it true that the defendant was registered at a Las Vegas motel in his own name?"

"Yes."

"Isn't it true that the defendant offered no resistance?"

"Yes."

"And that he waived extradition?"

"Yes, but—"

"Didn't even request counsel before waiving his right to fight extradition?"

"That's my understanding."

"So he went to Las Vegas," Nina said. "In what way does that constitute flight?"

"He was wanted for questioning."

"Did he know that?"

"How could he know that? He had fled the jurisdiction!"

"He might not see it that way at all. Isn't it equally possible that the defendant, who was mourning the loss of his father, just decided to get away for a few days?"

"That would not be my interpretation," Suntan said.

"Of course not," Nina said. "Well, then. In the sense that he has relied on his right to remain silent and you haven't located any witnesses who saw him somewhere other than the cemetery that night, Jason de Beers does not have an alibi. You find that suspicious?"

"It indicates he had opportunity. People who aren't up to something generally are in their beds at three o'clock in the morning. Where was he?"

"If he had an alibi, you think he would have come forward with it?"

"Certainly."

"What about his right to remain silent while the prosecution sets out the evidence against him? He's not supposed to be penalized for exercising that constitutional right, is he?"

"He has that right," Suntan said, his lips compressed.

"But he'd better not use it, or he'll look bad," Nina said.

"Your Honor!" Collier said.

"Don't get carried away with your own cleverness, Counsel," Amagosian said.

"Sorry, Your Honor," she said. "I did get carried away."

"You may continue."

"Okay, Deputy Beatty, the last factor you mentioned was motive evidence. What did you mean by that?"

"I was referring to the civil suit in which the defendant was pitted against his grandfather. *De Beers* versus *County of El Dorado*. The defendant submitted a declaration through your office stating that he opposed an exhumation of the body for any purpose. He stated that he believed the grandfather was using a pretext and actually wanted to satisfy a paranoid suspicion that Raymond de Beers did not die of natural causes."

"So what was the motive, in your opinion?"

"Well, the defendant's mother, Sarah de Beers, had changed her mind, which meant that the exhumation order would likely issue. The defendant thought his grandfather had pressured his mother into withdrawing her opposition. That made him angry at his grandfather."

"How do you know that?"

"His mother told us."

Jason, who had sat quietly up to now, muffled some sound.

"She said when he found out she was going to let them go ahead, he told her it would never happen. That's in her statement."

Now Nina was in a quandary. If she attacked the statement Sarah had signed, Collier would put Sarah on the stand and emphasize it. If she didn't attack it, it would certainly appear that Jason had a motive, however far-fetched, to murder his grandfather. She decided to let it pass.

"Let's say he was angry with his grandfather," she said. "Are you telling us he went to the cemetery and dug up the grave, knowing his grandfather would follow and planning to hit him with the shovel?"

"No. That would not be my reconstruction from the crime scene. I would say he was digging up the grave to frustrate the grandfather's plan to exhume the body. The grandfather followed and tried to stop him. The defendant attacked him with the shovel. It's all linked to animosity."

"So you don't feel Quentin de Beers's death was planned before the events at the cemetery that night?"

"I couldn't say that at this time, no. It was more a situational thing."

"All this is a reconstruction from what you call the motive evidence?"

"From all the evidence I've mentioned."

"Which is all really just supposition, isn't it?"

"Objection. Argumentative."

"Sustained."

"Just a house of cards?"

"I wouldn't say—"

"Same objection."

"Sustained."

"You don't have a single solitary piece of real evidence, do you?"

"Objection!"

"Withdraw the last question," Nina said. "I have nothing further."

"We'll take the midafternoon break," Amagosian announced.

The courtroom cleared. "Now I'm starting to feel like I have a chance," Jason said.

"In spite of yourself," Nina said, gathering up her papers.

"What do you mean?"

"Never mind. Collier!" Collier was just walking out. He waited for her, but he didn't look happy. Close up, it was evident to her that he was working from some reserve of energy that was draining away his health.

"I just wanted to say . . . I know the hearing isn't going well for you . . ." she said.

"You shouldn't have pushed me into a ten-day hearing," Collier said. "You know how short-staffed we are. In spite of what the law says, the other defense attorneys work with us, give us time to prepare. That's the way it's done, Nina. As usual, you'll do whatever it takes to win, to hell with protocol."

"I have to make strategic decisions based on what's best for my client."

"That may work for you this time around. But at some point in some case you're going to need an accommodation from our office. And you won't get it. That's how it works."

"So I'm not even supposed to use the one advantage the defendant has, a quick hearing," Nina said. "You have all the other advantages. Look, I don't want to get into an argument."

"What do you want? Hoping I won't take it personally?"

"I suppose so. I, uh, value our friendship."

Collier snorted. "Excuse me, Counsel," he said, and disappeared into the hall.

28

"CALL DR. STEWART CLAUSON."

The little man in the white shirt with the white skin and sparse white hair mounted the stand with his briefcase. Doc Clauson looked just like always, bloodless, bespectacled, and brisk, except for one thing—the habitual pack of cigarettes in the breast pocket was gone, replaced by Juicy Fruit gum.

Collier quickly established that Doc Clauson was the duly certified medical examiner for the County of El Dorado, in charge of all autopsies over the enormous area of the four-thousand-square-mile county; that he had performed more than five hundred autopsies within the last ten years, and that he taught forensic pathology at the University of California in San Francisco.

"On or about August twenty-third of this year, did you perform an autopsy on the body of a person subsequently identified as Quentin de Beers?"

"Yes. I knew who he was when I got him on the table. The skull was badly burned, but I recognized the features and body build. We played golf now and then at Edgewood for the last twenty years."

"And you prepared an autopsy report, a copy of which has been provided to Ms. Reilly?"

"I have it right here to refer to." Clauson adjusted his bifocals.

"Describe the condition of the decedent at the time of autopsy."

While Collier did his work, Nina looked around the courtroom, gathering her strength for the next big push. Sarah and Molly were still out in the hall waiting, where they would have to spend most of the hearing. She was relieved they wouldn't hear this. She squeezed Jason's hand, murmuring, "Stay cool."

"The skin was severely charred and much of the soft tissue of the arms and legs was gone. The body was in a supine position with both legs pulled up, probably from constriction of the tissues after death. The contents of the abdomen, including the large intestine, were visible. Other than some shoe leather on the feet, the clothing had been burned away. A stainless steel Swiss Army knife could be seen in the abdomen. Fell in during the fire, I'd say."

Clauson reviewed the crime scene photos that had previously been admitted into evidence and identified and described the body in additional detail, saying at one point, "I'm just giving you a gross summary now." Nina thought, It's gross all right.

"Please, continue," Collier said politely. "And you then performed an autopsy of the body?"

"I did. Took longer than usual, about three and a half hours. Took a lot of blood samples and tissue samples we don't have back yet, so all I can talk about is findings available at the time of the autopsy."

"Please summarize your findings for the Court at this time," Collier said.

"Well, first of all, I found fat globules in the lungs."

"What significance would fat globules have?"

"It's an indicator of soft-tissue injury. Everybody has a certain amount of fat deposited underneath the skin, in the abdominal cavity, and in the bone marrow. If you're struck by a violent blow, some of the fat will be dislodged. It's taken up by the bloodstream and carried back to the heart. From there it goes to the lungs, but here the blood passes through blood vessels so small that these fat globules are strained out. When I look at the lung tissue under a microscope I can identify the globules using a special stain. I found some in the victim's lungs."

"And what can you conclude from that?"

"Just from that, two things you're interested in. One, the victim suffered direct violence to some portion of his body. Two, he was alive when the wound was inflicted."

"Could the bleeding you observed have occurred in the fire?"

"I would say not, because the victim was dead at the time of the fire. I'll get into that in a minute."

"Go on."

"The next interesting thing I found was also in the skull area. The relevant findings are as follows: The victim had been struck from behind, at the base of the skull. No fracture, but the scalp at the base was bruised. Under the skin I found what you'd expect, an area of subdural bleeding about three centimeters in diameter. The scalp bore an imprint indicating contact with a sharp edge, not breaking the skin like a knife cut, but sharp like a metal tool edge. Here are the pictures."

They were truly gruesome. While Nina consulted her copies, Jason kept his head turned away.

The imprint on the shaved skull had been photographed next to a ruler, which showed the length and width of the contusion and the sharp edge Clauson was testifying about. Clauson was now, in his blunt way, concluding that the wound imprint matched the edge of the shovel. Ginger had already told Nina not to waste her breath attacking that finding. Without much doubt, the shovel and Quentin de Beers's skull had come into contact.

"Did you observe any other wounds on the victim?"

"Some superficial contusions with dirt in 'em. Consistent with the victim being dragged some distance. The victim must have just died, because there was less subdural bleeding than you'd expect if he was alive."

"Any other wounds?"

"Well, not wounds. But let me go back to the base of the skull. I already mentioned the subdural bleeding. Well, there was a much more extensive area further in, in the subarachnoid space. Bleeding and several large clots, exactly underneath the point where the shovel hit.

"There was so much bleeding that I looked for another source of hemorrhage. Found a cerebral aneurysm on the right upper portion of the circle of Willis, usual spot for berries. Confirmed by the fact that he had a couple of others, a cluster of them, really."

"Perhaps you should explain what a cerebral aneurysm is."

"It's a dilated blood vessel. Several arteries meet in an almost circular pattern at the base of the brain. That area's called the circle of Willis, and aneurysms are common there. The veins swell out in a weakened area of the vessel wall for any of a number of reasons: atherosclerosis, congenital weakness, other things.

"Berry aneurysms in the brain are common. I see 'em once in a while in the autopsies I perform. Unruptured, that is. Usually too small to cause symptoms, and seldom diagnosed while the patient is still upright. Little ticking time bombs. So one of the berries had torn, which caused most of the subarachnoid bleeding, I reckon. The victim would have probably suffered severe pain, then passed into unconsciousness quickly."

"And what causes an aneurysm to burst?"

"Sometimes no reason. They blow when they blow. Or trauma. I judged the skull trauma to have occurred at just about the same time as the aneurysm went. Cause and effect. Trauma, in this case."

He said it so casually. *Trauma.* Amagosian made a note. Trauma caused aneurysm, the note undoubtedly said. Nina held her fire.

"Could the bleeding that occurred after the rupture of the aneurysm have been fatal?" Collier asked.

"It was fatal. That's what killed him."

"What about the fire?"

Clauson shook his head, said, "It was all over before the fire started."

"And what specific findings do you base that conclusion on?"

"Well, no matter how badly the victim's been burned, you can usually determine whether he was dead first on autopsy. Two ways. First, if the victim was alive at the time, smoke will have been inhaled into the lungs. Small carbon granules will be found deposited in the bronchial passages and other air spaces. There was still plenty of lung tissue and I was able to make the determination that there was no smoke inhaled. Ergo, since there was no inhaling going on, the victim was already dead."

"And the second way?"

"Quickie blood test we did for carbon monoxide in the blood. It's produced in the fire. Has a strong affinity for red blood cells. If there was any breathing after the fire started, there would be an elevated CO level in the blood. There was no elevation. Ergo, same conclusion. The victim was already dead."

"Thank you, Doctor." While Collier consulted his notes, Nina jotted Clauson's statements down on her pad.

"Okay. Did you find anything else of significance relating to the cause of death?"

"Quentin was sixty-eight," Clauson said. "He had shoulder bursitis from his bad golf swing and he ate too much aspirin. Tended to make the hemorrhaging worse. He did have atherosclerosis from all those steak houses he used to eat at, all those martinis he liked to pour down, but I don't think that had anything to do with the cause of death."

"Anything else?"

"Time of death was hard to figure. I guessed it at somewhere between midnight and two A.M. That's it."

"Based on your findings during the autopsy and the additional information you were aware of, do you have a conclusion as to cause of death?"

"Problem is, I don't have all the lab results. Drugs, for instance. I don't know. But even if he was doped out of his mind, drugs would only have been a contributing factor."

"Keeping in mind that certain lab tests are not complete, and that you do not feel at this time they will materially affect your conclusions . . ."

"Correct."

"What is your conclusion as to the cause of death at this time?"

"Extensive subarachnoid hemorrhage, secondary to ruptured berry aneurysm, precipitated by blunt trauma."

"If the trauma hadn't occurred, would the aneurysm have ruptured, Doctor?"

Clauson's eyes went opaque behind the glasses. "No," he said.

It was Nina's turn. Armed with Ginger's comments on the autopsy report, she felt ready.

"Doctor Clauson, we met again recently out of court, did we not?"

"Yes, ma'am, at my informal inquiry into the death of the victim's son."

"Actually, you autopsied two bodies from the same fire on August twenty-third, did you not?"

"I did. Quentin de Beers. Raymond de Beers."

"How did Raymond de Beers die?" Nina asked as casually as she could, but Collier was already up and objecting that she had gone beyond the scope of the direct examination.

"What is the relevance of this line of questioning?" Amagosian asked.

"Well, there has been testimony that Quentin de Beers believed his son had been murdered," Nina said. "I believe the Court will want to know if that is true."

"Why?"

"If he was murdered, the defendant could be a suspect in such a murder, and would appear to have a strong motive to dig up his father's body before an exhumation," Nina said.

Jason tugged at her jacket. She leaned toward him. "What are you talking about?" he whispered fiercely.

"Don't worry, I know what I'm doing," she whispered back, then straightened up.

"Well, spit it out, Doc. My understanding is that Raymond de Beers was killed by lightning," Amagosian said. "Did the autopsy change that finding?"

"No, sir," Clauson said. "The man was directly struck by lightning. His heart stopped. No foul play there."

"All right. Does that cover it, Mrs. Reilly?"

"It does indeed, Your Honor." She glanced back at Jason. He had leaned back in his chair and closed his eyes.

"Now, Dr. Clauson. You say the blow to the head caused the aneurysm to rupture. Do I have that right?"

"It stands to reason. Cause and effect." Clauson looked startled. He apparently hadn't expected her to zero in on what he must consider a secondary issue.

"You also said aneurysms sometimes just choose their time for no known reason."

"Yes, but there was a contemporaneous blow to the head."

"Contemporaneous? What do you mean by that?" Nina said, springing. She felt almost giddy, bloodthirsty, as she leapt upon the word.

"Well, at just about the same moment."

"Just a moment ago, you used the phrase *cause and effect* to describe your notion—your notion!—that the contact with the shovel came first. But now you use the word *contemporaneous,*" Nina said. "What I want to know, Doctor, is, Why do you think you know which came first, the contact with the shovel or the rupture of the aneurysm?"

Clauson looked down at his notes as if some new words might come.

"Are your findings consistent with the notion that the deceased suddenly suffered an incapacitating headache and fell on the shovel, suffering the head trauma you've mentioned?"

"Fell on the shovel? Wouldn't that be quite a coincidence, that he'd fall right on the spot where a sharp-edge shovel was lying?"

"He had to fall somewhere, didn't he?" Nina said. "The area was circumscribed to a few feet around the grave, and the shovel was within that area, am I right?"

"Objection! Argumentative!"

"Overruled. Look here, Doc, could the victim have suffered that contusion falling on the shovel, rather than being hit with it?" Amagosian said, leaning forward.

"Would be quite a coincidence."

Amagosian's face suffused into a brick-red hue. He bellowed, "I don't want to hear any more editorializing! Answer the question!"

Clauson shrank back in the witness chair. "It's possible," he said.

Amagosian said with deceptive tranquility that fooled no one, "This cause of death issue is troubling. We have some evidence of a shovel strike, of a ruptured aneurysm, of a fire—it's not easy to figure out what happened, is it, Doc?"

"I never said that," Clauson said quickly, licking his thin lips. "Cause of death was the ruptured aneurysm. Caused by a blow."

Amagosian sat back, took a handkerchief from somewhere in his robe, dabbed at his forehead. His face had faded like a rainbow after a tempest. "Proceed," he told Nina.

"Dr. Clauson, we appear to be clear on one thing, that the bleeding in the brain caused by the ruptured aneurysm was the immediate cause of death."

"Well, heart failure was the immediate cause of death. Due to a sudden loss of blood pressure due to the bleeding."

"The question still remains, did trauma cause the aneurysm to rupture?" Nina said. "Or did the aneurysm rupture, leading to a fall?"

"Far more likely he was struck," Clauson said. "The shovel makes a good weapon in a sudden fight. I've autopsied several deaths where a shovel was a weapon."

"But we're not looking at those deaths. We're looking at this death. The question is, What can you determine from the autopsy? It seems to me you're trying to make the autopsy findings fit the police theory, come hell or high water."

"As coroner, I have to consider the environmental circumstances. Graveyard, late at night, grandson holding a shovel, discovery—"

"And all this entered into your thinking in deciding that trauma caused the aneurysm to rupture?"

"Naturally."

"Isn't it true that berry aneurysms are not nearly as susceptible to trauma as other types of aneurysms?"

"Doesn't mean it couldn't happen," Clauson said, his voice as sparse as his hair.

"Isn't it true that the weight of medical authority is that even a crushing blow to the head, such as might be found in a car accident, won't generally cause such an aneurysm to burst, because of the surrounding protective structures?"

"It's not logical any other way."

"The contusion to the head you noted wasn't a tremendous, crushing blow, was it? There was no skull fracture?"

"No."

"How come one of the berries ruptured, but not the other two? If the trauma was sufficient to burst one, why wasn't it sufficient to burst the others?"

"The other two weren't . . . weren't . . ."

"Weren't ready to blow? They would go in their own due time, right, Doc? At a time no one can predict? Isn't that right?"

Clauson was fidgeting in the witness chair. "Counsel," Amagosian interrupted. "Is it the position of the defense that the cause of death was natural causes?"

"That's right, Your Honor."

"In spite of the violent circumstances? The fire?"

"The defendant isn't charged with setting a fire," Nina explained. "He's charged with a homicide. And he can't be held to answer if there is no probable cause to believe the death occurred by criminal means."

"All right." Amagosian put his pencil down and listened intently.

"Given the other circumstances—I mean, the head trauma and the whole scene at the cemetery—" Clauson was trying to say.

"Wait until a question is asked," Amagosian told him curtly.

"I ask you to address yourself at this time solely to the medical circumstances, Doctor," Nina said. "Based on the autopsy you performed and your experience and education in forensics pathology, is it not possible that the head trauma could have been caused by falling against the shovel, rather than being hit by the shovel?"

"Pretty freaky accident, if so," Clauson answered.

"You testified that when the aneurysm ruptured, the victim would feel a sudden severe pain? And then become unconscious quickly?"

"That's the usual sequence. Not always."

"So a fall would be likely, if the victim was standing up?"

"Could happen."

"And the victim might fall on something lying on the ground, not be able to avoid it, right?"

"Objection. Calls for speculation."

"We're talking to the county coroner here," Nina said. "If I can't query him about the medical effects of a ruptured aneurysm, who am I supposed to ask?"

Amagosian said, "It is speculation. Try to get at it some other way, if you can. Sustained."

"All right, then," Nina said. "Let me ask you this: Can you determine, based on your medical findings, and I stress that, medical findings, whether the victim was struck by some human agency wielding the shovel, or whether the victim fell on the shovel?"

"No! But it stands to reason—"

"So all we have are the shovel and the skull coming into contact? We do have that?"

"In my opinion, yes."

"And we don't know which came first, the aneurysm or the shovel, do we?"

"You have to consider the circumstances!" Clauson said a little desperately.

"Now, please tell me this as clearly as you can, Doc," Amagosian said grimly, stepping in. "Is it as likely as not that the aneurysm ruptured on its own as it is that it was ruptured by a blow to the head?"

"As likely as not?" Clauson said.

"That's what I want to know. I know you can't be absolutely sure about it. I just want to know, is it as likely as not the aneurysm burst on its own?"

Clauson was looking at Collier, whose folded arms and black stare let Nina know just how upset he was.

"It's just as likely," Clauson said.

Amagosian settled back in his chair. "I see," he said, the two words indicating the heavy weight he had attached to that answer.

Nina had destroyed Collier's case. She had won.

She shouldn't look at him. She did anyway.

He was hunched over, pretending to make a note, just as she did when she received a body blow.

"Thank you, Your Honor. I'm finished with the witness," she said.

29

Collier asked for a recess until the follow-ing morning, and a little later Nina saw the coroner walking across the patio toward the DA's office looking smaller than usual and wearing a chastened expression.

Collier had not made any mistakes. He should have been able to rely on the medical examiner's conclu-sions without doing any independent research. But Nina had listened to Clauson slanting everything ever so slightly toward the prosecution during two previous trials.

Over the years, Clauson had become a creature of the prosecution. He couldn't content himself with the medical side: he had to read all the other reports, and he let himself be influenced by them. In this case, faced with a rather complex investigation as to cause of death, when it came down to a fifty-fifty question on the cause of the rupture of the aneurysm, he had come through initially for the prosecution. When challenged, though, he had done what he had to do and backed down.

Through Ginger, Nina had known Clauson couldn't arrive at a medical conclusion that the aneurysm had burst because of a blow. Common sense and police theory prescribed that outcome, however, and Clauson initially hadn't been able to resist going along.

The next day, two more officers were sworn and questioned in an effort to rehabilitate the damage to the prosecution case, but Nina held the line. She had that sense of quiet confidence that only comes with a sure thing.

On that Tuesday afternoon Collier rested the prosecution case, and Nina had her chance to bring Ginger in, but she didn't do it. She told Amagosian that she wouldn't put on any witnesses after all. The cops and Sarah and Molly, who hadn't been able to hear any of the testimony, were allowed in at last to hear the lawyers make their concluding arguments.

Nina and Collier argued their separate views of the facts. From there, they moved to arguing the meaning and intent of the law. Although probable cause was the lowest standard of proof the prosecution could have, Collier had to meet that standard as to both prongs of his case: that Quentin de Beers's death occurred by criminal agency, and that Jason was the perpetrator.

Nina had found a California Supreme Court case holding that when the circumstances of a case are equally susceptible of innocence as of guilt, a finding of probable cause could not issue. Each prong had to meet that standard independently, or the case had to be dismissed.

They went back and forth for an hour, both of them coming close to losing their tempers on several occasions. Collier really believed Jason had killed his grandfather, and he had to win this prelim. Nina didn't have that sense of moral certainty he projected, but she took her refuge in the law.

"All right," Amagosian said at four o'clock. "I've heard enough." He stroked an invisible goatee. "This is a close case. I am compelled to follow the rule set forth in California Penal Code section 871, which provides as follows"—he harrumphed and adjusted his glasses, then read—" 'If after hearing the proofs it appears that no public offense has been committed, or'—and I emphasize the *or*—'there is not sufficient cause to believe the defendant guilty of a public offense, the magistrate shall order the complaint dismissed and the defendant to be discharged.'

"Now. The circumstances surrounding this man's death are quite suspicious. There are obvious crimes involved in connection with this death, including disturbing a grave and arson. However, we are not here today to decide whether the defendant shall be held to answer as to such crimes. We can look solely at the evidence relating to the death of Quentin de Beers.

"I would believe that there was sufficient cause to compel the defendant to stand trial on some type of homicide charge, if I could satisfy the first prong of the test, which is to show probable cause that a public offense was committed. To put it in plain language, if I believed it was more likely than not that the deceased did not die a natural death, I would tend to feel the defendant was responsible for that death.

"However, I cannot make that prerequisite finding. I don't see how I can bind the defendant over when it's as likely that the victim died of natural causes as from being struck by the defendant. It appears that the cause of death involved the rupture of an aneurysm, and that the aneurysm might just as likely have ruptured on its own. I will quote the medical examiner's testimony: 'It blows when it blows.'

"Therefore, it is ordered as follows: There being no sufficient cause to believe the defendant, Jason Quentin de Beers, guilty of the offense set forth in the complaint herein, the complaint is hereby dismissed, and the defendant shall be discharged from custody as soon as the necessary paperwork has been prepared and executed."

"I intend to appeal this order, Your Honor," Collier broke in. "I request that the defendant remain in custody while the appeal is pending."

"You know I can't do that, Counselor."

"Then I request pursuant to the interests of justice that the defendant remain in custody for a period of a week while my office completes its investigation of the arson and other charges, and prepares an arrest warrant."

"If I did that, Mrs. Reilly here would have my rear end on a *habeas corpus* writ, Counselor," Amagosian said. "You should have had your other warrants ready to go."

"I haven't had time, Your Honor!"

"I sympathize, Mr. Hallowell. But the Fathers of the United States Constitution in their search for fundamental fairness saw fit to require a better reason than that before a person can be incarcerated. Court is adjourned."

Noise erupted all over the courtroom. Amagosian glided from the bench off into the subterranean caverns measureless to man where judges lurk during their downtime.

Jason looked dazed. Nina touched his arm and said,

"You'll be going home in about four hours, Jason. I'll go harass the clerks to make sure the judge signs the release order right away."

"I can't believe it. I'll be freed?"

"Yes! The charges against you have been dismissed."

Sarah and Molly, who had come rushing up, were embracing both of them. Molly leapt up, jumping on her brother's back like a monkey, hanging off Jason's neck. "Whoopee! This is so great!" she cried, and, caught up in her joy, Jason danced her in a circle, faster and faster, as they must have done when they were very small. The twins celebrated together, mindless of the sight they made, Molly's shining hair flying behind her like sparks, and Jason's expression as open and full of emotion as Nina had ever seen it.

Molly finally fell off, laughing and panting. Sarah glowed. She said, "I'm so happy. Nina, you and Paul—please come to the house tonight for a celebration."

"I'll take a rain check," Nina said. "You'll get no fun out of me until I've had a good night's sleep."

"Oh, please! Just come for a drink after dinner, and we'll let you go home. We'll all be there. Please . . . it would mean a lot." Paul was nodding, so Nina gave in, not wanting to spoil the mood. "Okay. I'm going to make a short statement on Jason's behalf to the reporters, then go over to the clerk's for a while. Then I'm going to need a nap. Is nine okay?"

"Fantastic. Oh, Jason . . ." Sarah hugged him again, her arms around his waist, he was so tall, but he didn't hug her back. His own moment of joy seemed to have left him as swiftly as it had come. He bowed his head toward his mother wearily, and she held his face in her hands, talking to him in that way mothers have that shuts out the rest of the world.

* * *

Nina slept through dinner. She couldn't even remember hitting the bed. At seven she woke up and
took a shower, dressed herself in jeans and a red cotton
shirt, and sat down with Bob on the couch. Matt and
Andrea wanted to know about the hearing, but they
sensed that she wasn't ready to talk about it yet and left
her alone to do sixth-grade math with him.

She felt completely drained, not sure she could haul
herself off the couch to go anywhere. But at eight
forty-five the doorbell rang and Paul came in with a
bunch of sunflowers.

"They're lovely, Paul. These must have cost you a
pretty penny."

"We'll go get our backs patted at the de Beerses',
then let's take in a show at Caesars."

"I don't know."

"You'll feel better when you see their happy, smiling
faces."

But there were no happy, smiling faces when Sarah
answered the door at the de Beers house, her hair in
disarray, a glass in her hand. "Please come in," she said.
"I'm afraid you've just missed the twins. They've gone
out." In the living room Leo was mixing up another
shakerful of martinis.

"Er," Paul said. "I've about had it with martinis, if
you don't mind. I knew I should swear off them when
I stopped down at Pope Beach after court and all I
could think was that the sailboat masts looked like
swizzle sticks and the lake was the color of very dry
vermouth."

"Yeah," Leo said. "Let's bag the martinis. How
about a beer? Coors okay?" He, too, seemed oddly
subdued.

"Now you're talking. Nina?"

"Anything," Nina said. Leo brought out the bottles and glasses and they all sat down in front of the fireplace. It seemed like a long time ago that she had sat there and talked to Joe Marquez, the day Molly . . .

"How does Jason feel?" Nina asked.

"Fine, fine. Here's a toast to you and Paul. Thank you so much. You were both terrific."

They all drank some beer. Sarah and Leo seemed to have run out of things to say. "This has been a big strain on you, Sarah," Nina said. "I imagine it hasn't sunk in yet."

"What are the chances Jason will be arrested again, Nina?" Leo asked.

"I don't know," Nina said. She really did not want to talk about law. "Is that what's bothering you?"

Sarah looked at Leo, and Leo said, "No. I'm sorry we're not more festive tonight."

Sarah opened an album that lay on the coffee table in front of her and pushed it toward Nina and Paul. "See that?" she said, pointing at a full-page portrait.

In the photograph Molly and Jason were about four years old. Laughing and playing, outside on a lawn in the soft haze of late afternoon, the two seemed entirely unaware of the camera trained on them. Molly hung on Jason's back, and Jason was spinning.

"Jason would whirl around like a top with Molly on his back until they fell down. Then they'd lie on the grass side by side," said Sarah. "Aren't they just the most beautiful kids?" Her voice was tormented.

Puzzled at her mood, Nina and Paul agreed that yes, they certainly were. Leo sighed. The room was heavy with sorrow.

"Sarah, what's wrong?" Nina said.

"Sarah—" Leo said.

"It's all right, Leo. Nina and Paul won't do anything to hurt Jason. I can't just sit here like this. . . ."

Paul said, "Where is Jason?"

"He's leaving, you see," said Sarah. "He packed two suitcases and said to give the rest to Goodwill. He told me . . . he told me good-bye. He's not coming back. Nothing I could say would change his mind."

"He can't do that," Nina said, shocked. "He must not understand. I've got it all worked out, about the cemetery and the fire. I haven't had a chance to go over it with him yet. I think we can keep him out of jail. But if he leaves, they'll issue a fugitive warrant and—"

"He's going away forever," Sarah said, her face screwing up. "And Molly went with him. She wouldn't let him go alone. I wasn't supposed to tell. He's breaking down, Nina! He won't even try to explain. He won't talk to me!"

Nina cast Paul a sidelong glance. Paul said, "Where are they right now?"

"At Kenny's. Would you . . . go there? Ask them not to go. Tell them what you said—that he has to stay home and face the rest of it. It's not a matter of fear, though, that's just it. It's like . . . like . . . he . . . ."

"I think Molly's afraid Jason wants to die," Leo said.

"Why don't you go?" Nina broke in.

"Kenny hates me. He won't let me in," Sarah said, weeping.

Paul said, "You can't expect Nina to go over there blind. You have to explain what this is all about. She's been working in the dark all this time, and it hasn't been easy. You want help, you fill us in on what's really going on."

"Kenny hates me b-because I'm his mother," Sarah said, the tears flowing down her cheeks.

"You're Kenny's mother?"

"His biological mother. He's their brother. They all know it."

"Ray was Kenny's father?" Paul said incredulously, but Sarah seemed incapable of answering. Nina and Paul stared at her, waiting for her to find her voice again.

"Sarah was only seventeen when she had Kenny, younger than Molly is now," Leo said, taking up the thread. "Ray was older. He dominated her completely. When he found out she was pregnant, he married her and took her up here to live. But when Kenny was born—he had spina bifida and clubfeet. Ray rejected the baby completely. He always had to have everything perfect. If it wasn't perfect when he got hold of it, he made it perfect. Except for the houses other people would have to live in, of course. He was a goddamn bastard. He took the baby down to Stanford and had the specialists examine him. When they told him the defects could only be partially corrected, he gave the baby away."

"I should have stopped him," Sarah said, "I was such a coward. I should have taken my baby and left."

"That was twenty years ago," Leo told her. "You were a child yourself."

"I signed the papers he put in front of me twice, once when Kenny was born and six months later when he was adopted. After they took Kenny away, I was sick for several months. When I recovered, I tried to look for him on my own but I couldn't find him. Then I found out I was going to have twins. Ray was thrilled when they were born."

"What about Kenny?" Paul said.

Sarah said, "I found out years later that Kenny was raised in the Bay Area. His adoptive parents divorced. The mother went on welfare. He had a hard time growing up. I kept looking for him over the years."

"Kenny's adoptive mother sat him down the day he turned eighteen and told him he was on his own," Leo said. "She told him that his biological parents were a rich couple up in Tahoe who wouldn't lift a finger to help him. Oh, yeah, she knew. She had even contacted Ray several times over the years about getting financial help to correct Kenny's medical conditions, but Ray refused. He never told Sarah."

"How do you know all this?" said Nina.

"Kenny told me," said Sarah. "He moved up here to finish school, I think with the intention of finding out more about us. Kenny's a very intelligent boy, but due to some physical complications that delayed him in school, he ended up in the same class as Jason and Molly. One day, he told them who he was. Jason thought it was a crock, but Molly came to me.

"I went to see him right away. Kenny said he would never forgive me, and to stay away from him. He needed money, that was all. So I sent him money."

"It's been three years since she found this out," Leo said. "She didn't feel like she had anyone she could talk to. She told me all of it one day. I had been staying away from the house before that because Ray and I didn't get along, but after that Sarah and I became friends."

"Three years," Paul said in a musing tone.

"Yeah. That was a very rough time, the roughest yet

until this year. Not long after she found out about Kenny, Sarah had the accident."

"Jason and Molly—they were very angry at Ray," Sarah said. "But he was their father, and they still loved him too. They were in so much conflict—Molly especially started acting out. They were still very young—they had just turned sixteen, though they looked older because of their heights."

Paul asked, "Where was Kenny in all this?"

"Right in the middle. The twins started hanging around with him. Kenny hated Ray. He's suffered so much."

"Tell him about Molly," Leo encouraged her.

"Molly provoked him. At the dinner table, she might say, 'Kenny's working on a bomb. Maybe he's gonna blow you up for what you did to him, Dad.' "

"Ray couldn't get rid of Kenny," Leo added. "He tried to bribe him to get lost, but Sarah was sending him money. He felt like Kenny was haunting him. Ray called him the Toad."

"I played my part," Sarah said sorrowfully. "I couldn't pretend he wasn't my son. It was Quentin who kept us going. Ray thought everyone was against him except his father. He knew Quentin would do anything for him, and so Quentin could influence him. Quentin kept Ray calm and he talked to the kids and tried to help them understand that Ray was going through a very hard time himself. He persuaded me"— she wiped her eyes—"that Ray would get better and I should hang on."

"And he kept Ray and me apart, but kept me in the company," Leo said. "It wasn't easy. Ray had started accusing me of having designs on Sarah and the company."

"It's called projection," Nina said. "He projected his guilt and self-hatred onto everyone else. It sounds like it all came back at him twice over."

"Anyway, we got past that awful time," Sarah went on. "I recovered more or less from the accident and Ray calmed down to a slow simmer. I'm one of those—you know, Nina? Peace at any price. I kept my fingers crossed and thought, Soon Jason and Molly will go off to college, and Leo and I—everything would come to its natural conclusion. I was so wrong."

Leo said, "The twins graduated in June, and Ray saw what was coming, and he didn't like it at all. He started throwing his weight around again, said the twins should go to school here so Jason could work part-time at the company. He started making life hell for me at the company again. He was getting out of control again, we could all see it, and Sarah was afraid to make a move. Even Quentin had thrown up his hands."

"That's how he controlled you," Nina said. "By going out of control himself. Why did you all agree to go on that hike with him?"

Sarah said simply, "He made me. The night before, I told Leo."

"I was afraid for her," Leo said. "It didn't smell right to me. But Sarah insisted she had to go, so I decided the twins and I would go up there too. When we showed up and I saw Ray's reaction, I knew I was right, that Sarah was in some kind of danger from him. The twins felt it too."

"I just can't believe he intended to harm me."

"We'll never know now," Leo told her grimly.

Nina's cell phone rang in her purse. She ignored the ringing. She had been taking all this in, nodding as, piece by piece, she found the understanding that had eluded her until now about the de Beers family. "And then . . . Ray was gone, but it wasn't over," she said.

"Jason and Molly haven't had a chance to get their balance," Leo said. "But now it should be close to over. We should all be sitting here, happy, relieved, talking about the future. And now Jason is the one losing it."

"He can't run now," Nina said. "You're right, Leo. We are too close to the end."

"Why is he doing this now, at this point?" Sarah moaned, hitting her hand against the arm of the couch. "He's always been the responsible one, the mature one! Except for that one time—when things were at their worst, just after I got out of the hospital, right after you had that fight with Ray, Leo."

"Yeah, I remember you telling me about it." Leo explained to Paul and Nina, "Jason signed Ray's name to a business check and the next day took off in a stolen car. He totaled the car near Carson City and Ray brought him back home. Jason told Sarah and Ray he planned to run away, but when he ran off the road and wrecked the car he gave up."

"It was so out of character for him," Sarah said. "To take that money. To take a car. I could hardly believe it, but he sat right there in that chair you're sitting in, Nina, and told me. Ray was there too. For once, Ray did the right thing. He just told Jason he'd made a mistake, and not to do anything like that again."

Paul had jerked to attention. He said, "When was this?"

"Oh, it would have been in August. Three years ago."

"Did you ever see the car?" Paul said, his voice tense.

"Not afterward," Sarah said. "Actually, it was Joe's old car. It was parked on the street behind the house. Joe never did find out who had taken it. Ray and Jason just left the car in Carson City. Ray mentioned later that he called somebody to haul it away."

"What about the money?" Paul said, leaning forward. Nina was thinking, Please, don't let it be for ten thousand dollars. . . .

She waited for the answer, a painful pressure in her heart.

And Sarah said, "Jason left it in the car, he was so upset, and it was stolen out of the car while it was sitting by the side of the road."

"How much was it, Sarah?" Nina whispered. Sarah turned to her.

"Ten thousand dollars," she said. "Why?"

Paul said, "I'm very sorry. But I'm afraid Nina here is all tired out." He stood up and pulled Nina to her feet. "Let me get this lady home."

Sarah and Leo stood up, too, surprised. "But will you go see them? Aren't you going to try?" asked Sarah.

"I'm sorry," Nina said. "I'm sick. I have to go now." Without having to act much, she tottered to the door, leaning on Paul.

While they were in the house, a squall had come up over the lake. They could see the rain under the moon, scudding toward them. A moist breeze pushed Nina's hair back and revived her a little. When they were safely out of earshot of the house, she said in a low voice, "Could it be? Could Jason have killed Collier's wife?"

"Is there any doubt?" Paul said. "Get in."

"An accident?"

"I'm thinking about that."

They rolled out the driveway, Nina also thinking furiously.

"He must have decided to kill Ray after his mother's accident," Nina said. "That has to be it. He must have tried to hire Ruben Lauria to do it, Paul! Joe had brought Ruben out to the house once and had told the twins how he was this big criminal."

"Maybe all of them were in on it," Paul said. "Kenny and Molly as well as Jason."

"Maybe. I don't know. He was just a kid, Paul! Ruben took the money, then decided not to go through with it. He told Jason. . . ."

"And Jason was trapped. He couldn't trust Ruben not to tell the police, or, worse, Ray. Jason would have to be terrified of that possibility."

"Jesus, Paul, do you realize what we're saying! Ruben didn't hang himself." She was staggered. "I—I just can't believe Jason could . . ."

"He told his mother a cock-and-bull story about the car and the money, didn't he?" Paul said. "He had to account to them somehow for the ten grand. . . ."

"He must not have realized it was Joe's car. . . ."

"Then Ruben had some drinks and went down to the probation office and spilled his guts to Anna—he probably told the kid that was what he was going to do—and Anna had to be shut up as soon as possible."

"But that makes Jason a monster, Paul! He's not like that!"

"Stupid kid," Paul said. "Throwing away two lives besides his own." He seemed almost as stunned as she was. He turned up Matt's street.

"Hey, what's this?" Nina asked.

"I'm going to take you home. You're exhausted."

"But what about Jason?"

"I'm going over there. But I'm going to tell Collier about this first. He has to know."

"But he's a DA!" Nina said in horror. "Wait, Paul, we don't know anything for sure yet!"

They had pulled into the driveway. Matt's house was dark.

"Get out," Paul said.

"Oh, no, you don't," Nina said. "I'm going along. Whatever happens, it has to be fair to Jason. I'm going to see to it."

"I said get out." He reached past her and opened the door of the van, then pushed her toward the door.

"Hey!" Nina said. "Don't you dare touch me!" She balled up her fist, not thinking at all anymore, and punched him in the ear.

"Ow!" Paul said, recoiling. His foot slipped off the brake, and the van rolled backward. The passenger side door was still open. "Watch out, you little—!" He got the van back under control just before they rolled into the street.

"I'm coming, do you hear, Paul?" Nina said in a low voice.

Paul's right hand covered his ear. She thought, Oh, God, he's going to punch me back, hold on— He gripped her shoulders and twisted her toward him, held her tight against him so she could hardly breathe, and put his mouth against hers. The kiss was hard and hurt her so that she tried to move away, but he wouldn't let her go, his hands like vises. After a long moment, he released her suddenly and she fell against the seat.

"You son of a bitch," she said, panting.

"Now get out," Paul said.

She didn't move. Paul made an exclamation of disgust and threw the car into gear. They didn't speak to each other all the way to Collier's apartment.

30

A GRAY EYE THROUGH THE KEYHOLE. A DISGRUN-tled noise.

"What the hell?" Collier opened the door and waved them in. He wore nothing but a pair of knit gym shorts, revealing a thick mat of brown hair on his chest. Although it was only a few minutes past nine P.M., his eyes were puffy from sleep. "Come on in," he said. "Join the party." They entered the kitchen, piled with dirty dishes and clumps of fast-food wrappers. He cleared a place for them at the table by pushing things onto the floor, put his head on his hands, coughed, and said, "This completes my total humiliation, I suppose. What more could you possibly want from me now, Nina?"

"We have to talk."

"Talk." He got up went to the sink, poured himself a glass of water, took a drink, and turned to them. "Do I need to be awake? I see I do. Hang on." He turned the cold water on, stuck a finger in to sample it, and dunked his entire head under the faucet, coming up sputtering and dripping. Reaching for the dry cloth hanging on a hook beside the sink, he said, "Go ahead. I'm ready."

"Sit down," Paul said.

Collier took up his position at the table again, yawning and rubbing his hair.

While Paul was considering his words, Nina said, "I made that 911 call from Wright's Lake."

"Yep," said Collier.

"You knew?"

"I know your voice."

"Why didn't you say something in court?"

"It's not a big priority in my life to bring you down," Collier said. "Although perhaps it should be." He gave his head a final rub, then tossed the towel toward a pile on the counter. The towel knocked a plate onto the floor, shattering it.

They all looked at it. Collier said, "Did you come here to tell me that?"

"I went inside and saw Quentin's body. And Ray's body. The flames were just starting to shoot up around the living room."

"I'm amazed you didn't leave fingerprints. Maybe you did. Did you see who set the fire?" Collier asked casually, as though they were talking about the weather. "Or Quentin's car?"

"No. Whoever did it was gone by the time I arrived."

"I assume you came here to tell me the truth," Collier said. "You wouldn't be covering up for young Jason, would you?"

"I never saw him. He wasn't there. But . . . when I went inside, I saw a pair of sunglasses—"

Paul groaned. "I knew it," he said. "I knew if you came, you would do this. . . ."

"I picked them up and ran out. I wasn't thinking. Smoke was billowing everywhere, and I was afraid I would be trapped."

"Hand them over," Collier ordered.

"I can't. No, I didn't throw them away. I put them between my mattress and the springs until I could figure out what to do with them. They were stolen from my room. I don't know by who."

"Describe the sunglasses."

"They were expensive Vuarnets with green shades."

"Know anybody who wears glasses like that?" Collier said, even more casually.

"I can't answer that."

"Attorney-client privilege?"

"I can't answer that either."

"God, I hate lawyers," Collier said. "As soon as the prelim is over you come bearing this confession to assuage your guilt. Looks like you were right anyway on the murder charge. If Clauson had been straight with me from the start, I doubt the case would have made it to the prelim stage. Oh, well, we can still use them on the arson charge."

"I—I'm sorry," Nina said. "I realize it's a crime. What are you going to do?"

"Nina's confused," Paul said, his eyes holding Collier's. "She's made up all that sunglasses stuff. Shut up, Nina. It's my turn to talk. Listen, Collier. Jason is thinking hard about leaving town ahead of the warrants that you will no doubt be preparing tomorrow."

"He won't get far. It'll only hurt him."

"Wait. There's more. Three years ago, in August, Jason took Joe Marquez's Catalina out for a ride without permission. He got in some kind of accident. Joe never saw the car again, which he didn't mind because it was about to self-destruct anyway."

Collier rubbed his hand on his bare chest. His hair stood up wildly. He would have looked a little comical except for the brutal expression on his face.

"He drove the Catalina? Jason de Beers killed Anna?"

"I'm afraid it looks that way."

"He was riding around, what? Sixteen years old in a stolen car, and he mowed down my wife? He did that? And I was in court with him for the last two days?" Collier got up, knocking over the chair, and seized Nina by the chin, forcing her to look at him. "I don't give a fuck about attorney-client privilege," he yelled. "I want to know, and I want to know now. How long have you known this?"

"I just found out! Honestly!"

"Hey hey hey," Paul said. "Take it easy, big fella."

Collier held her eyes for one more soul-searching instant, then dropped his hand, saying, "Don't move." He went to the phone hanging on the wall and punched in some numbers. "This is Hallowell." He put his hand over the receiver. "Where is he?"

"Stop," Nina said, gently taking the phone from his hand. "You can't prove anything. Ray's dead, and from what Paul told me the trail backward hits a dead end."

"I want him arrested. Where is he?" The phone rang. He answered it. His office had called back. Reluctantly, his eyes still locked on Nina's, he told them he would call later.

"Come on, sit down. I'm going to tell you a story," Paul said.

Collier sat down, shaking. The news had finally hit

him physically. He kept shivering as if he would never stop. "Do something," Paul told Nina.

While searching for a blanket in the bedroom, Nina let her eyes roam around the private domain she had never before entered. She looked for a clue to Collier, and found a bare lightbulb, a bed with no sheets, and a pile of laundry in the corner. There were no pictures on the walls, but she could see tack holes from when there had been pictures, probably dating back to his wife. His room had all the personality of a white wall.

Someday, Collier might be someone again. Right now, he was a husk.

When she returned, Collier and Paul were deep in talk, Collier still shivering. She put the blanket over his shoulders and sat back down.

"We go over there and get him to admit it," Paul was saying. "We tape him. Nina, he'll talk to you."

"For Christ's sake, he's my client! Yours too! Forget it!"

"You finished the job. There are no charges pending against him. He's not your client anymore," Collier said. "Technically. And you use technicalities when they suit your purposes, don't you?"

"I can't take advantage of him that way. It would be unethical."

"This is another crime entirely."

"I don't care!"

Collier said, "Will you defend me at my trial, then? 'Cause if the law can't get him, I'm afraid I'll have to kill him myself."

"Hang on, you two," Paul said. "Don't get your undies in a twist. I'll go in."

"I have to know, Nina," Collier said. "You understand that, don't you? If he wants to talk to Paul, do you really want to stop him?"

"Let's tape it. I've got a pocket recorder," Paul said.

"No tape," Nina said. "I won't let him be entrapped that way. It's illegal, anyway. And no intimidation. I don't like this. He's a suspect. You should read him his Miranda rights."

"You know what, Nina?" Collier said slowly. "Right now, I feel like gagging you and tying you to this chair until we're done. This is my wife we're talking about. My wife."

"It's always been your wife we were talking about, Collier," said Nina, shooting off her big mouth.

Paul said, "You could call over a couple of cops— and believe me, it would take a couple—and arrest her, Collier, get her off our backs."

Nina realized he meant it. Collier was thinking this over. "All right," she said. "Collier and I will wait outside. The door's thin. I could hear everything in the hall when I was over there. We'll listen. But don't trick him, Paul. Be fair."

Collier went into the bedroom and came out dressed, carrying a standard-issue .45. "In case he tries to run," he said. "Are you armed, Paul?"

"Always," Paul said, patting his shoulder holster.

"He would never try to hurt one of us," Nina protested, but they paid no attention to her. The three of them went back out and got into the van, Nina in the middle.

On the way to Kenny's apartment, Paul said, "A flash of green. Kim saw it on the driver. Just the color. She put it in her painting."

"His green sunglasses," Collier said. The way he said it, in an ugly voice that didn't sound like him, was spooky. Nina turned to look at him. His eyes were blind.

"Hold on." Paul swerved into the driveway of the funky apartment building, clicked off the ignition, and doused the lights.

"Nina, you've got your cell phone?"

She stopped to check her pocket. "Right here."

"Get a move on," Collier commanded, striding urgently ahead into the building. Quietly, Collier and Nina took up positions out of sight in the hallway, around the corner from the apartment.

Paul rapped on the door.

The pungent odor of marijuana wafted from under the door, and a heavy bass vibrated the deck through the hall. Kenny opened the door a few inches so Paul could see the chain.

"What do you want?" Kenny's eye peered up at Paul.

"I need to see Jason."

"He's not here."

"C'mon, Kenny. I just have to talk to him before he leaves."

"Did the lawyer send you?"

"No. His mother. This is personal."

"Jason!"

Jason came to the door.

"Your mother was afraid you needed money," Paul said. He patted his wallet pocket. "She sent me over."

A pause. "Hand it through."

"No way. I hand it to you personally along with a message from your mother."

"How much is it?"

"That would be telling." Paul heard a commotion,

then the door swung open, and Paul entered Kenny's living room, reminding himself about what it was like to be nineteen and too naive to know the oldest come-on in the book when it walked up and slapped you silly.

Only the lava lamp was lit, the waxen red droplets dribbling and re-forming endlessly in the hot solution. Molly stood behind Kenny, who leaned over to the stereo and lowered the music. Suitcases stood against the bedroom door, which was slightly ajar. Molly looked stoned and frightened.

"Hi, Molly. Hi, Kenny," said Paul.

"Hi," said Molly. Kenny sat her down on the couch.

Nobody spoke for a minute. Paul was feeling out the atmosphere, choosing his approach.

"There's no check, is there?" Jason said. He looked as if he were on his last legs. "What did my mom tell you?"

Paul sat down at the counter where he'd eaten his pastrami sandwiches with Kenny, making himself comfortable. "So you're leaving," he said. "Is that going to help your mother and sister? I thought you were a brave kid. Boy, was I wrong. The minute you get your chance, you run again."

"It's not like that."

Molly said, "Our mom'll be all right. She's got Leo. We have to get away from all this. We can't stay."

"I told you, Moll, you can't come," Jason said.

Paul said, "Nina cares about what happens to you, Jason. And what about your mother? She loves you. If your sister goes along, I don't think your mother will be all right at all."

"I'm telling you for the last time, Moll, we have to split up," Jason said. "We have to, Moll!"

"I won't!" Molly said. "Not in this town full of death! I don't care if we have to go to Timbuktu! I don't want to live without you!"

"You promised, Moll, never to try that again!"

"Why not just stay and pay the price, Jason?" Paul said mildly. "Going into exile can be a worse torture than jail. It's so very lonely out there. And you'd always be afraid."

"Because I can't. It's worse than Nina knows. She can't do anything. No one can. I have to go away."

"Because you're a murderer after all, right, Jason?"

Molly inhaled sharply. Kenny said, "Uh-oh."

"You did very well. You almost got away with it."

"You're bright to figure it out," said Kenny. "We're all bright."

"Why did you do it?" Paul asked, keeping his eyes on Jason. "You're going away, you might as well tell me. You have to tell somebody, sometime."

"You really want to know?" Kenny said.

"Kenny, don't!" Molly cried.

"Because of Ray," Kenny said. "He was killing them inch by inch. Molly, Jason, and Sarah. And me. He was going to put me away in some funnyhouse, just for sticking my ugly face into his life. He was going to kill Sarah. Everything came together at once and Jason knew it was the only chance."

"I still don't get it."

"Don't let Kenny say anything else, please, Jason," Molly said, but Jason didn't move. He had the abstracted look Paul had seen him wear in court, as if he were listening to a voice inside himself, an accusing, hateful voice. Molly got up and went to him, put her hand on his arm tenderly.

"Good, Kenny, good," Paul said. "Go on."

"That's enough!" Molly said. "Look what he's do-ing! We can't talk to him. Let's just go, Jason!"

"No," Jason said, pushing her away. "I pay. Not you. Not Kenny."

"How did it go down, Jason?" Paul said, his voice steady.

"Oh, Jason," Molly said tearfully. "Please don't say anything!"

"No one can hate me worse than I hate myself," Jason said slowly. "I hate myself, you know. I can't stand myself."

"Say it!" Paul demanded. "Say it!"

"I can't say it!" Jason said. "I'm too ashamed. I'm so sorry. I know I did what nobody could ever forgive." He hung his head. The lamp cast his shadow against the wall, the head bowed as if awaiting a guillotine.

Molly said in a tiny voice, "You did it to save us."

There was another pause. Then Jason went to the two suitcases and picked them up. "Wait," Paul said. "You haven't told me about your grandfather."

"He followed me to the cemetery. We argued. He clutched his head and he said, 'Jason, I have the most awful headache.' Then he fell. I ran over to him, but he was unconscious. I didn't know what to do. I couldn't call anyone. So I put him in the back seat. . . ."

"And Ray in the trunk."

"I thought, the cabin. I had to think. But when I got there, he was dead."

"The shovel with the blood, though, that puzzles me."

"It was right next to the rock. Like Nina said. He fell on it. I moved it away from him. . . ." Jason was reliving the moment.

Molly took one of the suitcases and said desperately, "Come on, I'm ready."

"I'm going now," Jason said, looking down. "Tell my mother—"

"Just one more thing. Don't worry, I won't stop you from opening that door," Paul said. "The thing that would bring all this together for me. Just this: Why did you dig up your father's body?"

Jason said, "Tell my mother I'm sorry. Tell Nina thank you. She tried to help. Kenny—"

"Good-bye," Kenny said softly, "bro." He edged over and gave Jason a shy hug, little Mutt hugging tall Jeff.

"Good-bye, Moll." But Molly wouldn't let him hold her.

"No! No!"

"Please, Molly," Kenny said. "Stay. I need you."

"What's that noise?" Jason said, pointing at the door.

"I didn't hear anything," Paul said. "Don't go, son. We'll try to help you."

"There's someone outside!" Kenny said.

Collier burst in, pushing Nina ahead of him. His gun was drawn and he was breathing in short gasps. "Get out of the way," he said to the air, and then he raised the gun and aimed it at Jason, who was standing not two feet from Nina.

"No!" Nina yelled, and threw herself in front of Jason. Paul had his own gun drawn now. "Put it down, buddy," he told Collier. "You're not going to shoot Nina, are you?"

Jason's arm shot out, knocking over the lava lamp, which whacked the vinyl floor, bounced once on its base, and cracked into smithereens, leaving them in complete, windowless darkness. Someone whimpered. Paul grabbed Nina, holding her still, and froze, praying that Collier wouldn't fire off a shot in the dark.

The apartment door swung open. Jason and Molly ran out into the hall. Paul's hand found Collier, but Collier whirled away from him and ran out too.

The outside deck held the only real light, all of forty watts beaming muddily down from above the doorway. Paul checked the gun in his hand. An eerie green glow surrounded it from the Tritium night-sights. Two figures fled like deer through the dimness, disappearing almost instantly, Collier already falling behind.

The rest of them waited a long, silent instant, until they were sure he and his trigger finger had gotten safely away.

Then Nina and Paul raced out into the parking lot, past the startled neighbors, Kenny hopping along behind them. They arrived in time to see the Jeep, followed by Collier's car, skidding around the corner of the street at top speed, brakes screeching, the people driving behind the steamy windshields wearing looks of equal determination.

They leapt into the van, Kenny jumping in back just in time, and chased the cars. At Highway 50, all three cars, one after the other, careened into a sharp left. Paul drove the van, and had no trouble in the light traffic keeping track of Collier in his little car trailing the Jeep in front. Nina was punching 911 for the third time that month. Paul pried the phone out of her clutching fingers and calmly described the Jeep, its license number, and the pursuing car, all the while driving at top speed up the street.

But there didn't seem to be any danger of the two cars ahead losing each other. Collier stuck to the car ahead of him. When he got close, he surged forward, slamming into the back of the Jeep. Jason skidded left, veering up onto the sidewalk, where he drove for what seemed like an eternity, narrowly avoiding posts, flattening some bushes, and causing two pedestrians to jump for their lives.

"Why's he trying to kill them?" Kenny said, hanging on to the back of Paul's seat.

"The probation officer Jason killed—she was his wife!" Nina called back, not turning her head away from the cars in front.

"Anna Meade? He never did that!"

"He just confessed, didn't he!"

"No! You're all mixed up!"

Down again onto the road in front of Collier, Jason jumped the curb with a thundering jolt, raising up a sheet of water from the half-flooded street. Nina could see Molly's hair flying behind her as the Jeep skewed once more, almost completely out of control.

Collier roared up behind Molly and Jason again. Again, he slammed them.

"Oh, my God! He's going to kill them both!" Nina cried, but they recovered somehow, returning to take the lead, their maniacal speed eating up the road before them. Her cell phone rang in vain somewhere near her feet.

"They're heading across the state line!" Kenny yelled, his hair brushing against Paul as he leaned over the seat. "It wasn't him! Stop that guy!"

"Damn it, Paul. Faster!" Nina shouted, and Paul gritted his teeth, pushing harder.

Somehow they had crossed the miles between Kenny's apartment and the casino district. Nina watched Paul, who must have had his foot glued near the floor already, edge forward, and listened for the sound that must come next, the sound of a crash. She closed her eyes, and almost instantly opened them, to the sight of Jason's car whipping into a left turn that had to be the closest thing to a right angle possible in a car, directly into the Prize's parking lot.

Collier shot past, skidded into a U-turn in the middle of the highway, nearly hitting a car coming from the Nevada direction, and hurtled up the drive into the parking area just ahead Paul. He cruised the lot rapidly, and they could see him craning his neck to examine the cars. Then they saw the Jeep, empty, windshield wipers slapping time, doors open, in the middle of the drive. Collier screeched to a dead stop and tore out of his car, running straight through the puddles into the brightly lit casino entrance.

"Oh, shit," Paul said. He grabbed his phone from the seat and barked out where he'd gone.

The van skidded to a stop. They all jumped out.

Brilliant and garish, full of busy people, the casino's raucous atmosphere quickly absorbed anything out of the ordinary. Blinking in the bright lights, Nina stood in one place until she caught a glimpse of Collier in the elevator near the door, gun waving as the doors closed on him. A couple of security guards from the casino punched buttons on the next elevator. Two others ran for the stairs, their own guns drawn. Kenny had dropped behind them, lost in the crowd.

Collier's elevator, an express car, stopped only at the rooftop restaurant.

"Police!" Paul yelled. The guards obligingly held the elevator door long enough for the two of them to run in, dripping and gasping. "All the way up!" Paul ordered. "Police are on the way. He's trying to kill a young man with a girl who must be just ahead of him. His gun's loaded."

The doors opened. They found themselves in a red-carpeted hall, the anteroom to the penthouse restaurant. A maître d' had shrunk his body tight against the wall. When he saw the guards, he stepped out and pointed, saying, "That way! He has a gun!"

"The roof!" one of the guards yelled. They ran after him to a small closed door, which led to a narrow flight of metal stairs.

On the roof, the rain-swept sky pressed down, heavy with unseen presences. Below, with its arc of gaudy light between lake and forest, the town looked as remote and frivolous as it had from the top of the mountain. Encrusted with brilliant neon signs, the walls of the neighboring casinos burned and hissed. Cylindrical shapes of ventilator casings and square concrete walls of unknown purpose broke the wet expanse of concrete, creating pools of complete darkness.

They spread out, searching for Collier, Nina staying close to Paul. Half-crouched as she moved beside him, her clothes already sodden and heavy against her skin, she was as exposed as she had been in that other storm, but this time she felt no fear. This time she felt that rocklike resistance rising in her against the tide that propelled them irresistibly from event to event, quenching every attempt to outwit it.

If only they hadn't told Collier . . . and what was Kenny blabbering about in the car?

Out of obstinate loyalty to Jason, Molly, too, was now in the line of fire. I won't let that idiotic girl die! Nina thought. But what could she do? Collier had cracked, and she felt tragedy rocketing toward them like a crashing jet.

Catching a movement out of the corner of her eye, she ran off to the left toward the edge of the building. "There they are, Paul," she shouted. He sprinted toward her, gun raised in his hand.

Fleet and light as birds, the twins made an unforgettable sight. Multicolored in the glittering neon, they moved swiftly toward the low wall of the building. Jason got there first. He twisted his head back toward Molly. "Stay back," he said. Then he made his move, leaping into a dive over the side. Nina's breath froze in her chest. In her mind, she watched the inevitable ending, Jason falling out of the sky, a man-bird whose wings have failed him.

"There's a ladder, Nina. There must be!" Paul said.

Out of a pool of blackness, Collier appeared, his gun silhouetted in front of a darker Tallac. In the dimness he crept along the edge toward Molly. Casting a terrified glance back toward the man who came after her like a hunting animal, she looked once below, then leapt over the side, following her brother into the abyss.

Collier ran after her, teetering along the building's edge, seemingly oblivious of the danger and the rain streaming down his back.

Nina waited for a blast, a shriek.

No sound. No sound at all.

Paul had followed Collier, and now, too late, Nina saw a new danger descending upon them, imminent and terrible. Paul would have to kill Collier to save Jason.

"No!" she screamed at Paul, but her voice was drowned by the harsh static of electronics and the cacophony of voices behind her as the security people caught sight of them and came running toward them from the other side of the roof.

Paul stood directly behind Collier, his gun pointed at Collier's back. Nina's eyes, sharpened by anxiety, saw his finger on the trigger.

"Freeze!" Paul shouted. But Collier ignored him. She heard a hoarse cry from beyond the wall.

And she lunged forward, seizing Paul's taut forearm, the one holding the gun. They were so close to the edge, and her balance was bad—God, it was a long way down. They wrestled furiously, until Paul finally flung her away. She felt herself losing her balance, going over, but Paul pulled her back toward the solid ground of the roof.

Gasping for breath, they looked toward the edge. Collier was gone.

Racing to the place he had disappeared, leaning over and straining to see over the side through the rain, they glimpsed the escape route, a metal ladder. Stretching down a hundred feet along the building, it ended on a flat extension of the roof spanning barely six feet. Molly was hurrying down the ladder to her brother, within twenty feet of the ledge where Jason stood, looking up into the rain. Collier was only a few feet above her, moving clumsily, an easy target for Paul.

A sound came, a tearing sound like a branch splitting off a tree. The ladder below Molly fell away, hurtling toward Jason, who raised his arms as a shield. "Omigod—" Paul had time to say, "Leo said—he planned to fix the fire ladders—"

The long length of ladder smashed onto Jason's ledge, still standing straight up. It stood momentarily on end, then tumbled off the ledge and fell again, pitching heavily into the power lines far below. Crackling and sparking, the metal section hung between the wires, glittering in the air like a stairway to hell.

Then it crashed to the street, splitting into several pieces, narrowly missing several Douglas County police officers sheltering under their cars.

Jason! Had the ladder hit him? Nina spotted him still crouched on the ledge, looking up, his mouth open.

It was Molly who was in trouble.

Molly had managed to hold on to the last rung of the ladder with her hands. The whole thing had pulled away from its supports except at the very top, and the ladder swung gently several feet from the wall. Her feet, unsupported, danced in air.

A few steps above her, where the ladder was still in one piece, Collier clutched the sides of the ladder. He pulled his gun from his belt and aimed at Jason, who was totally unprotected as he stood on the ledge below.

"Jason," the girl shouted to her brother. "You can get away. Go!" Was it rain or tears that trickled down her face? Nina couldn't tell.

On the ledge below, the boy stood up, swaying.

He seemed to jump toward the wall. With incredible strength and agility, finding invisible toeholds and fingerholes in the rough wall, he began to climb up the face of the building. "Molly, hold tight. I'm coming," he called.

"Jason, no! He'll kill you!"

"Hold on tight!"

He was up, just a few feet below her waving feet. He almost had her.

One of her hands slipped. Flailing wildly, she scrabbled for a hold, just as she had that night in her bedroom as she hung, fighting to live. . . .

"Molly!" Jason screamed.

The mass of people now surrounding Nina and Paul screamed in horror too, the din of their voices merging into one long moaning, crying sound that Nina would never forget. Rain broke the flashing neon lights into a hundred pieces.

Molly's other hand slipped off the rung.

In an impossible, superhuman gesture, Jason reached out one arm, the other hand clamped to one of the ladder supports still attached uselessly to the wall, bending his body out from the building, stretching. . . .

He had her. She was clamped tightly to his side, held with one hand.

They could not hang on. They couldn't climb. They could only wait for the inevitable ending. The boy's eyes bulged a little and the cords in his neck stood out, but he held his sister motionlessly. He had done all he could.

All Nina could see of Collier was the top of his head, slanting raindrops splashing against him and the bulk of his body. Paul must have realized he could not shoot now without endangering the two young people below him. He had stuffed his gun into his pocket.

The only sounds came from the rain splattering on the roof and the noise of sirens. Many heads now looked down over the side of the building, watching in an anguished hush. Nina felt the presence of death hovering in the air above the ladder.

All her muscles tensed as she held fast against the presence. "Collier." She called down to him in a rasping, guttural voice that wasn't hers.

"He killed my wife," Collier said, looking up, meeting her eyes. His were wide, innocent, filled with a terrifying light. "It's only right. Look at them. You see? They're supposed to fall."

"No," Nina said. "Anna would want you to save them. To be merciful, Collier. Please. For Anna."

A long, long second passed.

Collier looked down at the boy and girl, only a few feet below. "It'll never hold, Nina," he said absently.

Then he climbed down a few rungs. Bending at the waist, clinging with one hand, he reached toward Jason.

And a miracle occurred. The ladder held.

Collier clamped his hand on to Jason's wrist. He gripped it tightly until the rope could come down, and the helping hands.

Clapping, more shouting, a commotion as the three of them were hauled back over the side.

Nina put her arms around Paul's neck and buried her face in his jacket. She didn't want to see if that presence had receded. She was cold, colder than she had ever been before.

Kenny, dripping and leaning against the wall, said breathlessly, "Ray took the car. He lied to Jason. All he told Jason was that he'd totaled it and he asked Jason to take the blame with Sarah. He said he got drunk and lost a bunch of money gambling and drove the car into a tree. He . . . he . . ."

"He cried," Jason said. "He said he couldn't face my mom or my grandfather. He said he'd gambled away the money." He turned to Collier and said, "I'm sorry about your wife."

Collier's shoulders sagged. He bowed his head.

Molly fainted, and people crowded around her. Someone covered her up.

The rain still fell, silent and dark.

Epilogue

THE MAN AND THE WOMAN CAME TO THE SUMMIT of the great mountain just before two o'clock in the afternoon.

October had brought the cold with it, a still, windless cold. Snow would not be far behind. On the treeless summit, the slab of granite with its cairn of stones in the center, they stopped, threw off their packs, and lay down, gasping a little in the thin air.

Nina looked up into the sky just as she had on the day, two months before, when she and Collier had climbed the mountain in the midst of the threatening storm. All was clear and bright this time, and the crescent moon hovered like a ghost low in the sky, overshadowed by her big brother.

Paul, beside her, made a cushion for his head on his pack, and closed his eyes.

A month had gone by. Paul had spent the time in Carmel, and Nina had been picking up the pieces. When he called and asked her to go up Tallac again, she had refused at first, but he had said the most amazing thing, that they might learn something new about Ray de Beers's death at the summit. All the long way up they had avoided talking about the de Beers family.

And now, achieving the summit once again, she felt peace all around her. The mountain was at rest.

"Paul . . ."

"I'm here," Paul said drowsily.

"What are we looking for?"

"In a minute." He was quiet again, relaxing in full sun. Out there where Lake Tahoe glinted silver in the sun, a pair of eagles dipped and turned in the sky.

"I'll miss California," he said. "I've never worked in Washington, D.C. And three months is a long time to be away. But I'll be set for the year after this job."

"I wish you weren't going."

"We all need a rest. Try to stay out of trouble, will you?"

Nina pushed at him lightly with her boot. "I intend to," she said. "Now. Don't you want to know what happened to them? Jason, and the others?"

"All right. I'm ready now."

"First, Collier."

"How did our statements go over?"

"Perfectly. Jason and Molly and Kenny came through once I had a chance to talk to them. Collier's gone," Nina went on. "He took a leave of absence, dropped out of the DA race. I called him just before he left, and he didn't even know where he was going. He just said, someplace warm. He's a casualty, Paul. I wonder if I'll ever see him again."

"He'll be back when he feels better," Paul said.

"It's not just Anna. Looking for Anna's killer was only a symptom of his illness. He was burned out, Paul. Thank God he didn't kill Jason."

"He would have killed the wrong person," Paul said. "I really thought the kid did it after our talk with Sarah."

"Kenny told me the rest of it a few days later. Ray wrote the check, took the cash to Ruben, and hired him to kill Leo," Nina said. "Ray was paranoid. He thought Leo was taking everything away from him—his power on the job and his wife. He hated Leo enough to try to kill him. And when Ruben told him he'd talked to his probation officer and had a change of heart, Ray had to cover up, so he strangled him. Then he ran Anna down and dumped the car on El-Barouki. And he begged Jason to tell his mother he'd taken the money and the car, not telling him what he'd done. Incredible that Jason agreed, even so. He loved his father in spite of everything, Paul."

"When did the kids figure it out?" Paul asked.

"After we talked to Joe and Lucy, remember? Joe was at the house working and he told Molly how his missing car killed Anna. Then Molly told Jason on a visit to the jail. Jason didn't know what to do. It was just another blow among so many others."

"Did any hard evidence turn up?"

Nina said, "A long shot. Ginger matched prints in the car to Ray. There were no prints of Jason. Ray did it, Paul. There's no doubt."

"Tell me about the de Beerses."

"Sandy says Sarah's marrying Leo on Christmas Day. Kenny's going to be the best man. Then Kenny's starting Cal Tech in the spring semester. That's good, isn't it? Jason and Molly are both going to Columbia."

"What about the arson charge and the grave-digging charge?"

"I pled Jason guilty. He did dig up the body—I'm

still not sure why—and he did set the fire, Paul. But Amagosian took into account a lot of mitigating circumstances. Jason was convicted of two misdemeanors and has to complete a counseling program while he's at Columbia as part of his probation. He says he knows he can't run away from his troubles anymore."

"Good lawyering," Paul said drowsily, and Nina let herself bask for a minute in the warmth and his compliment.

"Oh, yes," she said. "Collier told me he sat down with Lucy Lauria and explained what we think really happened. It'll never be proven, though. Anyway, Sandy told me yesterday that Lucy Lauria had Ruben's body removed from the grave where it had been buried and reburied it at a Catholic cemetery in Reno. She still plans to marry Joe."

"Good," Paul said. "Joe's all right. Have they found Quentin's Mercedes?"

"No," Nina said. "It's probably at the bottom of some cliff somewhere around here. Jason won't say."

"A memorial," Paul said. "Did you ever find out who took the sunglasses?"

"Molly. Jason told her I had them. She was trying to protect him, and she didn't trust me. She waltzed into the house one afternoon while Andrea was picking up the children at school."

"It had to be her. Teenage girl, harmless, the neighbors would think."

"Oh," Nina said. "You'll never guess what I heard about Kim Voss."

"What's that?"

"I saw an article about her in the *San Francisco Chronicle* arts section. She's been discovered. Her series 'Synchronous Variations' is being shown at a big gallery on Sutter Street. She's suddenly famous. According to the paper, she was discovered by a gallery owner in Carmel who got curious because people were asking where to find her work."

Paul let out a hearty laugh.

"The flash of green wasn't Jason's sunglasses in the painting, Paul."

"I've thought about that," Paul said. "So Kim was wrong there?"

"No, she had that right too. Ray was wearing an olive-green golf hat that day on the mountain. That painting told the whole story.

"And that's about it," Nina went on. "That's my report."

"You missed one thing. Remember I asked you to try to find out who paid El-Barouki to leave the country? That's the one thing that's been really bothering me," Paul said.

Nina said, "That was easy. One call did it. To the *Mirror*. I gave the reporter the name, and she called back with the info five minutes later. Munir El-Barouki won one million, six hundred thousand dollars in the California Lottery Quick Pick game on the day before he left for Egypt."

Paul sat up. "You're pulling my—"

"True! I swear!"

Paul said, "Manifold are the wonders of the universe. He'll probably buy a gun store in Cairo. You know, this kind of case only happens once or twice in an investigator's career."

"What kind of case?"

"The kind where we're led around by the nose. A real honest-to-God mystery. The kind where it comes together, but in a way we can't build from logic."

"Well, I'll be doggoned," Nina said. "You're willing to admit there's something to the idea of—"

"Auspicious coincidence," Paul said. "Synchronicity. I admit it. But this kind of case is a rare thing, a very rare thing. I can't say that in all my years in homicide work I've ever seen the workings of fate so clearly exposed. It makes me feel—"

"Small," Nina said. "Collier said that once. About a storm."

"It's another kind of natural phenomenon," Paul said. "Beyond me."

"Yes. I feel that too," Nina said. "I feel as though we changed the way it was supposed to work out."

"We took on the gods, and kicked ass," Paul said. He laughed and scratched at his arm.

"I see you carried your gun up the mountain. What are you going to do with it, shoot the moon?"

"It stays with me," Paul said. "I may not have much control over anything at all, but at least I have my gun. I'd rather be judged by twelve than buried by six." Lifting up his water bottle, he took several long swallows.

"What I can't figure out is, why did Jason say all that stuff about the bad things he did at Kenny's right before Collier burst in? And why in the world did he dig up his father's grave?" Nina said.

"Well, let's do what we came up here to do," Paul said. "Maybe it'll answer your questions." He stood up and shook out his legs. "Up, woman. The search is on." He began circling around the granite, bending low, turning over rocks. "The bolt struck up here," Paul said. "There'll be some kind of mark." Nina followed, intrigued. She still had no idea what he was up to.

Near the edge of the summit rock, where the stony slope ran down to the unseen ledge where she and Collier had taken shelter that dreadful afternoon, Paul said, "Come here."

"What's this?" They both looked at the place where the rock made a shallow black depression filled with debris. Paul opened his pack and took out a pointed trowellike object. He put on leather gloves and began digging energetically at the debris. "Look," he said. He reached down and drew out a curious crystalline tube, about four inches long. Laying it carefully beside him, he reached in again.

Another bit of short tubelike rock came out, and another. They seemed to be made of fused rock, thin and hollow, wormlike in appearance. Nina had never seen anything like them before. They were alien. She found them frightening, as if they had unearthed something from outer space. "Paul," she said. "What are they?"

"The marks of the lightning," Paul said in a tone of satisfaction. "This is where the lightning struck Ray de Beers. The lightning literally melted the rock where it struck, down almost a foot, making this hollow broken tube to show where it passed into the earth. All the other marks have been obliterated by weather."

"How do you know this?"

"The Internet," Paul said. "Under 'lightning.' Try using one of the search vehicles, like Magellan. I've also been chatting with a forensics expert in electrical engineering, and he turned me on to a program on public television that I bet Kenny saw one night in his lonely apartment. And to think some people say public TV is boring!" He put each piece of the wormlike rock tube into its own plastic bag and carefully packed it into his pack. "Okay," he said. "Let's finish the job." He was on his feet again, head low like a dog sniffing out something.

"What are we looking for, Paul?"

"Burned wire," Paul said. "Any length." They moved in circles around the spot where Ray had died, looking among the jetsam left on the summit by wind and meteors for something like a burned wire. . . .

Nina found a small piece, about fifteen feet away, just at the drop-off. "Here!" she shouted. "I've got one!" Paul came over and they both looked at the six-inch length of black wire.

"That does it," Paul said. "Give it to me. Let's just see if we come across any more."

Fifteen more minutes of labor brought them three more bits of the same thin black wire. As they found each bit, Paul casually tucked it into his pocket.

They were both very tired of clambering around after such a long climb. "That's enough," Paul said finally. They sat down heavily. Already at three o'clock the shadows were lengthening across the faraway Nevada mountains.

"We have to go down, Paul," Nina said.

"Yes. As soon as I catch my breath again."

"Did we find what we were looking for?"

Paul nodded.

"Are you going to tell me about it?"

"It was the book you saw at Kenny's," Paul said. "About sugar rockets. Later, I asked Kenny what a sugar rocket was and his reaction made me curious. So when I started looking into lightning strikes on the Web, I looked up rockets too. Kenny gave me some help there."

"Well, what is a sugar rocket?"

"You'll find it under 'pyrotechnics' on the Web, if you ever want to look up the exact recipe," Paul said. "A fellow named Cloaked Guerrilla saw fit to post it for the world's benefit. It's a small rocket made with ingredients you can buy over the counter.

"The propellant is made with potassium nitrate, sugar, and sulfur. You put the ingredients in a plastic container and shake them. It looks like a yellowish powder.

"Then you make a casing out of brown package tape wrapped around a dowel, and a nozzle out of a plug of putty. You fill the hollow casing with the propellant, and take black powder purchased at a gun shop, make a paste with it, and smear it over the nozzle. You launch it from a guide stick made of wooden shish kebab skewers."

"Sounds like something some crazy kid might try to make."

"I think that's exactly what happened," Paul said. "The three of them were probably sitting around in Kenny's apartment, talking about Ray. And Kenny had his inspiration. Weather scientists have recently managed to send rockets up, trailing wires, into storm clouds. It is somewhat unpredictable, but every once in a while the damn things work. Lightning building up in the cloud is released, and travels down the wire to the ground. I'm sure Kenny knew all about it."

"You're kidding!" Nina said. "They called down the lightning?"

"It doesn't always happen," Paul said. "You have to have the right combination of circumstances. A mountaintop is the best place. The storm has to be right overhead, and the rocket has to hit the cloud just right."

"You're saying—I can't believe it! They planned to kill Ray with a lightning bolt?" Nina said.

"I don't think they ever thought it would work," Paul said. "Too many contingencies. I'm sure it was just a prank they thought they'd try out that day.

"But heaven cooperated. Remember how the party separated when the storm came up? I guess Jason and his father made it to the top. Somehow, Ray fell and was knocked unconscious. I can picture Jason looking at him, looking at the sky"—Paul was looking at the sky himself—"and thinking, what the hell. I think he tied the wire to Ray's pack, still on his back, and set off the rocket."

"The bang," Nina said. "Paul! I heard a bang! Just before the lightning struck!"

"The gods must have wanted it," Paul said. "Jason got out of the way just in time. The bolt blew Ray off the mountain. Jason must have been astounded it worked."

"He must have scrambled back up and picked up most of the pieces while Collier was going down the mountain after Ray," Nina said. "It's so ghastly, Paul!"

"That's a good word for it. I would add *awesome,* in the original sense of the word."

"He did kill his father! That's what he was confessing to the night Collier went after them!" Nina said. "What . . . what do you think we should do about this, Paul?"

"Do?" Paul said.

"Paul, listen. I looked up those names they called each other in a book on Greek mythology. You know, Phoebus was the god of the sun. Artemis was his twin sister, the goddess of the moon. The Romans called them Apollo and Diana."

"Hmm. But what about Kenny's nickname? Heff something."

"Hephaestus," Nina said. "Also known as Vulcan. He was a brother of the twins. They were all children of Zeus. He made Zeus' thunderbolt."

"Then he betrayed Zeus and made a thunderbolt to kill him," Paul said. "No wonder the gods . . ."

"What?"

"I'm not going to say it," Paul said. "It was just another set of murders, with perfectly logical motives, and solid police work solved it. Period."

Nina was silent. It seemed to her that she was floating in a great void, understanding nothing. She felt as though she had been practicing her trade in some other, greater court, blind and unknowing. They had interfered, and perhaps the gods watching were not pleased about it. She moved closer to Paul. "Let's go down," she said.

Paul said, "One more thing." He pulled out the burned wire they had so carefully gathered, dropped it into a hollow in the rock, and ground it up with his foot. "I just wanted to know," he said.

Three hours later, at the bottom, Paul held the door of the van open for Nina, who had limped the last half of the way down and looked wiped out. They drove down Highway 89, back toward town, eating pretzels they had found in the glove compartment, talking little, Nina's eyelids heavy in the passenger seat beside him. Passing the Y, they followed the highway a few miles farther to Pioneer Trail, where Paul turned left. At the streets with Indian names, they turned into the Tahoe Paradise neighborhood, and Paul drove down the steep driveway at 90 Kulow. The moon had come into its own, shining amid the stars as they got out, but the house was dark. Frantic barking came from within.

"Where's Bob?" Paul said.

"At Matt's for the night. I wasn't sure when we'd get back. God, I'm so tired. The barking you hear is Hitchcock, the dog Matt took in. Bob wouldn't move here without him."

"You aren't going to invite me in?" Paul said. "I haven't been inside since that day in court."

"If you hadn't brought me here that day, I might never have had the house," Nina said. "Sure, come on in." They trudged wearily up the stairs onto the porch, Nina fumbling with the keys. Once inside, the big black dog rushed around and tried to knock them down. Paul took him outside, howling with joy, while Nina turned on the heat and the lamps in the living room and disappeared into the downstairs bathroom.

Back in the warm house, Paul wandered around, looking at the orange-and-red rug on the floor by the wood stove and the new sofa and chairs, Hitchcock at his heels. "Very nice," he said when she came back.

"I'm all tuckered out, Paul. I'm even going to skip dinner," Nina said, yawning.

"Let's see the rest of it, then I'll be on my way," Paul said. She showed him the kitchen with its glass bottles and new pottery dishes, Bob's room, and then they went up the stairs, their legs like rubber after the climb. At the landing, Nina said, "My prize possession."

Inside the attic bedroom, occupying almost the whole space under the window, Paul saw something that made his eyes gleam, a high honey-colored four-poster pine bed, covered with a green-and-black Hudson Bay blanket. Hitchcock trotted right in, as he must do every night, and lay down on the rug beside the bed. "I couldn't resist," Nina was saying. "It's not what I thought I wanted at all, but I saw it at the store and I just had to have it. Has that ever happened to you, Paul?"

"Oh, yes," Paul said. "It's happening now." He reached for her and brought her close.

"Don't go, Paul."

"I'm here."

"Colleagues and friends?"

"Shh. No more talk, okay?"

And she must have agreed, because the whole night long, while the blue planet pursued its course through the dark unknown, and Tallac, crowned with stars, stood its perpetual watch, the only sounds from the bed were sounds to make even the gods jealous, sighs of dreams come true and cries of purest delight.

Turn the page for a preview of
Perri O'Shaughnessy's newest hardcover
Nina Reilly legal thriller

BREACH OF PROMISE

Now available at a bookstore near you.

Nina Reilly opened the window in her office in the Starlake building on Highway 50. Warm air smelling of toast and dry grass drifted in to mingle with the brittle cool of air conditioning. Outside, every shade of rust and gold shimmered in a hot October wind that rustled the papers on her desk. In the distance, bright colored sails waved like flags of the world against the blue backdrop of Lake Tahoe. She could sense a shift in the weather. The sultry air held a tang in it, like the end of something sweet, lemons in sugary tea.

Leaning through the opening to catch a ray of sunshine, Nina watched as a man and a woman in spotless white athletic shoes, plaid shirts tied around their waists, dropped hands so that the woman could stoop and gather some carrot-colored leaves from the littered road. She held her little pieces of autumn like a bouquet, dancing a quick step or two in front of the man on the sidewalk. The man continued walking, apparently unwilling to play the game. Giving up, she resumed her place beside him, dropping her leaves one by one to the ground like Gretel leaving a trail of crumbs.

"That's no way to keep this place energy efficient," Sandy said, standing in the doorway to Nina's office, hands on her womanly hips. Today she wore a fringed blouse and a shiny silver concha belt that jingled when she moved, khaki pants and cowboy boots, which made her look like an over-the-hill rodeo rider. Sandy enjoyed dressing for the office but she would never look the part of a legal secretary.

Two years earlier, she had worked as a file clerk at Jeffrey Riesner's law firm, a couple of miles west on Highway 50. In spite of Riesner's belligerent dissatisfaction with her work, her character, her looks and her air of superiority, Nina had hired her when she had begun her solo practice in South Lake Tahoe. It had been one of her more astute moves.

Sandy knew everyone in town, and had a strength of purpose that co-opted or crushed everything in its path. A lawyer starting up a practice in a new place needed to get clued in fast, and Sandy had brought in the vital first clients, invisibly organized the office and installed herself as Nina's keeper. Nina knew law. Sandy knew business. Everyone's business.

"What a day," said Nina. "Not that you'd guess it in here."

"High eighties?" Sandy said. "One of the last warm ones this year. Too nice to be inside."

"That's right. Let's blow this joint. It's four-fifteen and I can't think anymore."

"Not yet. You have a call on line two." Sandy jiggled her eyebrows significantly.

"Who is it?"

"Lindy Markov's secretary."

"Do I know Lindy Markov?"

"If you don't, you should. She wants to invite you to a party Mrs. Markov is giving this weekend."

"What kind of party?"

"She does a lot of charity work and hosts a lot of community get togethers. This particular shindig is a birthday party for her husband Mike Markov."

Nina closed the window, turning back to her desk. "Tell her I'm busy, Sandy. Give her my regrets."

But Sandy, a Washoe Native American whose people had hundreds of years of practice at stubborn resistance, gave no sign that she had heard. "Lindy and Mike Markov are the biggest employer in Reno. They live up here near Emerald Bay. This is a golden opportunity."

"Why? I'm too broke to be an asset to any worthy causes."

Sandy spoke again, her deep voice measured, reminding Nina of Henry Kissinger in his glory years, pushing governments around. "And that's exactly what you should be thinking about. We're in business here. And we need more money coming in. You've been tapping into your personal account to pay the office rent, haven't you?"

What could she say? The omnipotent Sandy knew all.

"Maybe they need a lawyer," Sandy said.

"I don't like going to things like that alone," Nina said.

"Paul's coming up this weekend. He called while you were in court this afternoon."

"He's back from Washington? I thought he was going to be gone longer. Anyway, what's that got to do with . . ."

Sandy shrugged. "I happened to mention the party. He's up for it."

"I see," said Nina.

"He'll pick you up on Friday at six. Don't be late."

"And if I still say no?"

Sandy heaved a fulsome sigh, her belt jingling slightly with the strain. "Then I'll have to go for you. Someone has to network around here. If you want to pay the rent and the Whitaker bill and Lexis, the new computer, my raise . . ."

"Which raise would this be?"

"I'll be needing a slight raise if I'm going to have to party for you."

"Okay, Sandy. You win. Which line is she on?"

"No need for you to talk to her." She turned to leave. "I'll confirm that you're on the list."

"You already told her I was going?"

"I thought you might. After you had time to think about it."

"Wait. Where is this party?"

"On the lake," said Sandy. "They're chartering the Dixie Queen. Taking off from the Ski Run Marina."

Paul picked Nina up early that Friday, treating her to a hug that bordered on the obscene. "Three weeks," he said. "God, how I've missed squeezing your cute little bum." While the words were light, she felt his scrutiny. Three weeks was just long enough for them both to feel the distance.

A good eight inches over her five feet four, blond, and forty, with two licks of gray around his temples and two marriages behind him, Paul seemed to have been in her life forever. An ex-homicide detective, he had his own business as an investigator in Carmel. They worked together sometimes. They also slept together sometimes. They were a lousy fit and grated on each other, sometimes. But every once in awhile, when they connected, they went deep down to a place that kept them coming back to each other.

As they drove to the marina, Paul quizzed her about her activities in the past few weeks. Nina talked about the house she and Bob had recently bought. "We're making it homey," she said. "It's just that none of us knows exactly what that means. I stockpile paper in every corner. Hitchcock has taken up residence in the ski closet and spreads kibble all over the kitchen floor. Bob rides his skateboard through the downstairs." When she turned the questions on Paul, he was un-characteristically close-mouthed. He couldn't tell her much about the Washington D.C. job, he claimed. And what was there to say about staying in a hotel?

Paul wasn't teasing her. She sensed his preoccupa-tion and wondered about it. Meanwhile, she could think of many things that might happen with him in a hotel and she spent at least part of the ride to the boat holding that thought, just enjoying his proximity and his big, comforting presence.

At the parking lot for the marina, not too far from Nina's office, Paul pulled his Dodge Ram van in tight beside a creamy white Jaguar.

"This is something," Nina said, stepping down into a parking lot crammed full of gleaming metal. "Oh, boy. Look over there by the dock. It's like a convention for chauffeurs. Maybe we should have rented a limo."

"You look terrific in that slinky blue stuff," Paul said, coming up beside her. He put a hand on her leg, squeezing gently to punctuate his point. "And if it makes you more comfortable, hell, I'll be your chauffeur. Can't do much about my chariot, but I've got a baseball cap in there somewhere. Anything to make you look less like you're about to jump out of your skin."

She shimmied a little, adjusting her pantyhose. "You're right, I'm nervous. I guess I'm just getting into the spirit of things, starting out with my foot in my mouth by insulting your car."

"You've talked with people before. I'm sure I've seen you do that. What are you so worried about?"

"I'm intimidated," she said honestly. "The Markovs are very wealthy. Their business is supposedly huge. They sell health aids of some kind. Mrs. Markov also raises money by the bucketful for the schools and recreation programs here."

Paul took her hand, and they walked toward the dock where a white sternwheeler trimmed in blue, rocked gently in the water. From the front of the boat, where Nina and Paul boarded, two black pipes tipped in gold shaped like medieval crowns framed a view of the rest of the boat. Silver lights of irregular lengths dangled like icicles from two of the three decks, and at the back an enormous paddlewheel, blades painted red, dripped water. On the bottom level, a wide swath of windows revealed a crowd of partyers already moving en masse to a tune Nina could not make out, bobbing between bunches of red helium balloons. The low bumping of bass traveled through the water to rumble up under their feet on the dock.

"Ever been on one of these before?" Paul asked her as they stepped onto the ramp that led to the lower deck of the boat.

"Once. I took a tour from Zephyr Cove with Bob when we first came here. He was only eleven. Very impressed by the glass bottom, even though there's not all that much to see under the lake, just sand and the occasional beer bottle."

"Did you say something about these people wanting to hire you?" he asked as they made their way to the exquisitely decorated party deck. "Because if they do, it looks like your ship has come in."

"I have no idea why we're here. It's one of Sandy's plots. Let's just enjoy ourselves."

They paused before going inside, taking a long look across the lake, toward the teals and peaches just beginning to tinge the sky and water. "When I see the lake like this, so beautiful, I think about the Washoe people camping on these shores," Nina said. "It wasn't so long ago, only a hundred years or so."

"I'm sure they'd love the hash we've made of the natural landscape." Paul gestured toward the casino lights. They had begun to gleam in the fading light, under the evening glow of the towering mountains.

"From far away," said Nina, "I think it's pretty."

A striking woman walked toward them, smiling. Several inches taller than Nina, Lindy Markov gave the impression of even greater height. Willowy, with warm coppery hair, she had expressive brown eyes over a prominent nose and jaw line. A golden, collar-style Egyptian necklace adorned her neckline, dressing up the rust-colored dress she wore over a body as muscular and wiry as an exercise guru's. She might be anywhere over forty. She had reached that certain ageless age.

"Hello, Nina Reilly. I've heard so much about you. I recognize you from the paper of course. Sarah de Beers told me you did good work for her family. Thanks for coming to join in the surprise for Mike."

"How are you going to surprise him? I mean, this boat . . ."

"Oh, he doesn't know I filled it up with friends. He just thought we were taking a dinner cruise to celebrate his birthday." She looked around. "He's going to love this. He loves surprises," she said. But the apprehensive expression on her face canceled out her words. Nina thought, uh oh. Something is not right.

"I hope everybody gets here on time. Mike's due at seven." She looked anxiously toward the door as another couple arrived, relaxing as she turned her attention back to Paul. "Mr. Van Wagoner." She shook his hand, holding it for a moment before letting go. "So you're a private investigator." Her eyes probed him in the dim light. "Do you dance?"

"Naturally."

She flashed a bright smile. Nina, who knew a stressed-out lady when she saw her, read worry verging on panic in it. "Save one for me." She turned away to look at the door again. More guests, not Mike Markov. She excused herself to meet the next crop.

Nina couldn't imagine how they could stuff more people inside. The decks were full of people, dancing, drinking and snacking. The usual casual tour boat had been transformed—waiters in black suits dipped and posed with silver trays full of hot treats for the guests, tables with white cloths and real silver had been set up in the midsection of the center deck for a massive buffet dinner.

What must be hundreds of people murmured and milled through the scene, dreamlike in the dusk. Once her eyes adjusted, Nina said hello to a number of them: Judge Milne, who was rumored to be considering retirement, Bill Galway, the new mayor of South Lake Tahoe and a few former clients. She stayed with the group where the judge was holding forth and Paul wandered off. Seven o'clock came and went, and the waiters made sure no glass ever emptied. But Mike didn't come, and the boat sat at the dock as the lake and sky flickered with the fire of sunset.

By the time Mike Markov finally appeared, everyone, including Nina, had had too much to drink. A lookout gave an advance warning, and a hush fell over the boat.

Nina saw him come aboard. Looking like a man with a lot on his mind, he walked right into Lindy's waiting arms. A stocky man with dark skin who was several inches shorter than Lindy, he embraced her quickly, his rolled-up sleeves revealing muscular forearms. "I'm sorry I'm so late," he said. "I was afraid the boat would be long gone." He looked around, puzzled. "Where is everybody?" he asked.

"Surprise!" the crowd shouted. The waiters popped another round of champagne. People poured out of the woodwork to pat him on the back.

For a moment, shock poised like the shadow of Lizzie Borden's ax over his features. Nina had time to think, God, he's having a heart attack . . .

He shuddered. In that first second he looked only at Lindy, suppressing some unreadable emotion. Then, like magic, as he turned to his guests, a cloak of good humor dropped into place. He began to stroll through the crowd accepting genuinely warm congratulations, shaking hands as he greeted each person.

"My God, Mikey. Fifty-five. Whoever thought we'd get there?"

"You look damn good for such an old fella!" This said by a bald man leaning heavily on a walker, who had to be teetering toward ninety.

"Great excuse to have a helluva good time, eh, Mike? Like old times."

Lindy trailed behind for a bit, then caught up with

him, taking her place by his side. Nina stayed behind as hands thumped him on the back and the good wishes floated on the air.

The engine started up. The paddlewheel at the stern began to churn up water, and a mournful low blast from the horn cut through the sounds of revelry, of wind, of evening birds and insects chirping away on land.

Just as the paddle started up, and the big boat began to move smoothly away from the dock, Nina saw the final guest arrive.

The young woman came on board quietly. In her mid-twenties, with black hair so long it hung almost to the hem of her dress, the girl wore strappy sandals that crept up her calves like trained ivy. Nina thought someone should say hello and show her the way to the bar. She started toward her, but after a quick glance around, the girl dropped her coat on a chair in the corner, collected a glass of champagne from a passing tray, and downed the first half of her drink, edging over to blend into a group of people standing by the door who apparently knew her. "Rachel, honey. Somehow we didn't expect to see you here tonight," a snickering, booze-laden voice called out to her.

Nina wandered off to find Paul, who was watching the great wheel make its waterfall at the back of the boat.

The enclosed main deck, a huge dark cave alive with undulant bodies, pitched with music from a live band. Far from deflating once the honored guest had eaten his cake and endured a shower of fantastic presents, the party was heating up. Nina dragged Paul to the dance floor, where they danced and danced some more. When a moment of clearheadedness intruded on her whirling brain, she moved outside to get a breath of fresh air, losing Paul somewhere along the way.

At the front of the boat next to the staircase, she leaned unsteadily against the wall of the cabin. They had reached Emerald Bay and the boat was circling Fannette Island, the rocky islet at its center.

In the shadow of the western mountains the water was indigo streaked with green, like shot silk. Fannette rose in solitary splendor out of the bay into a tree-studded, granite hill. At the top, the ruin of a rich woman's teahouse presided over the whole sweep of bay.

Nina had always wanted to visit the tiny island. The stone ruin at the top looked inviting under the fading tangerine glow of the sky. She imagined what the teahouse must have looked like back in the twenties, the rustic table and chairs for furniture, candlelight, a roaring fire; and Mrs Knight, coercing friends from the city into the steep climb up to her aerie, long dresses hiked up, waiters with trays and tea sets leading the way.

Someone on the deck above spilled a drink and laughed, then complained about the chill. Whoever was up there went back inside, and the night fell into the shushing of the paddlewheel and the drone of the boat's motor. Nina closed her eyes and sank into a woozy meditation on the high life, and what to do with Paul after the party was over. Questions swam through her mind as the night's cool air, balmy and soothing, wrapped itself around her.

The door opened, and two people stepped out. They didn't see her tucked away beside the stairway. She didn't feel like starting a conversation, so she said nothing. She would be leaving in just a sec, just as soon as she adjusted her shoe around the new blister forming on her heel.

"I thought you were going to wait for me at the marina," a man said quietly. "We would have been back in another hour."

"I just couldn't wait." The voice was a young woman's and it sounded a little defiant.

"Did you know about this crazy surprise thing?"

"No," said the girl. "Have you told her yet?"

"With all our friends around?"

"You swore!"

"Honey, how can I? I thought we'd be out here with strangers."

"Liar!" the girl said, sounding near tears.

"I will after this is over, later tonight," murmured the man. "I promise I will." The voices stopped. Nina started to rise, then heard whispers. They were embracing, kissing. Oh, great.

Now feeling the cold herself, she waited, hoping they would pack it in soon. Then she heard a cry, and the violent crash of a glass breaking close by them.

Someone new had entered the scene.

"Oh, no. Mike. Oh, my God, no." Nina immediately recognized Lindy Markov's voice. "What is this?"

Oh, no was right. Nina stayed out of sight behind the stairs, stuck like a fox with its leg in a clamp.

"Lindy, listen," Mike said.

The first woman's voice, younger and more highly pitched than Lindy's, interrupted. "Tell her, Mike."

"Rachel?" said Lindy, in a quavering voice.

Nina peered around the corner. No one was looking her way. Markov stood next to the dark-haired girl Nina had noticed arriving late. Lindy stood about four feet away, facing him, her hand over her mouth.

"Oh, Mike. She's got to be thirty years younger than you are," Lindy Markov said.

"Mike and I are in love. Aren't we, Mike?" The girl moved to take his hand but Markov pushed her hand away.

"Be quiet, Rachel. This isn't the place . . ."

"We're getting married! You're out, Lindy. We don't want to hurt you . . ."

"Oh, shit," said Mike. "Shit."

Nina, who for all the attention they were paying to her might as well have been invisible, silently agreed with him.

"Marry you?" Lindy said, her voice shaking. Nina didn't think she had ever heard such fury contained in two words.

"That's right," said Rachel.

"What kind of crap is this? Mike? What's she talking about?"

In a high, triumphant voice, Rachel said, "Look at this. See? A ring! That's right. A big fat diamond. He never gave you a diamond, did he? Well?"

"Get out of here before we both kick you from here to kingdom come," Lindy replied, her voice wobbling.

There was silence. "Lindy, I've tried to tell you," Mike said finally. "You just won't listen. It's over between us."

"Mike, tell her to leave so we can talk," said Lindy.

"I'm not going anywhere!"

"Calm down now, Rachel," Mike said, sounding remarkably composed, Nina thought. "Now, look at me, Lindy," Mike said. "I'm fifty-five years old tonight, and I feel every minute of it. But I have a right to choose my own happiness. I didn't plan this. I'm sorry it had to happen this way . . . but maybe it's for the best."

"Five minutes alone with you, Mike. That's my right."

"We don't expect you to understand," said Rachel.

"Who are you to talk to me like this! Mike loves me!"

"Oh, now she's playing that game, where she can't see the nose on her face," Rachel continued, lifting her words over Lindy's. "This is real life, Lindy. Pay attention for once."

"Shut up!" Did only Nina perceive Lindy's desperation, the menace that suddenly shot through the air?

"You had twenty years! Five more minutes won't change anything. Mike, come on. Tell her."

But Mike apparently could think of nothing to add to Rachel's remark.

"I said shut up!" Lindy rushed toward the girl, knocking her off balance against the railing. She fell. Nina and Mike both winced at the sound of her cry, then the splash as she hit the lake.

"Lindy!" Mike said. "Jesus Christ!"

Nina searched for a float to throw. She found one, but a rope was snagged around it. She fumbled to get it loose, her fingers working clumsily at a knot.

Lindy and Mike stood by the railing, their backs to Nina, too deeply engulfed in their own private hell to care what she did. Mike leaned over the side, peering into the darkness. "Rachel can't swim!" he yelled.

"Good!" Lindy said.

"Look what you've gone and done now, Lindy! My God, you just don't think! Now, listen. You keep an eye on her. I need to get help." Before he left he ran along the railing calling to Rachel, reassuring her.

"What I've done?" Lindy said, coming up close behind him.

Nina recognized that she was beyond reason, out of control. "Look at what I've done?"

The lifesaver suddenly fell into Nina's hands.

"Mike!" Nina said, preparing to toss it the few feet between them. He knew where Rachel might be. She didn't.

Mike turned to face her, putting his arms out to catch.

And Lindy, catching him completely off gurad, bent down and took his legs in her hands, heaved mightily and tipped him neatly overboard. "Go get her, champ!" she yelled, and the explosion of maledictions that followed was swallowed up by the sound of a second splash.